SLYE TEAM BLACK OPS

HONEYMOON TO DIE FOR

DIANNA LOVE

Praise for
THE SLYE TEAM BLACK OPS SERIES

FATAL PROMISE

"Fatal Promise left me speechless and in awe."
~~Heathercm, Amazon

"It was a slam dunk in terms of guns, international travel, romance, killers and resolution."
~~ Goodreads

STOLEN VENGEANCE

"This is one of those books where your body tenses, you stop breathing and you just can't read fast enough."
~~ Amazon

"If you love romantic suspense, you will adore Dianna Love's latest Slye Team."
~~ IMHO reviewer

DECEPTIVE TREASURES

"This may be my favorite book in the series so far. I swear they just keep getting better and better."
~~Heather CM, Goodreads

"Complex. Ongoing series. Nonstop action. Romantic suspense."
~~ Madison Fairbanks, Amazon

KISS THE ENEMY

"A FREAKING AWESOME continuation of the Slye Team series by Dianna Freaking Love!!! She did not disappoint."
~~Goodreads

"Kiss the Enemy is a high octane thrill ride through the high stakes world."
~~ J. Cazares, Amazon

HONEYMOON TO DIE FOR

"It seems with each book this series gets better."
~~The Reading Cafe

"…constantly believable and packed with intrigue."
~~Single Title Reviews

NOWHERE SAFE

"The love story is tender, steamy, erotic, and full of electricity, and the action plot will satisfy the reader's thirst for danger."
~~IndieReads review

"Blending taut pacing with sizzling tension, a little bit of James Bond with an engaging personal drama, this is a story for suspense fans and romance readers alike."
~~Goodreads

LAST CHANCE TO RUN [prequel novel]

"I could not put this bookdown...Once again Dianna has thrilled my suspense taste buds with an extra dashof spicy romance."
~~After Hours Rendezvous

"Engrossing, thrilling and wonderfully steamy...a pitch-perfect suspense that will keep readers breathless from the first nerve-racking scene to the last shocking revelation."
~~The Romance Reviews

Dedication

For Steve Doyle who is always willing to show me how to save the world. Thank you for the many times you've stood guard over us.

CHAPTER 1

PREDATORS INSIDE THE prison yard grew tense and quiet. They'd caught the scent of a weak prey—the overweight, middle-aged prison guard named Boyd. Sweat streamed down his face and his deep-brown skin had lost two shades.

Standing alone with arms crossed over his orange jumpsuit, Ryder Van Dyke kept an eye on Boyd *and* the other twenty Atlanta Federal Penitentiary inmates milling around during their hour of yard time.

The standard mix of killers, rapists, and thieves.

Present company excluded.

Ryder had never harmed a woman. He *had* stolen and killed, but only to protect the innocent. Actions he'd taken to preserve national security while on black ops missions for the Army before he was honorably discharged.

Operations that had resulted in saving thousands of lives.

Had that weighed in his favor when someone framed him for murder?

Hell, no. In fact, being an elite marksman—a sniper—was one piece of the circumstantial evidence that had put him in here. But he had a two o'clock meeting this afternoon with his attorney that he hoped meant positive news.

Forty-three minutes from now.

He eyed the guard and the players in the yard.

Ryder couldn't ask to go back inside early. Not at this point. If the guards picked up on something in the yard after he left, the other inmates would accuse *him* of snitching and turn on him even though he had no idea what was going down.

No, he was stuck until they were all called inside.

Survival to this point had been iffy. He'd spent the past four months, twenty-nine days and thirteen hours in this shithole. Given a choice, he'd have taken a bullet between the eyes instead of getting locked away in a space so small it would drive a dog crazy. He was lucky to have survived this long, and almost hadn't that first week.

The predators, led by the Beast, had turned on Ryder the second day.

Facing an undetermined stay here, he'd had only one option to stay alive. Take on the meanest bull in the yard—the Beast—and bust his balls, if he could, to make the rest think twice before testing him.

Ryder had ended up taking on three, and had hobbled away with cracked ribs, a bruised ball of his own, and peeing blood.

But he'd been upright.

The other three had left on stretchers.

Cost him thirty days of solitary confinement in the SHU, Single Housing Unit, aka the Hole.

A safe place. Physically. A wasteland of invisible land mines mentally.

The space would have been suffocating for an hour. He'd touched two walls when he stretched his arms across the space and the COs, Corrections Officers, controlled the fluorescent light that stayed on nonstop. Seconds turned into endless minutes that blurred into insanity while he waited to get out. His palms dampened just thinking about those thirty days.

When Ryder's breathing hitched, he ran his hand over his forehead to wipe away perspiration that stung his eyes. He drew a deep lung full of air. *Stay calm.*

In the past, he'd adjusted to any situation, but there was no way in hell he'd ever get used to being locked in a cage forever.

Movement in the yard tapped at his awareness. Shuffling around was normal. Choreographed moves were not and, all at once, it seemed as if everyone had new dance steps.

The predators were twitching.

Ryder eyed the sickly guard.

Fifteen feet away, Boyd panted in between wheezes from his two-pack-a-day habit. With a cool, late September breeze scurrying through the dirt exercise area, the temperature wasn't causing the excessive sweat that soaked Boyd's steel-blue uniform. Did he have the flu? He fisted his left hand then opened his fingers as if trying to work out a muscle issue before he gripped his rifle again.

Now Cherry Man turned toward Boyd. Bad sign that. Wide as a refrigerator, if they were produced in the color of burned oil, and just as hard to knock down, Cherry Man had been convicted on six brutal rape accounts. He gave a tiny head nod to the Beast.

His full moniker was the Rajun Beast. He'd climbed out of the Louisiana swamps and killed a two-hundred-pound man with his bare hands during a botched robbery attempt.

Rumor was, that hadn't been his first B&E *or* his first kill.

Cherry Man and the Beast moved slowly toward Boyd.

The rest of the jackals eased along behind their vicious leaders. All but four inmates who migrated away from the pack to the opposite side of the yard. What were they up to?

Ryder assessed the threat.

The Beast wouldn't be thinking to grab a sick guard's rifle and shoot his way out. He was a homicidal maniac with plenty of self-preservation instinct. Six weeks ago, Boyd had reported the Beast for harboring a homemade weapon. The Beast had been dumped in the Hole. He had the ruthless patience of a crocodile, waiting for a chance to make Boyd pay, and this was shaping up to be the perfect opportunity.

Fuck. Ryder had to keep his nose clean, so he didn't make it any more difficult for the attorney hired by Sabrina Slye, his former employer, to get his ass out of here. If not for Sabrina calling in favors, he wouldn't even be getting yard time.

He still couldn't believe Sabrina and her team of operatives continued to stand behind him even with a potential murder conviction.

His family sure as hell hadn't.

Except for his brother, Terrence, who'd visited three times and offered to bring in Van Dyke attorneys. Accepting that would have just put Terrence at further odds with their father, the one person Ryder did not want to owe.

Besides, aid bought with Hubrecht Van Dyke's checkbook would only play into the prosecutor's case against Ryder.

Smart money said to keep as much distance from the Van Dykes as possible. That same smart money also said Ryder should stay away from Boyd, who was looking worse by the minute.

Boyd leaned back against the wall, grimacing with each breath he took and white knuckling his weapon. His hand went for his radio, hesitated, then he drew a raspy breath, straightened up and pulled his hand back.

He was a decent guy who showed up and did his job without attitude. He'd actually dragged Ryder away after the fight with the Beast and his lackeys, before someone else could attack Ryder's broken body.

People who'd never been in a prison might assume Boyd's action had been standard protocol for a guard. Not even. The guards could have left Ryder to the other thugs, until his entire body had looked like hamburger, but Boyd had been standing close enough to know Ryder hadn't started that altercation.

Ryder spent thirty days in the Hole with nothing but time to think about that one act of consideration.

Forty-three-thousand, two-hundred minutes.

No clothes except underwear. Nothing but him, a bunk too short to sleep in, a toilet, and whatever rodent came by to steal a bite.

Dots swam in front of his eyes.

He squinted. *Stop thinking about it*.

Instead, he focused on Boyd.

What to do? Take the risk of saving a life, or live with the guilt of not lifting a finger?

Ryder began moving toward the guard with subtle steps as he searched the yard to locate all the players in the macabre show unfolding around him. He should back away, but his damn DNA was hotwired to his conscience. His odds floated right around toilet level. Interfering with the Beast's plan meant facing the Beast *and* Cherry Man.

The second guard in the yard was still observing what had turned into an intense four-man conversation.

Ryder looked back at Boyd, who sagged. *Stubborn bastard, radio someone to relieve you.* But Boyd had missed too much time recently while he cared for a diabetic little girl he was raising alone.

He was afraid to take another day of sick leave and risk losing this job in a sucky economy.

Ryder didn't want to know all that, but he did.

Don't take your eye off the goal, his common sense warned. Half an hour until the Slye attorney showed. Six minutes until exercise hour ended.

Come on, assholes, call us in early.

The predators closed the gap between them and Boyd to thirty feet. At five steps from the guard, Ryder paused because everyone else had stopped. Maybe he'd misread something and let his mouthy conscience interfere when he should be listening to his common sense. Just a couple more minutes and the Beast would lose his chance at whatever he was up to, this time at least.

Boyd looked right at Ryder then his face drooped on one side and his skin paled two more shades.

One of the inmates whistled a birdcall. A signal.

The foursome over in the corner cranked up the volume on their rumble-in-the-making discussion, which hadn't reached the point of an argument. No worse than a loud debate about sports. So far.

Whatever the Beast had in mind was on.

Ryder wasn't surprised at the crazy inmate going after vengeance, but how much was this going to cost him? The Beast had to pay the other inmates—and Cherry Man would not be cheap—plus he'd face whatever disciplinary action the warden dealt out.

When the other guard took a step toward the four noisy men, Ryder relaxed. That guard would call the end of exercise time and...

Boyd's left arm fell slack at his side. The rifle slipped in the grasp of his other hand. His knees buckled and Boyd slid helplessly down the wall, moaning.

Ryder took another cautious step. Sweat trickled into his eyes. Why wasn't the tower calling the other guard?

Because the four men in the corner had everyone's attention.

Everything happened within seconds.

A shrill birdcall split the air, then a shouting match erupted between the four men, but no contact or the tower would shoot. The second guard stalked over, weapon raised, and ordering the men to separate.

At the same moment, sixteen predators rushed Boyd.

Ryder cursed his stupidity and lunged for the guard, hoping like hell he didn't draw a bullet from the tower.

Bullets popped the ground around them. Sirens screeched and bullhorns shouted to break apart.

The guards *might* hesitate to shoot into a crowd *if* they realized a guard was at the bottom.

Boyd's pain-filled eyes locked on Ryder with a glimmer of hope that one person was not coming to hurt him.

Reaching the guard first, Ryder slammed his foot down on the rifle as he squatted to unclip the guard's radio. He got his fingers on the radio, then was body tackled to the ground. Feet and legs were everywhere. Dust boiled the air. Ryder choked and coughed. He sucked in the odor of stinking bodies. Fists punched *his* body, and a sneaker-covered foot bashed *his* face.

What the fuck?

The bigger the pile, the easier it was to cover up whatever went on underneath.

Sirens wailed and shots were fired.

Ryder yanked the radio free and dragged it toward his mouth. Calling medical aid for Boyd might save both their asses.

Two huge hands grabbed Ryder's forearm, knocking the radio loose and yanking his hand into the pile. His palm landed on cool metal. He closed his fingers to jerk his hand away. Another shoe kicked his jaw, knocking him dizzy. His captured hand slammed down on something. He couldn't breathe with the weight on his back. Stars crowded his vision. The inmate pinning him down rolled off. When Ryder felt his arm slip, he wrenched his hand back and found it empty. He shook his head to clear the ringing.

Gritty voices shouted orders. More shots erupted close by. Someone screamed.

An inmate clutching a rifle fell across Ryder. Guess that was the one who'd grabbed Boyd's weapon. The pungent smell of fresh blood stained the air.

Ryder shoved his elbows to his sides and pushed up to hoist the limp body off his back.

Boyd's arm stuck out of the pile with his banged-up Timex watch. His fingers flexed. Ryder grabbed Boyd's wrist, trying to drag him from the pile. If he could keep the guard alive then he had a chance to prove—

Another shoe heel slammed Ryder's kidneys. He fell down on his side, curled in pain. He tasted blood in his mouth.

More guards shouted as they poured into the yard, locked and loaded.

Inmates grumbled and cursed as they unpiled.

Clutching his gut, Ryder lifted his head and looked to his right.

Boyd's face was turned to him, eyes wide and blank. Blood trickled from where a homemade shiv had been jammed into his throat.

A vile laugh drew Ryder's gaze up to find the Beast grinning at him.

This hadn't been about payback to Boyd, but to Ryder.

There would be only one set of prints on that metal shiv.

Fuck.

CHAPTER 2

"I GOT THE NEW springs in that antique platform rocker."
FBI Special Agent Bianca Brady paced back and forth on
the manicured grass, fighting off the gut-wrenching ache that
lived in her chest. "It turned out great. It's goin' to Millie Fryer.
She needs it for rockin' her new grandbaby."

Bianca held a red velvet cupcake with "26" on the top, printed
in red icing. Sara Lynn's favorite.

"The upright freezer just needed a new cord. It went to a
raptor rescue center in North Georgia. Daddy's proud o' that."
Bianca continued with her progress report as she looked up into
the brown leaves clinging to the giant oaks scattered around
the area, at a few lingering patches of color in this part of the
Appalachian Mountains, anywhere but toward her best friend.

"I've got an entire pallet of Raggedy Ann dolls in the garage.
They didn't even hardly get wet when the Wal-Mart roof leaked.
The boxes are toast, but the dolls don't need much except new
dresses. Sewin' is *your* job."

Or it had been.

Bianca stopped in her tracks. She couldn't slide back into her
native mountain speech pattern. Not even here.

She finally gave up and sat down on the ground, crossing her
legs as thunder grumbled closer. "I better not leave here wet this
time, Sara Lynn."

Leaves rustled as the chilly, early October breeze kicked up,
but no other sound. Not even a bird chirped.

She hated the silence more than anything.

Missed the times when Sara Lynn would give her a shove and
say, "Don't be a wus, BB." *BB* for Bianca Brady. Sara Lynn had
started that in grade school, and she was the only person Bianca

allowed to get away with that, or with calling her a wus.

She missed Sara Lynn spending hours with her in Daddy's barn, refurbishing old furniture, appliances, toys—anything that could have a second chance—to give to somebody who needed it.

Bianca had a knack for seeing the value in something discarded and enjoyed the challenge of bringing it back to life. Her daddy had taught her how to work with her hands and use all kinds of tools.

Sara Lynn thought Bianca could do anything.

Bianca reached out and touched the cold granite headstone, squinting back another tear. "I thought I could do anything, too, as long as I had my best friend beside me. I hate celebrating your birthday here, dammit." A tear slid down her face. "God, I miss you so much."

Sara Lynn would swat her for taking the Lord's name in vain.

"I'm not holding up my end of the business right now, but I'm a bit busy. I'll get back to it when this job's done. I miss fixin' things almost as much as I miss you."

Sara Lynn claimed Bianca was drawn to all things damaged and abandoned, including people.

She'd only said that because Sara Lynn had been an outcast until the day Bianca met her in fifth grade and claimed Sara Lynn as her best friend *ever*. Bianca still didn't understand why others had never looked past the maroon birthmark that covered more than half of Sara Lynn's face, her full figure, or her kinky orange-red hair to see the loving soul inside.

Or the mind capable of running a Fortune 500 company.

The day Bianca handed Sara Lynn a small dollhouse Bianca had cleaned up and repaired in her daddy's backyard shop, Sara Lynn had burst into tears at the gift.

Bianca's throat tightened at the memory.

Even after high school, Sara Lynn had always been there with her, spending nights and weekends refinishing discarded furniture in the tiny living room of their ground floor apartment. When they had a load ready, they'd run it back to Thatcher for their neighbors.

When Bianca was recruited out of college to work as an

analyst at Quantico, Sara Lynn moved home to work for her church. But Friday afternoons at five, Bianca would head south on I-81 to spend her weekends with her best friend.

Until two years ago.

Bianca fingered the charm bracelet on her wrist. The six charms and bracelet links were shiny once again.

She'd rubbed a blister on her finger the first time she polished the second-hand jewelry and gave it to Sara Lynn for her sixteenth birthday.

The tear slid down Bianca's face. She wiped it away and sat up straight.

This should be like any other day on the calendar, but it would never feel that way unless she could turn back time. If she had that ability, she'd take back the words she should never have uttered that sent Sara Lynn to her death.

Swallowing against the knot stuck in her throat, Bianca said, "I brought your favorite cupcake." Sara Lynn was one month younger than Bianca. She placed the birthday cupcake on the ground in front of her best friend's headstone and tucked her birthday card underneath.

Thunder rumbled louder this time and the wind intensified.

She had to get through this and admit she was failing Sara Lynn. "Now that the party has settled down, I'll be honest with you. I have a favor to ask."

Was that rain falling in the distance?

She took in the clouds still piling together and lowered a narrowed gaze at the headstone. "I'm wearin' my good clothes today, but I'll make this quick if I'm holdin' you up."

Sarcasm was lost on Sara Lynn.

Bianca got back to her point. "Our investigation is stuck. I've searched everywhere for evidence on this case, but we still don't have any way of proving how the terrorists in your attack got their hands on those *specific* weapons."

Your attack.

As if everyone were allotted their own personal death squad when Sara Lynn had been nothing more than a warm body in a humanitarian group to those terrorists.

There were attacks—somewhere in the world—every few days now, but the one in Istanbul two years ago had taken Sara Lynn from Bianca and eight more victims from their families and friends.

A few wet sprinkles tapped against Bianca's arm. She sighed and hurried on. "I promised you I'd see this through, and I will, but I need help. I'm thinking you've got some pull and ... since your current Boss sees everything..."

Understatement of the year.

No flash of inspiration hit her.

Why should God help her when it was Bianca's fault Sara Lynn was dead?

She took a shuddering breath. "I am so sorry I talked you into going to Istanbul. I really thought it would be a great opportunity and it sounded low risk." Her voice cracked. "I'm more sorry that I got sick and couldn't go with you. We should've been together, just like always."

Bianca's cell phone buzzed. She scrubbed at her eyes and checked the display. "Really? I take one day off..." Another round of thunder boomed. She cleared her throat, sat up straight so she could sound professional, and answered, "Special Agent Brady."

"Murdock wants to see you in the Atlanta office pronto," Murdock's assistant Quinten said.

Pointing out that Bianca had taken a vacation day she'd put in for months ago was not a wise career move at this point. Not when Jason Murdock, her boss at her temporary assignment and FBI Special Agent in Charge in Atlanta, wanted to see her. "I'm about five hours north of Atlanta, but I'll head back right away. Can you tell me what he needs? I have my laptop so I can send him something immediately."

Water pinged her head and arms. Bianca glared at the headstone.

Quinten said, "No. Murdock wants, and I quote, 'his expert on the Van Dyke Enterprises case' located ASAP."

Bianca jumped to her feet. Did that mean they'd had a break in the case? "On my way. Please tell him I'll be there by three."

Rain gushed down as she ran for her Ford Explorer. She

turned her face up to the heavens. A regular frog strangler. "So *not* funny, Sara Lynn!"

Bianca dove into her truck and slammed the door. Soaked. Oh well, her hair and clothes had five hours to dry.

Rain pounded the roof of her sport utility, as it had every time she'd come to visit her best friend's grave.

Sara Lynn had to be laughing right now. She used to hoot at Bianca for fussing over her hair getting wet. Assuming Bianca was worried about her looks for some boy, Sara Lynn would say, "A man who *really* loves you won't care 'bout no wet hair, BB. Just let it go."

Bianca and Sara Lynn were going to be each other's maids of honor, but Sara Lynn wouldn't be getting married now. And neither would Bianca. Not after what she'd been through in her one serious relationship.

Sara Lynn had been there for her through that hell.

Bianca was here for her friend now.

The deluge of water came down so fast and hard, it blurred the cemetery, dredging up a memory of days long gone.

Sara Lynn would always stop whatever she was doing when they were inside, and the noise was deafening from hard downpours hammering the tin roof. Bianca would grouch about having to deal with a muddy yard. Sara Lynn would smile and look up at the ceiling with reverence, then say, "You can't have rainbows without a little rain."

I miss your sweet take on things, Sara Lynn. Bianca wiped the water off her face and cranked the engine, heading back to Atlanta.

And Sara Lynn, now would be a good time to ask your Boss about that favor.

CHAPTER 3

B IANCA RETRIEVED A file from her briefcase and placed the case on the concrete floor next to her feet. She tried to act natural, as if meeting with a murder suspect being held for trial was part of her weekly routine. Pretend this wasn't the first time she'd stepped inside a prison.

SAC Murdock sat on her left and Van Dyke's attorney had the chair on her right at the end of the dull-white table. The Atlanta Federal Penitentiary staff had provided a small conference room for this meeting.

No one chatted.

This was no social visit.

Murdock had made it clear on the way here that they had to wrangle a deal out of Van Dyke. Today. Intelligence reports indicated two terrorists suspected of being involved in the Istanbul and Italian attacks had dropped off the map. They might surface in the US, but by the time that happened whatever they planned might have already been executed.

Bianca straightened her file. It was more for show than anything. She had quick recall of written details. Not quite a photographic memory, but close enough that when combined with her dedication to this case, Murdock had chosen her to join him today.

A major step forward in Bianca's bid for a permanent position as an analyst on Murdock's anti-terrorism team.

But that wasn't her reason for being here. Her career moves fell down the list behind finding evidence of terrorist cells and justice for the victims of terrorist attacks. One would serve the other.

The day Sara Lynn died, Bianca had been ready to sign up to fight on the front lines as a field agent, but a person should know her strengths and weaknesses.

Ask her to lie and pretend she was something other than herself? Not her skillset. But hand her a keyboard and she'd infiltrate the enemy.

Ryder Van Dyke is not your enemy. He's a person awaiting trial.

Her job was to gather and analyze information, not pass judgment. That's what the court system was for, but her FBI research team anticipated a conviction based on the formidable stack of evidence they'd compiled. All of it pointed to Ryder Van Dyke as the shooter who'd killed J. K. Kearn.

Just over five months had passed since Van Dyke was arrested so that wasn't the reason Bianca and Jason Murdock were sitting here today.

No, it was Van Dyke's attack on a prison guard seven days ago that had changed everything. That had put Van Dyke's chances to beat a murder rap at below zero and given her boss what he needed to bargain with.

What was it with Van Dyke men and killing innocent people?

To be honest, Bianca had struggled to accept Ryder Van Dyke as a cold-blooded killer after digging into Van Dyke's military records, but the shot that killed Kearn *had* been taken from eleven-hundred yards away.

Making a shot that accurate and at night took an elite marksman, which Van Dyke was, but still, that was only circumstantial evidence.

It had taken the results of the ballistics report and months of playing devil's advocate for Bianca to finally accept that her team had a valid point in suspecting Van Dyke.

The distinctive sound of chains dragging the tile floor drew Bianca's head up sharply from where she sat writing notes.

The prisoner shuffled into the room. The small space smelled clinically clean in spite of the suffocating air. She'd been trapped once and had never liked being closed in. Even now her skin felt too tight with the urge to get out of here.

Not the time to allow old fears to crawl around in your head.

Bianca placed her pen on the plastic table surface and observed the man she knew inside and out on paper.

Ryder Van Dyke.

Twenty-seven, but he no longer looked like the vibrant ladies' man in Bianca's file photos. Where was the sexy playboy with an easy smile in the Facebook photos from when Van Dyke had spent a year at University of Georgia before joining the Army?

He'd been one year ahead of Bianca entering UGA.

Shaggy, sandy-brown hair now fanned his collar, and a beard one shade darker hid much of his face. His cheeks were hollow, but he did look physically fit beneath his orange jumpsuit, although a few pounds lighter than the weight in his file. Nothing weak looking about those wide shoulders or the biceps that he probably kept in shape in the prison gym. Thick forearms exposed below his short sleeves flexed when he curled his fingers tight, drawing her eyes to the metal wrist cuffs linked by a chain.

The guard walking behind Van Dyke held onto yet another chain that swung from where it connected to the length belted around the prisoner's waist.

Holding her mask of indifference in place, Bianca lifted the corner of her file to compare this prisoner with the man she'd researched.

Beautiful gray eyes in the file photos fit the image of a man with a reputation for charming the pants off women with little more than a look. In Van Dyke's military shots, that gaze carried the weight of maturity and a keen awareness honed by a long stretch in Special Forces.

A man of honor who had protected his country.

She closed the file and studied the live version again. The shadowed eyes now staring straight ahead were empty, as if they belonged to a stranger who didn't know the Ryder Van Dyke in Bianca's file.

Where was the smug criminal she'd come prepared to face?

This haunted shell standing before her made her heart catch. He'd had a promising career in the Army and had been rumored as first in line to inherit the Van Dyke weapons business at one time even though he'd been adopted.

What kind of man turned his back on a fortune?

Look at him now.

Did he spend his days thinking about what his life might have been like if he hadn't strayed to the dark side?

Why do you care?

She didn't. Her sympathy was reserved for the families and friends of the victims. Not the ones who caused the pain.

Prisoner and guard stopped at the same time.

Bianca waited for Van Dyke to acknowledge that he had guests.

Van Dyke's gaze ripped across the room, first to his attorney, then to Murdock and finally that silver gaze landed on her.

She held Van Dyke's chilling glare. Her daddy had warned her about the danger of staring down the wrong person.

But being a woman in a field populated heavily with men had taught her never to back down.

Van Dyke must not be impressed, because his gaze shifted to another more menacing level and still bored invisible holes through her.

In that moment, Bianca realized that the protection offered by guards, even the chains and cuffs, was nothing more than an illusion of safety.

She was thankful for Murdock's presence.

But she wasn't fooling anybody. She wasn't wired for this kind of encounter. She wouldn't even be here right now if not for impressing Murdock with her computer skills, her strong memory, and her commitment to this case.

An objective observer might call Bianca's dedication obsessive.

She'd been called worse.

Everything about Van Dyke sharpened to the attitude of a raptor on the hunt as he visually swept the rest of the room with brutal efficiency. She had no doubt that he sized up every person in proximity to him, every detail in his immediate space, the ever-present security cameras, and how many mundane items he could use as deadly weapons. Those were the kinds of things you learned while digging around on a man with his background.

Before her stood the lethal operator who had never backed away from a mission, according to his military record, no matter how impossible the odds, and returned every time with the same report. Mission accomplished.

When his gaze circled back to her, it slammed her with a load of condemnation.

She tensed and had the ridiculous urge to defend herself.

To a suspected criminal? Never.

"Have a seat," Murdock said to Van Dyke, then leaned back, arms crossed.

"No."

At forty-two, Murdock was turning into her mentor as much as boss, a rock she could depend on to push as hard as she did for justice.

He shot a pointed look at Ryder's attorney.

Mr. Finnick stood at the end of the table and greeted the prisoner, appearing undeterred by Van Dyke's arctic gaze as he explained, "I would have preferred a private meeting first with you, Mr. Van Dyke, but the FBI arranged this rather quickly and indicated they would share nothing until they spoke with you."

Van Dyke didn't even blink.

Bianca kept her poker face in place, curious to see how Murdock played this. He'd said little more once he'd briefed Bianca on the DA's intention to try Van Dyke for killing the guard.

"Would you like to sit down?" Finnick asked Van Dyke, repeating the question in a far more social tone, but the prisoner merely shook his head once.

As the attorney eased back into his seat, Murdock stood. Bianca's boss was not one to allow a criminal the advantage of looking down at him. "In that case, let's get to the point. I'm Jason Murdock, Special Agent in Charge for the FBI. This is Special Agent Bianca Brady and I assume you know your attorney. You're facing new murder charges, Van Dyke. You—"

"I didn't kill him." Van Dyke's words sounded hoarse, which made sense if he hadn't spoken much in the past seven days of solitary confinement since the guard's death.

Or had he screamed a lot?

Not something she wanted to think about.

Based on Bianca's notes, Van Dyke had spent his *first* thirty days after his conviction in the SHU. She couldn't imagine being locked in solitary confinement twenty-four-seven or wanting to go back a second time.

But Van Dyke had attacked a guard knowing he'd end up there as a minimum.

He didn't move a muscle when his eyes dropped to meet hers again as if he'd heard her thoughts. Fine hairs danced along her neck. She swallowed before she could stop herself from that show of nerves.

Van Dyke didn't smirk, but the tiny pull of his lips to one side televised the fact that he noticed.

Murdock gave a mirthless chuckle. "You didn't kill him, Van Dyke? Which *one*?"

Van Dyke kept glaring at Bianca. Was he recalling how she'd testified at his preliminary hearing? He uttered one word in reply to Murdock as if daring anyone to challenge him. "Neither."

"The facts say otherwise." Murdock shoved a look in Bianca's direction that she took to mean this was where she came in.

Bianca gave it a moment, because she'd figured out that a pause often worked well in the courtroom, then launched her counterpoint to Van Dyke's claim of having killed no one.

"Mr. Van Dyke, there may not have been any witnesses for the medal-winning shot that killed J. K. Kearn, but there *were* eyewitnesses when Corrections Officer Ernest Boyd was stabbed. If that isn't sufficient, your fingerprints were on the weapon that killed Boyd and we have a video that clearly shows you as the first one to jump the guard. That makes one murder conviction fairly simple."

Something dark flickered in the prisoner's gaze that sent invisible spiders racing up Bianca's arms, which were thankfully covered by a suit jacket. She clasped her hands in front of her to prevent any unintentional tremble.

Allowing a man to see her as vulnerable once had been enough. Never again.

Before moving ahead, Murdock gave Bianca a nod that said, "well done."

The door to the meeting room opened, and a beautiful woman came striding in. There was something familiar about her. She was close to Bianca's height, which put her around five-five. Black hair had been twisted up in a professional 'do that framed her exotic Latin face and exposed dangly silver earrings. She wore khaki pants and a plum-colored designer blouse that belonged on some willowy female, not a woman who moved her trim body with the confidence of someone with multiple belts in martial arts.

She paused long enough to whisper something to Van Dyke.

Whatever she said relaxed the tight muscles in the prisoner's face. The woman nodded at the guard, who unhooked the chain from the prisoner and left the room.

"Who the hell are you?" Murdock demanded of the woman.

"Sabrina Slye of Slye Corporate Security."

Ah, that explained it. Bianca had found only one blurred photo of this woman when she'd dug around on Sabrina and her agency. Slim pickins when it came to intel on that bunch, which said a lot. If Bianca couldn't find it, the information wasn't there.

Murdock's gaze tightened with recognition, too. "What're you doing here?"

"Watching out for one of my people." Sabrina Slye held up a hand to stave off Murdock's next comment. "If you have any issues with my presence, you're welcome to contact your superior, and just to be clear, I'm talking about *the* director."

The top man in the FBI had approved Van Dyke's prior boss attendance at *this* meeting? What did it say about Sabrina Slye that she supported a man facing a murder conviction?

Two murder convictions.

Bianca's conscience niggled that maybe there was a more revealing question. What did it say about Ryder Van Dyke that this woman was still supporting him?

Bianca would ask Murdock later about Sabrina Slye. Now was not the time to say or do anything that might undermine her boss's position.

Murdock stood there for several seconds until he finally said,

"I've heard about you and your *corporate* security. You can stay, but you have no say over what is decided here today."

"Never said I did." Sabrina walked over to the chairs that were across from Bianca and Murdock. When the Slye woman pulled two away from the table and flicked a look at Van Dyke, his eyes shifted with resignation, then he trudged forward. His wrists were still cuffed and linked to his chain belt. Ankle cuffs prevented him from moving fast, but Bianca noticed he worked to conceal a limp.

Once the prisoner was seated next to Slye, Murdock dropped into his seat, putting everyone back on the same playing level. "To bring you up to speed, Ms. Slye, we're discussing the fact that Ryder Van Dyke now faces another murder charge. One he hasn't got a snowball's chance in hell of beating."

Mr. Finnick interjected, "Once we hear what you have to offer, I'll inform Mr. Van Dyke of his options and—"

Murdock cut him off. "He has *no* options."

"Let us be the judge of that," Sabrina Slye said, ending that argument.

Murdock nodded at Bianca, who opened her file and looked at notes for show since she knew this case by heart. "Our research has produced strong evidence that points to Ryder Van Dyke as the person who shot J. K. Kearn with a 300-grain, match-grade .338 Lapua bullet discharged from a custom-built McMillan TAC-338 rifle with a special-order, one-in-eight-point-five-barrel twist. That exactly matches the weapon Mr. Van Dyke carried when he was in the Army, built to his specifications." Bianca glanced up at Van Dyke, who watched her with that penetrating gaze, but said nothing as she rattled off the ballistic details she'd memorized.

"Said weapon went missing from the armory," she went on, "the same week it arrived back in the United States from Mr. Van Dyke's last duty station. The same week he was discharged. Over the past five months, the FBI has accounted for all other relevant weapons and vetted the alibis of potential suspects who possess comparable expertise."

Sabrina Slye shrugged. "Still circumstantial and Ryder has a flawless military record."

Bianca mentally amended that statement to more accurately say that Van Dyke had left the military as a decorated hero. For that very reason, she'd worked twice as hard in building a file on this case. With no eyewitness and no murder weapon with fingerprints, Bianca had suffered nightmares over the possibility that she'd play a role in convicting an innocent man.

But Van Dyke's military record also raised the question of *why* he'd opted out early on a promising career, only to join a corporate security agency. Granted, the money was better in the private sector for a man with his skills.

Now that Bianca had deduced by Murdock's comment that this Slye group was not to be taken at face value, she had new suspicions about why Van Dyke would join up with a woman rumored to have once been a covert operative.

Was she still one?

Bianca had found no hard evidence to substantiate that rumor, which actually gave the spook angle more gravity. She asked Van Dyke, "Why did you leave the military only to take a job stateside doing similar work with Slye? A DA would bring up the point that covert operations with Slye offered you the ability to disappear to execute wet work."

For all that Van Dyke had relaxed his guard, he came to full alert with that jab. "I'm no one's hired killer."

Sabrina said with a lethal calm, "Careful how you word your accusations, agent. I might mistake that as suggesting I contract for wet work."

Bianca ignored the eyeball daggers coming from Sabrina. "I am accusing no one. Simply stating how this could be perceived in court."

Sabrina added, "I hired Ryder knowing he did not want to use his long-range expertise and he *hasn't*."

"According to what you know," Bianca clarified then persisted in pushing Van Dyke for an answer. "You still haven't explained why you left the military, Mr. Van Dyke."

Van Dyke's eyes narrowed to hard slits. He took his time answering, then finally uttered in a tight voice, "Because I couldn't make the shots anymore, Special Agent Brady."

Rolling her eyes, Bianca said, "Right. You all of a sudden lost the ability to hit a target in your crosshairs."

Van Dyke's penetrating stare turned frigid. His cheek muscles flexed above the beard that hid things like a clenched jaw.

Murdock shook his head and made a disgusted sound. "Trying to convince us that you woke up one morning without the ability to perform a function you knew as well as drawing a breath is wasting time. We have an offer for you that's good *right* now. Not an hour from now, tomorrow or at any later date."

Van Dyke glowered at Murdock. "What do you want?"

Murdock calmly answered, "In addition to the research our intel department has compiled on you, Agent Brady and her team have spent the last two years building a file on a suspected connection between Van Dyke Enterprises and illegal arms ending up in the hands of terrorists."

Suspected, my butt. But Bianca didn't let a muscle twitch at that comment, waiting for the fireworks to erupt.

Van Dyke muttered a soft curse.

Sabrina Slye shot Murdock a death glare. "You son of a bitch."

Finnick snarled at Murdock, "My client will *not* be held responsible if that information leaks out."

Murdock smiled with feigned politeness. "Agreed, but if Van Dyke doesn't accept my offer, he'll just have to stay in the SHU until our mission is accomplished. Might take a while."

At the mention of returning to the SHU, Van Dyke's flinty gaze faltered for the first time since walking into the room. His skin lost what little color he'd had. Anguish flooded his eyes.

Guilt clubbed Bianca, but she shook it off. Her team had built a file based on facts. Van Dyke would have a chance to dispute them and argue his innocence in court.

In the span of a second, Van Dyke's face shuttered again.

But in that tiny moment when his hard shell had cracked, Bianca had gotten a glimpse of the man in the military photos whose beautiful gray eyes had screamed *honorable* the first time they'd smiled up at her from his file.

Those eyes had tormented her dreams, accusing her of sending Van Dyke to his death.

Ryder Van Dyke's case would be decided by a jury. She had no reason to lose sleep but tell that to her mind at night.

And her daddy had taught her a simple rule a long time ago.

People lie. Facts don't.

Murdock continued, "Let's get down to business. We want to infiltrate Van Dyke operations. We're willing to offer you a chance to reduce the length of your sentence, Van Dyke, if you help us figure out how to insert one of our people inside the Van Dyke family compound *and* the headquarters of Van Dyke Enterprises."

"For what purpose?" Van Dyke asked, surprising Bianca when he didn't argue his innocence.

Was he finally accepting the future he faced?

"To gather evidence that Hubrecht Van Dyke is selling arms to terrorists."

Van Dyke sat back and looked over at Sabrina. "What do you know about this?"

"Just what you've heard."

Then Van Dyke lifted an eyebrow in question at Finnick, who said, "Any agreement here will be binding by law with all of us as witnesses."

"Bottom line," Van Dyke ordered.

Finnick nodded, understanding what was asked of him. "There is still no murder weapon in J. K. Kearn's death, but the circumstantial evidence is strong. Additionally, in the case of the guard's death, the eyewitnesses and videotape will bear significant weight with regard to the trial."

Bianca watched Sabrina, who stared at Van Dyke during a long silence then said, "We'll support any decision you make."

That seemed obvious based on Sabrina Slye having paid for his legal defense. So, what exactly had she meant by her statement?

Van Dyke addressed Murdock. "You can't get inside the family compound without me."

"Right." Bianca made a soft scoffing sound that brought the prisoner's attention to her.

Van Dyke's eyes gleamed with condescending amusement. "If *any* of your research is accurate, you would know that."

That got Bianca's back up. "My team's research is spot on. I *know* how tightly your father controls his world. I was commenting on was the fact that you think we'll just turn you loose."

He sat forward and when he did all that dangerous energy came with him. His voice lost any hint of civility. "I'll make this very simple so take notes if you can't keep up. If I agree to help you, I have to go with the agent being inserted for *any* chance of getting inside that compound, *or* the VDE offices that rival the Pentagon for security. If the agent with me makes a mistake, we're both dead. That means the person facing the greatest risk right now is me."

Murdock broke in. "You'd have to wear an RFID chip."

"Think I don't know that? But we *both* know they don't have much range."

"The new RFID-X does. It was developed for us."

Bianca clenched the pen in her hand, shocked that Murdock was considering releasing Van Dyke. She knew Murdock's number-one priority was to nail Hubrecht Van Dyke, but to risk giving this prisoner a chance to escape and vanish?

Asking Murdock about that right now would be the fastest way to put the kibosh on her hopes for a permanent position on his anti-terrorism team.

Sabrina interjected, "My team can back him up."

Murdock shook his head. "No. Our people only."

Van Dyke and Sabrina traded a look, a silent communication that resulted in Van Dyke saying, "No deal."

"What?" Murdock barked. "You're willing to give up this chance to reduce your sentence *and* spend an indefinite stay in the SHU? Think you'll get a better offer any time in the next millennium?"

Van Dyke lifted a shoulder, causing his handcuff chains to jangle. "You and I both want something, so it's a matter of who wants what the most. I *can* get you inside Van Dyke properties. Think you'll get a better chance at nailing Hubrecht Van Dyke *without* me?"

The stare down between Murdock and Van Dyke lasted thirty grueling seconds.

Murdock stood. "Give me a minute." He stepped away, punching buttons on his cell phone.

While he discussed whatever he was calling about, Bianca considered what Van Dyke was willing to do. She ignored the hard glint in his eyes and asked with sincere interest, "You'll really help the FBI nail your father?"

"Yes."

"Why?"

"Because someone set me up for a murder charge."

Did this guy expect Bianca to believe a former Special Forces soldier was "set up" by his father?

Bianca would have scoffed at that, but beneath the anger simmering in his words, she heard pain that poked at her again.

What was Van Dyke's true story? What had led him to this?

She could almost hear Sara Lynn reminding her, "Don't go trying to save the wrong person, BB."

Sara Lynn was right. Van Dyke's family had enough money to fund a small country and the resources to protect it. Bianca had a job to do. She trusted her team's research.

Murdock ended his call and shoved his phone into a pocket on his way back to the table. "Fine. Slye's team will coordinate with ours."

With a nod from Sabrina, Finnick began negotiating the terms with Murdock.

Bianca forced her jaw to lock so her mouth didn't fall open. She'd never trust Van Dyke not to run even with an RFID chip in him.

Grim amusement settled in Van Dyke's eyes.

Bianca maintained her indifference, refusing to let her disappointment show. Van Dyke would see that as a win.

Finnick paused in negotiating the length of Van Dyke's reduced sentence that would be offered only if he pleaded guilty. He asked the prisoner, "Is that acceptable to you?"

Van Dyke didn't appear to have been listening, but he answered, "Sure," without any debate.

He seemed too accepting. Something about that stirred the puzzle solver inside Bianca, but she couldn't put her finger on what had pricked her curiosity.

Van Dyke announced, "Now that we've got all that out of the way, there's another detail to get straight."

"What's that?" Murdock asked.

"As I said, the only way inside the family compound is with me and I can't take anyone I present as *just* a friend."

That was total crap. Bianca gave a sigh of disgust as she sat back. "Then there's no deal."

"I'm *not* finished. I *can* get a woman inside." Van Dyke studied Bianca too closely, then said, "Hubrecht and his people will spot an experienced field agent a mile away."

"We'll find someone suitable," Murdock said dismissively.

"I need someone who won't raise any more concern than a file clerk. I'll take *Special Agent* Brady with me," Van Dyke said with finality as if this were his show.

Bianca held perfectly still to keep from influencing how Murdock wanted to deal with this crap, but containing her reaction was a challenge. Basic agency training and her own hours at the range didn't make someone a field agent.

But I'm not a file clerk either, asshat.

Murdock shook his head. "No, she's not qualified."

That sounded as if she wasn't even up to Van Dyke's pitiful standards. She'd spent two years putting in constant overtime as she turned herself into the go-to agent for Murdock on terrorist attacks that involved weapons they believed were supplied by Van Dyke Enterprises. The position on his anti-terrorism team would give her clearance that was one step away from the highest.

She could make a real difference and find justice for Sara Lynn and all the others. Bianca had all of that in sight for the first time, maybe the only time.

Everyone had stopped talking.

Did this deal really hinge on her?

Mama warned you more than once to be careful what you ask for.

Murdock was not bending. "I'll screen for an agent who can put on a convincing performance."

How hard could it be to act convincingly? Bianca busted ass in the gym and proved she was more than competent on a firing range. That ability came from growing up shooting. She was no slouch. Weapons training and being in shape didn't qualify her as an undercover operative, but she was *not* without skills.

Was she trying to talk herself into volunteering?

Van Dyke's eyes zeroed in on her, but he addressed Murdock. "Thought Brady *was* an agent."

"I am," Bianca answered before Murdock could.

"Thought you knew everything about me and my family."

"I do."

"Are you any good with computers?"

"That's a stupid question."

He smiled. "Then who would be better at circumventing firewalls and layered security levels in the Van Dyke computer systems from the *inside* than you?"

"No one." She felt the shift inside her chest at that admission. Murdock needed someone with her skills inside Van Dyke operations to search for the information they needed. Was she really going to do this?

What would Sara Lynn do in her shoes?

Whatever it took.

For you, Sara Lynn.

Bianca lifted her gaze to Murdock, who was watching her intently. *Decision time.* "He has a point, Sir. I am the best suited and I do have training," she added, glad when Murdock didn't roll his eyes at that.

Murdock's frustration balled up in his eyes. "This is not part of your job requirement, Brady."

"I know, Sir. I'm volunteering." That sounded so much better in her head.

Murdock still wasn't sold, but Van Dyke pushed him to the tipping point with, "It's Brady or the deal's off."

She hated how he said her name. He made her sound like some robot he'd chosen off a shelf.

Tension thickened during a silent standoff until Murdock said, "You had better be able to do what you claim, Van Dyke."

Van Dyke came right back with, "I can if she can."

Bianca gave Murdock a nod of confirmation and hoped she could carry her part.

"Done." Murdock's gaze didn't move from her for a stretched moment. He finally started putting files back in his briefcase, so Bianca stood and followed suit with her own files. Murdock told Sabrina Slye, "We'll discuss strategy over the next couple of days, then—"

"One last thing," Van Dyke said in Bianca's direction.

Wasn't the negotiation over? Bianca let Van Dyke know just how much he was testing her patience when she snapped, *"What?"*

His eyebrows barely lifted, as if surprised to find the file clerk had claws. "The reason this requires a female agent who won't draw their suspicion is because there's only one way to get an unknown female inside the Van Dyke home and offices with me. We have to get married."

"What? No!" Her jaw dropped, because he had to be joking.

Why wasn't anyone laughing?

CHAPTER 4

THE MINISTER PAUSED in his droning and asked the groom, "You have the ring?"

Bianca offered Van Dyke a stiff smile and lifted her hand. *Not Van Dyke.* Ryder. Her new husband any minute now.

What had made her think she could do this?

Breathe.

Murdock and the team were depending on her.

Bianca's heart pounded loud in her ears.

Ryder grasped her fingers lightly with his much larger and warmer ones. She looked up to find a charming smile on his face. It was no more sincere than the one she'd been beaming this morning, but it was better than his restrained expression that hadn't changed in the past two days of manic planning for this mission. Ryder no longer looked like the scraggly prisoner she'd met in orange prison garb.

Shave him, give his hair a roguish haircut, slap a suit on that body and *bam*. Instant hottie.

Now, instant husband.

Her partner for a week. She had no backup out here. Not since walking out of the hotel suite this morning where the entire team had been inside with them all night going through last minute preparations.

With his eyes on her, Ryder slid an egg-shaped diamond in an antique-looking setting onto her ring finger.

She gave it a closer look. Timeless, elegant, and tasteful. Points to the team for coming up with something that certainly looked valuable.

He gave her fingers a gentle squeeze, drawing her attention

back to his face. He had another smile in place, but it didn't reach the gray eyes that seemed to hover in shadows.

The only time she'd noticed a different expression in those eyes had been when he'd seen her in a dress for the first time right before they left the hotel. The look he'd given her then had stirred with an awareness that had her practically tripping over her feet.

Until she'd realized that, hello, she was nothing special. Any man who'd been locked away in prison for five months would have looked at her like a dessert begging to be devoured.

Probably just one of the reasons doubt had set up camp in the minister's gaze the minute he'd laid eyes on her. If this man of God was already finding her unworthy, just wait until Ryder's family figured out that her blood ran Appalachian Mountain red instead of old-money blue, the way a wealthy wife's blood should.

Bianca knew first-hand how the old-money set worked. She'd been on the receiving end of judgmental snobbery and had the emotional scars to show for it. She slid the gold band into place on Ryder's finger.

The minister said, "I now declare you husband and wife. You may *kiss* the bride."

Bianca could swear that sounded like a dare.

Ryder lowered his head.

She could do this. She'd obsessed over this very moment for the entire two days they'd spent preparing. Two whole days to cram for the performance of her life—and prepare mentally to kiss the son of Hubrecht Van Dyke.

Bianca drew in a deep breath for courage and shouldn't have. She inhaled a mixture of his natural scent and sultry cologne that should come with a warning that brain cells incinerated with one sniff.

She would *not* be the weak link in this operation. If Ryder could do this, so could she. Bianca lifted on her toes to meet him halfway, her hands on his arms.

She'd expected to be ravaged by a man who'd just walked out of prison.

But his lips moved softly on hers, so gentle it took her by

surprise, and even if her mind knew he was a criminal, her body decided right there that it liked Ryder Van Dyke's mouth, and *crud*, she hadn't seen that one coming.

Dropping her guard was a mistake because Ryder apparently noticed the change.

He pulled her into his arms and proceeded to kiss the livin' daylights out of her, as they said back home. His mouth molded to hers, the bold kiss of a raider claiming his conquest without remorse.

Sensations flooded her body and sent her pulse racing fast as a hound after a rabbit. She could feel the thump of his heart, so he wasn't entirely unaffected either. Ryder kept kissing her, driving the embrace to an intimate level Bianca had never experienced with ... any man. Period.

Not like she'd been given a wide variety of kissers to judge against. Only two. But this kiss took the blue ribbon. Her brain fought for oxygen, blaring a warning that she couldn't hear.

Every fiber of her body tensed under an onslaught of excitement and emotions she had to get under control. Her nipples ached. She wanted to rub them against his chest.

Bianca gripped the lapels of Ryder's suit to give him a nudge to stop, but to her discredit she held on for just a few more seconds.

Someone cleared his throat. The minister?

Ryder finally ended the kiss, but the pandemonium spinning low inside her was still picking up momentum.

Holy smokin' chemistry! She had to gain control here. He was her prisoner, not her husband. Bianca used the hand she'd moved to his chest to give a discreet little push.

Ryder loosened the embrace.

But when he pulled back, his eyes burned with a feral hunger that quickly morphed into a smug arrogance. The fake besotted smile returned along with a glint of amusement in the silver-eyed devil.

She'd given an inch, unintentionally, but an inch all the same. To a man like Ryder, she might as well have handed over the code to her hormones.

That was not happening again.

What. The. Hell?

Ryder wanted to finish what he'd started with that kiss. Talk about stupid. How could he be *attracted* to the woman who led the charge to see him put away for life?

Not happening.

She referenced her team constantly, but *she'd* been the one to testify at his preliminary hearing. Convincingly.

Agent Brady had angel lips that were full and inviting, and a smoking pair of legs now that she'd traded her stiff suit for a dress. Ryder couldn't decide whether it was pink or purple. But she was the wrong woman to get hot over.

Good luck explaining that to his sex-deprived body.

Those big hazel eyes and the innocent look that sometimes crossed that oval face had pushed their way into the few hours Ryder had slept hard enough to dream during the past two days of non-stop prep work.

It was during those unguarded times, when his subconscious was free to screw with him that Bianca Brady came to him as a woman. Not an FBI agent.

But reality was that she was here to play a role.

Just like the women he'd known in the past, Special Agent Brady's only interest in him was as a means to an end.

That worked fine for him, because it would keep his body from convincing him to do something that would get his ass locked in the Hole for a year.

A warning flashed in his *bride's* eyes.

There came Special Agent Brady.

Thankfully, Murdock had agreed to include Sabrina in the crash planning for this op because Ryder had been given zero time to reorient after walking through the front gate of the pen. Murdock thought he could rush this and make it work, but he was wrong, and they'd just made their first misstep. There was no way they'd convinced the Van Dyke family minister that they were a real couple. If Bianca thought she could blow off what he'd said about the difficulty of earning Hubrecht's trust, she'd screw this whole thing before it even got started.

Ryder took the wedding certificate from the minister, who would be on the phone to his father the minute Ryder left. With the legal documentation for this farce tucked inside his jacket pocket and his Oakley sunglasses in place, Ryder offered his arm to his new wife. "Ready, Bianca?"

She thanked the minister, then shoved her own sunglasses on and curled her fingers around his forearm, sparing Ryder an indulgent smile. "Absolutely, Darlin'."

He led them outside where the sun had almost clocked out for the day. *Never lose sight of the goal.*

Hubrecht had drilled that into Ryder's head over and over while he was growing up.

Now was the time to take that advice to heart—no matter who had given it—and use it to bring down the mighty Hubrecht Van Dyke himself *if* he was behind the whole plan to screw Ryder.

And yet...

Hubrecht had plenty of faults and had been hard on Ryder his whole life, but the Van Dyke patriarch was the most patriotic man Ryder had ever known.

Time would tell.

But Ryder had only a week.

With his eyes shielded, he gazed at the woman walking next to him with stiff steps.

She had to ease up. If his family didn't accept her as his wife, this entire operation was doomed.

All the training in the world wouldn't matter if she couldn't hold herself together under pressure the first time on a real mission. Out here, she was a rookie.

No media appeared near the black limo waiting in the parking lot behind the church. One headache avoided.

Their strategic team had leaked to the media how Bianca had spearheaded the drive to prove Ryder's innocence in J. K. Kearn's killing after she'd uncovered conflicting evidence. How he'd fallen in love with the woman who had fought for him. The team had created "documented" visits to the prison she'd made over the past three months.

In the end, she'd succeeded in both freeing Ryder and becoming his fiancé along the way.

He'd fallen in love. What a joke. He *had* once told a teammate that when he found a woman who enjoyed the outdoors, he wouldn't let her get away.

That was BP. Before Prison.

All he wanted now was freedom and to be left alone.

The only reason the media was not here hounding him was because the strategic team had leaked Ryder's wedding to the media ... but at a different location.

The driver stepped out from behind the wheel of the Van Dyke limo and hurried to open the rear door.

Not the family driver.

When Ryder had called to inform Terrence about being released and his upcoming nuptials, he'd said it would be a quick ceremony with no guests. His brother had asked Ryder to come by once he returned from his honeymoon—just as Ryder had predicted to the team. Ryder told Terrence that he wanted to wait until the media circus died down to go anywhere, then he'd hung up and had to listen to Murdock rant that Ryder wasn't holding up his end.

Ryder had reminded Murdock that he knew what he was doing.

Sabrina hadn't said a word, willing to accept Ryder's take on the situation, but the wait had made for a tension-filled hour until Terrence called back.

Hubrecht had extended an invitation to Ryder and his new bride to come stay at the family home in Buckhead, the old money district of Atlanta.

Jackpot.

Even Murdock had been impressed.

Yep, this mission had been rocking along until now. Terrence had said Hubrecht was sending the Van Dyke family limo, which sounded considerate to people unaware of Hubrecht's rabid need for control.

So where was Carlton, the man who normally drove for them?

Ryder paused at the car door. "Who are you?"

Bianca released Ryder's arm and gave him an appalled look at his abrupt question.

The driver answered, "I'm Jacques. Carlton was required elsewhere."

A reasonable answer, and Carlton could be busy with someone else in the family since all of them ranked higher than Ryder, but Ryder trusted no one. He glanced around, checking for anything out of the ordinary, but how would he know what was normal after the past six months? He nodded at the driver, then took Bianca's elbow, helping her as she slid inside the car with him right behind.

When the limo pulled away, Ryder hit the button to engage the tinted privacy window.

Bianca pulled off her sunglasses and kicked off her spiked heels. She squeezed her toes, then flexed them, drawing his gaze to legs that were, indeed, smokin'.

For a federal agent.

She turned to Ryder, putting a hand on his thigh as she did.

Out of an ingrained reaction, he growled under his breath, "Get your hand off me." The muscles in his chest tightened and irrational thoughts burst into his head. He didn't allow anyone to touch him without invitation.

She snatched her hand back but didn't scoot away like he'd have expected.

"Jeez," she blew the pseudo-curse out on a frustrated breath.

He shook his head. "What?"

"I was only going to suggest we play some music, but it might be a wasted effort at this point."

She was talking about covering their conversation with music, and she was right. He punched buttons until rock music fed into their area at a low volume, but still she just sat there.

The longer she spent turned toward him, staring without saying a word, the more his frustration built.

He dropped his voice so low she had to lean forward again, just to hear him. "Look, two days is not enough time to decompress from a place where everybody you live with wants to kill you." He glanced toward the driver, fairly certain their conversation was shielded, but took care with his words. "*I* wasn't the one who pushed this timeline past the edge of stupid. So, what do you expect?"

"Nothing—"

He took a breath, anything to calm the tension ratcheting tighter across his chest by the minute. They had to make this work. He whispered, "Let's keep our voices down even with the music going. What do you mean by nothing?"

Lowering her voice even more, she said, "Right now I expect nothing and that's exactly what I'm getting, which makes me wonder how long it's going to take for this entire operation to go up in flames." She sat back against the seat but turned her head to him. "I'm not seeing the person who claimed he could make this work. Guess it's a good thing you got your *file clerk* who's *capable* of carrying her end of the load."

He angled his head down to her, his voice for her ears only. "Let's be clear. You seriously believe your performance fooled the family minister? Did you really think I was blowing smoke when I said he'd be on the phone with Hubrecht giving his report as soon as he sealed the deal?"

Bianca swallowed hard.

Ryder ran a hand through his hair. "We might have screwed this right out of the gate. I'm just praying he thought you were a nervous bride."

"Understatement of the freaking century."

He swung a look at her, really looked at her, and took a mental step back. She hadn't wanted to do this, just been in the wrong place at the wrong time when his anger was aimed at any FBI target.

This couldn't be easy for her either. He pinched the bridge of his nose and considered pulling her to him to protect their words, but he didn't know how she'd react so he quietly gritted out, "I get that no matter how much I said otherwise, you still believe you can yank me out of a cell, dress me up and trot me out as your front man and they'll let you waltz right through Van Dyke security."

A blush crept over Bianca's face. At least she had *some* shame.

He went on. "But this whole escapade won't last an hour if you cringe when I get close—"

She swung her face up to his, interjecting, "*Or* if your head spins around just because your *wife* touches you."

He'd always loved the feel of a woman's hands on his body and missed it. Had missed it for five long months, well, nine if he was counting before prison. He muttered, "Guess I didn't realize how hard it would be to fake caring for a woman who believes I killed a man in cold blood."

Pain flashed through Bianca's eyes before the poker face of Agent Brady fell back into place. Shit, this was getting harder by the minute when it should start feeling easier.

Swallowing against the frustration vibrating his skin, Ryder tapped his fingers on the seat between them.

If the two of them didn't find common ground for this op, it would be over before he had a chance to find the truth.

Every mission required some sacrifice.

Pretending to be *this* federal agent's happily married husband stretched the seams of his tolerance, but he'd have to push his anger away for any hope of making headway with her.

Still, he wasn't apologizing. "Let's back up. I hear you, and I've got my end of this, *Bianca*."

She snorted. "That's encouraging."

"What's your point?"

Turning to him, her face lost all humor. Her eyes flicked over her shoulder at the front of the limo then back to him. Her words were soft and full of passion. "My point is that this is important. A lot of lives depend on what we do. I thought you were serious about this deal. I need to know that you aren't just treating it like a week's vacation from prison."

He leaned toward her, noting how she didn't retreat. She had more backbone than he'd expected with her background. "I *am* serious. Dead serious." He paused, considering his next move, then cupped her face and drew her to him so he could whisper right into her ear. When she didn't shove him away, he said, "I have every intention of getting you inside the Van Dyke offices. But that won't happen unless they believe this marriage—from *your* end as well as mine."

Her breath brushed his ear. "Tell me something you haven't said before, Van Dyke."

"How do you plan to convince them when you can't even call me by my first name?"

She was silent for several seconds. "Okay ... *Ryder*."

He blew out a breath. That was as good as she could do? She was never going to pull it off. Not without him stepping up his game.

She offered, "How about a truce?"

"I'm listening."

"I won't spend the next seven days treating you like a murder suspect, and you don't spend that time treating me as if I'm the one who put you in this position. This wasn't something I wanted to do, but you refused anyone but me. I'm here. I'm ready, but I'm only willing to give to a point."

He'd been telling the truth when he'd told Murdock that his family and Hubrecht's people would spot an agent, but the only reason he'd refused to take anyone else was because Bianca Brady had been so passionate on the witness stand that he believed she really was after the truth.

He needed to bring a woman who would accept the possibility that someone else killed Kearn if she saw evidence with her own eyes.

What he hadn't planned on was to feel any remorse over forcing her to do something outside of her expertise.

He finally moved his head back to face her and said, "Truce."

She rolled her eyes.

Now what? "Thought that was what you wanted."

"It is," she admitted and placed a hand on his shoulder, tilting forward another inch. "This truce will move along much smoother if you give me more than one syllable answers."

"Like what?" He sank his fingers deeper into her hair, watching to see if she'd react.

She stilled for a moment then met his gaze without blinking and came closer until they were cheek to cheek again. "Let's talk about what we have to do, *Ryder*. How soon do you think we can get inside the Van Dyke headquarters?"

How was he supposed to think about anything except how much he'd like to feel more than that soft cheek with her so close to him? But he'd just accused her of not carrying her part. He had to keep his mind on track even if his body had derailed the second he'd touched her. "I'll know better once I speak to

Hubrecht and gain his trust. First, I have to convince him I *want* to be back in the family fold."

She pulled back. Her eyes sliced him into invisible pieces but she managed to keep her terse words discreet. "We don't have forever to do this, and your family obviously doesn't trust you any more than I do, or they wouldn't have required this dog and pony show."

He lost interest in the fine texture of her hair and cupped her head, drawing her in so she didn't miss a word. "Your lack of trust is exactly what I've been talking about. You're lousy at hiding your feelings, *Bianca*, and I'll tell you right now, it's *not* just me. The only people Lady Anne and Hubrecht allow inside their home are family in the truest sense of the word, staff that has been around since they married, or business associates that have been screened—"

Bianca broke in with, "While we're on that topic, why do you call your mother Lady Anne?"

"Because Dragon Lady was taken, and we *aren't* on that topic. I told you, Hubrecht allows no strangers near the Van Dyke properties, particularly the corporate offices. He might, however, agree to give my new wife a tour. *If* we can make him believe it's real," he allowed.

The silent pause convinced him he'd finally gotten the last word with her until Bianca said in a pert but hushed voice, "You better hope so or you're walking back into prison in seven days with no more deals from Murdock if this fails."

Breaking out of his hold, she dropped back against the seat and shoved her sunglasses back in place.

Yep, Agent Brady had shown up with guns locked and loaded.

Tossing prison in his face just pissed him off all over again. So much for a truce. He turned to get up close in her face again. "You're so sure about your research that you're willing to send an innocent man away for the rest of his life? Must be nice to have a flexible conscience."

She looked wounded for all of two seconds then came back with, "I only gather information, analyze, and follow the logic trail. Decisions are up to a judge and jury."

"Decisions are based upon the information provided by

experts, even if that information is lacking or jaded, or driven by the wrong motive."

Clearly, he'd struck some sort of nerve with that one, because she clenched her jaw shut and sat back. He dropped his head back, staring at the darkening sky through the sunroof.

She was wrong about him returning to prison.

He'd accepted the FBI's deal for one reason. He intended to use the next seven days to prove his innocence.

Once he did, he'd have a chance of convincing the Feds to look at evidence he believed would clear him of Boyd's death.

If that didn't happen, Ryder would disappear.

He was not going back in a cage.

CHAPTER 5

*H*OW COULD I have agreed to this?
   Give Bianca a computer and she controlled her world.

She hadn't expected a fake marriage to take a toll on her emotions, but Ryder was back to being just as quiet and dark as he'd been the first time she'd laid eyes on him.

He hated her.

Okay she got that, even if his being in prison wasn't her fault, but she had no idea what was coming around the next corner of this charade and needed more information than she was getting.

How were they going to do this if they couldn't even talk for ten minutes without sniping at each other?

He was right. He'd looked at her during the ceremony like he was crazy about her, and he'd kissed her like he meant it. All she'd managed was stiff compliance, because ... dammit, he'd rattled her.

Wouldn't that sound lame coming from a federal agent? She wasn't about to admit out loud that she was damaged when it came to men, but Ryder might be more forthcoming if she did a better job with her end of acting in love.

The only reference she had for marriage was her parents.

She and Ryder could never pull off an impression of *that* kind of love match, but they had to be able to convince people they liked each other.

Her lack of experience with men would be a liability if she didn't settle down. It wasn't as if she hadn't had a man in her life, only that her one foray into a deep relationship hadn't given her any tactical information to draw on for the role of *happy* bride.

That didn't matter.

Everyone was depending on her to come through.

Lives would be saved by finding the evidence Murdock trusted her to locate.

If that meant Bianca had to look at Ryder like a lovesick fool, she could do it. But with the loaded silence festering inside the limo, she wasn't sure how to bring Ryder back around to meet her halfway, especially when they were off stage.

Ryder lifted his right hand and reached over his left shoulder.

She followed the movement with her eyes.

He paused, looking at her. "What? The cut itches. Don't worry. Your people made sure I couldn't get to the chip from any position."

"I wasn't concerned about you getting to it—" she defended.

"Right." Sarcasm rolled off his tongue with that.

Mama would say, "*You'll catch more flies with honey than with vinegar.*" Bianca let out a long breath. "I *know* you can't reach it and I'm sorry the cut itches plus it probably hurts, too, but I heard they put the chip close to your spine. I was just going to say to ... be careful touching it."

He just stared at her for several seconds, finished scratching and lowered his arm.

Not even one word, but he'd stopped frowning and the tension in the car had dissipated past the point of strangling her. She felt encouraged a little and decided to show she could meet him halfway. "Look, I admit that this is tougher than I thought, but I'm willing to try harder if you are."

Ryder nodded. "Okay."

She kept thinking he'd say something else, but she should realize by now that this was not the man in the file who had been the life of the party when he was in his late teens.

His gaze wandered over to her then shot past her shoulder and his eyes narrowed. "What the hell is going on?"

She looked around, trying to place their location in downtown Atlanta, which wasn't easy. She'd spent a little time here back during her college days, but the campus was seventy miles east of the city, so those trips were rare. Her trips here to work with

Murdock's team had meant long, brutal hours at the computer with no time for sightseeing. She did recognize Centennial Park and the Atlanta Aquarium up ahead.

Ryder pressed the intercom button and asked the driver, "What are we doing here?"

"I was just informed by the CEO's office to deliver you to this Hilton," came through the speaker, "and that one of the Van Dyke pilots would meet you to take you up to the helipad. I'll deliver your luggage to your home."

What was Ryder's father up to? Were they going straight to the Van Dyke home or not?

Ryder released the intercom button and leaned over to whisper in Bianca's ear. "I'm betting Hubrecht changed the plan after the ceremony when the minister wasn't convinced."

That sounded so cloak and daggerish. Was Ryder just screwing with her to throw her off kilter? That was *way* over the top. But sharing her lack of belief would not move this tentative truce forward. "What do you think is going on?"

"Don't know yet. Just follow my lead and stay close."

She wanted to keep things on an even keel, but she couldn't let him start treating her like she *was* the little woman. She said under her breath, "Don't underestimate me. I can take care of myself *and* I'm part of *any* decision that's made."

He cupped her face gently, silencing her with his touch. His deep voice rumbled close to her ear. "We've had privacy from the limo driver, but the minute we step from this car we're going to be with people whose job it is to report everything they see and hear to Hubrecht. Every word, every action, no matter how subtle. This change in plans could be trouble, or nothing more than Hubrecht letting me know who's in control.

He glanced around before he went on. "Either way, this is showtime. If you can't be on the same team with me and *own* the role of Mrs. Ryder Van Dyke, say so now, because whether you believe me or not, I didn't kill Kearn, which means someone inside VDE either ordered the hit or knows who did."

She started to pull away, but he turned his face to hers and let his lips brush her cheek. The zing she felt stopped her cold. He said, "There's no replay in a mission, Bianca. If you can't—or won't—hold up your end of this, we'll be dead by the end of the week."

She wanted to doubt the part about ending up dead if not for the sincerity she heard this time that she hadn't heard before. Plus, this was *his* family and *his* territory.

She had to walk a fine line between being responsible for this mission, since she was the agent in charge, and deferring to the person with more tactical experience.

The limo pulled to the curb at the hotel entrance.

A tight ball of wadded up nerves bounced around in Bianca's stomach.

She nodded at Ryder rather than risk her voice, then lifted her purse and stepped out when the door swung open.

Ryder climbed out right behind her, his gaze scanning the area.

He looked formidable. There was the Ryder Van Dyke who wouldn't settle for anything but "mission accomplished." Time to appear happy for observers. She brightened the smile on her face and looked around expectantly, like a woman unfamiliar with her surroundings.

A man with short gray hair who wore a dark suit and mirrored aviator shades stepped forward and shook hands with Ryder, then dipped his head at her. "Hello Mr. and Mrs. Van Dyke. I'm Jonathan, your pilot."

Ryder asked, "Where are we headed?"

Jonathan said, "I haven't been given a final destination yet, but the flight plan will be filed by the time we reach the helipad."

Bianca hesitated. Apprehension shimmered through her. Ryder *had* tried to tell the team during the strategic planning, but nobody had believed him about how cautious Hubrecht would be, or that she and Ryder might be tested more than once. Murdock thought Ryder had been exaggerating to up his own value to this mission.

Bianca had, too. Until now.

Maybe not the only thing you're wrong about. Heaven help her if she'd blown off anything important he'd said that would end up getting them both killed.

Dammit, she should've spent their time in the limo ride

working out some signals for what to say in surprise situations like this. Should she just go along with this, or should she come up with an excuse not to board the helicopter?

But what excuse? She couldn't say she was afraid of flying when Hubrecht might well know she'd flown plenty of times for work with the FBI.

Ryder acted as if they'd blown it, but no matter how much this sucked, she wouldn't lay blame where it didn't belong. *She* might have blown it. She hadn't convinced the minister.

Time to bury the hatchet—and her real emotions—to reach her goal.

The question was, could Ryder maintain his calm if—*when*—she touched him?

Ryder said, "Let's go," with as much enthusiasm as someone instructed to jump from an airplane with no parachute.

Bianca reached for Ryder's arm, but she moved more slowly this time, giving him time to process what she was doing as she hooked her fingers around his elbow, channeling her best version of an excited new bride.

The pilot stepped into the elevator and slid a key card.

Bianca missed a step and stumbled.

Ryder moved with lightning speed to grab her arm. He said nothing, but when she looked up she caught him watching her with ... concern?

Embarrassed, she said, "Sorry. Haven't been in heels in a while."

She stepped to the back left corner and focused on breathing. The elevator was going up, not down. It wouldn't fall going up, right?

Ryder stepped over next to her.

The elevator lifted slowly.

She felt sweat dampen the collar of her jacket. *Come on, you slow piece of dog crap.* She hadn't realized Ryder had moved until his arm hooked around her shoulder.

Had he realized she was fighting a panic attack?

Or was he just trying look the part of her husband?

"Here we are," Jonathan announced as the door opened.

Should she move first? Or should she wait for Ryder?

He pulled his arm back, solving that dilemma, then he cupped her upper arm and gave her a little tug forward.

Once she was inside the helicopter, Ryder slid in next to her on the side behind the pilot's seat. That allowed Bianca to sit on the left where she could see Jonathon in profile.

The pilot pulled on his headphones and lifted off, constantly checking the airspace around the Bell helicopter as they zoomed above the city that was just starting to twinkle with lights. His story about not knowing the flight plan had to be bullshit.

Ryder had to know that, but he hadn't protested. Bianca wouldn't either. She had to follow his lead.

Jonathon did a visual check to his left-hand side and seemed to pause, as if sneaking a peek at her through those mirrored lenses.

It wasn't dark yet, but the sun had set. Did he really need those glasses to fly?

Ryder lifted his arm and hooked it around her shoulders again. Had he picked up on the pilot's subtle surveillance too?

Exactly what was up with this helicopter trip?

Ryder's fingers brushed across her shoulder. He gave her arm a little squeeze that felt like reassurance. Had he done it because he'd noticed her tensing up?

And why would he care since no one could see his action?

He didn't care. He was just a damned good actor playing his part.

She was out of her depth with a man like Ryder.

During the two days of strategic planning, every minute had been so intense and fast-paced there'd been no chance for needling doubts to poke holes in her confidence.

She'd assured Murdock she could manage the relationship part of this mission. She might have oversold herself.

When it came to the opposite sex, personal interaction was her weakest skill set.

In the office, she was fine. After hours, not so much.

And she was well aware of her own shortcomings. Her last relationship five years ago had shone a blinding spotlight on every single one. Bernard, the Gucci-addicted jerk she'd fallen for in college, had listed them thoroughly and often.

Bianca had gained a little acting experience out of that disastrous relationship, if nothing else. After the first month together, she'd *pretended* to be happy to make things work with him.

But that had been a child's game compared to this.

Now she had to co-exist with a man she'd convinced herself, and everyone else in the FBI on this case, was guilty of murder.

Doubt niggled at her conviction, though. Truth be told, it had been nudging her conscience since she'd first met Ryder in person at the prison. The pilot did another visual check, pausing on the left again then turning back to his controls.

She cut her eyes up at Ryder, whose forehead was drawn tight in thought. He glanced over at her then at the pilot then back at her again.

What was going on behind that glittering silver gaze?

Ryder's long fingers moved to the base of her neck and massaged the tight muscles.

Like most sexy guys, he was good at charming his way into a woman's good graces. Was he seriously trying to work that charm on *her*?

Maybe it was lack of rest and constant stress, but Bianca's muscles would not get on board with her indignation. They tingled with relief—and something else that bordered on an electric zing she was beginning to recognize every time he touched her. She let her head fall forward to hide the surprise she knew was on her face.

And she barely caught the moan before it slipped from her lips. Not that anyone would hear much over the engine and rotor noise, but Ryder might, and she didn't want him to know how much she liked his touch. Her stomach flip-flopped with guilt because—*truth time*—she'd been wound tight as a spring for days, and she wanted him to keep going.

What was *wrong* with her? Playing a role was one thing, but if Ryder was capable of murder, how could she actually experience any pleasure from his touch?

This is not the time for that kind of soul-searching.

Right now, she had to play along. Give back as good as she got.

Bianca considered several actions and settled on slowly turning to him then placing her hand on his chest and sliding it across to wrap his waist.

Ryder stilled, just as he had when she'd touched his leg in the limo.

Please don't yell at me right now. When he only continued to study her as if he'd just discovered a new species, she took a deep breath for courage and snuggled against his chest.

In her peripheral vision, she caught the pilot looking to his right, which meant he was going to turn to his left next.

Would this look real enough to make him report his impression of the happy couple to Hubrecht, even if Ryder wasn't returning Bianca's advances?

She felt like an idiot hanging on a man who was ignoring her. She gave Ryder what she hoped was a look of encouragement. *Come on, Ryder. I'm trying. Hug me back or something.*

Ryder hesitated a microsecond then must have read the invitation in her eyes.

But he sucked at interpreting eye messages, because instead of just putting his arms around her, he kept drawing her close until his lips touched hers.

She had no idea what to do now. Backing away would definitely give the pilot the wrong message, but kissing Ryder when she didn't have to was a whole other kind of wrong.

Regardless, her body was just as confused as her, because it clearly enjoyed being in his arms, and apparently, kissing him failed to disgust her.

Just the opposite.

For all his faults, the man had a lethal mouth.

And he really threw her off balance when his lips moved over hers with a tenderness that turned her mind to mush. That crazy, fluttery feeling returned to dance a jig in her stomach. For the first time since she'd opened her eyes this morning, the fist in her stomach began to loosen. Heat spread through her like wildfire. She should break this up and stop him from thinking he could just kiss her at will, but they needed to make up for the minister's report and make this look good for the pilot.

Besides, Ryder's family would notice if something as simple as a kiss looked forced. She and Ryder could use the practice.

Ryder hadn't pushed for more, just continued the gentle assault that was shredding her sanity.

Her fingers gripped his back, feeling cut muscle. What would this body look like without clothes? Maybe wet from a shower. Water dripping along all the contours, down his gorgeous, ripped male anatomy.

Naked?

She was thinking about Ryder *naked*?

That is so not happening.

Ryder's hand moved around between them. His thumb brushed her breast, and she made a noise that squeezed out part pleasure and part plea.

Holy shit.

She'd opened her mouth to speak when he kissed a sensitive spot behind her ear, and she shivered.

Ryder growled like a wolf on the hunt that had just gotten a whiff of his prey.

This was out of control. *Again.*

She put her hand on his chest and pushed back.

He let her but kept her within his arms. There was no way to read this man when he shuttered his expression the way he was doing right now.

But Ryder's gaze dropped to her mouth.

She caught her bottom lip between her teeth. What now?

He released her to sit back, but kept his arm looped across her shoulders.

She'd only been kissed by two men. One *man* actually, since the first one had been a high school crush. An amateur.

Bernard had been far more experienced sexually, but he'd never kissed her the way Ryder did. If Bernard had, she might not have been such a failure as a significant other.

Her heart thumped furiously. Okay, so, Ryder could kiss. Not a big surprise given his reputation growing up. She willed the crazy stirring in her body to settle down.

Nerves and the situation had to be causing that since she'd never felt anything like it before.

The rotor whine changed, and the pilot said over his shoulder, "Landing in five minutes, Mr. Van Dyke."

"Okay."

Bianca turned to Ryder as he dipped his head, watching her face until he was close enough to whisper in her ear.

"I don't know what Hubrecht is up to, but we're not headed toward the family home. I'm guessing we're going to VDE headquarters and that concerns me."

"Why?" She kept her voice just as soft.

"I have no idea what the minister relayed to Hubrecht. If Hubrecht has any reason to question the validity of our marriage, regardless of paperwork and vows, he'll think it's some sort of a set-up or sting. He's not stupid and I have no idea what kind of reception we'll have."

She hadn't expected a roadblock to their mission this soon and waited for Ryder to finish.

"I know you're trained, but let's be reasonable about this since both of our lives are at risk. I've had far more time in combat situations than you've had in the field. Let me assess the situation once we get there. If it goes bad, do as I say, and I'll get you out alive."

He was talking about splitting up? "I appreciate your offer to get *me* out, but I already told you, I go where you go, and vice versa."

Ryder's fingers tightened on her shoulder and frustration clouded his face. "The FBI is tracking me with the chip. It's not like they can't find me. What I'm telling you is that we'll *both* get out if we can. If not, you can't escape if you're dragging dead weight."

He thought his father would kill him?

Was Ryder really trying to convince her that he would step into the line of fire if *she* were in danger when her research had him practically convicted? To believe that would force her to see Ryder Van Dyke as an honorable man.

And then she'd have to question whether Ryder had really killed J. K. Kearn.

How was she supposed to even consider the possibility that someone else had shot Kearn? To do so would be admitting that her research team—her investigation—had produced faulty results.

The pilot's voice intruded. "On approach to land."

Before she could compose a reply, Ryder turned away from her, distant again.

Every time she thought she was gaining ground in understanding him, he sucked back into himself.

She looked straight ahead, gripping the edge of her seat for an anchor.

Was this what field agents had to do when playing a role? How did they manage to keep their feelings out of the mix and still come across as natural? Especially with a man as dark and confusing—not to mention sensual—as Ryder.

Bianca had better lock down her emotions or he'd use that weakness against her. He did have more experience in combat situations, but that didn't intimidate her so much as the fact that he was a pro when it came to seducing women.

He'd gotten further with her than anyone else had on the rare dates Bianca had agreed to in the last four years.

She hadn't prepared herself for the possibility of being attracted to Ryder, and at some point, she'd have to come to terms with how she *could be* attracted to a killer. But they could use this little burst of chemistry to their advantage as long as she kept her britches on, as Mama would say.

No reason to worry about that, is there now?

Shame brought a flush of heat to her face, and she quickly looked out the left side of the chopper to hide it. Bernard had hurt her in many ways, but the very worst had been when he'd laid the blame for his cheating on Bianca at her own feet. Because she was frigid.

How could she argue when she'd found sex painful at best?

Ryder sat back and she turned to see a dark shadow cross his face when he muttered, "Van Dyke Enterprises."

His jaw bunched with an emotion that filtered up to his eyes. She'd seen that look in the prison. The raw despair that had broken through his cold indifference when Murdock had threatened to leave Ryder locked in isolation if he didn't deal.

She could better handle Ryder's anger than his desolation.

No, no, no!

A feeling of empathy for this man was about as useful to her as socks on a rooster. She was *so* not going there.

She couldn't help her natural curiosity though. It had served her well in the research department, and it made her want to dig around in Ryder's mind. Finding out what made a killer tick would be endlessly useful to a law enforcement officer, no matter what agency she worked for. But the "not welcome" sign that had curtained his gaze for the last two days warned her not to go excavating.

The helicopter approached Van Dyke Tower in an area of Atlanta known as Buckhead. The thirty-two-story, glass-and-bronze structure designed by a Danish architect housed the brain center of Van Dyke Enterprises, or VDE, on the top ten floors.

Their weapons manufacturing plant was north of the city near Suwanee, Georgia.

Once the helicopter set down, the pilot killed the rotors, pulled off his headset and flipped switches to shut the engine down. When the rotors wound down, he climbed out with Ryder right behind.

Ryder turned to help Bianca, who cursed her narrow dress again. She'd have worn pants and a jacket, but the team felt a mauve dress said *wedding day* more than a dark business suit. Before she could step down, Ryder cupped his hands on each side of her waist and lifted her to the ground. Slowly.

His eyes held her gaze the whole way.

And there went her heart, beating fast as a happy dog's tail.

Wind batted hair around her face. Ryder lifted his hands and pushed the hair back, holding it there when he leaned down and kissed her lightly on the lips and whispered, "Ready?"

Not if he was going to keep stoking a fire in her gut. She hated to admit he was doing a good job in this charade, but it was true. And it was knocking her equilibrium out of whack. *No way out now.*

She nodded. "Let's do this."

On the way across the roof, Ryder leaned over and said,

"Don't look around as if you're watching for anyone and smile while we're talking as if I'm saying something intimate."

When she complied and glanced at him the way she thought a new bride would, he said, "From this point on, assume that everyone is suspicious of us." He paused to wave at someone coming out the access door to the building. "Except Terrence. He's a friendly, but don't lower your guard even around him since he's under Hubrecht's thumb. In a tight spot, he'll tell Hubrecht anything you say. Just a matter of survival."

"Good to see you." Terrence walked up with his hand extended. Ryder took it and shook.

Bianca had found it interesting that Terrence and Ryder were technically cousins, but Ryder saw Terrence as his brother because of Ryder's adoption. Terrence could be considered attractive in his own right, but he was too thin and timid looking for her tastes. Especially when he stood next to Ryder's imposing presence.

"You too, bro," Ryder answered.

Terrence's eyes were filled with sadness. "I'm sorry I didn't come more often."

Waving a hand to dismiss his concern, Ryder said, "I know you caught hell from Hubrecht every time you did visit."

"It was bearable." Terrence's narrow face widened with a polite smile. "I was thrilled when I heard about your release. Where've you been for the past couple days?"

Ryder quickly ended any further talk about prison when he put his arm around Bianca. "Are you really asking me that with a woman this gorgeous standing next to me and wearing my ring? Terrence, meet my wife, Bianca."

Bianca was so struck by Ryder's easy description of her as gorgeous, she almost missed Terrence talking to her.

His brother extended his hand with stiff politeness and judged her lacking with his next glance. "So nice to meet you, Bianca. We're all interested in finding out more about you."

That did not sound like "welcome to the family." It sounded like "what are you after?"

Crud. She'd been so worried about convincing everyone she was Ryder's new wife and not an FBI spy that she hadn't even thought about how they were more likely to see her as a gold digger.

But that's what she read in Terrence's chilly gaze.

How was she going to win over the only person Ryder considered an ally?

CHAPTER 6

R YDER READ THE lack of belief in Terrence's face. Not that his brother doubted the wedding, but Terrence had been burned more than once by women who were after the Van Dyke fortune, and his natural default would be that Bianca was an opportunist. Coming to her defense right off the bat would be the worst move for Ryder to make around family, but he didn't care for anyone slighting his wife.

Whoa.

Bianca was *not* his wife, his significant other or girlfriend. She wasn't even his *friend*. Not really.

She was his enemy, forced into this awkward alliance, and that was all.

Denied female companionship for half a year, then kissing her again and approaching second base in that helicopter had screwed with his head. The little head.

Yeah, he was letting his dick affect his perception.

Reality check. This woman hated him and wanted to see him rot in prison. Best to remember that, even when he was making nice for this little charade they'd set up.

Bianca was not any happier than he was right now. And she had to be tired of smiling, but she beamed expectantly at Terrence. "What? No hug?"

Terrence's expression slipped. He mumbled, "I, uh, we don't ..."

Ryder was just as shocked at what she was suggesting and could appreciate the panic on Terrence's face. This family did not display emotion in public and hugging was considered a plebian action.

"Well, Darlin', where I come from, we hug family," Bianca said with an accent that could sweeten tea. She stepped forward and put her arms around Terrence, who held his arms out from his body at first then curved them around her much like someone would hug a porcupine. A look of bewilderment flushed his face, but after a few seconds Terrence smiled, too.

Ryder would never have bet on that.

Backing out of the embrace, Bianca hooked her hand around Ryder's arm with a possessive hold and gazed up at him as if he'd just handed her the moon.

And damn if he didn't suffer a moment of stupid ego by speculating on how hard it would be to give it to her.

He'd had women bat their pretty eyelashes at him since he first grew hair on his face and had never let it faze him. Prison had short-circuited his brain.

He hadn't been exaggerating when he'd called Bianca gorgeous. She was beautiful.

She was also sworn to take away his right to breathe free air, and he'd fight to the death to keep it.

But their bodies had apparently held a détente in the back seat of that bird, because for the past few minutes, every time Bianca so much as brushed against his he'd start getting hard. And he couldn't keep his hands off her because he had to play the newly married game to the end. Make Hubrecht believe they were in love.

To keep them both alive.

Maybe he should just throw himself off the edge of the building right now and save Hubrecht the trouble.

"My, my, Ryder," Terrence murmured, saving Ryder from that decision. His brother arched an imperial eyebrow. "You've certainly found an affectionate one. Well done."

"Thanks, bro." Ryder had tasted her *affection* in the chopper when she'd given him the *do something* look after he'd caught her watching the pilot.

Okay, maybe she was a much better actress than he'd thought. Maybe she'd only been reacting to his kiss for show, but right now he didn't care. Ryder hadn't shared a kiss like that in so long he had the pathetic urge to do it again just to see if he'd been kidding himself that she'd been just as turned on as he was.

Terrence stepped to the side and lifted a hand toward the access door. "I hate to be the messenger, but Father is waiting for you."

Ryder snapped back into the game. "Why'd he have us come here first instead of going home?"

"He didn't say. I can only surmise that he has questions about what happened regarding your release. Plus, you haven't seen him since you were discharged from the Army."

That had been intentional.

Ryder hadn't wanted to see Hubrecht then and didn't want to now. In fact, he had a strange urge to convince Bianca to climb back into that helicopter and fly away. Out of danger.

An absurd thought considering she was here specifically to gain access to Hubrecht's inner circle and ultimately his files.

"Well then this visit is *looong* overdue," Bianca chided, sliding her hand down Ryder's arm to weave her fingers through his.

Heat surged in his groin at the feel of her hand stroking his body even though the jacket. Just went to prove that a man's body had absolutely no conscience and his dick had no loyalty when it came to the enemy.

Terrence tilted his head in deference. "Shall we go?"

Bianca smoothed down her hair. "I guess I'm ready if I don't look like I've been wrestlin' bears."

Terrence struck out, leading the way.

Ryder heard nerves that Bianca's down-home voice couldn't hide. He should tell her she looked fine, better than fine, but that was the sort of thing a man told a woman he wanted to comfort. There had to be limits to this pseudo-marriage.

She squeezed his hand a little and asked in a warm honey voice, "How you doing, Darlin'?"

Her soft Southern accent whispered across his senses. Made the wounds on his soul long for something he'd lost hope of finding again. He pushed that out of his mind and focused on her accent. The more he heard her talk, the more it sounded natural, but as if it wasn't pure.

Had she intentionally watered down her dialect? Why?

Uncovering female secrets had once been his favorite pastime, but when he returned from the military he hadn't wanted to dwell on secrets, his or anyone else's.

The time or two he'd gone home with a woman since then, he'd been straight up about wanting nothing more than one night. A few hours to drown his nightmares in mindless sex.

To be fair, that had fit the bill for those women who'd looked deep into his eyes and seen "fucked up" in his gaze.

That had been fine since there'd been no mystique to any of them and no interest past rousing sex.

Bianca raised his curiosity again. She ruled her universe within her comfort zone, which circled around research. But Ryder had caught moments of vulnerability peeking through when he'd least expected it, like the times—three of them now—he'd kissed her. Yep, he'd even noticed it with that quick kiss when he'd helped her out of the chopper.

Of all the women in the world, why did he have to be turned on by the one who lived to see him locked away?

"I usually take the stairs since it's only one flight down," Terrence said when they entered a hall with the elevator on his right.

Bianca had been silent until she heard that. "Let's definitely take the stairs."

Ryder didn't care one way or the other which road he took to hell. But something niggled at him. Why had *she* agreed so emphatically?

"All right. It's this way." Terrence changed direction, heading down the hallway of the business where he'd struggled to be accepted, to find a place in the face of Hubrecht's constant disapproval.

Ryder, on the other hand, didn't actually belong here. Never had and never wanted to. Bianca tugged on the hand that held hers. That's when he realized he'd been squeezing her small fingers hard in his much stronger ones and relaxed his grip.

Out of some inborn reflex, he lifted her hand and kissed her knuckles as apology.

He could feel Bianca's eyes on him, no doubt questioning the reason for that move. Even if she were free to ask him, Ryder had no answer. Hubrecht was almost certainly watching them on a security camera feed, but that's not why he'd done it.

Terrence held the door open as they descended the last two steps in the stairwell to enter the executive floor.

Terrence nodded to his left. "Same office. I have not been invited to this meeting, so if you'll excuse me, I'll see you at home."

Ryder wasn't looking forward to that any more than being here. "Depends on how this goes here and then if Lady Anne lets us past the front door at the house."

"The staff has prepared a room for you. I know she can be distant at times, but I told her I have high hopes that you'll come back to VDE and, well, give me a hand with Father."

Lady Anne might not want her sister-in-law's mistake back at the Van Dyke mansion, but she *would* tolerate Ryder if she thought Terrence could benefit. The idea of being under Hubrecht's thumb again was bad enough, but Ryder had been used as a patsy for Kearn's killing. Nothing happened that Hubrecht wasn't aware of when it came to his business.

Ryder had spent months in prison trying to sort through all the possibilities. He still had a tough time coming to terms with the idea of Hubrecht actually ordering a competitor's death as a business move, but who else in this group would have sanctioned the hit?

Ryder intended to find out.

And for that reason, he'd been honest when he told Bianca that a wrong move would put their lives at risk.

Would he be treated like a beloved son returning to the fold? Or a loose end—a threat—that escaped a murder conviction?

Ryder asked Terrence, "Who else knew I met Kearn that night besides you and Hubrecht?"

Bianca squeezed his hand. Ryder understood that she was warning him about moving too quickly, but some things couldn't wait.

Terrence's upbeat mood flattened. "I am so sorry—"

Ryder held up his hand. "Don't. My meeting with Kearn wasn't a secret and I was fine with you telling Hubrecht, but was he the only one?"

"No." Terrence stared off to his left toward Hubrecht's office, then pulled his gaze back to Ryder. "In fact, I announced it at dinner that night before you called to tell me the meeting was set. I had such high hopes and never doubted Kearn would meet with you. To be honest, I thought Father would be pleased that I'd asked you to help."

"So you, Hubrecht, Lady Anne and Janeen were at dinner?" Ryder would never admit it but he'd been hurt that his older sister hadn't tried to contact him in prison. Her silence had been more condemning than any words.

"Yes, the family, Sam Long and Kale Carter."

Sam Long was the Vice President of VDE and Kale Carter, a former Delta Force soldier, headed up VDE Security.

But they both worked for Hubrecht.

"Okay, thanks," Ryder said and added, "If I don't change my mind, we'll be at the house later."

Guiding Bianca along the top floor of the Van Dyke building, Ryder's boots sank into thick carpet. A few small changes had been made, but not many. There was still an air of understated elegance. Everything from the clean lines of contemporary teak furnishings to nineteenth-century paintings spoke of a Dutchman's stalwart personality.

His father appreciated fine art, but nothing showy.

Just like the man himself, who never showed his emotions.

Acoustic music floated through the air at an artificially adjusted volume. The hidden speakers were arranged to saturate the environment but not interfere with conversation.

"What was all that about not going home?" Bianca whispered.

"If things don't feel right after this meeting, we'll stay in a hotel in Buckhead."

She tried to pull her hand from his, but he wouldn't let go. When he glanced down at her, she mouthed the words, *That wasn't the plan.*

He paused and stepped around to face her.

Bianca's eyes widened with confusion.

Slowly, he slipped his arms around her and eased her up to his chest, lowering his head as if talking intimately with her when he whispered, "First rule of a mission is that you have to be prepared for anything unexpected and adjust. The minute we walked away from our support team we were on our own. If at some point I say we're not going to the Van Dyke house, it's because my gut's telling me it's not safe. I need you to work with me for us to be successful, and I need this to work as much as you do. More, actually."

He slid his lips in a light caress across her cheek and brought his head up just enough to see her face.

The rose color of her cheeks deepened. Her lips parted and moved, trying to say something, then she frowned, thinking. "Okay. Unless you give me a reason to doubt you, I'm going to take whatever you do and say at face value."

Ryder released the air that had backed up in his chest while he waited to see if she'd allow him this one small trust. He kissed her forehead. "Thanks."

"Stop doing that."

He cut his eyes around, knowing remote cameras transmitted their actions to Hubrecht, but he stood too far from anything that could be a mic. Their hushed conversation was safe. "Stop doing what?"

"Kissing me whenever you want."

Just to be contrary he asked, "Why?"

Her mouth opened then closed. "Because ... I don't like it."

"Liar," he teased, expecting Special Agent Brady to show up with her usual bravado and attitude.

But she didn't react. Instead, she blushed. That, and her hesitation confirmed what he'd seen in her eyes when he kissed her in the helicopter. She was definitely attracted to him, too.

That might be risky.

He could deal with her snark and hardass attitude, but knowing she felt the pull would make it damned hard to keep his hands off this woman.

Bianca's mind must have caught up to the moment and kicked her out of her mental haze. She cut her chin up at Ryder, hazel eyes flaring with cockiness and tone smug. "Fine. You win. I'm a woman who likes to be kissed, but I've enjoyed other men who were ... better."

Bullshit. She'd kissed him back too tentatively to be all that experienced, and he hadn't even warmed up yet. The male in him rose up, prepared to prove her wrong and make her recant those words.

Arrogance shimmered in Bianca's eyes. "Ready to meet *Daddy*?"

That hit the mark and doused Ryder's lust quicker than a dunk in ice water.

He stepped back, but before continuing to Hubrecht's office Ryder decided to give Bianca something to take the edge off of her cockiness.

Lowering his head, he whispered, "The only thing more dangerous than what we're here to do is challenging me when it comes to satisfying a woman. Challenge accepted."

CHAPTER 7

WHAT WERE YOU thinking?

Bianca hadn't been thinking. She'd just hated to lose, so she let her mouth get her into trouble, but to be honest she hadn't meant to challenge Ryder's masculinity or prowess with a woman.

And now she had to face Hubrecht Van Dyke with her emotions playing ping-pong with her brain.

They'd just passed a young man dressed in a crisp, dark-blue security uniform, but other than that, the top floor of Van Dyke Tower was pretty much empty and silent as a tomb.

Bad analogy if Ryder was right about how touchy this was, and she was about to find out how honest he'd been about the difficulty of earning Hubrecht's trust.

She stayed in step with Ryder, putting all her attention on not stumbling in the middle of the Van Dyke corporate offices after that thinly veiled threat.

She didn't believe Ryder would hurt her physically and maybe that was foolish, but her daddy had always said to trust her instincts about people.

Hers were telling her that Ryder wouldn't harm her, but those same instincts warned her she'd made a mistake by pushing his buttons.

What exactly had he meant by 'challenge accepted'?

Ryder slowed as he turned them toward a double-door entrance to a beautiful office decorated in white and black with dark green accents.

A small, gray-haired woman who looked like a grandmother in spite of her trim beige business suit stepped from behind a tidy teak desk and smiled with genuine pleasure at Ryder. "Mr. Van Dyke, how nice to see you again."

Ryder released Bianca and stepped forward to take this woman's hand. "Good to see you, too, Adelaide."

Bianca couldn't see Ryder's face, but his warm voice said he thought fondly of this woman.

"How's your grandson? Jacob?" Ryder asked.

"Still doing good, thanks to you."

Ryder shook his head. "Give him the credit. He deserves it. Is he in college?"

"For now. But he wants to join the Army, just like you did. He'd love to talk to you."

"I'm not the person to talk to him. Not now."

Adelaide's sweet face turned fierce. She put her hand on Ryder's arm and her fingers visibly tightened. "You listen to me. I knew you were never guilty. None of us believed that. And now everyone knows the truth." At that, she stuck her head past Ryder and back came the charming grandmother who asked him, "Don't you want to introduce me to someone?"

Ryder let go of her hand and turned around, reaching for Bianca's arm. "Sorry. Adelaide, meet my wife, Bianca. Bianca, this is the person who really runs VDE."

Adelaide gave him a push on the arm, laughing.

Bianca hadn't finished digesting Adelaide's heartfelt proclamation, or that Ryder had done something to help this woman's grandson that sounded significant. But it was time to flash her smile and go through new-wife motions again.

Bianca reached for the woman's hand and was surprised by the strength she felt. "Nice to meet you, Ma'am."

"Oh, a Southern girl," Adelaide noted with approval then told Ryder. "Your father is waiting in his office. Now that you're here, I'm going home."

Time to face the monster. Bianca's stomach cranked up an acid party.

Ryder muttered, "Sorry if we kept you late, Adelaide."

Like it was our fault we got hijacked by your father?

"Oh, posh," Adelaide said, walking over to lift her designer handbag. "I could have left earlier, but I didn't want to leave until I saw you again and knew you were safely here." She slowed on her way out and lifted up to peck a kiss on Ryder's cheek then she told Bianca, "Looking forward to getting to know you better." She patted Bianca on the upper arm as she passed. "You got a good boy."

With Adelaide gone, Ryder put his hand at Bianca's back and gave her a light push to get moving toward the next set of doors. "Shall we?"

Bianca nodded, too busy processing Adelaide's endorsement of Ryder and preparing herself for this meeting to answer.

Ryder didn't knock, just opened the next door for her as they stepped inside a room that was larger than her apartment back in Virginia. Floor-to-ceiling windows made up two walls of the corner office.

The word that came to mind was Spartan.

Everything in the room was neat almost to the point of feeling clinical.

Hubrecht Van Dyke stood across the room next to a window filled with the black night. Hubrecht was in a hushed conversation with another man Bianca pegged as Sam Long, Hubrecht's right-hand man, who had a distinctive Wall-Street profile from his tailored gray suit to the wavy black hair with a touch of gray at the temples.

Sam was no shrimp at a couple of inches over six feet tall, but Hubrecht topped him by at least three more inches. Hubrecht's dark gray suit, white shirt and conservative tie were streamlined and neat compared to Sam's fashion statement.

No fancy cufflinks on Hubrecht. No silk handkerchief in the pocket.

Just a businessman's armor.

Camouflage for a killer.

The meeting had ended the minute Ryder and Bianca entered.

As Hubrecht walked across the room toward them, Bianca mentally ran through her file notes on her main target.

Hubrecht Van Dyke, born in Holland, emigrated to the United States with his parents at age twelve, currently sixty-nine, engineer from MIT, married thirty-seven years to Lady Anne Lexton, daughter and heir to Lexton Aerospace and Defense

Engineering PLC, second largest defense contractor in the United Kingdom.

Hubrecht stopped two steps from them with Sam at his side. "Ryder."

"Father." Ryder's return volley was given in precisely the same cool tone.

Oh, boy. Talk about strained.

Until now, Bianca had doubted Ryder's claim that he and his father didn't get along, but if the air turned any more frigid between these two, tiny green leaves would start dropping off the Bonsai tree sitting on the glass-and-bronze pedestal.

Hubrecht's thick hair was more silver than caramel brown, and he weighed at least two-hundred-and-fifty pounds. But spread across six-and-half-feet, he was fit and, well, *imposing* wasn't nearly strong enough a word.

In the same matter-of-fact tone, Hubrecht said, "So this is your wife."

"Yes, this is Bianca," Ryder replied, another stiff response.

Where was the hug and jubilation over Ryder being freed?

Why was Ryder just standing there as if openly defying his father for some secret reason?

Hubrecht angled his head toward Sam. "Ryder, I don't believe you've met my CEO, Sam Long."

Sam extended his hand to Ryder, but his expression was hard and unwelcoming. "Ryder."

When Sam addressed Bianca, his face turned even darker if that were possible, and he did not extend his hand. "*Mrs.* Van Dyke."

Ryder bristled at Sam's snub.

Was that part of the show or some undercurrent between Ryder and Sam?

The room might seriously explode from all the tension.

Thankfully, Sam said, "If you'll excuse me, I have work to finish." He strode past them, pausing at the door to tell Hubrecht, "Kale is in his office monitoring tonight's security. Please let him know if you need anything."

Hubrecht nodded and Sam left.

Ryder practically vibrated with tension.

Bianca could understand why, since Sam had all but shouted that she and Ryder were considered a threat, but she'd extended a margin of trust to Ryder so he could rule this meeting. That wouldn't happen while he sounded downright surly and his face was shut down into a mass of sharp angles.

Hubrecht's expression was no more inviting than Ryder's.

What the devil was going on with Ryder and his father?

Screw it. She had to do something to break this stalemate.

Bianca sucked up her disgust at sharing the same air as Hubrecht Van Dyke and turned on her charm. "It's nice to meet you, Mr. Van Dyke."

"Please, call me Hubrecht."

"Okay, Hubrecht." She stepped away from Ryder and reached out to shake hands with his father. She'd been avoiding Hubrecht's gaze and dreading the moment she'd have to stare into the eyes of Satan. When she lifted her gaze, she couldn't believe what she saw.

Hubrecht's eyes were sky blue and ... friendly? They were nice eyes. How could a man that evil possess eyes that belonged on your local grocery store manager?

He addressed her in a pleasant tone that was a bit disarming. "You're as charming as I've heard."

Pleasant? How could she think the man who sold guns to terrorists was pleasant? She finished shaking his hand and broke out her I'm-so-happy-to-be-here smile. "Why, thank you, Hubrecht. I'm flattered."

Hold it. What he'd said finally registered.

Just as Ryder had warned, Hubrecht had been getting reports on them today. On her. He was every bit the enemy she'd peeled like an onion, layer by layer, through research. How many serial killers had friends and neighbors who had described the killer as "a nice man" who would never hurt a soul?

Had she really expected Hubrecht to look and sound evil?

He was a master at hiding his true colors, which made it so much easier to focus on running this game on him.

Lifting a hand to indicate the sitting area with a cream sofa and two cushy side chairs, Hubrecht said, "Have a seat."

She glanced over at Ryder who showed no signs of moving,

probably because that had sounded like an order, but too bad. If she could shake hands with the man who'd helped kill her best friend, Ryder could sit with him. With her back to Hubrecht, Bianca lifted an eyebrow at Ryder and, surprise, surprise, he actually moved to the sofa and sat down.

Let this get easier now. She took her place next to Ryder as Hubrecht moved to a side chair.

After what had happened in the limo, she wouldn't risk putting her hand on Ryder's thigh, so she casually bumped his leg with her foot when she crossed her legs. *Talk to your father.*

Ryder put his arm around her and shifted, getting comfortable. Much better. She took that as a positive sign until Ryder asked his father, "Why'd you have us brought here by chopper?"

Wrong wish. She should have wished for him to have a *civil* conversation with his father.

"The media has camped out downstairs here and across from the gate at home. Your false wedding location appeared to have thrown the media off your trail, but someone always finds out the truth. I thought having you brought here by helicopter on short notice would ensure that you slipped away undetected."

Having it explained in those terms would have sounded uber considerate if the gesture had been made by anyone else, but in light of what she'd seen and heard, she was giving new weight to Ryder's statements about this man. Given that, Bianca wasn't sure what to make of Hubrecht's explanation, but she stayed in character. "That was so thoughtful of you, Hubrecht. I don't have to tell you what a pain it was to get rid of the media the minute word went viral that Ryder was innocent."

"I understand that we have you to thank for getting my son released. How did you do it?"

Ryder's fingers had been sitting loosely on her arm, but she felt them curl at that question, one of the landmines he'd been warning her about. Their mission was going to go down in flames right here if she failed Hubrecht's first test. But she fully expected to be poked at verbally all week, to see if she'd slip.

She leaned forward, all serious. "How did I do it? With the God's honest truth. I mean, who could believe that a man with Ryder's military record killed J. K. Kearn?"

Ryder's fingers uncurled and closed around her arm, warming her skin. She glanced at him and saw something in his eyes she hadn't seen before. A vulnerability, as if ... he'd been waiting for someone to defend him.

To believe he hadn't committed cold-blooded murder.

She couldn't take on that role.

Did he think she could just deep-six months of research that supported a logical conclusion? Looking into his eyes, the answer was yes. He really thought he could convince her he was innocent. She wanted to ignore the power of his belief, but she'd be lying if she said it didn't get to her. Ryder's constant declarations of innocence—along with his heroic military record—continued to nip at her conscience as it had done since the beginning of her investigation.

"I know Ryder did not kill J. K.," Hubrecht said, drawing Bianca back around to catch the rest of what he was saying. Maybe hearing Hubrecht's admission would soften Ryder's attitude toward his father.

Hubrecht continued, "In fact, I think your agency's circumstantial evidence is an insult to someone with Ryder's training. If he was going to kill J. K., he would never have met with the man that same night, and Ryder would have had an iron-clad alibi during the time of the shooting. The whole thing was ridiculous."

Bianca smarted at Hubrecht's statement, but her puzzle-oriented brain started considering the logic until she realized Ryder's eyes had turned into ice chips when his father said, basically, that Ryder *was* capable of committing the perfect murder.

And *that* reaction from Ryder she could actually understand. Bianca's parents would have been stomping around, declaring her innocence without knowing any of the details, because, motive and means be damned, they believed in her and stood behind her no matter what.

Who had stood behind Ryder that way when he was growing up?

A subject for another time.

She slipped her hand down between her and Ryder to find his.

With a little prodding, she forced him to unclench his fingers and take her hand again while she said, "I'm glad to hear that I'm not the only one who believes in Ryder, but I have to admit that I didn't change my mind until I found conflicting evidence."

Hubrecht's unreadable blue eyes watched every move she made. He propped his elbows on the arms of the chair, lacing his fingers over his chest. "Why aren't you on a honeymoon, Ryder?"

"We'll take one once the media finds something new to focus on."

"What are your plans now?"

Ryder drew in a long breath and let it out, not rushing to answer. "Don't know. Not a lot of companies interested in hiring someone most people will still suspect of murder until the real killer is caught."

"If you had come to me when you got out of the Army, you wouldn't have ended up in this position."

"Getting arrested had nothing to do with the corporate security work I was doing for Slye. I got screwed because I was doing a favor, which was ultimately for you."

Ryder was still testy, but he was engaging Hubrecht, so Bianca stayed out of the crossfire. This was his part.

Shaking his head, Hubrecht made an impatient noise. "I told Terrence that not even you could get that snake J. K. to the table. The man can't do an honest deal."

That was an interesting comment since Hubrecht had said nothing of the sort about Kearn when Hubrecht had been deposed in this case.

Ryder's voice hardened. "J. K. might be a snake, but that doesn't mean he deserved a bullet in the head."

Bianca sucked in a sharp breath at the subtle accusation.

Hubrecht's expression never changed. "Are you insinuating that someone at VDE had something to do with killing J. K.?"

"The only people who knew I was meeting with J. K. that night were people connected to VDE."

Hubrecht dismissed that with a slight movement of his fingers, saying, "That sounds as paranoid as the media bent on convincing the public that I had my son kill a competitor.

Preposterous," he muttered. "Why would I kill someone I can crush in business?"

Nothing about this conversation between Hubrecht and Ryder fit with what Bianca had anticipated. She'd expected Hubrecht to welcome Ryder with open arms, which he hadn't, and for Ryder to be at home in this environment, which he wasn't. And Hubrecht knew that she was FBI, or former FBI for her new cover identity, but he hadn't brought that up yet. Now he claimed that Kearn was not a threat to his business.

But business news had speculated that Kearn had a new weapon coming out that would make a top selling Van Dyke weapon obsolete.

Hubrecht's statements wouldn't change the evidence her team had compiled, but it did give her reason to look at some of her research with new eyes, *if* what Hubrecht said was true and he wasn't just posturing.

Watching these two men interact was bringing up a whole pile of possible questions, starting with who was playing whom? Had Ryder really agreed to the FBI's deal to see his father convicted and sent to prison, too? Was this about Ryder getting his potential sentence reduced? Or was it about being free long enough to get back at the person Ryder believed let him take the fall for a killing?

If someone else in VDE had taken that shot, Ryder had a legitimate beef with more than one person here.

But if Hubrecht was the reason Ryder was arrested for murder, would Hubrecht trust anything Ryder said or did at this point?

She couldn't start doubting her research. Not now.

Both men were guilty. That was all that mattered.

Hubrecht broke the silence with, "What about J. K.'s people? They could have known about the meeting as well. His oldest son has taken over since J. K.'s death. How do you know *he* didn't arrange the killing to push his father out of the way?"

"They wouldn't kill their father. J. K. was close to all three of his boys."

"And that makes him a good man?"

Hubrecht hadn't sounded disappointed … or hurt. That would be too human an emotion to attach to this man, but Bianca was wise enough to understand that he was no longer talking about J. K. Kearn's death.

When Ryder didn't answer, Hubrecht sighed. "You've always had a place here."

Good time to get back to the reason they were here. She hoped Ryder would change his tune and be more agreeable.

Ryder made a *pfft* sound. "In sales? That's not me."

Bianca kept the idiot smile on her face but wanted to strangle him for killing the perfect opening for a job at VDE. She angled her head at Ryder. "Don't be so quick to discount yourself, Darlin'."

"I'm not. He knows I'm not wired for schmoozing."

She can get married and let a man accused of murder kiss her, but he couldn't schmooze a little to hold up his end of the deal? They were going to have a come-to-Jesus meeting real soon about everyone's responsibilities this week. If they made it that far.

Hubrecht glanced at her. "Ryder's right, but I wasn't thinking of sales." His gaze shifted back to Ryder. "I need someone in production. Would you be interested in that?"

The only sign Bianca showed of her thrill at hearing that possibility was squeezing Ryder's hand. She hoped he read hand squeezes better than eye messages.

"Maybe. What'd you have in mind?"

"I'll tell you tomorrow when we can talk more about this."

She got where he was going. Hubrecht didn't want to tell Ryder anything in front of her, which meant Ryder would be coming here *without* her. That couldn't happen, but Ryder was barely getting his foot in the door. Would he ask for Hubrecht to give Bianca a position as well?

Nope. Ryder didn't say a word about her.

She tried to look pleased when she said, "That is so nice of you, Hubrecht. I'm hoping I'll have as easy a time finding a position."

"I'm sure I could find a place for you here—"

Bianca jumped on it. "Really? That's wonderful."

"—if I could trust you," he finished with unapologetic bluntness.

"What ...?" she sputtered, ready to demand Ryder pull out their wedding documents.

Instead, Ryder stood. "I don't need a job here. Let's go."

He couldn't be serious, could he? How had this fallen apart so quickly? "Wait, Ryder."

"Why? So he can insult you again?"

Hubrecht stood. "I have no intention of insulting Bianca, but I didn't build a company this successful without vetting every person who works for me. I'm only being cautious. She's an FBI agent."

Oh, *crap*. Bianca jumped up. "I was."

"And you want me to believe you just walked away from the agency?"

Ryder pulled her to his side. Before Bianca could get in another word, Ryder ripped into Hubrecht. "Bianca lost everything when she stuck her neck out for me. As soon as she uncovered evidence that proved I couldn't have been in position in time to make that shot, the FBI let her go on the lame excuse that she'd gotten involved with a murder suspect. She fought them and everyone else to get me released. It cost her a job and her friends. Her entire department treats her like a pariah because she proved their research was flawed, which embarrassed all of them. Besides that, she's still the only one who believes I'm innocent."

That sounded like the speech *she'd* practiced, thinking she would be the one expected to explain herself, but Ryder's delivery was so spot on that even she believed him.

And he wasn't done. "With my notoriety, Bianca is severely limited in her options, especially with her background. Her chances of getting a job in law enforcement are nil and, even if she could, I wouldn't let her risk it because some law enforcement might retaliate against her for springing me. We come as a package deal. All or none."

Well, *that* threw down the gauntlet.

For all the anger pulsing from Ryder, not a flicker of emotion had surfaced in Hubrecht's face. "I don't want to fight with you, Ryder, and I do want you to stay. I was sincere when I invited both of you to reside at the family home, especially now when you'll be hounded by the media. Family is everything to me. I trust you because I know you. Bianca is welcome to enjoy doing anything she wants while you're gone from home, but how can you expect me to trust someone I've just met with VDE information?"

Hubrecht sounded so rational when he put it that way.

Bianca stepped in before Ryder had a chance to bomb this fragile relationship. She held her hand up, requesting to be heard. "I expected this. We both did."

She spared Ryder a glance then continued. "I do appreciate the offer to just take it easy, but I can't sit around and do nothing. I spent the past three years pulling twelve, sometimes fifteen-hour workdays on the cyber espionage team. That's why I was able to dig for so much on Ryder's case. I'm sure I can find some contract computer security work I can do from home for the time being."

If she thought Hubrecht was distrusting before, telling him she was going to spend her days on a computer while inside the family home clearly bothered him. *Now we're getting somewhere.* She told Hubrecht, "But regardless of what I do for work, having us stay in your home is going to be uncomfortable if you don't trust me, which means none of the family will. What can I do to solve this dilemma for you?"

Ryder growled, "You're not doing *anything* to prove yourself to them, Bianca."

"I like how you think," Hubrecht said, ignoring Ryder, his attention on Bianca only. "I could use someone with counter-cyber-espionage skills."

"I'm listening."

"I'll have my security department clear you."

Bianca said, "All right."

Ryder growled, "No! She's my wife. That should be enough."

She wasn't sure if Ryder meant that or was just playing up the moment, so she turned to him. "We talked about this. You know it's always going to be an issue."

"I trust you. That's all that matters." He cupped her face, holding her gaze long enough for her to see the struggle in his eyes. He really didn't want her to agree?

No. That was just great acting.

She put her hand up on Ryder's arm and put some pleading in her eyes. "But I want to fit in with your family and they aren't going to allow me to if Hubrecht isn't satisfied." *And I am not letting you come to work without me.*

Hubrecht interjected, "See? You married a bright girl, Ryder. It's settled." He paused before adding, "There's a car downstairs inside my secured garage that will take you both to the house. Meet me at ten tomorrow, Ryder."

"Don't you want me here, too, Hubrecht?"

"I'll let you know as soon as you have security clearance. It shouldn't take more than two weeks."

Two weeks? Hubrecht had managed to diffuse the issue and still bar her from VDE for the duration of the operation.

She needed Ryder to take the job with Hubrecht, but Hubrecht and Ryder might be the ones putting on a show for her right now, which meant she could not allow Ryder to come here without her.

How the blazes was she going to manage that?

CHAPTER 8

MUNK KEPT THE crosshairs of his night-vision-enhanced scope on the male target who, at half-a-mile away, hammered his mistress on the secluded balcony of a premier London residence—a private flat the man kept secret from his wife.

The same wife who'd paid Munk exceptionally well for evidence of her husband's secrets and offered a bonus to tidy up her dirty laundry.

An unfortunate arrangement for her two-timing husband, but a windfall for Munk.

Fog smoked around his body and the evening chill felt refreshing after the last two weeks he'd spent in an Iraqi desert hunting a political target.

Someone else's politics. Didn't matter which country or who the target was as long as they agreed on his price.

His cell phone vibrated in the pocket of his gray desert-patterned cargo pants. Munk's entire body lay hidden beneath tree branches that overhung the roof. His purposeful choice of clothing blended into the rooftop's bleak colors. He easily lifted his two-hundred-and-fifteen pounds an inch off the gritty surface to pull the phone out and slide his finger across the surface to answer.

"What?" he whispered. Munk disliked interruptions while on a mission but being an enterprising businessman, he didn't want to miss out on any lucrative projects.

"When can you be in the States?"

Ohh—his best-paying American customer. Annoying, but with deep pockets. Munk's pulse always jumped at the chance to work for this one, but he never allowed his enthusiasm to show. "Depends."

"This pays well."

"That's a given." Munk adjusted his Barrett Model 99 two millimeters to the right and fixed the crosshairs on his target. *Not yet.* Let the guy have one last good hump.

Professional courtesy from one potent male to another.

"There's paying well...then there's paying *exceptionally well*," his client said.

Munk sucked in a quiet breath. He never broke a sweat over a kill—that was sport. He fed on the adrenaline rush of the hunt, but money—big money—made him hard faster than a Shanghai whore.

Grinning, he spoke softly. "How soon do you need me?"

"Now would be ideal, but tomorrow is sufficient."

"Who's going down?" Munk started mentally calculating what he'd need for the trip.

"This is different."

"How so?" He liked clean kills, nothing fancy.

"I'll give you the details when you arrive."

"And it pays exceptionally well?"

"Yes."

"What do you want? Information extraction?" He had creative ways to reach a captive's physical and emotional limits that were almost as satisfying as killing.

Not quite, but almost.

Considering this client, Munk had an inkling of the target's identity. His lips curled up. A fat wad of money to inflict pain on a man Munk would dismember for kicks.

It didn't get any better than this.

His client interrupted his fantasy. "No. More like terror. I want her rattled until I get what I need. I have specific plans."

"Her? How old?" Munk wanted to make sure he'd heard correctly, but male, female, child—he didn't care as long as the jack came stacked high.

"*Her.* Twenty-six. Can you be here by eight tomorrow morning, ready to work?"

Munk checked his Glashutte wristwatch, admiring the new

timepiece that had set him back twenty thousand—chump change. With a little luck he could make the last flight out of Gatwick.

"I'll be there. No killing, huh?" Munk asked, a little disappointed.

Silence filled the line for a few seconds before his client answered. "I didn't say that, but I have a specific timeline for this itinerary. I'll call you at eight eastern time."

Munk slipped the phone back into his pocket and checked the target. The mistress twisted in her lover's arms, allowing a clear view of the man's face, contorted as he neared ecstasy.

Slowing his breath to reptilian, Munk centered the crosshairs on his target's right eye.

Too bad, Romeo. Time to go.

CHAPTER 9

R YDER SHOULD HAVE mastered patience after sitting in
a tiny cell day in and day out, wondering if that was all
he'd do for the rest of his life.

He definitely should have gained extraordinary tolerance from
the two times he'd spent in the Hole. But he evidently hadn't,
because he'd come damned close to screwing this mission when
he'd been forced to act pleased to be offered a job at Van Dyke
Enterprises.

That came from having spent his youth under Hubrecht's
grinding thumb. Ryder had never wanted to return.

*I spend five months locked away like an animal and Hubrecht
acts as if it were nothing. Cold-blooded bastard.*

Had the Van Dyke patriarch framed Ryder for murder?

Ryder would never have thought so back when he'd first gone
into the Army. At one time, Ryder had credited his extreme
discipline to the time he'd spent working with Hubrecht.

Back when he'd had time away from this place to consider
all the things Hubrecht had done for him, the bastard child of
Hubrecht's dead sister.

Now Ryder wasn't so sure of anyone anymore.

"Ryder."

He blinked at the sound of Bianca's voice breaking through the
haze that blanketed him. Immediately sweeping a look around
them, he realized he'd been frowning as he walked through the
top floor of Van Dyke Tower. Not a wise move with security
cameras everywhere.

Cutting his eyes over at Bianca, he felt like an ogre when
she managed to keep a pleasant expression on her face as they
headed to the elevators. "What?"

She whispered out the side of her mouth. "I'm going to have a bruise if you don't let up, *dar*-lin'."

His fingers were gripping her upper arm. Damn. He loosened his hold and felt a sick punch to his middle when he saw pink blotches where his hand had been. "Sorry."

"It's okay." Her words were too terse for that to be the truth.

"No, it's not." He'd never put a mark on a woman who hadn't attacked him first in a combat situation, but this was not the time to discuss the injury. Bianca probably wouldn't believe someone who'd just been in prison anyhow, would she?

Regardless, he rubbed his thumb lightly over the injured skin.

She glanced up at him with that look again, the one that questioned what he was doing.

Did she think he'd held her that tightly on purpose?

Sometimes everything around him faded away and his world changed to a different place with little notice. He had a moment of wanting to explain that to her so she'd understand, but telling Bianca that he disappeared from reality at times might only freak her out.

That wasn't her fault. Ryder had demanded someone with no field experience. She was a brilliant researcher and he'd called her a file clerk.

He cringed now, thinking back on what an asshole he'd been.

But he'd walked into that room on the heels of seven days in the Hole, took one look at Murdock, who represented the power of the FBI, and Ryder had seen red, as in *wanting-blood* red. He'd needed someone to be as miserable as he was, but with some distance, he was now cursing a decision made in anger.

Bianca had compiled a ton of evidence against him. For that reason, he *had* hoped that he could get her into a position where she could see the evidence differently, but in truth she was here partly because she'd just been in the wrong place at the wrong time the day Ryder had walked into that meeting.

The FBI owed him for turning a blind eye to the possibility that Ryder had been framed, content to let Ryder go down in flames for someone else's crime. He'd wanted Murdock to see how it felt to lose control of a situation, so Ryder had forced Murdock's hand in demanding Bianca partner with him.

She'd been an easy target to manipulate.

By the end of two days in intensive planning, Ryder had realized just how dedicated she was to her job and how much she believed in what she did, which was a good thing for him on this mission. But the longer he was around Bianca, the more it was becoming evident that he'd chosen the wrong person and was regretting his hasty decision made in a moment of fury. She could end up getting hurt, and she didn't deserve that just because she worked hard at her job.

They should've given him some downtime to get his head screwed back to something imitating normal before having this offer shoved in his face, but Murdock had set a brutal pace and dared Ryder to balk.

Bianca was a decent woman with a passion for her mission and for justice.

If only he could point all that passion and dedication toward hunting for the real killer.

As his anger had cooled, he'd realized one thing for certain. Jabbing at her for her role in this wasn't going to bring her over to his side.

She shouldn't be here, but she couldn't leave now. It wasn't as if Ryder could swap out for a new wife.

Wife. He would never put a woman he cared about in this situation.

As they neared the elevator, Bianca slowed her pace. He moved his hand to her back to keep her heading forward, but her feet took shorter steps.

Ryder nodded at the security guard who would have already been alerted to use his keycard that was needed to activate the elevator. That was the only way to ride all the way down and access the secure underground garage that was available to only a select few.

Bianca asked, "What floor are we on?"

"Thirty-second. Why?"

"Just curious."

Ryder took a look at her. She was pale.

Why now? She'd been fierce with Hubrecht, surprising the

hell out of Ryder when she'd held her own with the man she believed sold weapons to terrorists.

Ryder hadn't wrapped his head around *that* accusation yet, but it seemed there was a lot he hadn't realized about this company or his family.

Bianca stopped short five steps from the elevator and muttered, "Guess it's too many stairs."

Was she nuts? Ryder looked at her then at the elevator door, then he remembered her quick decision to take the stairs down from the helipad. "Are you saying you can't—"

She swung around on him with a smile too bright to be real. "I said I'm ready to go home."

Was she afraid of elevators or claustrophobic? If so, why wouldn't she tell him? Did she think he'd use that against her somehow?

He could, but he wouldn't.

Bianca had been through her share of stress today and it was only day one. He wasn't going to push her to ride an elevator when she clearly had some fear of it.

What the hell? In prison, he'd sometimes run in place in the cell for an hour at a time. How long could it take to walk down thirty-four flights of stairs?

When Ryder lifted his hand to wave off the guard who had stepped inside the elevator to key it, Bianca caught his arm, holding it down and said, "Don't."

He dipped his head close to hers and shouldn't have. He got a whiff of whatever she used for shampoo that smelled like lilac and his dick took note. "Don't what?"

"I'm good with the elevator," she whispered on a shaky breath. "Please. Let's just go."

The guard now held the "open doors" button and watched them.

Everyone watched them. It would be this way all week.

Ryder couldn't wait to get out from under the microscope. Bianca probably wanted that even more. He put his hand lightly on her back, careful not to make her feel pushed, as he followed her into the elevator. His fingers itched to slide up into her thick auburn hair and pull her against him. That would lead to his dick sliding in somewhere else and based on her reaction to his touch in the chopper earlier, it wouldn't take that long to get there.

He closed his eyes and pulled his hand away from her before she felt it shaking with barely restrained lust.

When he opened his eyes, his gaze landed on the slats of mirrors between the rosewood panels that were intricately carved with mountain and waterfall scenes. He had a memory of making faces in the narrow mirror sections and Hubrecht calmly telling him to turn around and act like a young man should. Ryder used to like getting away from Lady Anne on the weekends and coming to the office with Hubrecht. Been a long time since he'd thought about that.

The guard exited the elevator and the doors closed on a whisper.

Ryder asked, "Okay, what was that about?"

She wouldn't look at him.

In fact, she was rigid as a board and her lips were moving like she was counting or reciting something. Still pale as a hotel sheet. The elevator was descending so gently you couldn't feel the change, but it would take a few minutes to get down.

He started to put his arm around her, but he wasn't sure she'd appreciate the gesture or if it would make things worse for her.

Her purse started buzzing, but she didn't notice it with her attention locked on the buttons lighting up slowly as they passed each floor.

"Bianca?" When she didn't say anything, Ryder brushed his hand over her hair.

Touching her usually brought some reaction even if it was a death glare.

There it was.

Her pretty lips pursed in annoyance, but that failed to hide the fact that something bothered her. "What, *dear*?"

He mentally smiled at the attitude loaded in that *dear*. "Your purse is buzzing."

"What?" She scrambled to dig her phone out and pulled it to her ear. "Hello? What's wrong, Mama? I couldn't hear all that. Are you talking about Daddy?"

Mama and Daddy? Was this some bogus phone call from Murdock? And hadn't he warned her about not bringing a cell phone, because it might get confiscated at some point and traced back to the FBI? One glimpse at Bianca's ashen face pushed Ryder's annoyance aside. She barely contained her distress, which was saying something for a woman who strived to prove she was tough.

Her face took another radical change when she slapped a hand on her forehead and moved the phone away from her ear, muttering, "This can't be happening." She pulled the phone back and said, "Calm down, Mama. The connection is breaking up. I can't understand what you're saying."

A soft ding sounded and the doors to the elevator opened.

Bianca kept trying to say something but either couldn't get an opening or hesitated to speak freely.

Ryder put his arm around her and ignored the new bout of lust brought on by touching her. He kept his voice low. "You'll have privacy once we're in the limo."

She didn't snap at him or jerk away.

Gratitude filled her eyes at his suggestion. "I'll call you back in five minutes," she promised the caller, Mama, then pressed the off button.

A potential family crisis might be the opening he needed to get her out of this mission.

Did he really want that? If Bianca got pulled, how would Ryder find what he was after without her computer expertise? He didn't know, but this might be the chance to right a wrong. He didn't wish her family any harm, but if that phone call turned into a family emergency, it would provide the perfect reason for Murdock to pull Bianca without raising Hubrecht's suspicion.

But would Murdock want evidence of Hubrecht funneling arms to terrorists badly enough to leave Ryder out here running solo?

Logic said yes.

But Ryder's gut said, *not a chance.*

CHAPTER 10

DID EVERY DISASTER in Bianca's life have to strike at one time? She sank into the creamy black leather seat of the second stretch limo of the day—of her life.

How was she going to explain to Murdock that Ryder had been welcomed back into VDE, but *she* wouldn't be until Hubrecht had a full background check run on her that would take two weeks?

And now Mama called saying something about Daddy and a heart attack.

Had she meant Daddy was *having* one or was Mama just using one of her sayings like, "Lord have mercy, your skirt's too short. You're gonna give your daddy a heart attack."

Tell me Daddy isn't sick. Bianca fought against the panic of losing someone else she loved. She'd never been this way until Sara Lynn was killed. Daddy had suffered a mild heart attack eighteen months ago and Bianca was just now getting to the point she could get through a day without the fear of losing him or Mama.

Bianca would put up with anything to get inside VDE, but if her Mama or Daddy truly needed her, she'd start walking home now if that was the only way to get there.

Ryder told the driver, "Head downtown. We'd like to ride a bit before going home." Then he raised the privacy window and turned on the stereo just enough to shield their words again. He put his hand over Bianca's that held her phone. "The Van Dyke home is ten minutes away. This drive through town will give you some time to talk to your family without having to rush."

"Thank you." Why was he being so nice? Shouldn't he be gloating over getting inside VDE without her? He was crazy if he thought he was leaving her at home tomorrow, but she'd handle one crisis at a time. Family first.

Ryder watched her face that had to be showing all the pain in her chest right now. He asked, "Is something wrong?"

Where to start with that list? "Just need to return this call."

The minute the limo was underway, Bianca hit speed dial on her prepaid cell phone. She'd gotten it just for an emergency. She covered her conversation with her cupped hand.

"Hello?" Her mama always answered the telephone like she expected bad news.

Deep breath. "You weren't serious about Daddy, were you? He's not in a hospital, is he?" Nothing could happen to the one man who hung the moon in Bianca's world.

"Baby, your daddy's right here. You know we don't go to hospitals except that one time. He's too ornery to have another heart attack."

Bianca closed her eyes and dropped her head. "Mama, how did you find me?"

"I tried your cell phone, but it didn't work. So I called that emergency number you gave me, you know for that girl, Sandra, you used to work with? She said you might be on an airplane heading out for a honeymoon. You know I don't like airplanes. They ain't safe."

Bianca sighed. This was a perfect example of why no one except Sandra had her temporary cell number. She'd trained under Sandra, who'd worked for the agency ten years and left four months after Bianca had started. They became fast friends, and Sandra was the one person Bianca had figured would understand when Bianca told her she needed someone to funnel a call to her if an emergency arose while Bianca was out of pocket on agency business. A safety valve if her parents had a problem because she knew Murdock would not tell her until the mission was done.

Bianca could not live with herself if her family needed her and couldn't find her.

But having a call routed to her prepaid phone was better than her mother being patched through to Murdock.

"Mama. Back to Daddy—is he or is he not sick?" Bianca threw a glance at Ryder who acted as if nothing at all was out of the ordinary. Bianca closed her eyes again to concentrate on what her mother was babbling on about.

"No, Baby, your daddy's never sick. You know that. Of course, he did get a cough two weeks ago, but I gave him some honey with salt. Remember when I used to give you that?"

Please, God, help me out here? "Then what is this call about, Mama?"

"Oh, your daddy got a call from Elbert who heard from Sadie's sister in Toccoa that her cousin the hairdresser—you know the one that permed Betty's wig and fried it—anyhow she heard from her brother in Conyers that they had a picture of you on the television and said you were a gittin' married. Your daddy got all worked up, well I did too, but your daddy started hollerin' at the phone, so I hung it up before Elbert sent the loony wagon. Just tell your daddy that it wasn't you they was talkin' about and he'll be okay."

Not now. Bianca hesitated, debating on what to say. She'd planned to complete the mission then recap the non-classified parts of the assignment for her parents before they heard rumors. A simple plan based on solid logic until the Appalachian network had rolled into action. Her parents hadn't even heard about Prince William and Kate's marriage until Kate was pregnant.

Bianca had felt safe for a week.

One week. That's all she'd needed.

Her gaze drifted to her skirt. She fidgeted with the hem, unable to avoid the truth and finally admitted, "That *was* me getting married."

"You married that man you helped put in jail? They said you got him out, too. Honey, don't tell me you're one of those women what fall in love with convicts."

God, it sounded awful put that way. "No, I didn't fall in love with a convict."

Ryder made a sound that could be a muffled chuckle, but he had yet to even laugh. Now would be the wrong time for him to get a sense of humor.

When Bianca flashed him what she hoped was a look of don't-give-me-a-reason-to-hurt-you, Ryder merely lifted an eyebrow in disregard.

"But you married that fella?" her mama said with total disbelief. "Why would you do that? You didn't even invite us."

Bianca rubbed her head. What had she done in her life to be punished like this? "I did marry him, but it's not what you think." She couldn't divulge the truth, even to her mama, *especially* to Mama. "This was a last-minute thing, and you never know. It may not work out."

"Now, baby, you know we don't believe in divorce. If you marry a man, you make a lifetime commitment. He may not be our first choice for a son-in-law, but the news said you convinced everyone he was innocent so he must be and if you think so we do, too. If you're his wife, then he's part of this family."

No safe way out of this conversation.

Bianca would just have to keep her parents in the dark until the assignment was over. She might be bound to Ryder by law right now, but after Bianca was done with this mission, she'd drive up to her family's home with her annulment papers and explain everything.

But Mama was on a roll. "When you bringin' your new husband up to meet everybody? We'll have a get together just for you two."

Bianca envisioned walking Ryder Van Dyke, raised amidst the Van Dyke fortune, into an old wood-frame house with few amenities beyond indoor plumbing and the smell of home cooking. For a fleeting moment, the idea of him seeing her poor origin embarrassed her. *Like hell.* Her family might not be the Van Dykes, but they gave unconditional love—the same love that had backed her when she left to study at the University of Georgia.

"We're on our honeymoon right now." Bianca almost choked on the lie. She felt Ryder stir next to her. "Give me two weeks and I'll come visit. Tell Daddy to stop threatening to have a heart attack. I'm going to be out of touch for a while, so don't worry and I'll call soon. Okay?"

"What about your job? They said you left your job because you said the government didn't give him a fair shake and they're not happy with you. They should be proud of you for standin' up to everyone and provin' this Van Dyke fella innocent. Why'd you leave?"

Please, God, just strike me with lightning. It would be so much less painful. "Things changed at work. It just wasn't a place I wanted to stay, but I promise to explain everything when I see you." That was as close as Bianca could dance to the truth for the next week.

"All right. We're going to look for you *both* in two weeks. But I'm still hurt you didn't invite us. They said his family's rich. Is ... that why we weren't—"

Pain like a knife struck Bianca's heart. She'd never intentionally hurt her parents and hadn't now, but they didn't know that.

"No, Mama. I don't care that his family's rich. When I come up, I'll explain why we had to get married so quickly and, before you ask, no, I'm not pregnant. It's complicated. We just did a simple service with no family, his or mine. I'm sorry for not telling you and I know it's confusing, but just trust me for now and I'll explain it later, okay?"

"Okay, Baby. We'll wait to talk to you. We love you." Her mother sounded more sad than worried.

Bianca squeezed her eyes to stave off tearing up at her mother's wounded voice. No matter what she said, her parents would still probably believe she hadn't invited them to the wedding because she was ashamed of her roots. Nothing could be farther from the truth, but until this mission was over, she would have to haul around a truckload of guilt.

Swallowing hard, Bianca said, "I love you and Daddy, too, with all my heart. Bye." She shoved the phone into her purse.

Amused, Ryder asked, "When do I meet Mama and Daddy?"

Kidding or not, he needed to know right now that some areas were off limits. She was not going to spend a week with him taking shots about her parents as if they were some joke. Bianca set her jaw and set him straight. "You are *not* meeting my parents. Ever."

He was undaunted by her anger. "Is the media's hounding them?"

"No media. The Appalachian Mountain drumbeat reached them."

Ryder studied on that for a thoughtful moment. "They haven't seen *any* media yet?"

"My family doesn't have an address. You can't find them without really good directions and it's a close-knit area. If the media started up that way, they'd get sent in circles until someone got word to my family and they gave the okay."

She could—would—protect her family from anything.

Ryder nodded. "That's one less worry."

Why? Did he think they'd say something that might blow her and Ryder's cover?

Bianca waited on him to taunt her again about her family or criticize her for having a cell phone, but he didn't.

Just who was Ryder Van Dyke? He'd been annoying and abrupt at times, but he'd also been considerate today, even pleasant now and then.

But there were the other times—the times when she'd looked into his eyes and known he'd retreated to a dark place. It happened during those moments when something triggered his anger.

Something like facing Hubrecht.

Tough. If Bianca could ride *down* thirty-four floors in an elevator, Ryder could sit in the same room with his father without going off on the senior Van Dyke. But it had been a close call.

Stepping inside that elevator had been a close call too.

So stupid for her to still be terrified of elevators.

She wasn't twelve anymore.

Elevators were fine. Rotten wood covering old wells was not.

It was that sickening fear that the bottom was going to drop out from under her that brought on crippling panic when she was in an elevator. But her mama's phone call had distracted her on the way down from Hubrecht's office.

"You traded the country for the big city?" Ryder asked, distracting her from elevators and old wells.

She considered his question that had been presented almost

as a criticism. "Not a lot of colleges or jobs like mine where I grew up."

"If there were?"

"What are you asking, Ryder?"

He shrugged and didn't answer at first. "Nothing."

Why didn't she believe him? She started to dig into it when he asked, "Murdock know about the phone?"

No. Guess the confrontational Ryder was back. "I'll deal with Murdock when this is over, but my parents would not understand being unable to reach me."

"Guess that's the downside of having parents who care about you," he quipped.

Bianca considered his words and the way they came out as a brutal taunt against anyone who was loved. "There is no downside to being loved by my parents."

"I wouldn't know."

"I can understand that it was tough to be adopted, but there are worse things."

"*You* can understand? Really?" His attitude took a nasty downturn. "You with parents who miss you and beg you to come home? How can you possibly understand what it's like to grow up as the bastard forced on a woman who blames him because she's in a wheelchair and for her *real* son's health issues?"

She managed not to flinch at the bitterness in his words. "I thought Lady Anne was driving the day of the wreck. If anyone was to blame, that would make her at fault for the wreck because she lost control."

"Not when she can blame *me* for my mother going into labor and distracting her. If not for *me* being in the womb, then there would have been no labor pains."

Ryder had gotten on Bianca's nerves all day, but she was appalled at Lady Anne's blaming him for that. Talk about screwed up.

Putting aside Hubrecht's being suspected of dealing with terrorists, the man had adopted his sister's child and given Ryder a home. Bianca admitted, "Okay, Lady Anne sounds like a roaring bitch, but Hubrecht must have cared about your mother to take her in when she was pregnant, and to adopt you.

Sometimes bad things happen and you just have to accept your lot in life and make the best of it."

His laugh was dark and warned against pushing this topic too far. "Don't play psychologist with me. And don't kid yourself about understanding what it was like to grow up a bastard in that family."

Bianca shoved her face right up to his. "Oh, you're right. I have no idea about growing up in *that* family, but you're wrong on the rest, because I'm just as much a bastard as you."

That punched the wind out of his anger.

She nodded. "That's right, I'm adopted. In fact, I don't even know who my mother was, but I do know she didn't want me. Someone left me in my daddy's barn in a stroller that cost as much as Daddy made in a month. There was a box of fine baby clothes you didn't find in a Wal-Mart. Inside the stroller was an envelope with ten-thousand-dollars in cash and a typed note that said no one would *ever* come hunting for me."

Ryder's throat moved with a hard swallow, but he didn't try to pass off any useless sympathy.

Her voice softened as she recalled the story she'd been told. "Just that week, Mama had lost her third baby and couldn't even look at me, but Daddy said she was still full of milk. By that night, she finally picked me up to stop me from squalling for food. She fed me and after that, she never let go."

Bianca shook after that rant. She hadn't meant to lose her temper, but Ryder at least knew who his mother was and that she'd wanted to keep him.

He frowned. "I had no idea—"

She held up a hand. "Do *not* feel sorry for me. I was raised by two people who loved me even though they'd lost their natural child. I don't think about the wealthy woman who tossed me aside and could have kept me. I think about the two people who shared what little they had because they believed God had given them a miracle. Maybe you were so busy looking at the negative you missed some of the good things. That's not psychology. It's just plain common sense."

"You're lucky."

His words had been uttered with sincerity that mollified her anger. Nice Ryder had shown up again. "Yes, I am. As for the phone, it's a pre-paid, with no link to the agency. A trusted friend forwards the calls, and obviously she thought this was an emergency." Bianca felt the heat in her face and looked away. "I won't be where my parents can't get to me."

The limo slowed to a crawl, but Bianca felt Ryder's silver gaze on her. To avoid continuing that conversation, she asked, "Where are we?"

"Middle of downtown." Ryder sighed. "Traffic sucks no matter what hour here."

Bianca caught flashing lights. An accident had just occurred, and traffic was being diverted to the left.

She didn't know metropolitan Atlanta well, but they'd been traveling south on Peachtree Street and were now headed east on Edgewood into a much older area. The limo was detoured again a couple of streets later. She lost track of where they were, but the four-lane road they motored down had a desolate feeling.

The limo slowed in the left lane to stop behind an old beater that managed to miss the green traffic light even though there'd been plenty of time.

Bianca grumbled, "Waiting on a favorite shade of green, buddy?"

Ryder didn't move, but Bianca could feel him tense right before he muttered, "Shit."

The way he'd said that one word sent chilly fingers clawing up her spine.

Ryder grabbed her hand. "If anything happens, do what I say. Please."

The "please" from a man who probably hadn't said that word in a long time sent her pulse racing. But she was too busy taking in the changing landscape to answer him.

With perfectly executed timing, a white panel van pulled up tight behind them, then another one blocked the right lane beside them, and a third matching van made a fast left hand turn in front of the beater and stopped short on the driver's side of the limo. White panel vans with no windows. Even a computer geek knew that meant *agency*.

Or agency look-alikes.

Professionals.

Ryder was talking calmly as the scene unfolded. "I'm sorry you're here, Bianca, but I'll find a way to get you out alive. Don't do anything to put yourself in more danger, no matter what."

"You're my responsibility," she said, even if her heart was thumping wildly in her chest. In spite of her words, she was hoping between the two of them they could get out of this.

He cursed as he physically lifted her and tossed her onto the seat closer to the front of the limo. "Don't fight them, Bianca. Don't give them a reason to hurt you. *Please.* Just do what they say."

Six masked figures jumped out of the vans. They surrounded the limo and used sharp-ended batons to smash the rear windows of the limo, then they reached in to pop the rear doors on each side.

Everything happened in seconds.

Ryder fought two people on his left.

Someone lunged in and grabbed Bianca's leg, dragging her out the right side while she kicked wildly to free herself.

Booting his attackers away, Ryder dove for Bianca. She reached for him but was snatched out of his grasp.

She hammered her attacker with every strike she could make, but whoever had her was far more powerful, and anticipated the moves. He knew what he was doing. In less than twenty-five seconds, she was inside one of the vans with a gag shoved in her mouth, and with her wrists and ankles flexi-cuffed. The last thing she saw before a black bag descended over her head was Ryder. He was also cuffed, but still struggling against the three figures tossing him into the van.

Please don't kill him.

Fear for him hit her in the gut like a battering ram. She couldn't have explained that to save her life, but there it was. That, and what these people might do to *her* sent her into alien emotional territory.

Murdock was right. She wasn't trained for this.

What did these people want?

Had Hubrecht found out what she and Ryder were up to and sent a team to eliminate the threat to his activities?

She didn't want to die this way.

Would anyone even find their bodies?

God, this would kill her parents.

Doors slammed shut on the van and it started moving.

Ryder asked, "What the fuck do you—"

His words were cut off by the sound of a thud, like a fist or boot hitting his body. He sucked in air and grunted.

Bianca had been acting badass with Ryder, but this was the real world. This was what happened to *real* field agents. She'd never been so afraid in her life, and if Ryder couldn't fight these people with his skills, there was no chance of her surviving against a professional black ops team.

Her lungs squeezed tight with fear. The FBI unit tracking Ryder's chip would find *him*.

But by the time they did, there might be nothing left but a body.

CHAPTER 11

A PROFESSIONAL SNATCH JOB.

Ryder could hear Bianca breathing hard, terrorized rasps. She was right. He'd forced her to do this, and she was in danger because of him. He cursed his miserable ass over and over again for dragging her into this mission. If he got her to safety, he'd find a way to get her pulled off the mission.

She had parents who loved her. They would be devastated by losing her.

Ryder couldn't hold that against her even if he did feel a deep envy he'd never experienced before.

But would he have a chance to negotiate her freedom with the kidnappers?

If this group had been sent to make a hit, Ryder and Bianca would have already drawn their last breaths. This was a professional team, which hopefully didn't include bottom feeders who would take advantage of a female hostage. If one of them laid a hand on her, Ryder would make sure the pig regretted it in the most excruciating way.

Whoever sent this team wanted something. Ryder was ready to trade even if it meant Bianca was the only one who walked away alive. Boyd had died just because the Beast had wanted to get back at Ryder.

Ryder did not want another death on his conscience.

Bianca sniffled and the sound cut him worse than the knife he'd taken to the chest back when he'd marched toward danger by choice.

Mind in the game, Van Dyke.

He forced his mind off Bianca so he could focus on using the skills that had saved his ass more than once in the military.

This bunch hadn't handled him as roughly as they could have. The boot he'd taken in his side had been just sharp enough to shut him up. He'd gotten the message.

The chip embedded near his spine would bring in the FBI and Slye's people.

If this bunch didn't know about the chip.

If they did, they'd carve up Ryder's back just to get rid of it.

Noises and movement changed. The van slowed, turned sharply and moved along a ... driveway? No, they were entering a building. Ryder heard the squeal of an overhead door being lowered.

He wanted to reassure Bianca, but speaking right now might end with a boot to his head. Getting knocked out, even for a short time, had to be avoided. He had to stay cognizant of time and surroundings for any hope of getting back to Bianca if they were separated and he managed to escape.

They were hustled out of the van and up metal stairs based on the hollow echo of heavy footsteps. A set of hands on each side of Ryder guided him down a walkway then sideways, probably through a doorway. The door clicked shut behind him.

The air smelled old and dank.

His heart had picked up speed with every change, more so now because he didn't know where Bianca was. He didn't hear her. In fact, he'd already become accustomed to her scent and didn't smell her anywhere nearby.

Someone cut the flexi-cuffs on his hands then ordered, "Sit."

Feeling a chair shoved against the back of his legs, Ryder sat. The black bag came off next.

Sabrina and Slye team members Josh Carrington and Margaux Duke stood with their arms crossed, staring down at him. Dingo Paddock's wiry frame sat in the corner with his head dropped forward, as always, over a laptop open on his knees. Chopped blonde hair stuck out in all directions. He typed furiously.

Behind him, rectangular shadows from missing pictures covered the faded blue walls. The only other furniture Ryder could see was a wooden desk that looked too heavy and beat up to have been worth dragging away from the abandoned office.

He shook his head. "Are you out of your fucking minds?"

"No more than usual," Josh answered in his cultured voice, but Ryder had learned recently that Josh, Sabrina and Dingo had grown up on the streets of New York as miniature hoodlums. Then Josh had hit the adoption jackpot with a technology family.

"Where's Bianca?" Ryder wanted to know before he'd listen to anything they had to say.

Sabrina answered, "Safe."

"Terrified," Ryder snapped, reaching up to unbutton his collar and jerk his necktie off. He stuffed it in the pocket of his suit, which needed serious cleaning since he'd drawn blood with at least one punch. But no one in here was bleeding. He passed a hard look at everyone in the room. "Is she hurt?"

He'd asked that in a quiet voice that promised pain if she had so much as a scratch on her, and he didn't have time to figure out why the hell he cared so damn much. Bottom line was that he did. He wasn't sure what this was all about, but Bianca didn't belong in the middle of it.

Your fault, asshole.

True.

"She's fine." Sabrina looked at her watch as she spoke. "Nick's watching her to make sure she doesn't hurt herself trying to escape. Tanner is with the limo driver at another location until I give him the all-clear to vanish. We don't have a lot of time." She shifted her steel gaze back to Ryder. "The FBI will be swarming the area where we snatched you."

Dingo looked up at Ryder. "Now you feel better about my midnight surgery?"

"Not really." Ryder shuddered at the memory of Dingo showing up in Ryder's bedroom at the strategic planning site two hours after the chip had been surgically inserted in his back his first day out of prison. Dingo had explained what he was doing and there was no time for any anesthetic. He'd cut the fucking wound open again—and deeper—to attach a tiny piggyback electronic on top of the FBI's tracking chip.

Dingo had told Ryder if it came down to a choice between getting the information Murdock wanted and keeping Ryder alive, Sabrina wanted to ensure Ryder's survival.

"Just remember," Dingo said, typing as he paused. "Try not to get slammed back against something hard. With the chips so close together, you might damage one or both of them. Disarming theirs will bring the feds down on your head and this mission will be over. Plus, they inserted it close to your spine for a reason."

Ryder had no desire to cripple himself or cut this mission short. "Got it."

Sabrina had the patience of a gnat and wasted no time moving ahead. "Dingo has overridden the transmitter in the chip in your back and is forwarding the signal around the area as if you're moving, but he can't do it for long without someone figuring out what's going on."

Ryder rubbed his wrists. "When they do, they can tell *me* what's going on."

"I don't know who set you up, and after the CIA screwed my team two years back, I'm not willing to trust the life of one of my people to *any* alphabet agency. Murdock doesn't care whether you live or die, and he would never allow you to be privy to everything on this mission, but I do and I will."

Talk about a resounding vote of trust.

Ryder had wondered why Sabrina had supported him for the last five months, even arranging expert legal aid in spite of every piece of evidence stacked against him. He'd appreciated that, expecting to have her support pulled at some point, but Sabrina's determination to help him and the show of the team's backing left him without words when he should have said something.

Sabrina said, "Everything still points to you having killed Kearn, which is *way* too easy and damned insulting. As if I'd hire anyone who killed for money and was too stupid to make that hit and get away clean."

In a screwed-up way, that was flattering, as opposed to Hubrecht's similar comment that had sounded more like condemnation. But that still didn't explain why Ryder was sitting here. "I know you didn't grab me just to rant. What's going on?"

Sabrina asked Dingo how he was doing. He nodded, so she

turned back to Ryder. "Do you know that Nanci Tyler is the FBI agent Murdock assigned as Bianca's contact?"

"Bianca hasn't said a word, but then I'm not exactly on her FBI team. Is Nanci a friend of hers?"

Pacing in front of him, Sabrina continued. "No. Bianca has never met Nanci. Murdock wanted to use someone from Bianca's unit as her contact until I convinced him he'd be taking a risk. That someone in her unit might talk to another FBI agent, because Bianca's research team was very close. If this mission slipped out, you'd both get burned."

"I'm still surprised Murdock didn't balk."

"He did until I told him our people were the ones who found the mole in the DEA task force in Miami last year. That got his attention. He finally agreed that it would be safer to find someone not connected to Bianca's original team." Sabrina nodded at the only other woman in the room as she spoke. "Margaux pulled a personal marker to get Nanci in place."

Ryder had worked with Margaux Duke, aka "The Duke" on a couple of ops. Tall at five-foot-ten, and with legs a mile long under those black knit pants, she had dark auburn hair styled in a careless cut that slashed down against her black turtleneck and fell around an olive-skinned face with high cheeks. Blistering green eyes dared anyone to test her. She was tough and hot in a camo-Amazon kind of way. Ryder didn't know her background, but then he didn't know much about anyone else's since he'd still been the FNG—the Fucking New Guy—when he was arrested.

He asked Margaux, "Were you with the FBI before coming to Slye?"

Leaning a hip on the desk, Margaux said, "No, but Nanci is my cousin. We grew up like sisters. I told her what was going on and that I needed someone to watch my back in this. She put in a request to change departments just before Murdock and Sabrina had their conversation. She was in the perfect place when he looked inside the agency for someone with no connection to any of Bianca's team."

"Nice move."

Margaux accepted the compliment with a nod. "Nanci is loyal

to the FBI and intends to do whatever Bianca or the agency needs, but when I told her what had happened to you and that you're innocent, she agreed to help us as long as she believes we're acting in the best interest of the FBI and this country."

Sitting back with his arms crossed, Ryder asked, "She just accepts that I'm innocent?"

"If I say so, yes. We're that close."

Considered innocent until proven guilty. Wouldn't that be nice?

Ryder nodded. "I'm guessing Murdock doesn't know you're related?"

Margaux shook her head. "But then Murdock doesn't know I exist."

Sabrina cut in, telling Ryder, "You need to make sure Bianca gives you any information passed from Nanci."

"I'll try my best, but we still have a few bumps to work out," Ryder muttered.

"Then unbump them," Sabrina ordered.

Josh shifted his stance, dropping his arms to hook his thumbs in the pockets of his black cargo pants. "We grabbed you for a couple of reasons. One was so we could tell you about Nanci and to bring you up to speed on new information we have. But you'll have the added benefit of what this will do to Bianca."

Ryder scowled. "Give her nightmares?"

"You'll be there to soothe her because the minute we're done here, you get to play hero and escape with her. If you can avoid the FBI picking you both up."

Josh had a point, because people bonded when thrown together in a stressful situation, but Ryder still didn't like Bianca having to suffer through this. And the FBI probably hunted him as they spoke, but Ryder grunted his understanding rather than share his concerns about Bianca and bring all conversation to a screeching halt. The team would look at him as if he'd grown a third eye and he wouldn't blame them.

In their shoes, he'd be wondering what kind of fool he was not to take advantage of Bianca when she was vulnerable.

"Talk faster, people," Dingo ordered without looking up from his computer.

Sabrina moved them back on topic. "Like Josh said, there are other reasons for this meeting. Josh, tell him what we've learned about Czarion that we couldn't discuss during the strategic planning."

Ryder asked, "Wasn't Czarion the name Leanne Witherspoon gave Trish before Leanne died? Something to do with an artifact Trish was appraising for that reality TV show?" Talk about a nasty mess. That was the last mission Ryder worked with Josh and the team.

Leanne had been a mole in a Miami DEA task force. Everything went to shit for her when Josh and Ryder stopped a plan to take down an airliner with a laser device activated near Miami International Airport. Trish Jackson, Josh's future wife, had been on that flight with a senator Leanne wanted dead. Pissed off, Leanne kidnapped Trish, who managed to wreck the car into one of the deep canals along Alligator Alley. Ryder and Josh showed up in time to shoot the gator that had Leanne in its jaws, but she'd died anyhow.

"Yep," Josh confirmed. "We'd searched in every direction for intel on Czarion and found nothing. Trish was actually the one to put us on the right track."

Ryder gave Josh a long look. "Speaking of Trish, you owe me for telling you what a fool you were for even thinking about not keeping her." Ryder paused. "Did you *ever* marry her?"

Josh sighed. "No."

"You really are a dumbass."

Josh flicked a look of impatience over at Sabrina. "He has to look roughed up before he leaves here. I call dibs."

"Dream on," Ryder countered.

Sabrina snarled, "Would you two *try* to get along—just long enough for us to do this? Josh and Trish haven't married yet for a reason."

Ryder frowned. "Why's that?"

Sabrina arched an eyebrow at Josh that would be the equivalent of an executive order if she were president.

"Fuck." Josh looked over Ryder's head when he answered. "Trish won't get married until you're free so you can be there."

Dingo spoke up while still typing. "Trish was not the only one who wanted to wait, mate. True?"

Well, hell, if Ryder walked away from this with his freedom, he was going to find Trish and give her a big kiss. Right in front of Josh just to piss him off.

Arms crossed again, Josh demanded, "Can we get back to the mission?

Ryder conceded. "What did Trish find out about Czarion?"

Sabrina took over again, clearly in no mood for any more jawing. "Trish said she kept trying to figure out something from the night she was kidnapped. Leanne brought up the rare Amber Room panel Leanne had made available to the television show. Leanne told Trish that the panel was authentic, but not the one the Czarion were searching for. When Trish put feelers out for an Amber Room panel as if she had a buyer, she mentioned it to her brother Zane, and he got testy."

"Testy?" Josh asked, eyebrows shooting up. "Testy is mouthing off. Zane threatened to make Trish a widow before she said I do."

Ryder smirked.

"Not funny, asshole."

"Trish will protect you," Ryder taunted, remembering what a bear Zane could be. Trish's brother had a temper that exploded when it came to his sister or his wife, Angel.

Josh scoffed. "I can hold my own with Zane, but I'll be sleeping on the couch indefinitely if I put a scratch on Trish's sainted brother. Once Zane understood that I didn't want Trish involved in our missions any more than he did, he settled down and told us that Mason Lorde had a deal with someone in Germany. The German buyer wanted the Saint Gaudens gold coins Mason had stolen, so they could use them to trade for an Amber Room panel. A very specific Amber Room panel."

Ryder frowned. "Who's Mason Lorde?"

"It was before you came along. He ran an international theft ring that specialized in rare art and collectibles. Whoever he was dealing with killed him after he escaped a dragnet in Miami."

"Okay, what does all this mean?" Ryder asked, directing his question at Sabrina.

"Trish thinks this Czarion might be connected to the Orion Hunters, an ancient, secret group that has passed what they consider their divine roles from one generation to the next. They're searching for five artifacts that when brought together will somehow reveal a message called Orion's Legacy. There's a specific panel from the original Amber Room that's considered one of these artifacts."

Ryder tried not to roll *his* eyes, even though Margaux's practically disappeared into the back of her head when she did. He asked, "And that would matter why?"

Josh explained, "Trish says once Orion's Legacy is unlocked, translated or whatever has to happen, it will predict the Final Conflict, an Armageddon that will end all other wars."

Dingo raised his head and faced Ryder. "I had that same look on my face that you now have, mate. I thought it was a big joke, but Trish is quite clever and when she explains it, I get chills. Even if this Orion's Legacy is nothing more than some legend, these people believe. Few things are more dangerous than those who believe in some greater cause. Zealots."

Sabrina raised her watch up to her eyes and asked Dingo, "How are we doing?"

"Getting close to the two-minute warning. Might be a one-minute warning."

"Got it." Sabrina told Ryder, "All we care about right now is how this affects you gaining your freedom and whether it impacts national security in any way. With Czarion and the Orion Hunters as starting points, we've turned up some things about Van Dyke weapons that have been found in the hands of terrorists over the past twenty-six months."

Ryder murmured, "That's bizarre."

Sabrina didn't pause. "Two terrorists were wounded and captured. They admitted to being Orion Hunters before dying. One said he knew nothing about Van Dyke Enterprises. The other one was kept alive long enough to say that he'd heard their benefactor was connected to the Van Dyke weapons, but he didn't know how other than a vague reference he'd overheard."

In other words, the CIA person who waterboarded the second

terrorist was skilled enough to interrogate without actually killing him.

Sabrina continued, "What Murdock didn't tell you was that the Van Dyke XM-28 Woden rifles being sold illegally are pretty much sterile. They don't have serial numbers or markings on the lower receivers."

Most modern rifles built for military use were made in two main parts—upper and lower—so they could be taken down easily for cleaning. The lower receiver held the critical trigger and firing mechanisms—and was *normally* stamped with the manufacturer's name and government-mandated serial number for tracking that weapon.

"With no serial numbers, how can they be sure these are Van Dyke weapons?" Ryder might accuse Hubrecht of being the hardest son of a bitch any person could grow up around, but he'd always been just as tough a patriot.

Aiding terrorism did not fit the Hubrecht that Ryder knew.

Sabrina pulled a manila folder from inside her jacket and handed it to Ryder. "There's a close-up photo inside of a flaw on a lower receiver. That flaw is *always* present on the weapons found in the terrorists' hands. The only legal weapons that have that flaw were made during the first batch of Wodens that Van Dyke created—the experimental models they were testing. They corrected the flaw before the Woden was put into production and out to the marketplace.

Sabrina paced as she talked. "All those legal experimental weapons have been confirmed as under lock and key at VDE. *But ...* sixty-seven *other* identically flawed lower receivers with no serial numbers have turned up so far. Murdock doesn't want you to know any of that."

Huh. More Woden rifles had been made from that original Van Dyke mold than had been reported to the government, and those rifles were going to terrorists.

Ryder took in every face, watching for some indication that they were concerned about sharing information that could be given to Hubrecht Van Dyke. This team was giving Ryder far more trust than anyone in his position deserved.

Sabrina, Dingo, Margaux, Nick, Tanner and Josh were taking a risk that could land them all in prison if Murdock found out.

His team.

Ryder hadn't realized until now just how much their support meant. He gave a short nod of understanding. "Murdock thinks I'll tell Hubrecht. Won't happen."

"We know," Sabrina waved it off in a way that said she'd never thought otherwise. "That's all we've got so far, but we're still digging, and we'll get information to you when we have it."

"That's more than I could have expected." Ryder looked around and added, "Thanks. For everything. I mean it."

Not one to go gooey, Sabrina snapped, "You're not out of the woods yet. And right now, you still have to get out of here with Bianca, make it look good and avoid getting picked up by the FBI. We'll know when Nanci is passing information to Bianca, but not what it is unless the info comes from us. If we turn up intel you need, Margaux will feed it to Nanci if we can't get it to you any other way. It's going to be hard to back you up from a distance, but we'll try. At least Dingo will be able to track you the same as the FBI can."

Ryder considered something for a moment then asked Sabrina, "What's the chance of Murdock letting me run this solo and pulling Bianca out?"

"Having buyer's remorse?" Sabrina could do sarcastic with the best of them. "Murdock wants something, and he wants it bad. Something he's not sharing, and it's more than just evidence on Van Dyke selling rifles to illegal factions, which is bad enough. But he won't consider letting you run solo if he has to pull Bianca."

"I may have to take that risk."

Fire stoked in Sabrina's steel-blue eyes. "Before you go all protective, keep in mind that Bianca accepted this role voluntarily. Murdock gave her the option to pass after they left the prison, and she chose to stay in."

Ryder hadn't known that. "Really?"

"She may be a rookie, but Murdock assures me that she's trained and understands the risk she's taking. Besides, you need her tech skill to get inside the VDE network unless you've gained all her computer talent by osmosis."

No, Ryder hadn't, but he *was* having buyer's remorse for putting Bianca in this situation.

Dingo announced, "*Shit!* FBI locked onto the bounced signal and is backtracking. Time to escape. Everyone out in ninety seconds."

Ryder stood as Margaux snapped into ready-mode along with Josh and Sabrina. Josh rattled instructions off for Ryder. "Here's your story. You were grabbed by Kearn's people and worked over to tell them who ordered you to kill Kearn, but they were amateurs, and you fought your way out, grabbed Bianca and escaped. That should play well with the Van Dykes and Murdock."

"Ah, hell." Ryder stood up, thinking about all the bones and bruises that had barely healed from his prison battles.

"That's right, FNG." Josh grinned. "And I called dibs."

"Let's get this over with."

CHAPTER 12

THINK ABOUT ANYTHING except being locked in this little room.

Bianca worked feeling back into her wrists, glad her flexi-cuffs had been removed. She rubbed her arms. Now was not the time to be wearing a knee-length dress with princess sleeves.

So *not* feeling like a princess at the moment, and she'd been locked away on ground level instead of a tower.

The walls are not closing in. Think about escaping.

Six-by-ten concrete floor. Ten-foot-high, concrete walls. One tiny horizontal window eight feet up. Streetlight struggled to cut through the dirty pane. Stained drop ceiling. Not a stick of furniture that she could use to climb or turn into a weapon. No rope. No levitating ability.

Escape plan examined.

Analysis: Screwed.

Where had the kidnappers brought her and what were they doing to Ryder? She doubted he was sitting alone in a room by himself. Those people wanted something and given the reason she was even on this mission she didn't think she was their target.

As an introduction to working undercover, this sucked hooey. And it didn't rate any more points as a honeymoon.

The only memorable parts so far had been the ones when Ryder kissed her. If she was ever on a real honeymoon, she wanted a man who kissed like Ryder.

And she'd bet a woman would enjoy sex with *him*.

That's the impression she got every time he touched her.

Or when he looked at her as if he actually found her desirable, which was more than she'd ever seen in Bernard's eyes. All she'd seen in Bernard's eyes was the desire to dominate and abuse.

He'd never had a gentle touch, not like Ryder who had only to touch her hair or put his arm around her and her hormones held a party just for him.

A siren whined, but in the distance.

This was not the time to think about sex. She'd managed to ignore it for five lonely years. Why not now?

Because as much as she denied it, ignored it, and fought it, she found Ryder attractive.

If they'd met in a normal situation, would he even be interested in a woman like her?

Is that ever going to be a real concern?

No.

Then stop dwelling on anything except surviving this.

Her gaze wandered over the room cast in shadows with only that thin slit of light coming in. The well had been completely dark except for a single ray of sunlight that climbed the round wall above her as the sun crept lower in the sky.

Her teeth chattered. She fought the panic trying to seize control.

What if they came for her? What would they do?

She wouldn't kid herself into thinking she would be tough if they tortured her, but what if they tortured Ryder in front of her? Or threatened to shoot him?

Noises erupted outside the door to her room.

They were coming.

Her next breath came fast, then another one. Hyperventilating would end in her passing out. She forced herself to calm down and maintain control.

The sound of at least two people fighting, maybe more, pounded and grunted for a moment then something crashed.

She backed as far into the corner as she could and mentally ran through the simplest strikes she'd been taught in self-defense classes. The ones most likely to work on a bigger, stronger opponent.

Shaking her arms loose, she rolled her shoulders in an attempt to shed some of the tension that knotted them so she could move. Her heart was clearly trying to beat its way out of her chest. The kidnappers should have tied her up, because even though they would eventually get her, she was going to make sure someone bled first.

Two gunshots were fired right outside the door, shoving her heart up in her throat.

Oh, God.

The door crashed open.

Ryder raced in. Holding a handgun.

She stared at him for one second of shock then dove into his arms.

He gripped her close with one arm, whispering, "Are you okay, Sweetheart?"

She was now. Her heart turned warm and squishy at the endearment, and she didn't have the energy to chastise herself. "I'm good."

"I'm getting you out of here. Please, just do what I tell you."

"I will." At this point, she might be doing the equivalent of jumping off a cliff to hand her trust over to a man with the charge of murder hanging over his head, but she believed one thing about this man above all.

Ryder Van Dyke had the skill to escape a group of operatives.

If he said he was going to get her out of there alive, he would.

He kissed her hard and fast, then took her hand and hooked her fingers inside his belt at his back. "Don't let go of me."

With the weapon raised in both hands, he led them to the doorway, checked both directions then out into a pitch-black hallway. She stayed with him step for step, doing her part by watching their backs for any threat. He was weaving around a corner when he jumped back, pushing her behind him as bullets ripped through the drywall at the corner, inches from his face. He leaned around, returning fire until it was quiet.

Tossing the weapon aside, he said, "Empty."

Bianca didn't wait to be told to grab his belt again.

He squeezed her arm as a signal, then moved out.

When they reached the street, she had no idea where they were, but from the short distance they'd traveled by van they had to still be somewhere in downtown Atlanta. Once Ryder had them a couple blocks away from the building, she said, "We have to contact Murdock."

Ryder pulled her into the dark doorway of an old building, turning her so that his body shielded hers. "How do you plan to call Murdock? Your purse and phone are still in the limo—if it hasn't been torched. And the minute you call in Murdock, he'll pull us both." He drew in a deep breath and let it out. "But if you want to de-ass this op, that's what we'll do."

Part of her screamed, "Yes!" but the part that was even more committed to seeing this through pushed her to say, "No, I don't want to quit."

Ryder brushed his lips over hers.

"Why'd you do that?"

"Because you're amazing."

She smiled, a real one for the first time that day.

Butterflies were holding a flutter convention in her stomach again. She had no idea how to reply and glanced around to hide the quick flash of nerves she got at the intense way Ryder was staring at her. "I'm surprised Murdock hasn't swarmed us by now."

"Something might have interfered with the radio frequency for the chip. I heard one of the kidnappers say they sent someone to keep the limo moving, because they suspected it was being tracked."

"Who grabbed us? And why?"

"Kearn's people. His sons are out for vengeance. They wanted to know who contracted me to kill J. K."

"What did you tell them?"

Ryder was quiet for a moment. "That I have no idea who contracted the hit because I didn't kill him. They didn't like that answer."

Bianca's determination to back the findings of her team warred with her gut, arguing that Ryder might be telling the truth.

"You didn't tell them you thought Hubrecht was behind the hit?"

"I suspect Hubrecht, but then I suspect *everyone* at VDE, but I won't condemn another person until I'm absolutely certain and have evidence. Someone was sent to kill J. K. and they used the timing to finger me for it, which points to everyone in my family, plus Sam Long and Kale Carter. From your perspective, everything points to me. I could be just as wrong as you are."

Her conscience was taking a beating from the constant, knocking accusation that she was, indeed, wrong. That this time, facts *had* lied.

Could Ryder be as innocent as he claimed?

If so, what had she missed in her research? The doubt that had pecked at the back of her mind from the moment she'd started digging into Ryder's case returned. One question had gone unanswered despite all the other evidence gathered.

Just as Hubrecht had pointed out, wouldn't someone with Ryder's skills have known better than to use the very weapon he'd preferred and used consistently throughout his career as a sniper?

She didn't have answers and couldn't figure out anything while she was running through the hood, trying to avoid associates of the men who'd grabbed them. A mugging should concern her, but after watching Ryder in action, any mugger stupid enough to jump them tonight would be in for a rude surprise when he stepped into Ryder's path.

"We need to find wheels," Ryder said, scanning the light traffic moving along the street.

No handy limo hanging around.

She'd been searching while they stood there and finally spotted the illuminated top of a Yellow Cab and tried to step past Ryder. "A cab. Let's wave it down."

"You stay here until I call you out."

Arguing would only waste time and Ryder was too tense to push right now. "Okay."

The cab took its time coming over to the curb. It slowed long enough for the driver to take a hard look at Ryder and the blood on his tux, then the taxi peeled off.

Bianca ran out of the doorway, shouting, "Come back here, you miserable, egg-sucking prick!"

Someone chuckled.

She turned around, sure it couldn't be stone-faced Ryder, but he was the only one standing there with amusement glittering in his eyes. She might have taken a moment to enjoy this break in his hard-ass veneer, but he was laughing at her. "What's so funny?"

"That was impressive adult language."

She covered her mouth. Add potty mouth as another newly acquired skill for an undercover agent. Mama would've had a fit if she'd heard that.

Daddy would have another heart attack.

Bianca stopped in her tracks when she finally got a good look at Ryder with streetlight catching his face. "Holy crap, no wonder the cab took off." She came over, putting her hand on his jaw. "Does it hurt bad?"

"I'll live." He wiped his cut mouth on the sleeve of his ripped-up jacket as he walked her back over to their dark doorway.

"I know you'll live, macho man. My question was whether it hurts." She'd been sweating from their fast escape, but now that she wasn't moving and the adrenaline rush was dying down, the night air chilled her.

He must have noticed her shiver. He pulled his jacket off. He draped the coat around her shoulders, keeping himself between her and the street the whole time.

He pulled the lapels together, using them to draw her in close and asked in a deep voice, "If I tell you my booboo hurts, will you kiss it and make it better?"

Now she understood why women fell at Ryder's feet.

She wasn't falling at any man's feet, but he was so adorable in that moment she couldn't help her reaction. Lifting up on her toes, she gently kissed his swollen cheek then his abused mouth. She was being careful not to cause him any more pain.

But Ryder made a noise that sounded like a jungle cat on the hunt and wrapped her in his arms, not holding back when he returned the kiss. His tongue ran across her teeth then played with her tongue. If this man could bottle his ability to kiss, he could take over the world. Well, half the world.

The female half.

She heard a car motor puttering toward them right before

Ryder shoved her deeper into the recess and stepped out to approach the cab. He had frighteningly fast reflexes.

The cabbie shouted out through his open window. "You folks okay? Need a ride?"

Bending down, Ryder answered, "We got mugged, but I've got a hundred-dollar bill hidden in my boot. It's yours if you let me use your cell phone to make a call and drive us back to Buckhead."

"In the words of my favorite actor, show me the money."

Ryder pulled his boot off and produced a one-hundred-dollar bill, then he waved Bianca over to the car. He kept watch until she was inside and slid in behind her, telling the driver the address.

When the cabbie handed Ryder his cell phone, Ryder punched numbers quickly. "Terrence, are you at home?" He paused, nodding. "I'll explain when I get there, but I need you to clear me through the gate. I'm in a cab. Did our driver call in?" Ryder listened. "Great. We're safe, but a little scuffed up. No, I'm good. Don't send anyone. We'll be there soon."

She could see blood seeping where the front of Ryder's white shirt had a rip at chest level, and he'd have a black eye tomorrow. Scuffed up? Kearn's people had worked him over. When Ryder hung up, Bianca took the phone from him. "Let me tell my people that we're okay, too."

He hesitated but handed the phone to her.

She dialed the hotline she had for Nanci Tyler that Murdock had given Bianca for a dire situation since they couldn't send Bianca out with a secure line. But no one would have a tap on a random cabbie's phone.

Nanci had been brought in from another division in the FBI to be Bianca's contact. Murdock had wanted to limit the number of people who knew the truth about what Bianca was doing, and figured if he brought in an unfamiliar agent the team wouldn't get anything out of her.

Ryder had been telling Hubrecht the truth about Bianca when he'd said she was considered a pariah in her department.

To convince the media—and her department—that this was all bona fide, Bianca had announced flaws she'd found in Todd

Dolan's research. Todd was removed immediately, but in truth he currently sat in an undisclosed location with no Internet or cellular connection until this was over.

But Todd would be well compensated, and they'd probably put him at the beach, his favorite vacation spot.

When Nanci answered her phone on one ring, Bianca said, "Just want you to know that I'm fine and all is okay on this end, but this is a quick call." She'd let Nanci know she could only say so much on this end even if the cabbie didn't know her.

"I'll pass that along to the boss, but he'll want a report. Go for a run tomorrow morning and use your tricked-out iPod."

She could feel Ryder trying to figure out what was being discussed, but Murdock had told Bianca to share nothing with Ryder that she didn't have to, including when she picked up or dropped intel. If she couldn't go into VDE with Ryder in the morning, assuming he was still going, she could at least pick up information from Nanci once Ryder left. "Sure."

"Do it at daylight."

What? Bianca sighed, "Okay, good talking to you."

She handed the phone back to the cabbie, thanking him.

How was she going to get away from Ryder that early in the morning?

CHAPTER 13

BIANCA MENTALLY PREPARED to get out of the cab. She wished he'd drive her anywhere but here.

She still had to meet the rest of the Van Dyke clan. The car rolled along a brick-inlaid drive lined with Magnolia trees. Elegant wood sentries lit by architectural lights hidden around the bases.

The driver circled a stone fountain where a bronze sculpture rose from the center. Water streamed from graceful metallic orchids and flowed over the dress of a gaily dancing girl, reminding Bianca of her childhood. Carefree.

Aerial photos she'd reviewed didn't do the estate justice from ground level. The film of this estate that had aired on *Fabulous Homes of Famous Families*—that was before the Van Dykes had taken ownership—had provided her FBI team with a view of some interior rooms and the surrounding grounds. After watching that recorded videotape—fifteen times—Bianca knew those rooms better than her own small apartment in Virginia.

After all, she wasn't here because of spending endless hours in combative training at the gym and honing her gun skills at the range. Bianca enjoyed being in shape and shooting. With those skills, she'd thought she was somewhat prepared.

She'd found out tonight that all her extra training had been useless against a real threat.

No, she wasn't here because of the new muscles she'd developed or her ability to double tap a moving range target with her weak hand.

She was here for one reason. To do what she did best with her exceptional memory for details and her ability to circumvent computer security shields most considered impregnable.

But Ryder *was* trained for what they'd gone through tonight.

He hadn't abandoned her when he could have. And by rights, maybe he *should* have, based on the way she'd been treating him.

It was time to stop fighting him, stop mistrusting every word he said, and act like a partner. And maybe it was time to consider that he just might be telling the truth.

But for now, she had to prepare to step out of this limo as the new Mrs. Ryder Van Dyke, who would be expected to appear clean and tastefully dressed.

Not some woman who looked as though she'd been in a barroom brawl.

Ryder's jacket hung to mid-thigh on her and hid the rip in her sleeve. She rubbed at the dirt smudge on her arm and brushed at her dress, where grime clung like metal shavings to a magnet.

She smoothed her hands over hair that hadn't fared much better than the rest of her.

Ryder had his arm around her and gave her a little squeeze. "Ready?"

Not even. Her simple roots hadn't prepared her for stepping into a world of opulence, even if she'd had on her best church clothes. She could only hope bulldog determination would make up for lack of a pedigree.

As the cab stopped, Bianca nodded. "As ready as I'll ever be at this point."

Ryder handed over the hundred-dollar bill he'd promised the driver and climbed out before helping Bianca to her feet.

She stared up at the monstrous house and suffered a moment of serious insecurity, but she'd just survived being kidnapped at gunpoint. Could meeting Ryder's family be any worse? Half of this place could hold most of the people from her hometown. If *they* visited, it would look like a remake of that old show the Beverly Hillbillies.

"Bianca?"

"Huh?" She ripped her attention from the gigantic house.

The cab drove away. No one could hear her talking to Ryder, but she still needed to act like they were a couple, or someone watching from inside might suspect a problem.

She tried, and was pretty sure she failed, to pull out a new rendition of her I'm-a-happy-bride face as she turned to Ryder. "Yes, Darlin'?"

A swirling breeze lifted several tendrils of hair that flicked across her cheeks. She'd almost convinced herself she had everything under control until Ryder brushed her hair back, his knuckles lightly fanning across her cheek.

She stilled.

"Sure you're ready?" His low, husky voice wrapped its sexy fingers around her comfort-deprived senses.

No, she wasn't sure of anything right now. She'd been fine until he'd touched her *again* and sideswiped her composure. Anxiety brought on a bout of vulnerability. That made her feel weak, and she hated to feel weak, so the end result was anger.

She bit back the urge to snap and quietly ordered him, "Would you stop doing *that?*"

"Doing what?" His mouth curled just a little.

She had a feeling she was witnessing something special when his lips lifted further, into the beginning of a smile. A real one. There was the rascal who had smitten women when he was the hottest eligible Van Dyke before the military and ... prison.

She liked seeing his eyes crinkle, as if he were almost happy, but telling him that would only give him license to keep twisting her nerves into a heated ball of frustration. "Let me save you a lot of trouble."

"How?"

"You're attractive, but I'm not wired for seduction." Not that she was immune to sexy men, but after having Bernard tell her, "You could turn a rock into jello," she'd decided to forget about a relationship until she retired from the FBI. By that time she'd be older and would find a man who wanted only a companion.

Someone who wouldn't accuse her of lacking spontaneity and being the one to ruin sex. No one would ever humiliate her again by claiming she was frigid, then sharing that with half the college, which was so unfair when the pain of intercourse had been just plain unbearable.

She hadn't considered sex since then. Especially once Bernard told her he'd made the mistake of slumming with a hick, and tossed Bianca aside for a new woman better suited to his social standing.

Ryder had flipped a button on her libido, but so had Bernard at first. Regardless, this whole attraction thing was not happening with Ryder. Plus, he was a prisoner in her custody.

Ryder had been frowning at her, but then his eyebrows shot up as if he'd realized something.

"What do you mean by not wired for seduction?" The surprise on Ryder's face was comical. "Do you prefer ... women?"

"What? No." Was he really going to make her explain? "I don't like sex."

"Why?"

"What do you mean why?" Were they really having this conversation standing in a driveway? "I was in a relationship and found out I wasn't cut out for that." There. Done.

Ryder nodded.

What did that knowing look on his face mean? She didn't care as long as the topic ended there. "Glad we're clear." With that out of the way, she turned to head for the front door that might as well be the gate to hell.

"Bianca?"

"What?" she snapped, turning back.

Ryder leaned down and kissed her, holding her face between his hands. He didn't touch her anywhere else, but it sure felt like his hands were running over her breasts and down between her legs.

Something had to be causing the ache in both places.

When he lifted his head, he had that half-smile tugging at his lips again, as if he'd answered a question. Taking her hand in his, Ryder turned her toward the house.

She'd been stunned silent by another Ryder kiss. How could his feel so different from any other, so intense?

If Bernard had ever kissed her with that much heat, Bianca might have stuck it out longer, but that would've been a mistake. Rich guys wanted toys to play with. Once the toy was no more fun, they tossed it aside.

Everything was disposable to those with money.

Even hearts.

Ryder led her up the steps to a pair of leaded-glass doors beneath a high canopy supported by huge columns.

The door on the left opened before they reached it, and an owlish man with thinning gray hair and sunken cheeks appeared. Had to be the butler, Edward Harken. Bianca prodded her tired mind to dredge up his details. Age sixty and he'd worked for the Van Dykes for thirty-four, no, thirty-five years. He wore a dark charcoal suit with a matching gray bowtie on his five-foot-nine body.

Edward didn't so much as blink at Ryder's unkempt appearance, saying only, "How nice to see you, Mr. Van Dyke."

Did the butler need glasses or was it bad manners to say, "What in blazes happened to you?" Bianca's family would have been raisin' cane over who had dared to harm one of theirs, be it family or friend.

Ryder answered the butler as if he showed up every day looking beat to hell. "Hello, Edward. I'd like to introduce my wife, Bianca."

If she didn't know better, she'd be flattered by the warm introduction that sounded as though Ryder was proud of her and their alliance.

Every time she thought she had Ryder figured out, he'd kick his game up a notch. But he was in his natural environment, had come from wealth.

Edward gave a half bow. "So nice to meet you, Lady Bianca."

"*No!*" Ryder snapped.

Bianca flinched at the wrath behind that word.

"My apologies, *Sir*." Edward stiffened.

By God, Ryder appeared chastised by the butler's response.

"Sorry, Edward," Ryder said. "Been a long day."

Eyes tracking across Ryder's ripped clothes and bruised face, Edward answered, "It would appear so."

Ryder's voice was full of warmth when he said, "You haven't called me *sir* since I was old enough to tell you to use my name, which you know is *not* Mr. Van Dyke. I'm still fine with Ryder." He ran his fingers through his hair and expelled a hiss of breath. "You may call my wife Bianca or Mrs. Van Dyke, but—please—do *not* call her Lady anything."

"As you wish." Edward backed into the foyer and managed a guarded smile. "It's good to have you home, Ryder. Your room has been prepared and your clothes have been unpacked. Dinner will be at eight unless you'd prefer it in your room."

"Thank you, Edward. Given the day we've had, I think we'll eat in our room." Ryder took Bianca's hand and towed her toward the stairs on the left.

"Good God, are you alright, Ryder?" Terrence came hurrying down the curved stairs. A young woman followed more slowly, and several steps behind him.

Ryder raised a hand as Terrence hit the landing. "Nothing ice, a shot of Jack Daniels and a few Band-Aids won't fix."

Bianca disagreed on Band-Aids fixing some of Ryder's injuries, but kept quiet and observed the woman just taking the last step. Had to be Ryder's sister, Janeen, in snug black pants and a gold sweater that clung to her lithe shape. She moved with the grace of those born to wealth and good genes.

Bianca had practiced hard to emulate that grace in college.

Dark blonde hair fell around her shoulders, lying as smooth and straight as her bangs.

Janeen had Terrence's pale skin and narrow cheekbones, but her gray-blue eyes were more like Hubrecht's intense, sky-blue gaze than Terrence's faded green eyes.

Terrence said, "Father is at a business dinner tonight. I'll inform him of what happened as soon as he arrives home."

Janeen swept up to them, but spoke to Terrence. "Have Kale put a security detail on these two."

Bodyguards would be a disaster for this mission. Bianca waited to see how Ryder would handle this.

Ryder shook his head. "No, Terrence. Don't mention this to Hubrecht tonight, or he'll want details, and I'm too tired to go over everything. I'll inform him tomorrow at the office." Turning his head to address Janeen, Ryder said, "I don't need a security detail. Kearn's boys were behind this. He'd be a fool to try it again and I'll be driving myself next time."

Bianca studied the two biological children and one adopted sibling. She noted the concern in Terrence's worried eyes and what she could only describe as irritation in Janeen's.

Janeen shrugged. "But you will give Kale a full report, right?"

"Probably."

The conversation died with Janeen and Ryder staring at each other until Janeen said, "I suppose congratulations are in order."

His sister didn't make specific whether she meant Ryder's release from prison or his getting married. Bianca had a strange urge to hug Ryder, since no one had embraced him or cheered for his release from prison.

Family should be happy. They didn't know his release was temporary.

You're not supposed to be encouraging him either.

Bianca was going to need therapy when this was over to untangle her jacked-up emotions.

Ryder didn't ask for clarification from Janeen, instead saying, "Speaking of that, this is Bianca, my wife. Bianca this is our sister Janeen."

Terrence smiled at Bianca and told Janeen, "I had the pleasure this afternoon."

Janeen studied her a moment then extended her hand. "Nice to meet you."

"You, too." Bianca shook hands, hearing the total lack of sincerity in Janeen's voice.

Janeen gave Ryder a malicious smile. "You haven't lost your touch."

Ryder's eyes turned so frigid there should have been icicles hanging from his lashes.

What had Janeen said that insulted Ryder?

Bianca ran back over Janeen Van Dyke's file in her mind. Oldest Van Dyke child at twenty-eight, enjoyed the nightlife, several semi-serious relationships since entering Yale for a business degree she'd never finished or put to use. She'd had no one man in her life for the past year and a half, which might be to preserve her party girl image. And no visible means of support other than being independently wealthy by virtue of birth.

She *was* on the boards of several charities, and she was the face of the Van Dyke family at major social or community events, so Bianca couldn't write her off entirely as fluff.

"What are your plans now, Ryder?" Janeen asked.

"Looks like I'm back at VDE."

"When you swore never to work there again?"

Ryder gave her a wry look. "I don't have a lot of career options at the moment."

Terrence managed to look pitiful in spite of smiling.

Janeen's eyes skated over to Terrence, then back to Ryder. "In what capacity?"

The question had held a warning of some sort, but Ryder brushed it off with, "That's up to Hubrecht."

Bianca had noticed how Ryder constantly addressed Hubrecht as *our* father or Hubrecht, or just *Father* on very rare occasions, but never as *my* father, as if he refused to accept any part in having Hubrecht as a father.

Another disconnect of Ryder's being adopted?

Terrence rubbed his hands together in a blatant attempt to ease the tension. "We'll have to find a night to go out and celebrate once you two are settled in. We know where *you* will be tomorrow, Ryder, but what about your new wife?"

Everyone turned on Bianca so quickly she blurted out, "I'll be looking for work."

Janeen's cool attitude couldn't have switched to surprise faster if the giant bouquet of fresh flowers on the table in the foyer had started talking. "Ridiculous. You just got married, and to a Van Dyke, no less." Her eyes lit up with some idea. "I know. We'll go shopping and have lunch. We can leave around ten. Give us a chance to get to know one another."

Murdock would be pleased since he'd told Bianca to insinuate herself as quickly as possible into the family, but she still didn't like the idea of being split up from Ryder.

And something in Janeen's voice made jackhammers go off in Bianca's gut, which Daddy would have said meant trouble.

Ryder put his arm around Bianca's waist. "What do you think, Sweetheart?"

Bianca was all set to beg off until he'd called her sweetheart. Again. Why that caused her a mental stumble, she didn't know, but everyone was waiting for her answer and she didn't have an acceptable reason to refuse.

She beamed a smile, which made it easier to grind her teeth. "That's very nice of you. I'd be delighted." Ryder's fingers had tightened on Bianca's hip, but they loosened and he let out a weary sounding breath when he told his siblings, "We're eating in tonight, so if you two will excuse us." He'd tugged Bianca toward the stairs, but Janeen stopped him with one more thing.

"Lady Anne wants to see you now."

Ryder paused. "We clearly are not up for socializing."

"She's been waiting in her solarium for an hour and said she wanted to see you the minute you stepped through the door if you intended to stay here. She gave that stipulation to Father when he announced that he'd invited you here. He saw no problem with that requirement, but if you want to blow her off ... "

Janeen's voice trailed off, leaving it clear that Ryder would be defying Lady Anne if he didn't go now.

What a bitch. Dressed as she was Bianca did not want to meet the woman Ryder thought of as the *Dragon Lady*, but Murdock expected her and Ryder to stay at this house. Murdock would not understand any refusal to meet with Ryder's mother, short of their landing in a hospital.

But Bianca had spent enough time around Ryder to see he was ready to fight. Mission or no mission, he was not a man who allowed anyone to push him around.

She cupped his arm. "If Lady Anne doesn't care what we look like, I don't. Let's get this done."

"This is bullshit."

"We'll stay a couple minutes and be out of there."

He finally ripped his angry gaze from Janeen and looked at Bianca.

She didn't say a word, hoping this time he got the eye message right. She was trying to remind him how much was at stake.

That wasn't working. She raised up and kissed him, just a brief touch of her lips to his.

The fury migrated out of his face. He took a breath. "Okay. Let's go."

When they stepped away, Janeen called out, "Lady Anne said

if she's not there she assumed you chose not to meet with her and prefer staying elsewhere."

Bianca picked up the pace, but if Ryder lost his temper with Lady Anne this could fall apart in seconds.

CHAPTER 14

R YDER WANTED TO climb into a car and drive as far away from the Van Dyke home as he could.

If Bianca wasn't standing next to him, he'd have walked out. She was the levelheaded one here.

He needed this more than she did, but she was the voice of calm when he would have screwed up the plan by snubbing Lady Anne. Not that he cared about pissing off the cold bitch, but creating conflict between Lady Anne and Hubrecht could end with Ryder out of a job at VDE tomorrow.

Ignoring the deplorable state of her clothes, Bianca carried herself as a lady. But she kept glancing at the Remington sculptures and priceless art.

Bianca's fingers kept gripping his hand and releasing the pressure, fidgeting. She asked, "Would Lady Anne really toss us if Hubrecht wants you here?"

Regardless of Janeen's callous warning about being late, Ryder kept the pace easy for Bianca's shorter stride. Screw Lady Anne. "She runs the estate with a gloved fist. Hubrecht may control a multi-billion-dollar enterprise, but even he defers to Lady Anne in her home, and rest assured, all of this is *hers*."

"Have you always called her Lady Anne?"

"She prefers the title and, frankly, calling her *Mother* never would have worked. She doesn't fit the image." Resentment leaked through Ryder's words, ruining his attempt to sound matter-of-fact.

He pulled his temper back under control as they neared a room at the end of a long marble corridor. Golden light from Italian wall sconces washed across the solarium.

"That is the revered Lady Anne," Ryder whispered in Bianca's ear when they moved into the doorway and Lady Anne came into view wearing a funeral-black dress. She sat in repose next to a delicately carved antique table. Soft light accented her pale-blond hair styled in a graceful upsweep. She gazed out a window that faced the gardens behind the house, which were lit for night viewing.

Her long, thin fingers were placed delicately in her lap ... elbows propped on each arm of her wheelchair.

A classic beauty in her youth, Lady Anne held so much power because she'd brought the money to this marriage, and that money had staked Hubrecht in his first venture.

Without Lady Anne's money, Van Dyke Enterprises would not exist.

As Ryder and Bianca stepped into the private parlor, Lady Anne lifted her sharp chin. Stern lines replaced the smooth ones of only a moment ago, rearranging her high-cheeked features into an unmistakable composition of disapproval.

That brought back memories.

Many journalists had wanted to interview the reclusive Lady Anne, but she kept the private affairs of this family buttoned up tight. Ryder wished he could enjoy how much his notoriety as a prisoner had infuriated her, but he wasn't proud of any of that.

Pausing close enough to be heard, Ryder called out, "You wanted to see me?"

Poor Bianca dragged out her new-wife expression for what she had to hope was the last time today. In the ensuing silence after Ryder's question, Bianca smiled with charm that he should've warned her wouldn't work on the bitch queen.

Bianca spoke up. "So nice to meet you, Lady Anne. Your home is spectacular. I have to admit, I'm a bit overwhelmed by all this. Thank you for having us here. The peace and quiet will be wonderful."

Ignoring Bianca entirely, Lady Anne pointed her attention at Ryder, raking her gaze over his disheveled appearance. "Must you continually disgrace this family?"

"If that's all you wanted to see me about, we're done."

"No, we are not." Lady Anne's contemptuous gaze swung to

Bianca. "This is your *wife*?" She'd said that as if it had taken a supreme effort not to gag on the word wife.

"Yes."

"You see this as acceptable?"

Ryder shrugged. "If my staying here is an issue, say so. I'll be happy to reside elsewhere." He'd snapped out those clipped words as an open challenge.

Bianca squeezed his hand.

"You're not going anywhere," Lady Anne threw back at him. "Yet."

Bianca exhaled a breath that sounded full of relief.

Lady Anne swung her intimidating gaze to Bianca. "You, on the other hand, have made a major miscalculation. You may have fooled the media, the world, and quite possibly Hubrecht, but I know exactly who you really are and what you think you're going to find here."

Bianca's knees threatened to give out.

Could Lady Anne really know why she and Ryder were here? If so, had she said anything to Hubrecht?

Did that mean Hubrecht had uncovered something while Bianca and Ryder had been busy having tea and scones with their kidnappers?

If so, that would mean a leak from the team. Had it been Slye? What about the FBI? Murdock had kept her research team in the dark about this mission, even to the point of making them hate her, but they were research geniuses and every agency had leaks.

More questions zinged through her brain than she had any hope of answering right now. Her heart collided with her breastbone over and over again.

And her left hand hurt.

She blinked when she finally realized Ryder was squeezing her fingers to shake her loose from being stunned. She let out a calm breath she didn't feel and wiggled her fingers in response. She owed him a thank you if they got out of this.

When his grip relaxed, Ryder gave a dismissive snort to Lady

Anne's announcement. "How would you know anything about my wife when you haven't known a thing about me since I enlisted in the Army?"

Lady Anne swung her formidable gaze from Bianca to Ryder. "I have resources that would rival your employer's."

"If you're talking about Slye, we parted ways the day their attorney suggested I take a plea. Their idea of damage control meant sweeping me under the rug. If not for Bianca, I wouldn't be standing here."

"Of course not, but you don't really expect me to believe this ridiculous marriage, do you?"

Acid churned in Bianca's nervous stomach. She clenched Ryder's fingers to caution him on how he answered that, since Lady Anne had not divulged exactly what she actually knew. Now that Bianca had a moment to consider that, maybe Lady Anne only questioned the amount of time Bianca and Ryder had spent together.

Ryder's tone turned stone cold. "I am here by invitation of Hubrecht Van Dyke, *not* by request, so I *expect* you to respect my marriage and my wife, regardless of what you do or do not believe."

"*Do you* now."

Way to go, Ryder. That should get us tossed out the front gate any minute. Bianca had no way to stop this train wreck, so she held her peace and waited for the track to run out.

He'd helped her a minute ago, but he ran too hot and cold for Bianca to have any sense of comfort. Still, this household was his area of expertise, the whole reason he was on this mission. He should be able to fix this, but that might be tough when he was pissing off the queen bitch.

Ryder added, "Out of curiosity, just *who* do you think Bianca is?"

Bianca managed not to flinch when Lady Anne turned a caustic glare her way and said, "I don't *think*...I know who she is. She's a backwoods-nobody with her eyes on the gold ring. Help the poor little rich boy overturn his conviction in trade for the chance to be a 'somebody'."

Yes! Lady Anne was just being a snob.

Until now, Bianca had never thought being snubbed would be a blessing. She'd hated being ostracized in college because of her Appalachian twang that had labeled her a hillbilly and she'd spent time with a voice coach learning how to shift her speech. She could have no accent—or a classy southern one.

Ryder's entire body tensed from his rigid jaw to his locked shoulders. A vein pulsed in his neck, aggressive body language that said a war was brewing.

Whoa. Why wasn't he laughing that off and acting happy their cover hadn't been blown?

"You know nothing about Bianca," he challenged.

"Oh? You think not?" Lady Anne countered with hands calmly placed in her lap. "I have a file compiled by a reputable firm, but I admit that there are some gaps in the information I want filled."

"No."

"Why not, if she has nothing to hide?"

Bianca said, "I don't mind an—"

Without a blink, Lady Anne fired a question. "Who are your people?"

"No," Ryder snapped. "My wife will not be interrogated."

The female side of Bianca appreciated his gallant defense, but they weren't in a real relationship, and this was all about winning.

What would a new wife say? Bianca licked her dry lips, and Ryder's eyes shot to her mouth then up to her face. At least she'd managed to distract him. She lifted a hand to his cheek to take him another step off balance.

"I'm fine, Darlin'," Bianca said, leaning heavy on the Southern this time. She even let a little of her natural country dialect come through. "I wouldn't have made it through Quantico if answerin' a few questions would rattle me."

Bianca lowered her hand and turned back to the bitch who had better be as prepared as she claimed. If Bianca was going to be interrogated by the society police, she'd give as good as she got.

Lady Anne raised her chin, the equivalent of ordering Bianca to continue, so Bianca lifted a finger to her chin in thought.

"Let's see. I grew up in a small town called Thatcher set in God's country, the Appalachian Mountains. I went to a school where I knew everyone, their parents, and extended families. During the summers, I split my days between part-time work with local law enforcement and helping the Calhoun family with their farm."

Lady Anne broke in. "I have a dossier on you with those insignificant details."

Bianca recalled the old hound dog she'd named Lady and said a silent apology because *that* bitch had been a sweet dog. Those details were not insignificant to a young girl whose family toiled day in and day out to give her a chance to have more in life. "Well, if that's not what you're after, just what can I tell you?"

"Explain your interest in Ryder."

He growled something that sounded like another "no," but the future of Bianca's mission could turn one way or the other on this meeting. She was starting to see why he'd left at seventeen.

At least, she could answer this question truthfully. "As for my interest in Ryder, I'd have to tell you how I came to meet him. I was raised by loving parents, who taught me the importance of being fair, and that the truth is what matters most in any situation. The Sheriff was my daddy's fishing buddy and thought I'd be content to file and help out in his office one summer, but I liked law enforcement. Just before I graduated from the University of Georgia, the FBI approached me about entering their intelligence gathering department because of my aptitude and mad skill with computers."

Ryder's harsh breathing settled into an easy rhythm.

Bianca took that to mean she was doing okay and continued. "Through the diligent work of our research department, Ryder was singled out as the person most likely to have shot J. K. Kearn. But I have a reputation for never stopping until I have the truth. To the point my peers often complain that I don't know when to let something go, but my tenacity resulted in finding something that no one else had."

"And this was what?" Lady Anne asked, no hint of acceptance in her voice.

"A time discrepancy in statements by people who claimed to

have seen Ryder in person right after he left Kearn the night of the killing." Bianca felt Ryder's fingers twitch at that, but he showed no other outward sign of reaction. "I pursued that lead and interviewed those witnesses again, corroborating a time element that proved Ryder couldn't have been in place to make that shot."

"Why did you leave the FBI?"

Bianca affected a shamed look. "Unfortunately, my team felt betrayed because I'd basically embarrassed them, plus someone at the prison leaked that more was going on between me and Ryder than ... just finding justice." She'd let her voice drift to whisper soft and raised adoring eyes to him. When he looked down at her with those startling silver eyes, she forgot where she was until he gave her fingers another gentle squeeze.

Bianca finished. "My superior was not happy to find out I had fallen in love with a prisoner that the majority of the intelligence gathering department believed was guilty."

For just a moment, Ryder stared at her as if she really had done all those things. He lifted his hand to her cheek and leaned down to kiss her forehead.

Butterflies did an Irish jig in her chest.

"How nauseatingly sweet," Lady Anne remarked, killing the moment when Ryder dropped his hand.

Evil woman. Bianca answered cheerfully, "I admit it. I am head-over-heels about this man."

Ryder sounded bored when he said, "Bottom line is we're married. Anything else?"

Lady Anne looked out her window so long that Bianca thought they'd been silently dismissed, but the matriarch wasn't through yet. She said, "She'll have to get rid of that twang. She'll need a tutor to groom her before we entertain."

I don't have a twang, dammit. Bianca had smoothed out the country twang to be a sophisticated Southern dialect and had thought Lady Anne would realize Bianca was intentionally pulling it out a moment ago. Bianca felt heat creep up her neck just like when she'd overheard someone mimic her speech the first time in a bathroom at college. She didn't need a tutor. She was not some backwoods bumpkin who couldn't be trusted to act properly in a social setting.

Ryder reacted as if someone had cursed her. "How dare you insult my wife?"

"Better that than insult guests. Hubrecht has requested a party in two weeks for you and *her*. I won't have our family shamed."

"I won't have Bianca subjected to this."

"Oh? Then leave if you want, but be sure to tell Hubrecht that you chose to do so. Show him your true colors. Show him you ran away, which should convince him of what I've been saying since you were released. That he would be a fool to bring you back into the family business." Lady Anne did have facial muscles capable of smiling. Like a cobra. "He doesn't need you when he has Terrence."

After listening to what Ryder had said about his brother, Bianca read between those lines quickly enough. Lady Anne saw Ryder as a threat to Terrence's position. She didn't want Ryder here and insulting Bianca was the perfect way to make him back away.

Ryder turned to leave and Bianca had no doubt he'd follow through, even if he regretted it later. Every person had a limit and Lady Anne was clearly a pro at testing Ryder's.

Bianca held firm without moving.

Ryder turned back to her. "What?"

Lady Anne smiled with the pleasure of someone who had gotten the best of an underdog.

Bianca matched her smile, prepared to show her how they handled bullies back home. "Are you sure you don't want to ask Ryder to stay, Lady Anne?"

"Why would I do that?"

"Because I did learn a *great* deal while researching Ryder's background, which included a detailed file on you as well." Bianca paused to let that settle in, gratified when Lady Anne's smile disappeared. "I found very little information about the private homelife of this family."

"That's because unlike the *poor*, we avoid being in tabloid news," she sneered.

Bianca ignored the dig about poor people and said, "Then

I'd think you wouldn't want someone talking to those media outlets, right?"

The first sign of concern flitted through Lady Anne's cold eyes. "What are you threatening?"

"Me? I'm not threatening. I'm just saying it will be much harder to avoid the media with us staying in a hotel. Just can't get away from them. And being that I'm so clueless about social graces and such, I might just make a mistake and share something I shouldn't."

No one said anything for a moment, then Lady Anne unclenched her jaw to tell Ryder, "You can stay."

Ryder squeezed her hand as if high fiving her for out-playing Lady Anne, but Bianca was determined to make this bitch treat Ryder with regard. "That didn't sound like an invitation for the both of us."

Lady Anne stared holes through Bianca for a drawn-out moment. "You and your wife are invited to stay with us, Ryder."

Bianca beamed her new bride smile and whipped out her Midwestern American broadcaster's accent. Which was none at all. "Why, thank you, Lady Anne. We accept your hospitality. And, just so we're clear, I don't need a speech coach, and I'll be happy to share some of my charm school tips with you any time you'd like." She turned to Ryder, who was staring at her, too, but with something akin to admiration. "Ready?"

"Ready, Sweetheart."

Her heart quivered at the way he said the endearment this time. As if it really were reserved for her only.

He got them out of there pronto. When they were alone, Ryder said, "That was an impressive maneuver. Impressive as hell."

Bianca grinned. She was pretty thrilled with herself.

"But it raises a new concern."

"What?"

"Lady Anne is not one to suffer embarrassment. I don't want you going anywhere near her without me."

"You think she's dangerous."

"I think she's powerful enough to be dangerous, especially when threatened in her own domain."

Well, crap. Another front she had to fight on.

When they reached the top landing, he turned to his left.

She kept track as Ryder wove them through this hall and that one until she gave up. How did anyone get around in this place without a map?

Ryder stopped and pushed a door open. "This is our room."

When Bianca stepped inside, she forgot about confusing floor plans, standoffish sisters and crazed kidnappers.

The room was huge. So was the king-sized bed.

She was alone with a man who had been locked away from women for five months. "Who else stays in this end of the house?"

"No one but us."

CHAPTER 15

R YDER URGED BIANCA further into the suite so he could close the door. She didn't say or do anything to indicate she was uncomfortable, but he could sense it in her silence as she took in her surroundings.

He hadn't missed this room after leaving to join the Army.

Not until he was arrested.

Looking around now, he had a better appreciation for the large suite that covered more square footage than some apartments. Far more than the ten-by-six prison cell Ryder had shared with a man who'd been caught in the act and convicted of stabbing his wife twenty-three times.

Ryder's gaze ran over every detail, searching out the familiar. Nothing had changed. His king-sized bed was still covered in the same simple brown-and-blue comforter he'd chosen to keep his room from looking like the rest of this designer showplace. His computer desk still had his magnifying glass on a stand that had allowed him to have both hands free when he'd painted model car parts sometimes no larger than his fingernail.

But with one glance at the doorway to his bathroom, his chest tightened.

Of all the things he hated most about prison, he'd never gotten used to the lack of basic privacy. There was something degrading about being on display while using the toilet.

This suite had been his sole respite during the seventeen years he'd spent doing time in the Van Dyke manor. He'd refused entry to all but the housekeeper, hoarding his privacy like a man rationing water to make it across a desert. Counselors at the private high school he'd attended had tossed about terms like "outsider" and "introspective" when they referred to him, as though they'd had a clue what his life was really like.

Looking back, they might have known him better than he realized since both traits played into choices he'd made in the military.

"Someone unpacked my clothes?" Bianca asked without turning around.

Ryder shoved his hands into the pockets of his slacks. "One of the staff."

"Guess that's expected ... in places like this."

"Sometimes." In this instance, Ryder was sure security had gone through everything he and Bianca had brought, to check for weapons or electronic gear. But saying that out loud without knowing whether the room was bugged would be careless.

"Interesting." She'd said that one word as if he belonged to a family of aliens.

Bianca had quieted. She hid her discomfort beneath a shield of confidence that didn't fool Ryder for a minute. He grudgingly admitted that, for a rookie, she'd held up her end even when they'd been kidnapped.

He would curse his soul for eternity if anything happened to her after he'd put her in this position, even if she had volunteered.

With Sabrina and the team sticking their collective necks out for him, Ryder couldn't pull back at this point either. Plus, he wanted freedom more than anything he'd ever wanted in his life. As long as he kept Bianca safe, the possibility to clear his name and have a life again was within his grasp.

Thanks to his team, he had new information about the Van Dyke Woden rifles being sold with no serial numbers. What was the possibility of a connection between the person inside VDE selling those weapons to buyers the United States had on a terrorist watch list and the contracted hit on Kearn?

Could be connected or totally unrelated.

"Is this a guest suite?" Bianca asked, still wandering around the room.

"No, this is actually my old room."

"Oh. I see." She didn't have to say more.

He'd never had a woman in this room, but having Bianca here didn't bother him as much as he'd expect.

Why not?

What had happened to the burning hatred of all things FBI he'd lived and breathed every hour in prison?

Bianca had happened. She'd made him take a look at himself and he hadn't liked what he found. He did have every reason to be ruthless and cruel, but staying this angry was tiring and unproductive.

He still had a hard-on against Murdock and the legal system, but Bianca was in her own category now. And if Ryder wanted to win his freedom, he had to gain her trust.

She stopped in front of the window that overlooked the rear of the property filled with landscaped gardens and a resort-level pool he'd stared at during breaks between homework assignments. She squatted in front of a short, half-round, antique curio. Out of curiosity, to see what had caught her attention, he peered over her shoulder at the contents, and did a double take.

Bianca angled her head. "Are these yours?"

"Yes." Who had unpacked his model car collection and arranged them for display?

Sure as hell wouldn't have been Lady Anne.

Bianca stood and swung around. "Is it a special collection?"

"Just a bunch of model cars I put together." The miniature automobiles had meant much more when Ryder had painted the details with a brush no thicker than a toothpick and adhered tiny decals with a pair of tweezers.

"Really?" She turned back and bent low, studying them closer. "They're beautiful. I can't believe the paint jobs."

Her admiration for his childhood hobby spawned an unusual touch of pride. No one outside of the family had seen his models and no one in the family had ever given a damn about his passion for old muscle cars.

He'd thought.

Who in his family had arranged the models in the cabinet?

When she stood up, her gaze fanned over to his brass bed, then boomeranged back to him with a we-need-to-get-something-clear look. "About tonight—"

"Sure. What do you want for dinner?" Ryder put a finger to his lips and tapped his ear.

"Something light. Whatever you're having." Once she glanced from side-to-side and then up at the ceiling, he knew she'd figured out his warning that they might be heard. She raised her eyebrows at him, demanding to know what his plan was.

He held up a finger for her to be quiet and to wait, then made a quick sweep of his suite. He found nothing, but the ceilings were twelve feet high. He had no way to check the light fixtures or the ceiling fan.

He pointed to her left and spoke clearly, crooking his finger as he walked toward the bathroom. "I need a shower. Let's figure it out while we freshen up."

Whiskey-colored eyes narrowed in suspicion. She didn't move at first.

Was she afraid of being in here with him?

Even after what they'd been through with the kidnapping?

Drawing on a limited supply of patience, Ryder motioned again with his finger for her to follow. Once inside the bathroom, he spun the shower knobs to full force. Nine gold-plated showerheads pulsed a torrent of water at the center of the stall. He turned around to find her right behind him and could have just leaned down to speak in her ear, but a sudden desire to see her eyes light up again like they had during his faux rescue sent his hands to her waist.

Passion flashed in her hazel eyes, but she recovered to whisper, "What are you doing?"

Destroying what sanity he held onto by threads because his balls were ready to explode from wanting to bend her over the vanity and bury himself inside her. *Not fucking going to happen.*

He already missed the feel of her body next to his, molded against him as she'd been on the way home in the cab.

He drew her into a snug embrace.

"Ryder." She'd muttered that with indecision that made his mouth twitch.

"Just a moment," he whispered so close to her ear he could touch it with his tongue.

Shit. He wanted to touch a lot of her with his tongue, he realized, but Bianca Brady was the only person who could help him regain his life. He wouldn't abuse the position she was in even though he knew he could unleash the passion she feared.

Someone had convinced her that she didn't like sex.

Bullshit. What idiot had been that screwed up?

But he would not take advantage of the vulnerability she'd shown him.

Ryder whispered next to Bianca's ear, "We can't take any chances. Someone could be listening."

He inhaled her sweet scent, closing his eyes to let it flow over him. He'd missed simple things like holding a woman in his arms. Breathing in Bianca pushed out the scent of misery that had permeated Ryder's lungs for five long months. They'd felt like decades.

She eased against him.

Man, she was so hot. Not in a runway model way, but in a wholesome, spend-a-night-making-out way that he hadn't been around in a long time.

Maybe ever.

"You think someone in your family would bug our room?" she asked, sounding curious and amused at the same time. "Are you accusing Hubrecht of being a voyeur?" Her soft breath warmed his neck. The confining area in this bathroom was quickly becoming too hot, the steamy shower not entirely at fault for the sweat beading on Ryder's forehead.

"No, but we can't take the chance that someone might have a transmitter in this space. Since we couldn't get any electronic gadgets past the VDE security and I'm sure our luggage was gone through with a fine-toothed comb, we should act and speak as if we're in front of an audience at all times unless there's music playing or water running."

"Agreed." She had her hands on his chest. One finger moved in a circle as if she was lost in a thought, but that slight touch was driving him crazy.

Should he warn her that she was tempting a desperate man?

She said, "Take your shirt off."

"What?" He was already perilously close to making a huge mistake. He had a handful of soft female he wanted to drag under that raging waterfall.

A vision of Bianca naked with water cascading over her shimmering skin sucked the breath from his lungs.

This might not have been one of his more intelligent ideas.

"Earth to Ryder."

"Hmm?"

"Take off your shirt and sit down so I can clean you up."

"Oh." He released her and stepped back. "I'm fine."

"No, you aren't." She crossed her arms. "Would you please change the water to cold so this doesn't turn into a sauna?"

He did as she asked and unbuttoned his shirt far enough that he could pull it over his head. He tossed it to the floor, watching her as he did.

She was busy all of a sudden, her eyes going anywhere but to his body.

Liked what she saw, did she?

He wanted to smile over the way she fumbled around. He was only allowing her to deal with his injuries for one reason. His cuts and bruises would be fine but having Bianca in nurture mode meant she had to finally be seeing him as more than a cold-blooded killer. This was a step forward.

She dug around in the vanity. "Don't you have any antibacterial ointment?"

"Second drawer on the left if nothing has changed."

"Got it."

After wetting a washcloth, she turned to him. "Sit on the edge of that swimming pool you probably think is a tub."

When he was seated with his hands at each side, she came over and knelt, setting the tube of ointment aside. Using the damp cloth carefully as she washed his face, she murmured, "That might be a black eye tomorrow."

Ryder dismissed it with, "I've had worse." Shouldn't have picked at Josh about not getting Trish to marry him yet. Ryder would make sure Josh paid for that down the road.

If he wasn't in the Hole.

She paused, staring into Ryder's eyes with something he wanted to call remorse. Could it be that she was rethinking her position on the evidence against him?

Whatever had caused that look disappeared.

When she had his face cleaned up to her satisfaction, she moved down to clean dried blood from the cut on his chest. That wouldn't have happened if he'd been a little faster when he and Dingo had pulled down an old metal cabinet to make it sound as though Ryder was fighting his way to Bianca.

Good thing his tetanus shot was up to date.

Bianca put ointment on her fingers, then rubbed the antibiotic gel gently over the cut that looked bad but wasn't all that deep.

He hadn't been prepared for the shock of feeling her hands on his chest and sucked in air along with his stomach muscles.

Snatching her hand back, she raised worried eyes to his. "Did I hurt you?"

"No." He hadn't meant to sound angry, but he couldn't say more without it coming out like a croak. A gaping wound in his chest wouldn't lose a drop of blood right now because it was all pooled in his groin.

He had to be crazy to let her do this.

If she didn't finish soon, she'd see just how much he was hurting in a different way. He didn't want to worry her about sleeping in the same room with him tonight, but it wouldn't take long for her to see how much he wanted a woman.

Not just any woman. *This woman.*

Bad idea. One that had so many repercussions he'd need an adding machine to tally them.

Bianca tossed the washcloth aside and stood up. "That's as good as it gets until we can put some ice on that cheek."

He stood up, but before he could say a word, where her gaze had avoided him moments ago it now traveled from his face, down his chest to his waist.

She chewed on her bottom lip and her tongue peeked out the corner of her mouth as her gaze dropped lower.

Ah, fuck. That did him in. His crotch bulged more under her attention.

Her eyes widened then shot back to his face.

"That," he said, "is *not* my fault. You can't eye me like I'm your new favorite dessert and not expect me to react."

"I didn't do that."

"Yes, you did." He stepped up and put a finger on her cheek. "Thank you."

Bianca should end this conversation and get out of the bathroom.

Away from Ryder's seductive voice and way-too-tempting body, the one causing her brain to implode from overheating.

Why had his icy silver eyes turned into molten pewter?

Awareness thrummed under her skin. "Why did you thank me?"

Lips cut from perfection drew closer to hers as he said, "Because it was nice to be looked at like a person. As a man and not a criminal. I've missed that."

She tried to listen to what he was saying, but she couldn't take her eyes off his mouth that was close enough to kiss her. Would he do that again? Did she want him to?

A smart woman would say no.

Her IQ was losing points every second that she took her time considering whether she wanted to be kissed again.

Why would he want to kiss her after she'd explained she didn't like sex?

His fingers were grazing her face and brushing her hair back behind her ear. He lowered his head.

She stopped him with her fingers on his lips. "I told you, Ryder, I'm not ... I don't ..."

"I heard you. Not wired for seduction. Then I can't seduce you, right?" he asked her in a deep voice that put her into a heady trance where thinking wasn't possible. "Because seduction requires a certain amount of chemistry. Since you're not wired for chemistry, you're safe from anything happening, right?"

"I, uh, suppose." She tried to follow his logic, but he was standing so close that all she could think about was kissing him, which meant her hormones had hijacked her brain.

He kissed the corner of her mouth and trailed a finger lightly down her throat. "Just so we're clear on one thing," he said in that deep voice between peppering kisses along her neck that had her melting.

One of his hands cupped her hip, then slid around back to draw her up against that powerful body, then he kissed her lips.

No, he devoured her.

His fingers threaded into her hair, holding her head as his mouth went to work ripping through any puny resistance her brain put up. She'd never been held and kissed as if she was the most desired woman on earth.

His tongue mated with hers in a sensual dance. He caressed his way to her breasts, holding one in his hand and running his thumb across the nipple that tightened into a hard nub.

She felt moisture between her legs where a tightening sensation had her clenching her legs together, wanting more. Ryder's mouth kissed her intimately, dragging her to the edge of no return. Making her want to stay here, suspended in time.

Being in Ryder's arms was like the world's greatest rollercoaster ride. Frightening, exhilarating and addictive.

The world disappeared.

Nothing mattered but the two of them.

A worry niggled at the back of her mind. She shouldn't be doing this, but she couldn't think when he massaged her other breast and teased the nipple.

"God, you taste like heaven," he murmured between kisses, stroking her female ego to life. His lips stroked a hot trail along her chin to her neck. She leaned her head to the side, craving his touch everywhere.

How could this be so much better with Ryder than it had ever been kissing Bernard?

Bernard had been worldly and handsome. Women drooled over him everywhere they went. Women far more attractive and sophisticated than a geeky college girl with the aspiration to join law enforcement.

Law enforcement like the FBI? You know, that group you're working for right now?

So *now* her brain comes back to roost?

Bianca put her hands up on his chest. "Ryder. Stop."

He stilled immediately and raised his head, looking down at Bianca with need burning in his eyes.

For that one second, she wanted to be the woman for him, to be desired by a man like Ryder, but her senses were coming back to remind her he was in her custody. Not a man she was really involved with.

This was all make-believe.

Ryder took a step back and shoved his hands in his hair, cursing under his breath. "Guess I should say I'm sorry, but that would be a lie."

How could she berate him for that when it felt so powerful to have a man as seductive as Ryder admit that he wasn't sorry about making out with her?

He dropped his hands. "Why don't you shower first?"

Should she say something?

What? Like ... please do it again?

Afraid to trust her voice, Bianca nodded. She'd have to discuss the "rules of engagement" later. As she stepped away, Ryder caught her by the arm and lowered his mouth to her cheek. "If you didn't like sex, it wasn't you. It was the moron who didn't know what he was doing. You're sexy as hell. Don't ever let any man convince you otherwise."

Then he walked out.

She stood there staring at the door, experiencing an emotion she hadn't felt the entire time she'd been in a relationship with Bernard.

Appreciated and cared for.

CHAPTER 16

CHATTON IGNORED EVERYONE she passed as she stayed in character with each step, leaning on the walking stick and limping her way down a long hallway in the Pentagon. No one questioned the ID on her chest that identified her as Alexander Zaran, a reclusive male military strategist who had SAP, or Special Access Programs, clearance. Alexander was eighty-three and had gotten his limp while serving in the Army as one of the first to wear a Green Beret.

He'd been born fifty years before she'd been a glint in her parents' eyes.

A difficult man to locate, but not impossible for someone with her MI6 skills.

At the moment, Alexander Zaran was in a deep slumber. When he woke, he would be hesitant to say he'd lost two days sleeping. That might suggest he suffered from dementia.

Chatton had a detail of her men watching over the old guy so nothing happened to him while she borrowed his identity, including his fingerprints on the false skin covering her fingertips.

She'd come to collect on a debt.

All she'd asked for was the name of the person who'd killed a descendant of Clan Macintosh, though few of them went by that surname these days. Someone was systematically killing everyone with a drop of blood from that ancient clan, her family.

Chatton stopped at the desk of the plump, middle-aged assistant to the man she'd come to confront.

"May I help you?" Esther Shorter asked, squinting up in annoyance until her eyes lit on Chatton's stolen ID. "Colonel

Zaran? I'm sorry, I didn't realize it was you. I haven't seen you in a while ..."

Chatton lifted a hand covered in Zaran's favorite black gloves he wore any time he traveled. She reached into the inside pocket of the brown tweed jacket that hung on her slouched shoulders, which made her look as hunched over and frail as he did.

Withdrawing the crinkled paper she'd written on with Zaran's scribbly handwriting, she let her hand tremble a little when she dropped it on Esther's desk.

Esther covered being flustered by squaring her shoulders and stepping back into the role of assistant to a high-ranking pentagon official. "Let me get you something to drink and I'll inform ..."

But Chatton lifted a hand, waving off the assistant and started limping toward the door, just as Zaran was rumored to have done more than once when he came to share his unsolicited opinion.

As Chatton opened the office door, she heard Esther's rushed voice behind her speaking into an intercom. "I'm sorry, sir, but Alexander Zaran ..."

But Chatton was inside, and the door closed by the time The General hung up his phone. He was not a true general. It was a moniker he used when meeting with Chatton and Wayan as part of a secret three-person group known only as Czarion. Wayan was the pseudonym of a powerful man inside the inner circle of the Chinese Party Chief.

Of the three who made up Czarion, she was the only one who didn't buy into their fanatical drive to fulfill Orion's Legacy. She'd write the other two off as insignificant if both men weren't in positions to influence world conflicts. Wayan was one scary buggar when he got on his soapbox about how five rare artifacts told of a final international throw down.

Wayan and The General had let her join them in their sandbox of crazy because she possessed one of the five artifacts.

The three of them never breached each other's security. Never crossed the line of entering each other's countries unannounced. But The General had not made good on a deal with Chatton. It was time to pay the bloody piper.

The General took one look at Chatton's impersonation, and his eyes sharpened. He spoke into his intercom. "I don't want to be disturbed, Esther."

"Yes, sir."

He punched the off button on his intercom and leaned forward, coiled and ready to pounce. At forty-nine, The General was still an impressive man who managed to stay fit in spite of aggravating back problems. The buzz cut prevented his short red curls from being odd looking in contrast to his coffee-brown skin, but grey peppered the tight beads of hair on his head.

Chatton shuffled forward, still hiding her identity even though doubt was entering The General's gaze. He hadn't decided for sure if she was Alexander Zaran or not.

"What do you want?" he asked, more as an order than a question. No matter how hard he studied her, he would not be able to recognize the attractive thirty-two-year-old woman with honey-brown hair—her normal appearance.

Hell, some days *she* didn't even recognize her new face. She let her natural voice come through when she told him, "The same thing I wanted the last time we met. A name."

Light bulbs went off behind his eyes. "Son of a ... what the *fuck* are you doing here?"

She sat down in the chair across from him and removed horn-rimmed glasses that appeared an inch thick to someone looking at her. Not real glasses. She'd had perfect vision all the way here. "I've been patient, something I'm not known for."

His voice came out in hushed stream of fury. "You screwed up coming here. You may think you've got me in a vulnerable position, but I can have you killed three steps outside my door."

Oh, she did have him by the short hairs. He just didn't know it yet. "You wouldn't do that. Not when you know I'd never come here without plenty of insurance."

That gave him pause. "Like what?"

When she didn't answer right away, The General's nostrils flared as he realized why she waited. He leaned back and tapped on his keyboard, glanced at his monitor then back at Chatton. "We're secure."

She lifted an electronic unit that was concealed inside a hard phone case so it could pass as a phone, but when she pressed a button it played the audio of the General and Wayan from one of the Czarion meetings. Both men incriminated themselves in the sixteen seconds she played before thumbing it off. "I shouldn't have to point out that this is a copy. Now back to our unfulfilled deal. I want the shooter who killed Edward Abbott."

Edward Abbot Macintosh, a British diplomat and cousin to Chatton's murdered father.

The General slapped his hand down on his desk and ground his words. "I gave you Van Dyke. That's who our intel fingers as the most likely candidate."

"Lot of Van Dykes in the world and our deal wasn't for a *candidate*. I wanted *the* killer." She'd known inside an hour who the only possible Van Dyke suspect could be.

"One Ryder Van Dyke was arrested for shooting J. K. Kearn with the same .338 Lapua round that killed Abbot, which indicated the same McMillan rifle was used in both shootings," he said as though instructing an imbecile. "I would think even you could put that one-and-one together on your own."

She'd come up with that same conclusion right away. Too easily. In her business, easy equaled flawed thinking. "If I had handled my part of our agreement as carelessly as you handled yours, Wayan's shipment would not have arrived intact and on time in Miami. I expect more in return than just Van Dyke, but I would have let this go if I had found satisfaction by now."

"Speaking of Wayan's unit—"

"Were we?"

"We are *now* since this was more his debt than mine," The General pointed out.

But The General had set the parameters and made the commitment. She was not here to quibble and let her silence hammer that home.

He made a gritty sound in his throat and leaned back. He eyed her for a tedious moment. "Your part wasn't as clean as you'd like to pretend."

"You're wasting my time trying to claim fault on my end."

"You delivered the packages to Miami, but someone undermined the project and the unit got destroyed."

"Not my problem." She used this break to stretch her legs and back from holding Zaran's balled-up posture. "You said those three boxes were booby-trapped if I tried to open any of them during transport. They were delivered on time, intact and unopened. What happened with them after that point is not my concern."

"Don't act as though you don't know what was inside the boxes."

"Oh, I realized when I heard the news about an airliner almost being taken down on approach to Miami International that it was very likely Wayan's *unit*, but you saw me on television in a live broadcast on another continent at that moment, just as we'd agreed. You should hire better people next time."

The General's dark eyes turned black with frustration. "My man made no mistakes. He said a specialized security team found him as he was activating the laser unit, and in the battle, they triggered the destruct mechanism on the unit, preventing the airliner from crashing into a Miami suburb. Wonder how that security team knew where to look for my man and the unit?"

She knew exactly how Sabrina Slye's team had found Wayan's evil little toy, because Chatton had added a special tag of her own to those three boxes. When The General's man cut the hair-thin wire concealed along the edge of the packing tape, he triggered a signal that could be tracked by software inside a laptop she'd slipped into a surveillance vehicle belonging to one of Sabrina's agents.

But the General and Wayan would never figure that out.

Cocking her head, Chatton asked, "So now you're insinuating that I had something to do with exposing your man's location and destroying a laser device? Even with evidence of me off continent? Seriously, General? I don't care what you and Wayan do as long as it doesn't affect me negatively. What motivation would I have to get involved when our deal was an exchange, which brings me back to why I'm here."

"What more do you want? Ryder Van Dyke's your man. Has to be."

"He's out of prison, no longer suspected of the Kearn killing. Sort of blows the simple math on your theory."

"A prison romance and legal jockeying does not absolve Van Dyke of guilt. The facts support his being the shooter for both targets."

"Van Dyke's alibi—which checked out iron-clad—proves he couldn't have been in Colorado for the Abbot shooting." She'd been far more thorough than US law enforcement in investigating Van Dyke's alibi and had to admit she'd found a weak spot in it.

Ryder Van Dyke had been observed from a distance at a rented lake house in central Georgia when the Abbot killing happened. But he could have had someone of similar build taking his place while he made the hit.

The General snarled, "I don't give a flying fuck about any timeline difference. We're talking about someone trained in black ops and he was working with Sabrina Slye's bunch. They're not just corporate security."

"That wouldn't be the team that shut down your man in Miami, would it?" She let the fact that they both knew who got to the laser device sink in. "Is that why you put me on Van Dyke? Take care of a little vengeance for you while I'm at it? Not going to happen. I don't terminate anyone unless they've given *me* reason to act."

"So, you've got a conscience now?"

She smiled, letting him see how much that amused her. Much like a cat who enjoyed watching a mouse consider his possible escape route when they both knew he had none. "Do you really expect me to believe that Van Dyke would allow himself to be caught after a hit on Kearn?"

The General growled something vicious, clearly not happy to constantly be pushed deeper into a corner. "Hell, Van Dyke probably set himself up to get arrested, figuring that it would look too easy for someone with his expertise to be the real shooter."

Thin logic at best. Why would Van Dyke shoot Kearn to begin with? Van Dyke had been on the Slye team that Chatton had covertly tipped off about the laser unit. The Kearn killing was completely out of character for a man with Van Dyke's history. He'd been honorably discharged with an exceptional military record. Then he signed on with an agency that had actually stopped a terrorist attack, but out of the blue he decides to kill an innocent man in cold blood?

On the other hand, was Kearn innocent?

Something just didn't add up right.

None of that mattered so much as Van Dyke's getting arrested.

With her background, Chatton would never put herself in a position to risk getting trapped in prison. Why would Van Dyke?

And what about FBI agent Brady who'd made a complete about-face on Van Dyke's guilt?

Chatton countered with, "Bianca Brady testified for the DA at Van Dyke's preliminary hearing, then changed her tune five months later. She must have found something significant to sacrifice her career as an FBI agent."

"Bullshit. I read the report. Brady's young, single and an overachiever. Perfect patsy for a player like Van Dyke. He comes from money. Sent someone to convince her to dig harder into the timeline, probably guided her to find exactly what Van Dyke had set up before he got grabbed." The General shrugged. "Van Dyke meets with Brady a couple of times and convinces her she's his soul mate. Next thing you know, she's found proof he couldn't have been in two places at once. Two weeks later, he's free and getting married. Smooth."

Chatton never dismissed any possibility. She let The General ramble on with his theory while she considered how she wanted to satisfy their deal.

Opening his hands in a dismissive move, he said, "Van Dyke is playing the I'm-so-innocent role all the way, but only a fool would buy that. He ran some ops for the CIA when he was in the military." The General leaned back, arms stretched behind his head, signaling this meeting was pretty much over. "Mark my words. Van Dyke is no easy target and he's probably planning to disappear. In his shoes, I would whether I was guilty or not, because the government isn't the only one who believes he pulled the trigger both times."

There was some truth in what The General said, and the ballistics matched on both killings. Chatton leaned forward and placed a burner phone on the General's desk.

He glared at the phone. "What's that for?"

"I'm going to be around until I get the answers I want. I'll contact you if I need intel. You'll give it to me. I'll call from a different phone each time. I'll let you know when this is done so you can destroy that one. Until then, keep it with you."

She lifted her walking stick as she stood and turned to leave.

"I'll help you until you determine it *was* Van Dyke, but once that happens, you're going to owe me much more, Chatton."

A warning with an unspoken threat that he'd take payment when she was least expecting it. He wanted the last word, but she would never allow him to think he intimidated her. She turned around. "Like what?"

"A termination. Someone my government considers a danger."

He thought he'd found a weakness when she said she'd only eliminate someone *she* deemed necessary.

Chatton made a scoffing sound. "Done."

"What about Van Dyke?"

"If he pulled the trigger on Abbot, I'll save your government the cost of trials and prison expense."

CHAPTER 17

BIANCA LAY ON her left side, using the full extent of her adult language to curse Ryder in her head.

The nightlight glow seeping through the doorway from the bathroom washed a pale outline over Ryder's muscular body. He at least wore a pair of shorts, but the lightweight material outlined his lean hips and the bulge that had been in a half-aroused state for the past hour.

How was she going to get any sleep with him so close?

Sharing the bed had sounded better when she was too tired to come up with an alternative to sleeping on the floor. Taking Ryder's battered body into consideration, she couldn't ask him to do that either.

Just like she couldn't pull her eyes from the slow rise and fall of his chest. Bare chest. Muscles moving with each slow breath.

Her head ached. Her body complained. She should be catatonic by now, but she couldn't convince her mind to stop imagining what he might do if she just passed out.

Ryder had spent five months locked away from women.

Five months with no sex.

She'd awakened one time with her hands and feet tied spread eagle on the bed and Bernard leaning over her. She flinched just thinking about that again.

"Bianca."

She jerked at her name ghosting from Ryder's lips. Was he awake or talking in his sleep? "What?"

"Go to sleep."

So, he wasn't really out after all. See? How was she supposed to rest knowing he was alert? What would he do if she *could* reach deep REM sleep?

With a fluid move, he rolled up on his side, facing her with a hand's width between them. The man moved like a shadow. After a moment, he scratched his head then extended that hand toward her as he lifted up.

She froze, unable to breathe.

But his hand kept going as he reached over her for something. When he dropped back down, he had a remote in his hand and punched a button. Haunting guitar music, something new wave with a Latin flare, flowed through the room, then he tossed the remote on the other side of the bed.

He whispered, "What's wrong?"

"Nothing." She was not going to admit she'd been lying awake for the past hour thinking about all the things a man desperate for a woman might want to do. Of course, according to Bernard, it would take a desperate man to want anything Bianca had to offer.

Was Ryder that desperate?

Ryder's voice had a tired rasp. "That's one of those trick answers, isn't it?"

"No."

"Yes, it is." He sighed. "You don't want to tell me that you're afraid to fall asleep because you think I'll take advantage of you."

Had she been that easy to read or did he expect that from women now? The sad note in his voice had her leaning toward the latter. Hearing that tugged at her and made her want to say something to convince him that she wasn't concerned.

But that would be a lie since she had been.

His face gave away nothing. Eyes as alert as when he'd been watching for a threat when they'd run from Kearn's people. He probably expected a denial.

Just waiting for her to lie about being worried.

She spread her hand out on the sheet between them and tapped a finger then met his gaze. Should she admit that she was so *not* the worldly woman expected to play this role? That she felt as though she'd lied to Murdock when she said she could do this?

Just stick to the truth. "I admit that I might not have thought all this through during the planning stages, like sleeping in a room with ..."

"A dangerous convict."

"I was going to say with a man who hasn't been with a woman in five months."

"Nine."

"What?"

"It's been nine months."

"Why?" She wanted to bite her tongue. No man wanted to talk about a lack of sexual activity and now wasn't the time to remind Ryder of how long it had been since he'd had sex. But it couldn't be for lack of female interest.

His gaze honed in on her as if he saw through her barriers to all her insecurities. The longer he stared, the more she wanted to take back that one word. "You don't have to answer—"

"I slept with a couple of women when I first came home from overseas. It was adequate. Not their fault. I was too ... numb for a while to agree to something I just didn't feel."

"You *turned down* offers?" she asked with more incredulity than was polite but *come on.*

"Find that so hard to believe?"

"You're a guy." Didn't that explain any man's decision making? Bernard had thought so. *I'm a man, Bianca, with needs. You can't expect me to turn down an offer when you're not putting out.* As if she hadn't felt inadequate enough as a woman at that point, hearing him blame his infidelity on her had crushed what little ego she'd still had.

Ryder blew out a breath. "Guess you've got a point, but after I let a flight attendant convince me to spare her from boredom on a layover, I realized I had to get my head straight before doing that again."

Bianca should be pressing for more, trying to get closer to Ryder like Murdock told her to do, but she couldn't bring herself to dig around for intel when Ryder was so relaxed and talking. He was not someone who opened up easily. That he was doing it with her meant something, touched her in a way that made her want to soothe the pain that clung to the edges of his eyes.

He'd buttoned up, so she prodded a little more. "You never saw the flight attendant again?"

"She made it clear she only wanted what I could give her that night. I'm pretty sure she had a boyfriend back in Chicago."

"Didn't you feel used?" Bianca asked, not sure why she felt indignant on his behalf.

"Nothing new, but it didn't matter."

"You don't mind being used for your body?"

Ryder stayed silent for so long that Bianca wondered if he was going to answer her. "Women have come to me since I was in my teens. It was always just to scratch an itch, except for a couple of gold diggers who couldn't find their way inside the Van Dyke Dynasty through Terrence." He shrugged, moving all those muscles in liquid symmetry when he did. "I've yet to meet a woman without an agenda."

Bianca couldn't argue that point when she was here only for what he could do to get her inside the Van Dyke family, but he'd known that from the start.

So why was she feeling this creeping sense of guilt?

Ryder lifted his fingers to her cheek, and she held her breath. His touch was light and careful, his voice a low rumble. "I came home from the military with my head cocked sideways, but functioning. After spending five months locked in that hellhole ... I'm pretty fucked up, Bianca, but I will not hurt you. Ever. Go to sleep. Can you do that for me?"

She wouldn't have thought she could until he asked her to do it for him. He needed someone to trust him.

To believe his words.

They had to get through this week. He could have overpowered her without even waiting on her to fall asleep, so how hard could it be to extend this small olive branch of trust? "Okay."

She rolled over on her back and felt the bed shift as he did the same. She really did want to get some rest, but she couldn't help thinking about the man in her file who'd been portrayed as a playboy with a different woman all the time.

Had Ryder wanted only one woman at some point? Someone who cared about more than the Van Dyke money.

Information from her files flipped through her mind for a few more minutes, then she drifted off to sleep.

Bianca hadn't slept long when she came awake, disturbed by a deep mumbling. She'd been out cold until then.

"Get radio ... killin' him ..."

She looked to her left.

Ryder's jaw was tight. Neck muscles flexed. His fingers gripped the bed next to his hips. He jerked his head back and growled. Sweat beaded on his forehead. "Fuck no ... don't ..." His body arched as if stabbed. The mumbling sounded tense, and his shoulders thrashed.

He was in one hell of a nightmare. Sweat popped out on his forehead. His fingers twisted the sheet.

Music still played through the room, a steady background sound that should be relaxing. Ryder was anything but.

Bianca reached over to touch his shoulder and shake him awake.

Ryder shot up and over her like a lightning strike, pinning her wrists to the bed at each side of her head, with his body holding her in place. He had a wild look in his eyes, like that of a cornered animal ready to attack. His chest heaved, straining for every breath. The muscles in his arms trembled with fury.

She held her breath, afraid to move an inch.

Ryder had said he wouldn't harm her, but the eyes staring at her boiled with rage. This was not the Ryder who had made that vow.

This one didn't recognize her.

CHAPTER 18

I MAY NOT GET out of the Hole alive, but neither will those two.

Ryder's hands and feet were tied. Fucking guard locked him in isolation with the Beast and Cherry Man. The guard knew those two had homemade knives, but he'd just turned his back and walked away.

No one paid attention to screams from the Hole.

"You're safe, Ryder."

Who said that?

He fisted his hands tighter until his arms shook from trying to break the bonds. Cherry Man was snickering. *Smile, you bastard. You die first. Come a little closer and I'll bash your face in. Think me being cuffed will save you?*

The Beast would wait and let Cherry Man take a few shots, make sure that Ryder was badly wounded before he came for his pound of flesh.

Didn't matter. The Beast was dying too.

"Ryder ... look at me."

He shook his head. That sounded like a woman. Cherry Man was messing with his mind.

Something soft brushed his chest. He flinched. It touched him again. The images blurred. He had to clear his eyes, or they'd sneak up on him and get the advantage.

That female voice was saying, "It's okay. You're safe."

He'd never be safe again.

Not in this prison. Not in this lifetime.

Fog rolled into his mind, distorting the room. Where was Cherry Man and the Beast? Had to be a trick. Ryder had to shake it off.

"Look at me, Ryder. It's me, Bianca."

Who? He blinked his eyes and shook his head, heaving one hard breath after another. When his eyes focused, he was staring down at a woman.

Bianca.

Swiveling his head left then right, he searched for the other prisoners. This wasn't the Hole. New age music swirled in the air, just loud enough to push out silence. He took in everything, breathing hard as pieces fell into place in his mind.

He was in his old room. In his own bed.

With Bianca. He knew her. FBI researcher. *Wife*.

He really looked at her this time. She was trying to act calm, but she grimaced as if she was in pain.

She whispered, "Please, let go."

That's when he realized he had something gripped tightly. Her wrists. He released her immediately then dropped his head. "I'm sorry."

She wasn't safe around him. He'd have to figure out something else, even if it meant him sleeping in the bathroom, far away from her at night. She'd trusted him and he'd—

Fingers touched each side of his face, lifting gently until he faced her. She swallowed. "You didn't hurt me."

"Yes, I did. You'll have bruises on your wrists tomorrow." Just the thought of putting a mark on a woman disgusted him, but hurting Bianca kicked him in the gut. She hadn't been the raving bitch he'd expected on this op. Once they'd come to an understanding, she'd been just the opposite. She had spunk and a gentle nature that drew him to her and triggered his protective instincts.

Considering what he'd just done, that was laughable.

And he was still stretched over her, using his arms to bear his upper body weight. He should move, but he couldn't.

She held him captive with the tips of her fingers sliding over his cheeks and down his throat, soothing him. When was the last time anyone had tried to soothe him?

No memory came to mind. Not one.

Massaging her wrists, he tried not to grimace when she tensed.

He deserved that. When she didn't order him to move, he ran his thumbs over the pulse points on her wrists, apologizing with his fingers when words wouldn't come.

She relaxed beneath him.

Her fingers brushed his skin again. Nothing had ever felt so good. He gazed down, waiting on her eyes to fill with loathing. For her to shove him away. One push and he'd move. But she continued staring up at him as if she could see past all the darkness shrouding his soul to the person hiding inside. The feral being that knew he'd never be free again.

Would never know the joy of life the way he had before.

One who did not deserve to breathe the same air as this innocent woman who he shouldn't even be touching.

But she was so soft and smelled like nothing that belonged in his world.

Fresh, sweet and so damned kissable.

Bad idea. His body was onboard, but those parts had no conscience. He still had a smidgeon of one, though it was vaporizing with her so close.

She put her hands back on his cheeks, forcing him to look at her when she spoke. "I didn't mean to startle you. I just wanted to wake you. You were having a nightmare. Was it from when you were a soldier?"

He could understand why she'd go to PTSD for his reaction, but the trauma he'd suffered for the past five months was a whole different level than what he'd brought home from the military. He could lie and give her an answer she'd accept, but she hadn't lied earlier when he'd expected her to deny being afraid to sleep in the same room with him.

She'd trusted him and he'd broken that one small trust.

Shaking his head, he said, "Not from the military. We all come back with some form of that, but this was ... from prison."

Guilt spread across her face. "I'm, uh, I—"

Ryder moved a finger to her lips. "I don't think you got up one morning wanting to destroy my life. I know you were just doing your job and I can see how damning the evidence is." He took a deep, unsteady breath, hoping against hope that he could convince her to do one thing. "I don't blame you, but if we find something that points to someone else as Kearn's killer I *need* you to consider that possibility."

She reached up and grasped his hand, moving it away from her mouth and didn't let go as she gave him a long, thoughtful look. She gave herself a little nod, as if making a decision. "I've never had PTSD, but I do have nightmares about putting away an innocent person. I'm one of the best in my field. Get me inside VDE and I'll look at everything with an open mind."

Some of the pressure in his chest eased at that one concession. "Fair enough."

This would be a good time to apologize again and get the hell off of her.

Clearly, he had no sense of timing, because he hadn't moved an inch.

She nibbled on her lip then the pink tip of her tongue peeked out between her lips. Her slender fingers still stroked his neck. What was she thinking?

That if she stopped soothing him, he might get angry, and she'd be dealing with a crazy man again? She needed more than two hours of sleep. He had to convince her she was safe, but that was going to be tough at this point. "Can you go back to sleep?"

She shook her head.

Damn. He'd frightened her. "What if I leave and promise to stay away tonight?"

"Don't leave. I'm not afraid of you."

Was she telling the truth or just placating him? Didn't matter. If he could get her back to sleep, he wasn't shutting his eyes again. Not tonight. He'd figure out something else for tomorrow night. Normal sleep would never be a part of his life again. His fingers had wandered over to play with her hair, sifting the fine strands.

Everything about her was so feminine and understated.

Gentle. A kind of gentle he never thought he'd touch again.

Making the conversion from life as a prisoner whose every minute is controlled, to living as a free citizen took more than walking through a doorway without chains on his wrists and feet. He'd grown a chip on his shoulder the size of a boulder that had the initials FBI carved into it.

They may not have set him up, but they'd built a case against him instead of hunting more suspects. Someone had to pay for the injustice he'd suffered and still faced.

He felt her eyes roving over him, watching him until he cut his gaze back to hers.

Someone owed him, but not Bianca. Right now, he didn't see her as an FBI agent.

He saw her as Bianca, the woman who had every reason to scream and bring her agency down on his head but had shown him compassion instead. Even when she'd wanted to pry deeper earlier in the day, she'd held back at times when he'd needed space.

She'd back off and give *him* space, but she was a tigress when she went after anyone else.

Lady Anne had never been outmaneuvered that Ryder knew of, which made the bitch someone he'd have to watch for retaliation.

His blood churned at the idea of Lady Anne, or anyone else, harming Bianca. That was crazy, but he'd had crazier thoughts.

He owed her for not running screaming from the bedroom when he'd been locked in a nightmare with her pinned beneath him.

His body took that moment to realize it *still* had a soft female beneath it and reacted. The boys were up and ready for action.

Her eyes flared with surprise.

Had he finally frightened her?

Her lips parted, but she said nothing. He'd tasted those lips today, and not nearly enough. He wanted to kiss her so badly he couldn't think past that want, a primal need that was more than just having a woman so close.

It was *this* woman.

That mouth.

She should order him to get off her. He hoped she'd do it soon, before he could screw up any worse.

Why was she staring at him as if she expected something? What did she want?

He ran a finger down the side of her cheek, and she moved against his touch, as if asking for more. Ah, hell. That was dangerous, because he wanted to give her more.

Maybe one kiss in apology.

He lowered his head and sealed his lips to hers carefully, ready to move with the slightest push of her hand.

Her hand hooked around his neck.

Fuck it. He was a goner.

He kissed her and even after having tasted her mouth all day, he hadn't been ready for her to kiss him back with gusto. She'd been sucked into responding a couple of times, but nothing like this. With absolute abandon, with a female craving that reached inside him and seduced his soul.

A foreign feeling exploded in his chest. One he knew he should be backing away from, something that would turn into pain when this week was over, but he hadn't felt this good in so long, ever, that he couldn't let go.

Her hands were everywhere, on his shoulders, his neck, in his hair, clutching him. He'd had other women, but none had ever given with such honesty.

Hooking his arm around her waist, he pulled her to him, shuddering at the feel of her body beneath him and the brush of her silk-covered breasts against his bare chest. He cupped her breast and she moaned into his mouth, just the opening he'd needed to slide his tongue past her lips and play with hers. She had such a dainty tongue, and it moved with a timidity he found sensual. So different from the confident FBI Agent Brady.

The vulnerability he'd sensed in her was sexy and sweet, and reminded him that he had to be that much more gentle because of it.

Every touch was crossing a line he shouldn't, but all those amazing sounds she was making and the way her body moved kept encouraging him. He had no idea what tomorrow would bring, had learned tomorrow could be taken away in an instant.

He'd gone without feeling anything for so long that he couldn't give this up. Didn't have the power to back away.

Until she said stop, he was on go.

His hand moved under the silk camisole, running over smooth

skin to her breast. He cupped the soft mound and scraped his finger over the hard tip.

She arched up at him.

Holy mother. His hard-on and loaded sac screamed for release.

There were reasons he couldn't do that, and he was doing his best to remind himself that this was an unexpected gift that came with dangerous consequences. But when a man held pure passion in his arms, he wanted it all.

To feel everything with this woman.

His survival instincts were trying to warn him away from this temptation, but they didn't have a chance against his need for Bianca.

CHAPTER 19

HEAT RACED FROM Bianca's breast to her womb. Her body strained, reaching for something just out of her grasp. She was lost inside this onslaught of sensations.

Ryder's hands were like lightning and hot oil on her skin one minute, and light as a feather the next.

She'd only meant to ease his guilt over jumping her. To calm him down so they could stick out this week together.

But then he'd looked at her as if he were a starving man and she was a gourmet feast. As if he couldn't take another breath without kissing her.

She should have ordered him to move back across the bed or roll off of her at the very least, but her body had launched a little campaign in his favor, racing around to shake up her hormones and invite them out to play.

Ryder had a mouth that should be licensed as a lethal weapon because he was killing her. Kissing him was crazy, like being shot up to the stars on a burst of light. His lips kissed her face and neck, pausing to linger and drive her insane with stupid thoughts like what it would feel like for Ryder to touch her everywhere?

His fingers thrust into her hair and held her head to lift her lips back to his for another deep kiss. Then his fingers were moving down her side and up under her silk top until he covered her other breast and tweaked her nipple.

Muscles at the juncture of her legs clenched. She sucked in air and bowed up, muscles clenching.

He muttered, "You're so fucking amazing."

With her body twisted in knots she shouldn't have been able to smile, but she grinned, reveling in the way he'd said that.

He lifted his head and stared down at her so long she came back to earth and started feeling self-conscious until he whispered, "I love looking at you. You're beautiful."

No one had ever really looked at her with that intensity. Ryder made her feel things she couldn't explain. How could she be so hot for him and not for anyone else before?

Not in the entire four months with Bernard had she been this turned on. Not once.

Bernard had pursued her and charmed her until she thought she'd fallen in love. What a laugh. She'd fallen for a psychopath. A narcissistic misogynist who wanted only to control her and humiliate her when she'd failed sexually.

She'd been too naïve to understand all that then.

Studying profiles of psychotic individuals for the FBI had caused her to see Bernard in a new light.

Away from home for the first time, she'd allowed someone with a sick need to control her and dominate her to reach his orgasm. He'd destroyed her from the inside out and had ground her femininity into the dust along with what little female ego she'd possessed.

Even knowing what she'd later learned about him and his warped psyche, she hadn't been willing to take that risk with another man.

Not until now.

She didn't want to analyze why. That might just be exhaustion beating down her resistance, but she didn't think so.

Ryder kissed her again, gently, which was in total contrast to the chaos his hands were causing on her breasts.

"That feels *so* good." She moved, rubbing her hips against him.

He growled and moved a hand down to her abdomen.

As if a switch had been thrown, that brought up a memory of Bernard pressing down on her abdomen to hold her in place while he shoved inside her.

She gripped Ryder's wrist, the one at her abdomen. Reality crashed in with a sour taste. Would she really allow him to take this further?

Allow him? You're encouraging him.

Then he would accuse her of being a tease.

Bernard had screamed that at her all the time, telling her he'd been forced to sleep with other women because Bianca teased him, then turned into an ice sculpture.

She squeezed Ryder's wrist. "Stop."

He did, moving his other hand from her breast.

Why had she let this happen? Ryder hadn't done anything wrong. Nothing she hadn't opened the door to. Now she'd humiliated herself with him and had a week to suffer it. "Uhm, I didn't mean to—"

"My fault."

"What?"

"I told you I wouldn't do anything, then I keep breaking my word. I've never broken my word." He shook his head at himself. "I won't again."

"It wasn't all you."

His silver eyes were dark and shadowed. "We both know you didn't start that. Like you said, you didn't mean to do it."

She'd always taken responsibility for her actions, but Bernard, that bastard, had taken advantage of her by convincing her she really had been at fault.

Ryder wasn't manipulating her.

He was shouldering all the blame, which fit the man she'd read about when he was in the military. She couldn't let him. "That's not what I was saying."

He frowned, confused, so she clarified, "I was saying, I didn't mean to act like a tease. I just ... had to stop."

That must have surprised him because the harsh lines of his face softened. "I can't figure you out. You tell me you don't like sex, but you're so smoking hot and passionate that the only thing I can guess is you were brainwashed by an idiot."

His heartfelt words stroked her heart. She still admitted, "I don't know about being hot or passionate—"

"I do. You are." He seemed determined for her to believe his assessment. One of his long fingers grazed her cheek. "You should get some sleep. I'll find a spot to rest somewhere else."

"No."

"Yes. I *will* keep my word this time."

Why did hearing that vow fill her with disappointment? Because she was a mass of trembling nerves that wanted to be touched again, which meant Ryder was the only one thinking clearly. She should be setting the example by acting professionally and agreeing to the distance, but where she had been uncomfortable with him earlier, she now wanted him to stay close.

He'd convinced her to share the bed earlier by telling her there was always a chance that someone would open the door during the night even with it locked just to see if they were in bed together.

When he moved to the side, she reached over and cupped his arm. He paused, staring at her with those unyielding eyes. "What?"

"Stay." She glanced over at the door. "In case."

He considered her words for several long seconds then nodded. "Don't touch me if I'm in a nightmare. I'll deal with it."

She nodded. He'd know she was lying if she spoke. Her Uncle Jerry had shoved her against a wall once when she'd snuck up on him and tapped his shoulder as a joke.

At thirteen she hadn't known any better.

The glazed eyes and dangerous face Uncle Jerry had turned on her hadn't found her joke funny. Mama had walked in and ordered her brother in a calm but firm voice to stand down.

Mama had told him Bianca was a friendly.

That had gotten through to him.

Uncle Jerry's vacant eyes had flickered with recognition, then confusion and, finally, guilt so heavy Bianca had wanted to hug him. But he'd backed away and run out of the house, not stopping until he'd disappeared into the woods.

Mama's eyes had gotten shiny then she swiped a hand over them and told Bianca not to worry, that he'd return in a day or two.

He did, but it had taken a long time before Bianca could hug him again. He'd shied away from her for a while. After Mama explained about PTSD, Bianca spent hours reading up on it, anything to help her Uncle Jerry come back to a point that he'd trust himself around her again. Mama coached Bianca that Uncle Jerry needed to be touched and reminded that he deserved to be loved.

Mama had been right.

After a while, the light had slowly returned to Uncle Jerry's eyes. He'd even helped Bianca and Sara Lynn with their repair-refurb charity. He was the one who'd taught Bianca how appliances were put together and what made them run.

Everything had a value, especially people.

Uncle Jerry's eyes had that haunted look less often now. But it had shocked her to recognize that same look in Ryder's eyes as soon as he realized he had Bianca pinned down.

Nobody was that good an actor. She'd seen the real Ryder Van Dyke in those unguarded moments.

At the VDE offices earlier in the day, when he'd worried about bruising her arm, she'd dismissed his concern as just trying to play nice, but not tonight. His self-disgust over harming her when he hadn't been cognizant was real.

And he'd been willing to sleep in the bathroom on a hard floor or in the tub to keep from breaking his word.

A man who'd spent the last five months sleeping on a hard cot would give up his awesome, soft bed rather than hurt her or break his word.

Ryder stretched out on his chest, arms folded around the pillow and his face turned away from her.

Would a man with no conscience care how he treated you? Would he care about his word to you?

Would he kill someone in cold blood?

Oh, God, had she made a mistake?

Had she been blinded with anger and hurt to the point she'd committed her worst nightmare and helped to convict an innocent man?

She felt sick to her stomach.

Who was Ryder Van Dyke really?

If he didn't pull the trigger to kill Kearn, then who did? And more importantly, if Ryder was innocent, how was she going to prove it?

CHAPTER 20

MUNK HIT THE speed dial on his phone. He stretched out on the deep mattress, enjoying the plush surroundings in his room in Buckhead, with its picture window overlooking Atlanta's famous Peachtree Street. Daylight glowed behind the sheers. It was nice to get a cushy spot for an op. Unnecessary, but nice.

His client answered, "Are you in place?"

Munk grinned. "Ready to go. The minute the little wife is on her own, I'll be there."

"She has plans to shop tomorrow, but she won't be alone."

"Keep her away from Ryder and I'll find my moment."

"Remember I have two goals. One is to terrorize her and the other is to convince her that Ryder is behind the attacks. Try not to kill her until I give the word."

Munk smiled. There was a lot of latitude between terrorizing and death. "Your nickel."

CHAPTER 21

B IANCA WALKED OUT of the bathroom in a robe with her
hair pulled up on top of her head. "What time is it?"

"Not even daylight yet. An ungodly hour for this household."

"Not me. I'm an early bird." *And I've got somewhere to be.*
"You can shower first."

Ryder waved a hand from the bed. "Nah, I'm not in a rush."
But I am and I can't get out of here until you're preoccupied.
"But you're the only one with a job."

The perpetual music played overhead, but they'd agreed not
to push their luck even with the music on, and to avoid risky
conversations unless they were necessary.

Smoothly changing the subject, Ryder got out of bed and
asked, "Would you like some coffee? I'll have a pot delivered."

"You mean we don't have to go to the kitchen or somewhere
to get it?"

He gave her a wry smile that said he'd just discovered a
weakness.

Guilty. Want an instant human? Just add coffee.

He stepped over to the desk phone on a side table and punched
a button, then requested a tray be sent up. Turning back to her,
he shrugged. "Having anything delivered to your room is a perk
of wealth. Take advantage of it while we're here."

What she wanted to take advantage of was the VDE computer
system. It would take all her acting skills, which were limited,
to play the happy wife around Janeen today. Not that she
had anything against Ryder's older sister, but Bianca ranked
shopping right up there with scrubbing toilets.

She did it only when she had no other choice.

A tap at the door broke into her thoughts. Ryder spoke to

Edward then took a large tray filled with a sterling silver coffee server, two mugs and a dish of pastries.

"Oh, croissants," Bianca crooned.

"They're all yours. Edward knows I don't do breakfast."

She lifted the pastry to her lips and her robe parted an inch. She snagged it closed, but not before Ryder's eyes had shot to the gap with laser accuracy.

His eyes darkened with a clear message of what he wanted and that's all it took for her body to react. They stared at one another, each waiting on the other to make a move.

Striding into the closet where he grabbed some clothes, Ryder avoided looking at her on the way to the bathroom. He muttered, "I'm taking a shower."

Good. Stay in there for an hour.

That should be enough time for what she needed to do. Bianca dashed into the closet and changed to her running top, shorts and sneakers. Next she dug out her customized iPod and hooked it on her hip, then ran the earphones up to her ears.

She slowed near the bathroom door on her way out.

The shower sounded like Niagara Falls with all those water jets on.

Ryder had spent a long time showering when they'd been with the team. She could understand that after having no privacy in prison.

She wouldn't need much time for a quick two miles. Hopefully, that's all it would take to make contact with Nanci. Bianca tiptoed down the stairs, then laughed at herself. As if anyone would hear her in this hotel. O-dawn-thirty might be an ungodly hour for this household, but not for a girl raised in the country.

Adjusting her earphones as she reached the front door, she slipped outside where she stretched a little, then jogged down the tree-lined drive. Would the guards allow her to leave? When she reached the gates, she ran in place and waved at the security guard who shot her a surprised look then nodded at her and opened the gate.

No media sitting outside today.

Maybe she and Ryder were old news.

Breaking into a jog, Bianca flipped on her music, hoping the reconfigured iPod worked the way Murdock intended and that she'd be hearing Nanci's voice soon. Murdock must not trust the Slye group since she'd been warned not to let Ryder know when she spoke to Nanci via radio transmission. Lengthening her stride, Bianca was actually enjoying the time alone in spite of not being a dedicated runner. Clouds littered the predawn sky that glowed red with warning of rain on the way.

Halfway down the block the sidewalk wound to the left past homes just as massive as the Van Dyke manor.

To think her parents had raised a child in a two-bedroom house. Their one-level home was a little rough around the edges, but always clean. Her mama mopped wood floors that had never been varnished. After seeing where Ryder grew up, Bianca would take her loving home over his any day.

A few cars passed her, traveling in both directions. Too busy to be the quiet road Nanci had indicated, Bianca took a right and slowed her pace as she headed down a hill.

She caught sight of a dark, four-door sedan turning behind her in her peripheral vision.

The car moved slowly toward her.

Was it Nanci?

Note to self, get more information next time such as what vehicle to expect.

***

Margaux held her temper as she strode through the street level offices at Slye headquarters. The civilian area up here functioned as a bona fide high-level corporate security business. Sabrina could have set up camp in a shiny tower in downtown Atlanta, but Sabrina Slye had chosen a spot in the older area of College Park to be near the Atlanta International Airport. Plus the property provided an underground space for black ops planning.

Sabrina might have turned her back on the CIA after her team barely survived a bad op, but she'd never turn her back on her country when it came to protecting national security.

Bumping Sabrina's open office door with her knuckles on her way in, Margaux announced, "Bianca is on the move."

Sabrina put down the file she'd been holding. "Did Nanci tell you about it?"

"No." Margaux shouldn't be pissed since Nanci was FBI and had made it clear there were limitations to what Nanci would do to help her cousin, but Margaux had expected a heads up on any movement with Bianca.

"Dingo's hidden cam picked it up," Sabrina stated.

"Right."

"And Ryder isn't with her?"

"No." Margaux had been standing close to Dingo when he cursed and pointed at his wall of monitors. She'd stayed long enough to determine that Ryder was absent from Bianca's early morning run, which wouldn't have happened unless Bianca had snuck away.

"I knew that son of a bitch Murdock wouldn't keep us in the loop," Sabrina muttered.

"No more than the basic information we share with him."

Tapping a pen against her file, Sabrina thought out loud. "What the hell is he up to?"

"Nothing that will work in Ryder's favor, that's for sure. We need ears on Bianca. Murdock wouldn't risk having her meet Nanci in person, which means they're going to work with a limited radio transmission. She had earphone wires running to an iPod. I'm betting that's the radio."

"We can't put anyone in fast enough if Bianca is trading information while she's running."

"Right," Margaux agreed. "If we saw Bianca leave, then so did anyone else watching that house. Murdock won't put anyone close enough to be on scene and risk burning her cover, which means she's out there with no one watching her back."

Sabrina raised a sharp eyebrow at Margaux. "That wouldn't be the case if Nanci had told us about this meeting. What can you do?"

Besides strangle my cousin to get answers? "I'll know once I talk to Nanci."

"She may not be as willing to help us as you thought."

"She will be." With that, Margaux turned to leave, ready to use a marker she'd told herself she'd *never* use. But Sabrina believed in Ryder's innocence and he was part of the team. Failing to pull out every trick to save him would be no different than leaving a fallen team member in the field.

Never happen.

Bianca's iPod music coming through her earphones faded to almost nothing as a voice broke in saying, "This is Nanci. I've got eyes on you."

Bianca had been singing along with songs while jogging so that it would look natural when she started talking. "I hear you. Where are you?"

"Coming up behind you now."

The sedan Bianca had noticed passed her with a woman holding a cellphone to her ear and nodding as she talked, ignoring Bianca as she passed by.

"That was me," Nanci said. "I'm going to park up ahead. Keep jogging. We'll have until you get a half-mile away to talk before the connection breaks."

"Got it." Bianca jogged slowly in warm up mode to keep from moving too quickly.

Nanci asked, "What happened last night?"

"We were grabbed by Kearn's people."

"Were you harmed?"

"No, they separated us and locked me in a room. They worked Ryder over pretty good, but he managed to escape and got us out."

Nanci clarified, "*Ryder* did?"

"Yes. He said they weren't trained very well."

"Did he have a chance to run?"

"Yes, but he didn't." That kept playing over and over in Bianca's mind. He faced going back to prison for a long time. He could have left her, but he hadn't.

Silence answered her for a couple seconds then Nanci continued in rapid fire. "You have to get inside VDE today."

"Going to be tough to do. I'm stuck shopping with Ryder's

sister. Hubrecht gave Ryder a position in the company, but he doesn't trust me for obvious reasons." Bianca didn't even glance at Nanci's car as she jogged passed.

"Stand by." Nanci went off the air for fifteen seconds then came back on. "Murdock said for you to find some way to get inside the VDE corporate offices this afternoon and he'd have something in place to help you gain their trust."

"Like what?" Bianca didn't care for surprises, especially when it came to dealing with Hubrecht Van Dyke.

"He didn't share specifics. Just said for you to be there before five."

How am I supposed to do that when Hubrecht made it abundantly clear that he did not want Ryder's new former-FBI wife inside the building? But Bianca wasn't about to say that and have it repeated to Murdock. "Understood."

"Carry the iPod anywhere but into VDE. On a standard security check of your luggage they wouldn't find anything unusual. But if they took it from you and gave it to someone who knows what they're doing, they'd figure out the unit has been modified as soon as they disassembled it."

"I'm pretty sure everything I brought was scrutinized before we got to the Van Dyke house so it's probably a good sign that they didn't confiscate it."

"Right. You'll be out of range in another hundred feet. We'll know when you enter VDE today. Be careful and don't say a word about this to Ryder."

"I will." How could she convince Ryder she had to get inside VDE without telling him about her communication with Nanci? Bianca took the next right, intending to circle around back to the main road. As she rounded the corner, she glanced over to see the sedan gone.

At the bottom of a very long hill, she realized the roads did not work in a square pattern, but continued twisting and turning.

Turn around and go back up that hill or go forward and find another way out of the area? No sane person liked to run up hills. She jogged on and took a right at the next turn that wound around and up a more gradual incline.

She'd been so focused on finding her way back that she hadn't noticed steps falling on the pavement not far behind her. It could be another runner out to take advantage of the ideal temperature in the low seventies.

When someone backed out of a driveway ahead of her, she sped around between the front of the car and the driveway, tossing a look over her shoulder as if she was looking at the car when in reality she was checking for the runner.

The road was empty except for the luxury car puttering away.

She believed in being prepared, not paranoid, and didn't like feeling paranoid now, but after being kidnapped she felt justified. Laughing at herself for a case of nerves, she turned once more and jogged along a secluded street bordered by tall walls and thick bushes. Looking ahead, she recognized a huge house down at the corner that she'd seen while talking to Nanci.

Her shoulders relaxed. That meant she was about a mile and a half from the Van Dyke estate. Piece of cake to get back.

A figure all in black exploded from behind a line of bushes as she passed by and grabbed her arm, yanking her off balance.

Not again.

CHAPTER 22

RYDER WALKED OUT of the shower dressed in a pair of shorts and drying his hair. Hubrecht expected him to wear a suit. Ryder would compromise with a button down shirt and slacks.

The stillness in the room stopped him.

He called out quietly, "Bianca?"

Ah, shit. Where was she?

Tossing the towel down, he rushed to the closet and shoved his feet into a pair of sneakers then snagged a T-shirt and bolted from the room. At the bottom of the grand stairway, he tugged the T-shirt over his head on his way to the door where he found Edward. "Do you know where Bianca is?"

"Have you lost your wife?"

Yes. "Not exactly."

Edward cocked his head. "What exactly then?"

That was the Edward he knew, full of sarcasm. Ryder was too worried about Bianca to care how foolish he looked trying to find Bianca. "Where is she, Edward?"

"She passed me a half hour ago in running clothes and wearing an iPod. I'm no Sherlock Holmes, but my guess would be—"

Ryder was already out the door and running toward the gate where the security on duty confirmed that Bianca had left the compound. Taking off in the direction security indicated she'd gone, Ryder kicked it into high gear to find his wife of one day.

Wife.

The single word used to send a shiver of fear down his spine. Yeah, that was there, but now there was a streak of irritation shooting alongside it.

Whoever she married for real would have to deal with an

unpredictable, strong-willed, hardheaded woman who would drive him crazy.

But he'd also get a body made for loving and lips that were sweet as honey. Her husband would overlook any irritating habits every time he walked through the door and realized Bianca was his. He'd be one lucky bastard.

Ryder hated him already.

Which only proved that Bianca was making *him* crazy.

What was she thinking to leave like this?

Why hadn't she told him she wanted to run? He'd have gone with her. Didn't she realize that as his wife, she could be a target for anyone angry about his release?

Or a kidnapper wanting a quick payday?

When he got her home again, he was setting ground rules. She could shop as long as she was with Janeen, who would have security with her. Ryder would inform security that Bianca was to be returned to the Van Dyke compound once she finished shopping and she was to stay inside the property until he came home.

No argument. No exceptions.

Adrenaline slammed through Bianca the minute the attacker touched her. Head covered in a stocking cap, he was close to six feet tall and solid as the old oak trees lining the street.

He yanked her through bushes, scraping exposed skin on her legs and arms.

A thick branch whacked across her shin. She stumbled and he reeled her in harder. She'd trained over and over with self-defense moves and went on autopilot.

Taking advantage of her momentum, she swung around with an elbow to his throat. He turned in time to miss a direct hit and twisted her wrist in his iron grip. He slapped her with his free hand.

That just pissed her off.

She whipped a knee up at his groin and collided with a hard protective groin cup that felt like it cracked her kneecap. Dammit. She stomped his instep and shoved him backwards.

Using the heel of her hand, she hit him in the chin and he grunted, but wouldn't let go.

Sweat poured down her face as she landed strike after strike. He cursed her and grabbed a handful of hair, wrenching her head back.

A siren shrieked nearby. Sounded as if it was coming toward them.

She felt his hesitation at the distraction and kicked backwards hard, hitting him in the knee. He howled and lost his hold on her.

The best defense was to be fast.

She took off at a dead run. At the top of the street, an ambulance raced past on her right, heading in the opposite direction.

Footsteps pounded behind her.

Ryder had slowed his pace again as he approached a street on his right that intersected with the road he ran along. He'd been glancing down every side street, pausing only long enough to check for an irritating auburn-haired female with too much grit for her own good before he moved on. One more street then he'd turn around. In fact, he'd send out a team of security to track her down. That would probably screw up things with Hubrecht who would immediately think she was up to something, which she probably was, but Ryder would deal with any fallout once he found Bianca.

He angled his path of travel to the right as he neared the next street.

A body flew around the corner and slammed him in the chest, knocking him sideways into a yard.

Bianca. She was fighting him with all she had.

He grabbed her arms as they rolled over wet grass. "Stop before you get hurt."

"Oh, thank God it's you," came out on a rush of air. She slumped against him, damp and breathing hard.

He wanted to yell at her for scaring him worse than hitting a trip wire on a land mine, but his arms went around her, pulling her close instead.

She was safe. That was all that mattered.

He ran his hand up and down her back that moved with ragged breaths. "Are you okay, Sweetheart?"

Pushing against his chest, she lifted up on shaking arms and slung sweat-soaked hair out of her eyes, but it fell back into her face. Her pupils were dilated so much her eyes almost looked black.

Something—or someone—had scared her. Would the hardheaded woman admit it? Doubtful.

He was just calming down when his gaze swept over Bianca's upper body and stalled at her arms that were bleeding from scratches.

And now he could see a red mark the size of a hand on her cheek.

He wanted to kill someone. The idea that she could have been killed herself brought all that fury to the surface. "What the hell were you thinking to leave without security?"

"Do *not* raise your voice to me or you're going to look worse than I do," she warned. She slid off of him then sat back on her knees and used both hands to finally shove the wet hair off her face. Lowering her hands, she tugged down the tank top that had ridden up and checked the iPod clipped on her shorts. When she lifted her earphones into view, one side was missing. "That bastard."

Ryder had pushed up on his elbows. He ground his back teeth. "Bianca, you have two seconds to answer my question."

Someone jogged past them tugging a small terrier along on a leash. The dog paused to sniff Ryder's shoe then ran on when his leash jerked tight.

Bianca huffed out a breath and cast a wary look around. "We're in someone's yard. People are probably watching. Let's start back."

Ryder's hands shook with the need to find the person who had done this. But ranting at Bianca wasn't going to get him answers any quicker and she was right about getting off the street. He shoved up to stand and hooked his hands under her arms, lifting her to her feet.

She took a step and limped.

He cursed. "You're hurt."

She glared at him. "I don't know why you're so angry. *I'm* the one in pain and I'm not cursing a blue streak." She moved off at a slow limp, muttering under her breath about overbearing men.

Ryder rolled his eyes and caught up to her. When he put an arm around her waist she stiffened until he said, "I know you're tough, but you need ice on that. Lean on me until we can get it."

Heaving out one long breath, she relaxed.

"Tell me what happened," he coaxed in a calmer voice than he'd thought possible

"I got jumped down the road, but I got my licks in and managed to break away."

"Got a description?"

"Caucasian male. Six feet. Two ten, maybe two fifteen. All muscle. Smokes strong cigarettes. Something European. Wore black all over and a stocking cap."

That could be anyone. What was the chance that someone on the Slye team got a look at Bianca's attacker? Sabrina had said the FBI didn't want Slye anywhere around the Van Dyke home, but that wouldn't stop them from setting up an observation point.

"Must be Kearn's people again," Bianca offered and grimaced when she stepped wrong.

Ryder tightened his hold on her to take more weight off her leg. He wished he could tell her that Kearn's people hadn't kidnapped them, but he couldn't betray Sabrina's trust. He seriously doubted Kearn's boys would have sent someone to grab Bianca. They might not be happy about Ryder being out of prison, but he just did not give J. K. Kearn's sons that much credit for initiative.

He fully expected them to sell the company at some point.

Of course, if they did and Hubrecht bought it, that would only improve the government's case against Ryder.

He circled back to his original question, but changed it up. "Why did you leave without telling me?"

She tried to shrug, which was hard to do when he held her so close. And it was forced. "Just needed to get some air and exercise."

Lie. Had to be about her job, but Ryder was shocked that Murdock would set up a meeting when someone could have seen her.

Unless ... Ryder's gaze went to the iPod.

So she had a way to communicate with the FBI. Slick, as long as no one in VDE figured it out. But she couldn't do this again. He would not have another person's death on his head. He couldn't have prevented Kearn's, but he could keep Bianca alive if she'd just do as he told her and tell him what the FBI was up to.

When the guard gate for the Van Dyke home came into sight, Ryder leaned over and said, "Don't leave the house alone again."

She bristled, muscles tightening across her shoulders and back. To her credit, she smiled when she told him, "I am the one calling the shots. Not you. And I can clearly take care of myself. You should just worry about getting me inside VDE."

"Be patient. If we push it now, Hubrecht and his security will get suspicious of me then *I* may lose access. Give me today to figure my way around there and I'll get you in by the end of the week."

"That's not soon enough. I can't spend a week playing trophy bride."

Just as they reached the gate, he said, "Trust me. You're not trophy bride material."

Bianca would never be some man's arm candy.

She was too much woman for a man who wanted a subservient female. Ryder liked that about her even when she frustrated the hell out of him. She'd handled some cretin who'd jumped her and taken Ryder's head off when he'd yelled at her.

She could be so damned adorable sometimes.

She turned to him with a clenched-teeth smile. "Don't be late getting ready for work, *Dear*." Then she stepped away from him, entering the gate.

Why was she pissed off now?

What had caused that?

Women could be so damned *aggravating* sometimes. Most of the time.

Ryder paused to inform the security guard that Bianca was

not to leave unescorted again. He hurried to catch up with her. But the minute he put his hand at her back, she hissed, "Don't touch me."

Facing a hostile enemy whose language he didn't speak was easier to figure out than a woman on a good day.

CHAPTER 23

BIANCA FINISHED A long shower. Her muscles felt better but her temper still threatened to explode.

Trust me. You're not trophy bride material.

She glanced over at the mirror. Scary wet hair stuck out everywhere. She had the blistered-red splotch of a handprint on her cheek and cuts everywhere from shoulder to ankles.

Granted, she wasn't prime runway material, but did Ryder have to put her shortcomings in such blunt terms? She was having enough trouble keeping her footing in this operation without him echoing Bernard's words.

Not specifically, but the insinuation was clear.

Bernard had said she was too uptight, too much of a prude, too critical ... too everything a man didn't want and not enough of what men liked. He'd been a jerk, but she still wondered how much of what he'd said was true.

When Ryder had hovered above her last night, she'd been swept away in the moment. Clearly caught up in a fantasy of her own making.

She must have imagined that look of desire in his eyes.

If that's so, then why'd he kiss you?

Because he'd felt guilty about waking up out of control. For those few minutes, she'd imagined she was special. That he saw only her and no one else.

And that she'd been enough.

She looked away from the mirror, unable to stare at the fool who'd fallen victim to Ryder's crazy-hot silver eyes. Must have been lack of sleep and getting kidnapped that had turned her brain to mush.

That and having Ryder's ripped body covering her from head to toe.

Her nipples puckered at the memory.

She shook her head at herself. She was law enforcement and he was a prisoner. Possibly one who had been wrongly accused, but until she had hard facts she needed to keep her head straight about their roles.

Flipping her towel into the corner, she pulled on the robe she'd grabbed on the way in here rather than take the time to figure out what she wanted to wear today. To shop.

Kill me now.

Murdock would probably go nuts later when his people reported that Bianca was putting in hours of research at Sax Fifth Avenue when she was supposed to be breaking into the VDE computer network.

Using her computer skills wouldn't happen unless she got inside the building.

She ran a brush through her hair enough to get it off her face, wrapped the thick navy blue robe around her and walked out of the bathroom. The perpetual acoustic music had switched to blues. Bonnie Raitt was singing about loving a man.

Dressed in a white button down shirt and gray dress pants, Ryder leaned against the wall next to the window. He held a cell phone at his ear. "She *is* an amazing woman."

Bianca walked toward the closet, acting as if she hadn't heard him. Was Ryder trying to get on her good side by talking her up to the team?

Wait a freakin' minute.

He didn't have a cell phone.

She spun around. "Is that my phone?"

He was smiling at something being said. "Okay, here she is."

She was going to murder him in his sleep. Marching across the room, she snatched the phone out of his hand and glared a death threat at him. "Hello?"

"Hi, baby." Bianca's mama bubbled over with happiness. "I sure do like your young man. He's a sweetie."

Bianca changed her mind. She wasn't going to kill Ryder. She would take her time coming up with a slow and painful way to make him pay for talking to her family. "He's something all right. Why'd you call, Mama?"

"I need to know when you're comin' home. Everybody wants to throw you a party."

Bianca rubbed her forehead where the mother of all headaches had set up camp. "I'm going to call you on Monday to let you know. Remember?"

"Yes, but we're so excited. You can't come home this weekend? Everybody is anxious to meet him and see you."

"I'm tied up right now."

"But you're on your honeymoon."

The honeymoon from hell. "Something came up that I need to take care of. Let me get that done and I'll call. Promise. Just wait for me to call you, please?"

"Okay, baby. I don't mean to be botherin' you."

Just give me the worst daughter on the face of the earth award. "You're never a bother, Mama, but it's hard to talk with people around. I don't like them to know my personal business."

"That's fine. I'll wait. We're just bustin' a gut to show you two off. Daddy's braggin' to everyone that you're all grown up and married."

Bianca should have talked to them before doing this, but even if she could've shared any of this, the FBI deal had gone down so quickly there'd been no time to go home before starting the mission. She hated lying to her parents, even for national security.

Bianca ended the call and turned on Ryder. "Why did you answer my phone?"

"Because I didn't want you to miss the call if it was your parents."

She'd been prepared for some smart comeback, not a sincere reason, though she wasn't certain why she'd expected that. Ryder had proved over and over that he wasn't that way. Why did she keep going to the worst possible scenario as a default when it came to Ryder?

He watched her as if he braced himself for a rant.

She wanted to hold on to her anger and nurture it, but if she took an honest look at everything she'd have to admit that he'd only told her the truth about not being trophy material, and he'd acted with consideration by answering her phone.

Underneath all the turmoil in her head, she knew where the anger originated. She wanted to be the woman a man like Ryder looked at as if he couldn't live without kissing her and making love to her. She'd let her insecurities get a foothold and mistaken a simple kiss for more than it was.

Dropping the phone in the pocket of her robe, she nodded. "Thank you for catching the call."

From the surprise that broke through his stern features, she'd robbed him of whatever reaction he'd planned on. He blinked, then straightened away from the wall. "You're welcome."

She chewed on her lip then decided *what the hell?* "I really would like to come to VDE today."

Ryder crossed the room, stopping inches from her. "I know you would, but you don't know how quickly Hubrecht can change his mind about even my being there. I thought you'd have realized by now I wasn't kidding about his security measures. This could turn ugly in the blink of an eye. Give me a chance to make sure it's safe for you—to find a way to get you in."

It wasn't that she didn't believe him but she had Murdock breathing down her throat. She had orders to get inside VDE *today*. Period.

She whispered, "You think Hubrecht ordered Kearn's death, don't you? Otherwise you wouldn't be worried about my safety." She turned away with her arms crossed.

Ryder's arms came around her. He lowered his face next to her ear. "I know you need to get inside and I'm not saying Hubrecht is guilty of anything to do with Kearn, at least not yet, but when I was seventeen I had a friend I ran the streets with. Hubrecht made it clear he didn't like it and told me to cut him loose. I refused. Two days later, Larry and his family disappeared."

She turned in his arms to face him. "Did anyone report it?"

"Larry wasn't kidnapped or killed—at least I don't think he was. He left me a note written in his handwriting that his father had a job materialize on the other side of the country and the family had to move in twenty-four hours. House sold. Gone. Larry said keeping in touch would be too much trouble."

She tried to come up with a reasonable scenario. "Maybe a headhunter came through with a job offer his father couldn't turn down."

"Larry's father stocked machinery parts in a warehouse. Not a lot of head hunters broker labor positions. I had no way to find Larry once he left, which means Hubrecht paid to get rid of my friend."

What kind of parent did that?

One with more money than parenting skills.

No wonder Ryder trusted no one. Her hands were flat against his chest. She felt the steady thud of his heart. How was she going to get inside VDE without putting Ryder in a tight spot or drawing unwanted attention from Hubrecht?

Ryder moved his head until they were nose to nose. "If I thought it was a better idea to bring you into the office, I would."

"I understand."

"I'm not just saying that, because I don't like leaving you on your own today." His hand came up to her injured cheek then he gently kissed the puffy skin. "You have no idea how much I want to kill the person who hurt you. If you came in the office and anyone threatened you, there would be bloodshed."

Her heart banged her ribs at that declaration.

How had he managed to twist her heart into a pretzel with so few words? Because Ryder didn't say something unless he meant it and, when he spoke, it came out with steel conviction.

She didn't doubt that he'd back it up, too.

Why would he jeopardize his freedom by igniting a conflict at his father's office?

For the same reason he came to free her from Kearn's people when he could've escaped.

She had better get over this ridiculous attraction, but that would be easier to do if he didn't have his hands on her and wasn't saying things that turned her insides to mush. She'd become immune to sexy-looking men after her time with Bernard, so it wasn't Ryder's undeniable hot looks that drew her to him.

It was the man inside that packaging. Ryder's character was carved with a lethal edge and confidence ran through his blood.

And he was honorable.

In all the pages of research Bianca had pored over, there had been only one dishonorable act—killing Kearn—and Ryder denied having pulled that trigger.

Daddy had taught Bianca she had sound instincts and to trust them. Hers were telling her she held the destiny of an innocent man in her hands.

Believing that in her heart was one thing.

Proving it to the FBI and the justice system was another.

She was saying nothing to anyone, including Ryder, until she had hard evidence. "I'll wait."

He squeezed her waist and pecked a kiss on her forehead. "Thank you. I'll do what I can to come up with a plan today. Just be careful and don't let your guard down." He glanced over at the Bose clock radio. "I'm going to head over and go in early before everyone shows up and I have to run the gauntlet. And for the record, I do know you can handle yourself or I wouldn't leave you alone with Janeen."

She rolled her eyes and muttered, "Now you've really insulted me."

Ryder had started for the door but stepped back and kept his voice down. "No, I haven't. At this point, I'm not sure who is behind killing Kearn and who wanted to see me spend my life in prison. I would never have expected that of someone in this household, but I've come to realize I never really knew everyone here. Janeen was angry with me when I left for the military and I can see it's only worse now that I'm back."

Bianca huffed at him. "How dangerous can the party girl of the household be?"

"You saw my marksmanship records from the military. You know I was a sniper."

"Yes. Impressive."

"Janeen taught me how to shoot and, as a target shooter, is every bit as good as I am," he said. "I've seen her hit moving targets at eight hundred yards." Then he walked out.

CHAPTER 24

SABRINA PICKED UP her Starbucks coffee and moved to the condiment area. Someone entered her personal space.

She paused, putting the cup down, prepared for the threat in spite of people laughing and moving through the crowded area.

"It's me," a baritone said at her ear.

She cursed the sizzle of heat that raced along her skin and picked up her cup, turning to face Gage Laughton. "You, of all people, should know how dangerous it is to sneak up on me."

"The last time I arranged for a lunch meeting you had a sniper in position with crosshairs on my head."

As a CIA agent high on the food chain, he should have expected that after the CIA sent her team into a trap two years ago. He claimed no one at the agency was behind the busted mission, but someone had traded her entire team for the captured undercover agent they'd gone to rescue.

That agent and the person who'd picked him up had disappeared.

When someone bumped into Sabrina, Gage passed a dark look at the kid and suggested, "Let's find a seat outside where it's not so cramped."

Sabrina kept stirring her coffee, but she narrowed her eyes, watching him. Let him think she was suspicious of his motive. She was.

She'd seen his brown hair in every length, but now he wore it cropped short. As if he didn't already have rugged appeal, the bomber jacket, black T-shirt and worn jeans that showed off his muscular body took it to a deadly level. The beard shadow meant he was growing it for an upcoming mission.

That shouldn't make her stomach clench, but it did.

Stupid emotions that she kept tucked away where they wouldn't interfere with her life.

His gaze kept moving around the room as he said, "If I wanted you dropped, you wouldn't be here now."

Cold hard truth from a man who had claimed to love her at one time. Back when she'd said something equally stupid to him.

She led the way outside to where she could better appreciate her own leather jacket. The crisp air held enough chill to start turning leaves on trees in Atlanta.

After scoping out her options, she located a spot where a table and umbrella had been shoved into an alcove created by the shape of the building. She tilted the umbrella to block them and took a seat with her back to the bricked-in corner.

Gage took the other metal chair next to her.

Sabrina should have moved further away, because she could feel his presence—the energy around him.

That's what had drawn her to Gage in the first place. He hadn't inherited pretty boy genetics. Nothing about that face was magazine worthy, but put him in a room full of alphas and his sheer force of presence would mark him as the top of the pack.

"What do you want, Gage?"

He swung his hazel gaze to hers and she should have turned away before she saw the longing. "I want to see you again."

Sabrina waited until she could answer with nothing in her voice that would betray how much she missed him. "Then you wasted your trip."

"Why?"

"You don't want to make me talk about the UK."

"Are you going to hold me responsible for that forever?"

She didn't want to have this conversation. "You were my handler. My entire team trusted you, because I did. If you don't want the burden of blame, hand me the names of everyone in the CIA who knew about our mission. But someone has to answer for burning my team."

Gage took a drink of his coffee. "There is a reason I came by."

He was never going to give her those names. How could he

expect her to spend a night making love with him ever again without thinking about what had happened to her team in the UK? If he could keep moving on, away from what they'd had, she could, too. "I'm listening."

"What is one of your people doing inside VDE?"

She slowed her breathing in the same way she would if she was about to take a long range shot, because that was the last thing she'd expected him to ask. "*Whom* are you referencing?"

"You mean, there's more than one?"

She closed her eyes then opened them again. "I don't have an op going on."

"So Ryder isn't with you any longer?"

Fuck. "Don't screw with this, Gage. It's important."

"That's my point. We're working on something major and I can't have your man interfering."

She waited for more, but Gage had said all he would until she gave him something. She'd trusted him with her life at one time, but could she trust him with Ryder's?

"Talk to me, Sabrina, or I can't help him. Whatever he's up to can get him killed."

She leaned toward him and quietly shared what had happened to Ryder and why he was in VDE. When she was finished, she sat back. If Gage didn't give her something in return, the fragile truce they'd formed since he'd shared intel with her on an op last spring would take a huge step back.

He shifted his body toward her, turning so no one could read his lips. "We know about the illegal weapons exports, but not how they're getting into the terrorist countries or who's funding the operations. I need that information. Soon."

Time to put the negotiations on the table. "I'll share anything related to that if you will."

"Agreed."

He stood, but before he left, he leaned down, placing a hand on the arm of her chair so that he was only inches from her. There was a time when she wouldn't have lasted ten seconds without kissing him when he was this close. He still used the same soap, and the scent was going to stay with her after he left.

Meeting his unrelenting gaze, she asked, "What else?"

"I'm still turning over every rock to find out who screwed you. When I do, you'll have your chance to exact justice, but holding me responsible is only hurting both of us. I won't push, but I'm not giving up. I want to hold you so much its killing me not to touch you, but when I do it'll be because you want me just as much. I'll always love you."

Then he straightened and walked away, leaving her heart in shreds again.

CHAPTER 25

RYDER PARKED HIS black 1968 Mustang in the covered corporate space in front of the sign with his name. Finding this car in the garage at the Van Dyke home had dragged emotions to the surface that confused and aggravated him. Edward had confided that when Lady Anne ordered the car sold, Hubrecht had overruled her, warning anyone against so much as scratching the car.

Then Hubrecht had it moved to a temperature-controlled storage space so nothing accidental happened to it.

Who was the Hubrecht Van Dyke who had saved one of Ryder's two most cherished possessions?

Edward also shared that *he* was the one who'd arranged Ryder's model car collection inside the antique cabinet, per Hubrecht's orders.

Ryder rode the elevator up the tower, feeling empty handed after seeing so many briefcases being toted through Buckhead, but he didn't really know what his job description was or what he'd put in a briefcase at this point.

Ryder had just stepped into the receptionist's lobby when Hubrecht's assistant came around a corner and walked up with a genuine smile. "Mr. Van Dyke, nice to see you again so soon."

"Good to see you, too, Adelaide."

"Your office is ready. I'll show you." How had this sweet grandmother stuck with Hubrecht for so many years?

The office she showed him was bigger than he'd expected, with a rosewood desk and matching credenza. A wall of glass offered an unobstructed view of Peachtree Street's busy traffic bustling between Lenox Mall and Piedmont Road.

"Is there anything I can get you?" Adelaide asked.

A governor's pardon would be nice. "No, thank you."

She smiled and withdrew.

He'd never anticipated what his shooting ability would one day cost him. If Hubrecht hadn't forced Larry's family to leave, Ryder might never have joined the Army. So determined to prove his value, he'd worked his ass off and finally been chosen for Special Forces, then his natural abilities got him into sniper school. He'd excelled at long range shooting as if he'd been born with a rifle in his hands.

All that because he refused to work for a man who would upend a family and send them across the country to get what he wanted.

The door opened. "Ryder." Hubrecht's normal salutation never changed.

Ryder nodded, returning his standard greeting.

"Find everything acceptable?"

"Of course." Ryder's life with his family had always been just that—acceptable. Not warm and loving, not a hellhole, but tolerable. "What am I supposed to do? I don't see any files."

Combative silence charged across the room. Bianca would be exasperated with him if she were present. But she didn't understand the dynamics that had always percolated between him and Hubrecht.

Hubrecht strolled into the room, parking himself in front of the windows, a wall of dark clouds forming a backdrop. "We have an opportunity to pick up clients from a struggling company."

"Thought we agreed that I wasn't a salesman."

"Yes, but your knowledge of this particular client will be valuable so I want you to be familiar with the project. You'll be given information pertinent to your specific role." Hubrecht sent Ryder a pointed look. "The rest of the files will not be available."

Ryder didn't need a sledgehammer over the head. Hubrecht was making no bones about not trusting him with sensitive material.

"What struggling company?" Ryder concealed his irritation. Not too tough. He'd learned how to mask his emotions from the very best—Hubrecht Van Dyke.

"Kearn."

The son of a bitch was going to shove his face in it and put Ryder's handprint all over picking up Kearn's business. Had Hubrecht set him up to take the fall after all?

"Don't you think these clients will be a little wary of the person charged with shooting Kearn?"

"Absolutely not. You've been cleared and released. I would think they'd be interested in meeting you."

So I'm to be a novelty? Ryder clenched the arms of his chair, restraining his anger. He'd love to throw this back in Hubrecht's face and walk out. Then what? Go to prison for the rest of his life while a murderer lived free?

He could do anything for six days. Besides, how much could really be expected of him?

"What about Terrence? He might be a better choice."

"Terrence now works for you."

"That's bullshit."

Hubrecht turned to him. "I've kept Terrence on the payroll in deference to Lady Anne, but he's gone more often than he's here. And when he is here, he does little."

"He's sick."

"I know. And I do sympathize with his struggle, but that doesn't change the fact that we're in a highly competitive business. I need people who can produce. You'd think it would be simple to find highly qualified individuals in this job market, but it's not."

There was the opening Ryder had been hoping for to bring Bianca on. "If that's the case, you should consider hiring my wife. She's not just good with computers, she's exceptional."

"Bianca appears to be a nice girl, Ryder, but I didn't make it to this point in business by being a fool. It's going to take longer than a few days for me to trust someone from the FBI inside my company. Ask me after your first anniversary."

Hubrecht walked out.

Ryder would argue that Hubrecht had led Bianca to believe she could come in once security cleared her in two weeks.

But two weeks might as well be a year from now on their supposed anniversary, because either would be too late.

CHAPTER 26

BIANCA SMOOTHED THE front of her white-and-black pinstriped skirt suit. No more wrinkles there than the last ten times she'd checked.

She followed Terrence to a high-back booth the maître d' selected specifically for Mr. Van Dyke, his favorite customer. Janeen had bailed on her, which had felt like a blessing until Terrence invited her to lunch. At least she could use this time to find out more on Terrence. Hushed conversations carried through the swanky restaurant doing a booming business at mid-afternoon hour. Terrence said it was his late day for work, but Bianca had a feeling any day could be his late day.

Several heads turned as they passed.

Bianca could imagine the Buckhead buzz above white linen tablecloths and china place settings.

"That's her. She put Van Dyke away, then got his conviction overturned and married him."

"And she's with his brother. Wonder what that means?"

"A cozy pair if you ask me."

"Guess old Ryder wised up and seduced someone who could do him some good instead of another sex kitten. Picked the right one from the looks of it."

Bianca told her insecurity to shut the hell up. For the past two years she'd had no life. She'd first put her all into finding the evidence to prove someone at VDE was selling weapons to terrorists, then she'd taken on researching and analyzing evidence in two killings the FBI believed were connected.

With Ryder the number one suspect in Kearn's.

Now she was married to the man everyone in her research unit had toasted her for helping to put away.

Had everyone, including her, been so caught up in fitting the evidence pieces into one neat little puzzle that they'd stopped questioning that evidence?

She slid into the booth after the maître d' shifted the table away. Terrence scooted in right after her, a little too close. Bianca moved around the curved booth closer to the other side.

She couldn't see the rest of the room from this position, which meant no one could see her and Terrence in this secluded alcove.

Terrence reached into his coat pocket and withdrew a prescription bottle. What pain or ailment was that for? He'd climbed out of his Jaguar sedan with stiff, labored movements.

She scanned the menu. No prices. Fine by her. She'd rather not know just how much money it cost to eat a meal in a place where hand-tooled copper chairs had cushions covered in needlepoint—each chair a different landscape design.

"Nice place," Bianca observed. "Was it tough to get a reservation on short notice?"

"For most, but I'm a regular." Terrence gave her face a slow perusal. "You have beautiful eyes, Bianca."

She'd been taking in the décor until he said that. The compliment was sweet. Right? So why did it feel weird?

"Thanks." Bianca half-smiled and lifted the menu to hide behind. Once the drink orders had been taken—Diet Coke for her and some French wine Bianca couldn't pronounce for Terrence—she engaged Terrence in a discussion of family and travel, hoping to make better use of her time with this Van Dyke.

"Tell me about your father, Terrence?"

"He's intense, as you can imagine someone with his success might be." Terrence paused thinking. "He's not the most nurturing person."

"Was it tough growing up with him?"

"It was for Ryder."

Bianca took a risk and pushed a little harder. "I got the impression from Ryder that your father was harder on you."

"Maybe." Terrence stared off. "But that was because he measured Janeen and me against Ryder, even though we all knew I could never measure up to Ryder."

That was so sad the way Terrence described their relationship.

"Ryder speaks highly of you and thinks his father doesn't recognize your value."

A smile touched Terrence's lips as if he agreed but wouldn't put words to the thought.

"Your father can be very intimidating."

"Not to Ryder. He butted heads with Father all the time. He was the Mighty Komodo."

"The what?" She laughed.

"Father traveled to the Indonesian Islands in search of a rare orchid for his greenhouse. He faced off with a giant Komodo and admitted that he feared for his life. I'd never heard my father admit a weakness. When Ryder went toe-to-toe with him, we nicknamed Ryder the Mighty Komodo. My father wasn't a fan of it, but the name stuck."

Bianca filed away the information about Hubrecht—wild orchid collecting?—and Ryder for later, then turned the conversation around to Terrence.

Throughout the meal, he regaled her with stories of his travels to one country after another, never mentioning his frequent trips to Switzerland. Why not? She'd understand trips to see family in the Netherlands since Hubrecht was Dutch after all, but Bianca had found no immediate family connection in Switzerland.

Her intel showed that Terrence traveled there often to visit a medical facility where VDE had funded an expansion.

She'd only noticed because he hadn't mentioned it.

Bianca waited for their server to clear the dishes away before she pressed Terrence. "What an amazing amount of traveling you've done. What about Switzerland? I saw in a file at some point that you'd visited there if I'm remembering correctly. I've always thought it must be the most beautiful country." She composed her face into rapt attention.

He quieted for several seconds then said, "I've made several uneventful trips there, but as those were for medical treatments there's nothing of interest to be told. Are you finished, my dear?"

Huh. Switzerland was evidently off limits as a topic.

Now she was even more intrigued.

Bianca unconsciously dropped her hand back to the cushion between them and realized that was an error when Terrence

covered hers with his. Every muscle in her body tightened
in nervous reaction, but she didn't jerk her hand away. She
deserved bonus pay for keeping her smile in place.

He lifted her left hand. "This ring says it all."

"I love it." The agency did better than good for Terrence to
pass approval on the ring.

Terrence touched his lips to the back of her fingers.

Uh uh. They weren't kissing cousins, kissing in-laws or any
other mouth-sucking relation.

"Terrence..."

"Lady Anne can be harsh at times, but she's right about one
thing. You are a trophy worth winning. Ryder did well. I'm
envious."

Was he making a pass? Crap. And what in blazes did he
mean by suggesting Lady Anne considered her *a trophy worth
winning?* That had to be total bullshit. What kind of family
did Ryder have? One the word dysfunctional didn't begin to
describe.

"Terrence, I'm married to your brother. This is inappropriate."

"Oh, don't take me wrong." He released her hand. "I have no
designs on you. I realize you two are deeply in love, right?"

In love? With Ryder? No, absolutely not.

"Deeply," she sighed. Ryder wasn't the only person capable
of theatrics.

"He's very lucky."

She slowly returned her hand to her lap and didn't even wipe
it off on the napkin. Another bonus-pay credit earned. What had
possessed Terrence to behave this way?

"As your brother-in-law, I'm concerned for you, Bianca."
Terrence leaned toward her, and she had to work not to cringe.

"Why? What's wrong?" *Make another move on me and you
can be concerned about keeping that hand.*

"Nothing is wrong, but I just want you to know you can turn
to me if anything happens to Ryder."

"What...what do you mean 'if anything happens to Ryder'?"

He grimaced, hesitating as if he didn't want to say more,
but he finally explained. "Ryder was always a loner, even in
school. I'm sure you know from the research you've done for

the FBI that after leaving the Army, he was involved with some corporate security group. A lot of them were ex-military from what Kale said."

"Who's Kale?" She knew exactly who he was.

"Kale Carter, head of VDE security. I don't believe Ryder committed the murder, but I have a bad feeling that he might know who did or *suspect* who did."

Terrence sounded sincere and worried.

"Ryder would never listen to me," Terrence continued in a low monotone. "I tried to convince him to disappear for a while. Don't look surprised. I'm worried about both of you. Whoever did commit that murder and set him up as the fall guy might be out to get him now that he's free. I just want you to be careful and know I'm here for you should something ... happen."

Guilt slapped her over misreading his consideration. Maybe Terrence was just the touchy-feely type. She got the message loud and clear. He thought Ryder was in danger.

Ryder had been lucky to get away from Kearn's people, but if her niggling conscience was accurate about her missing something in her research, and Ryder truly wasn't guilty of the shooting, would the person behind killing Kearn want Ryder dead?

Her gut said yes, and that it was time to sit up and pay attention to her instincts, like her daddy had taught her.

Although, in spite of her instincts saying Terrence was acting a little off, he'd just proven himself to care about his brother.

Terrence watched quietly with a studious gaze.

Bianca patted his hand to let him know she understood his concern. "Thank you for sharing your concerns, Terrence. I'd hoped this was all behind us, but you're right. A killer is still out there and Ryder's vulnerable. I'll talk to him, but I don't think he'll hide. It's not in his personality to run from a threat."

Her words rang with sincerity because everything she knew about Ryder indicated he was a fearless fighter.

By the time Terrence paid the bill and ushered them from the restaurant, it was getting close to four in the afternoon. Murdock expected her to get inside the VDE offices before five.

Bianca suggested, "If you need to go into the office, I don't mind riding over with you."

"Missing your husband already?" Terrence asked, smiling.

Answering that with a yes would make her sound like some lovesick newlywed. But wasn't that technically her role? Still, she couldn't play it that sweet without throwing up. "I'm not quite so needy, but I would like to see him in an office environment."

"I doubt that you've been cleared through security yet."

What could she say to that? Time to go big or go home. Bianca reached over and put her hand on Terrence's arm as he started the car. "I understand that, but do you mean I can't just walk in with you and say hello to Ryder?"

Terrence sat back for a moment, thinking, then sighed. "I'm not staying long so I don't see the harm in taking you up with me for a quick visit."

Hallelujah. She pulled her hand back but gave Terrence a bright sister-in-law smile. "That would be so nice."

At the Van Dyke building, Terrence guided Bianca through security as his guest. She managed to ride up in the elevator without hyperventilating, barely, only because she mentally worked through her files, recalling details on every employee in key positions. She used the mental exercise to distract herself and kept her eyes on the mirrored slats between the wood panels, working hard to keep Terrence from seeing her distress.

Terrence led the way through the top floor of offices, pointing out his on the way then pausing to tell Ryder's female assistant—cute, collegiate-looking blonde that she was—that Bianca wanted to surprise Ryder.

"Thanks again," Bianca said when he excused himself outside Ryder's door then strolled away.

Bianca tapped on the door. A muffled "come in" sounded from within the office. Inside, Ryder sat with his head down, monitor on his right and his nose stuck in a file on his desk. "Be with you in just a minute," he mumbled.

"Take your time," she said.

His head jerked up.

"Bianca." Ryder's face broke into a smile. Big, sexy smile. Like he was genuinely happy to see her.

Scary thing about it, she was happy to see him, too. This whole pretending to be married had some major pitfalls. She got to glimpse something she would never be offered—marriage to a man who lit up her day.

Back to business.

Ryder stood, looking past her as his expression changed to one of concern. "How did you...?"

"Janeen had to cancel on shopping, so Terrence took me to a late lunch, and he brought me up here."

He came around the desk and stepped past her to the doorway. "I don't want to be disturbed, Jenny."

Closing the door, Ryder took Bianca by the arm. He used a remote from his desk to switch on soft music, just as he had last night in his room at the house, then he moved over to the window where he whispered, "Hubrecht won't be happy if he finds out you're up here."

She whispered right back, "Then let me on the computer now."

"I've asked for a laptop to take home."

"We've tried that," she said, indicating her FBI research team. "I have to access the network from inside here."

A beeping started at Ryder's desk.

They both looked over. Ryder squinted at the monitor. "What the hell is causing that?"

Jenny's voice outside the door said, "He has someone in there."

Ryder cupped Bianca's face and said, "Kiss me like you mean it." He crushed his lips to hers and she kissed him back, loving the way he tasted.

The door burst open. "Ryder!"

He took his time ending the kiss then put his arm around Bianca's shoulders when he turned them to face the man who had barked at Ryder. Sam Long stood there.

Sam passed a scathing look over Bianca then that feral gaze moved to Ryder. "You two in Hubrecht's office now."

Ryder didn't move. "Why?"

"I have security coming who will escort you there."

Bianca's stomach hit the floor. What had she done by coming here against Hubrecht's orders?

Worse, what had *Murdock* done and how did he see this as gaining anyone's trust?

CHAPTER 27

RYDER KEPT HIS arm around Bianca until they reached Hubrecht's office. What the hell was going on with the computers? Every office he passed had computers making a beeping sound or flashing monitors.

Sam walked into Hubrecht's office and kept going until he stood with Hubrecht. Next to them was a man with an earpiece and throat mic. He was five-ten, and his hair was buzz cut except for the short black curls on top of his head that fit his dark, Polynesian look and build. A Glock 17 was holstered at his hip. Intense eyes scoped everything while he watched Hubrecht's monitor and spoke softly, letting the sensitive throat mic pick up the words.

Had to be Kale Carter, head of security.

Kale paused, pulling the radio away when he spoke to Ryder. "What'd you launch into the network?

"Me?" Ryder didn't have to act incredulous at that. "I just figured out how to set up my email. Do you really think I'm computer savvy enough to cause whatever is going on?"

Sam cut in. "No, but your *wife* is."

Ryder wanted to kick himself for handing them a reason to point their trigger fingers at Bianca. "She just walked in and wasn't anywhere near the computer." He glared at Sam. "Right?"

"I have no idea what she was doing before I walked in."

Kale went back to monitoring whatever was going on with the computers and communicating with his security staff.

Hubrecht raised his gaze to Bianca then slapped it at Ryder. "What is she doing here?"

The cold bite in his tone let Ryder know this situation could escalate quickly and dangerously. "She just stopped by to say hello."

Kale raised his hand, drawing everyone's attention. He told Hubrecht, "Level One files are being deleted."

Ryder asked, "What does that mean?"

"Someone is trying to destroy our intelligence infrastructure. We have everything backed up." Then Kale told Hubrecht, "Security personnel are outside your door, Mr. Van Dyke."

Ah, shit. How could this be happening? Ryder hoped Bianca really hadn't started this. If she had, Hubrecht might turn them both over to law enforcement as a best-case scenario. Ryder didn't want to think about worst case.

Sam roared at Bianca, "What the hell did you do?"

Bianca stepped forward, even as Ryder tried to hold her back. She surprised him by snapping back at Sam. "Am I capable of breaching your firewalls? *Yes!* But even I have to type on a keyboard and need more than the sixty seconds I was in Ryder's office to get inside your system." She jutted her chin at the three men. "And what's my motivation to destroy files at a company where my husband has his only opportunity for a job?"

Man, she was so hot when she got all high and mighty, but Ryder wished she'd hold her tongue and not make this any worse.

Kale announced, "Twenty-eight percent of Level One files deleted and the attack is picking up speed. We've tried shutting down the system, but we can't risk what we'll lose in a major crash."

Sam was pacing and changed direction, striding over straight for Bianca.

Ryder stepped between them. "Touch her and you'll never regret a decision more."

"You brought a fucking FBI agent into this place. Why?"

The door opened and Terrence walked in just as Sam made that remark. Terrence said, "Ryder didn't do that. I brought Bianca in to surprise him."

Ryder appreciated his brother owning up to that but wished he hadn't because the fury in Hubrecht's eyes turned chilling.

Hubrecht ordered Terrence, "Leave us."

"I'm sorry, I didn't think—"

"Now," Hubrecht ordered.

Ryder sent Terrence a sympathetic glance, but his brother was already pulling the door closed behind him.

Sam raked his hand through his hair. "This is bullshit. What does the FBI want?"

Bianca pushed past Ryder and got in Sam's face before he could pull her back. "Your conclusions are irrational. Unless you're doing something illegal here, the FBI would have no interest in breaching your electronic systems. And if they did, why would they *delete* files? And, trust me, you'd never know if they did, because the team I was on would run circles around your best people."

Fuck, that was not going to help, but Bianca wasn't done digging that hole.

She looked over at Hubrecht. "Your people should have found the intruder by now and stopped it."

Hubrecht exchanged a look with Kale who shook his head and said, "Everyone in the building has been told to stay off their computers and we have the whole IT team working on it. No luck yet."

The neck muscles visible above Sam's collar flexed with tension. Ryder wanted to get Bianca out of this building now, but he hadn't expected to need an exit strategy when he came to work today.

When Kale muttered, "Sixty-three percent," Hubrecht shoved a raging glare at Bianca.

Ryder took a step toward her to pull her back. Before he could get to her, Bianca spoke up. "Has anyone considered that this attack could be to keep everyone busy trying to protect the files being deleted while a secondary assault goes after the backup files?"

Hubrecht, Sam and Kale were quiet as stone at that suggestion. Then Hubrecht's expression turned to one of a general going into battle. He ordered Bianca, "Show me how much better qualified you are than my people."

Kale and Sam shouted, "No!" at the same time.

Hubrecht addressed them both with a harsh, narrow-eyed

look that silenced the two men. Once he was satisfied with their reaction, he turned to Bianca again. "Well?"

"I didn't say *I* specifically was better."

Ryder told Hubrecht, "She didn't create this problem."

"I have not accused her of such. Yet."

Bianca raised her hand to Ryder. "I'll try."

Bad idea. He caught her hand and pulled her to him. "You don't have to do this."

"But I want to help."

"If anything goes wrong—"

"What, like all the files being deleted?" she quipped. "At this point, anything I can do is better than nothing."

"Eighty-seven percent of Level One gone," Kale announced.

Sam scowled and sent all that fury at Bianca. "Is this the FBI or not?"

She snapped at him, "I have no idea."

"You have two minutes to find out."

"Are you crazy? I can't just type in a few keys and determine that. This is not the movies or TV."

"*Enough!*" Hubrecht shouted. "Come here. Please."

Hubrecht never raised his voice. Never lost control.

That, more than anything, said how dangerous this was for the person who had caused the attack on Hubrecht's system.

Bianca told Ryder, "Let me try."

He didn't want to let go of her, but with security waiting for them outside the door, he didn't have a way out. Yet. Ryder released her so she could buy him time to come up with a plan to get them out of there.

Bianca pulled her hand free and walked over to sit in Hubrecht's chair.

Kale asked Bianca, "What exactly are you going to do?"

"I don't know for sure until I get inside the system, but I'm thinking of attacking the Level Two files—"

"What the fuck?" Sam bellowed.

Bianca had a pretty menacing look when she wanted to use it. "Think of an attack like this as starting a wildfire. What's the best way to stop the fire from taking your house? You start one that heads back toward the first fire and hit it head on."

"Just do it," Hubrecht said calmly.

Ryder started over to stand beside her, but Sam stepped in front of him. He met Sam's gaze, not blinking. "Get out of my way."

"You're of no use right now. I can have security remove you."

"You can have them *try*," Ryder replied softly.

"He stays, Sam," Hubrecht said.

Ryder walked past Sam and stopped at the side of Hubrecht's massive teak desk. Bianca looked small in his father's wide leather chair. Vulnerable. *All my fault that she's in this mess.*

No matter what happened, he had to get her out of the dangerous position he'd put her in.

Bianca looked up. "I need someone's access code."

Ryder rattled off his access code, expecting Hubrecht to blast him. But instead, he got a nod. But if the computer system continued to go down in flames, Ryder expected retaliation from Hubrecht, who did not suffer betrayal by anyone.

Ryder told Hubrecht, Sam and Kale. "You're no different than the FBI who charged me with a crime I didn't commit. You treat my wife like an unwelcome stranger. No, worse. Like an enemy. Know that as soon as this is done, we're gone."

<hr />

If Bianca hadn't been busy concentrating all her effort on trying to figure out what the FBI team had done, she'd push her fingers down Ryder's throat to shut him up.

What the hell had Murdock done to her with this cyberattack?

Her fingers flew across the keys, typing codes she hoped would unlock the program and give her an opening to stop it. She found the secondary level of files, noting that it went to level five, which had to be classified.

Her palms were damp.

Her heart thumped so hard in her ears everyone should be able to hear each thud.

She typed furiously, hitting dead end after dead end. What if this wasn't from the FBI? If she didn't find a way to block it, would Hubrecht believe she'd really tried or that she *was* responsible for the attack?

"Level One is down, and Level Two files are being attacked," Kale announced, keeping everyone aware of the progress.

"You have one minute to do something or get out of those files," Sam warned.

Bianca caught the curl of Ryder's fist. He was preparing for battle. She typed faster and barged into the second level of security, which had to be where she'd find the Level Two files. "Give me an update."

"Level Two files still deleting."

Crap. She typed again, sure she'd located Level Two and searched for a file to lock down.

Sam walked to the door and opened it, ushering in two security personnel. He called over, "Time's up."

Ryder cursed lividly.

Bianca muttered, "Would you chill out, Mr. Long, and leave me alone for one damn minute so I can actually work without you distracting me?"

The two security personnel walked forward.

Bianca spared a fast glance.

Ryder stepped in their path and said over his shoulder in his father's direction, "Call them off. Now."

"I need an update," Bianca shouted, hoping to diffuse the tension if there was good news. If not, bad news might light the powder keg of posturing going on.

There was a brief hesitation then Kale said, "Level Two is frozen."

"Yes!" Bianca kept typing.

In the myriad lists of numbers scrolling across the monitor, one numerical string caught Bianca's eye. She recognized that and started typing a code off the top of her head, praying she was right and not triggering another launch code unintentionally.

She hit ENTER and waited, holding her breath.

All the numbers halted movement.

"*Come on, baby ...*" she muttered. *Please work.*

One pair of numbers in the middle of the screen started blinking.

Hubrecht leaned close. "Now what's wrong?"

She held up a finger and studied the second hand on her watch. Twelve seconds later, she typed a sequence of numbers and paused over the ENTER key in indecision. If she was wrong, this could crash their entire system.

When in doubt, she was going with Daddy's advice to trust her instincts yet again. She pressed the key and sat back, exhausted by that mental sprint.

First, she looked up at Ryder whose steady gaze told her he was backing her no matter what. That flooded her with a warm pleasure she hadn't expected. She lifted an eyebrow at Kale.

He was grunting at whatever was being said into his earpiece then finally said, "The attack has stopped."

Hubrecht's sigh of relief was loud in the quiet room.

Sam scrubbed a hand over his forehead.

Ryder smiled at Bianca. A real smile, filled with pride that lit a glow in her soul.

She returned the smile with one that she hoped would smooth over the friction this had caused.

Kale said, "What?"

Everyone turned to him. He shook his head in disbelief and Bianca's happiness fled until he told Hubrecht, "The destroyed files are reforming."

Now everyone looked at Bianca who shrugged. "While I was trying to find a way to stop the attack, I found a mirror of the program copying files first then deleting."

"What'd you do?" Ryder asked.

"I got lucky and when I found the leading edge of the attack, I stopped it then thought I'd see if I could turn it around." She held Ryder's gaze that began filling with comprehension as she finished explaining, "I used the codes in the program to send it in a counterattack, reversing the process."

Kale asked, "Can you tell where it came from?"

"No. I have no idea how long it would take to trace it or that what we'd find would be the true origin."

Ryder took in all three men now that Sam had moved back to stand next to Kale and Hubrecht. "You owe my wife an apology."

She cringed at that ultimatum and wished someone would

utter a quick "I'm sorry" to appease Ryder whose easy smile was gone, replaced by a hard line of anger.

"We still don't know what she did," Sam countered.

Bianca sent Ryder a look, begging him to let it go.

Hubrecht said, "Sam. Kale. I want a word alone with Ryder and Bianca."

Sam headed for the door, saying, "I'll be outside with the security team." Kale followed him out.

Hubrecht directed Ryder and Bianca over to the sofa and chairs arranged next to the windows overlooking the Buckhead business district.

Once they were seated, Ryder started in. "I thought I could work here, but I can't. Not when you're going to treat Bianca this way."

She had her hand on his thigh and dug a thumb into the hard muscle to stop him. All that did was hurt her thumb. He lifted her hand off of his leg and enclosed it in his hand, giving her fingers a gentle squeeze in return.

Did he think that was going to appease her? She'd just pulled out every stop to save the VDE computer system to gain some trust and Ryder was tossing in the proverbial towel.

What was with that?

"You're right," Hubrecht agreed. "Bianca has not been treated well."

For crying out loud. "I understand protocol for security, Hubrecht."

He continued as if she hadn't spoken. "But that is going to change now that I'm clearing her to work for VDE."

She held perfectly still when she wanted to jump and shout. Murdock would be over the moon with this news.

"Your top people don't trust her, and I don't trust them around her. I don't want her working here," Ryder argued.

Ryder was going to be the death of her. She squeezed his hand and told him, "You don't get a say, *Darlin'*."

"Yes, I do."

"Ryder," Hubrecht interrupted. "Hear me out."

That a boy, Hubrecht. This is your company after all.

When Ryder started to speak, Bianca cut him off. "I have no

intention of us living off your money alone, Ryder. I'm not cut out for shopping and lazing around the house. The fact that I went up against my agency to free you should have told you I'm not a woman who needs anyone to speak for me and I make my own choices." She took the edge off her words when she asked with all sweetness, "Are we clear, Sweetheart?"

That last word must have done it because Ryder turned to her with a strange expression. "You're right. I shouldn't have spoken for you."

Hubrecht watched the byplay. "I like her, Ryder."

Ryder said, "I do too."

Those three words didn't stun her so much as the honesty in his voice and the warmth heating his gaze. Had he meant that?

Ryder winked at her, and she lost any idea of what was going on around her.

"Bianca?" Hubrecht said, snapping her attention back to business.

She smiled at Hubrecht. "What did you have in mind?"

"I want both of you to do something specifically for me," Hubrecht stated. "I believe someone has been selling our plans to Kearn. Our weapons have shown up in the wrong hands, and that's the only logical reason I can come up with for how they got there. I'll give you what you need to uncover the traitor, but I don't want anyone to know that you're doing this for me. That means no one here, and in particular, no one in the family."

Bianca's lips parted. She hadn't seen that one coming.

This could be a golden opportunity.

Or a deadly trap set to catch her and Ryder if they made a mistake.

CHAPTER 28

RYDER LIFTED HIS gaze from the printed pages he reviewed and watched Bianca roll her shoulders for the twentieth time. "That's it. We're out of here."

"No, I still have more to check," she murmured and kept typing on his keyboard.

The constant overhead music was making him nuts. "You may be able to take being in an office all day, but I hate it in here."

She muttered, "Me, too. I go a little loony trapped inside too long. I'll take a day hiking in the woods over this anytime."

She liked the outdoors. He was head over heels in lust now.

He stood and walked over behind his chair where she'd been sitting for hours. When he started massaging her shoulders, she stopped typing, dropped her head back with her eyes closed and moaned, "Okay, I'm yours."

No, but he wished she was.

Ridiculous thought generated by an exhausted mind.

"It's after ten. Let's go home and get dinner, some rest and we'll come back early."

"We can't waste this opportunity. Tomorrow's Friday. Will Hubrecht let us come in this weekend?"

"You're in and with Hubrecht's blessing. The hard part is over. I'm sure he'll be fine with us in over the weekend, and you'll do better if you're fresh."

"I suppose you're right." Her stomach growled. "I am hungry."

"I'll call Edward on the way, so we'll have food waiting."

"I could so get used to a life of luxury."

He could get used to pampering her. If he ever saw the day when he would be free, he'd reconsider tapping into the funds that had been put aside for him at his mother's death. Since he'd left the Van Dyke household to join the Army, Ryder had lived on whatever pay he made in the military or at his job with Slye. During those years, more often than not, he'd been on missions and slept in the dirt or on an army cot or in a sleeping bag holed up somewhere.

He appreciated the nice things money could bring, but the bottom line was that being wealthy had never mattered much. He was just as content to live on a little as a lot, but now he realized how nice it would be to treat Bianca to special things.

If she found a clue to who killed Kearn, Ryder might have that chance.

Her unmarred brow scrunched.

He worked his fingers deeper into her tight muscles. "What's wrong?"

"Guess I got my hopes up ..."

He dropped his head down next to her shoulder when her voice trailed off, and kissed her slender neck. He smiled when she shivered. Bianca might have been concerned about being heard in spite of the music playing in the background so he kept his voice soft. "Got your hopes up about what?"

"Finding something tonight that would point us to the real killer."

His fingers stilled on her shoulders. His breath caught.

She'd said that so casually, he was stunned.

She believed he hadn't killed Kearn? Was he dreaming?

He started breathing again, then started massaging again, but he wanted to yank her out of her chair and kiss the breath out of her. He was unbearably touched to hear *us* and *real killer* come out of her mouth. Did she really, *finally* believe he was innocent?

Better to let it go and not push her for more right now.

Bianca's neck and shoulders were getting looser by the minute. He'd like to finish this massage with her stretched out on the bed. Full body. No clothes.

Stop thinking with your dick.

That was asking a lot when he had his hands on *this woman.* Sabrina and Margaux were hot women and, yes, his sex-deprived body had taken note of both, but for no more than a mindless release after a long dry spell.

Touching Bianca was becoming addictive, a craving so strong he should be backing away because he had a real fear that once he had her he'd never be cured.

He already dreaded withdrawals once this was over and he never saw her again.

She yawned. "We're missing something, but I don't know what it is."

"You're beat. Let's go. We'll tackle it in the morning."

Not making a move to leave yet, she kept pondering. "There has to be another file, a link to a bank account, something. If not here then in someone's personal files."

"That's going to take some digging."

She opened her eyes and looked up at him. "I know it sounds overwhelming, but this is what we did in my department. This is what I did."

The fire in her eyes reminded him of her on the witness stand and her passion. Sabrina's attorney had hammered Bianca for being obsessive in her research, suggested a personal vendetta. She'd held her own with the seasoned attorney, impressing the media.

Now—with less subjective eyes—Ryder understood why the judge had believed her. It was the desire to find the truth that drove her, not obsession.

"We still have a few more days," she pointed out.

Five days. Sounded like a lot of time, but Ryder knew better. Unless they got a break soon or Bianca hit on files that might not even be in the system, that time would be gone faster than it took to snap his fingers. "Right. Let's get moving. You've had a tough day."

Once Bianca had her purse, she stepped out of the office into the hallway. Ryder locked the main door and trudged behind her to the elevators.

He'd watched her dig through files for the past five hours and nothing had shown up. Not the first hint of anything illegal or a communication that would indicate who had been contracted for the hit on Kearn.

Hubrecht was going after clients of Kearn's company. Was that just one step before he went after the entire company?

Would the FBI ever believe Ryder wasn't involved in Kearn's killing? Ryder's only defense at this point was lack of motivation, regardless of his being a Van Dyke. Based on the way all this had gone down, he had a sick feeling that an *unexpected* motivation might be discovered right before the trial.

As unbelievable as that seemed, it was no more bizarre than his being arrested for murder and held in prison. With enough money involved, anything was possible.

Ryder hadn't told Bianca about Hubrecht going after Kearn's clients yet. Not when she was finally thinking someone else could have killed Kearn.

Besides, he had bigger concerns.

Was the killer in this building?

If Hubrecht *was* behind the contract killing, he could be testing Bianca and Ryder with this "search for a traitor" task.

Either way, the minute Bianca found anything concrete in the files, Ryder had to be ready to get her out of here.

This time, he'd have an exit strategy.

At the elevators, Bianca's pursed buzzed. She dug out her phone, but it stopped ringing before she could answer it.

"Who was that?" Ryder hit the button for the elevator.

"Has to be Mama since no one else has this number."

The elevator doors slid open. Bianca stepped in and turned to see Ryder's hand when he ran his card through the security keycard slot. "Where's your ring?"

"Damn. I left it on the credenza. Not used to wearing it. I'll run and get it."

"I'm going down to the lobby so I can call my mother back," Bianca said. "It's awfully late so I'm worried that something's wrong." Better to talk to Mama now than later when Bianca might be in the middle of something important. "I lost a call in this elevator earlier today so I don't want to start talking with her and deal with starting the conversation over every time the cellular signal drops." And she didn't want to have this conversation on the Van Dyke floors where, if Ryder was right, the walls had ears.

Ryder had his finger on the door button, holding it open. He looked like he was going to ask her to wait with him.

"Just go, Ryder. It'll be quicker this way." And she'd have the elevator ride over without him seeing her turn into a wus while riding down.

"Okay, but just go down as far as the lobby, and stay in sight of the guard and wait for me to take you down to the garage." Ryder stepped all the way out.

"I will." The doors closed and Bianca tapped the phone against her leg as the car began its imperceptible descent. Her shoulders were tightening up again, but this time it was from nerves. She tried to breathe calmly, but a quarter of the way down she was breathing fast and hard.

She needed to carry a paper bag with her—or get in shape to walk thirty-two flights of stairs.

Fall down a well at twelve years old and fear elevators forever.

She'd been sure she could overcome this fear on her own, but she might have to go talk to someone about it after all.

For now, she tried to focus on what she'd discovered today. She'd wanted to tell Ryder about finding a suspicious monitoring system inside the VDE computer network, but she hadn't and her conscience was attacking her from all sides. Murdock had specifically ordered her to keep anything relevant she found from Ryder. That warred with the loyalty she felt for Ryder, and what would Murdock say about that?

Nothing she wanted to hear.

Murdock believed Ryder might be in league with Hubrecht, of course. Bianca had pretty much trashed that as a possibility. But she was still an FBI agent and had to find a way for that to live alongside her growing feelings for Ryder, which was why she *would* share anything with him that pertained to helping prove his innocence. At this point, she had no idea who was running the monitoring program or why, which meant the information was of no use to Ryder. Yet.

When it was, she'd cross that bridge.

But she was not telling Hubrecht a damned thing.

It appeared to be a custom security program and, if it had been presented as such, anyone in the company would accept that at face value and not tamper with it.

But she'd been given carte blanche to do some snooping and had paused the program long enough to observe it for all of a minute. When she'd activated it again, calendars for the executive level of VDE personnel opened in alpha sequence.

Someone *was* spying on VDE executives.

The panel of numbers slowly blinked on and off when the elevator passed each successive floor.

Bianca had not yet been given official security clearance or an access code, so she'd used Ryder's, and she'd noticed something interesting. Hubrecht's cyber-security personnel were tracking what she did when signed in as Ryder. She could have mentioned that to Hubrecht, but decided if she gave security enough to watch under Ryder's sign in they wouldn't see what she was really doing signed in as Sam Long.

Sam had stopped by to tell Ryder that Hubrecht mentioned a special project he'd given Ryder. He'd fished for details and when Ryder had stonewalled, it obviously did not sit well with Sam. Then Sam had made it clear that he would be watching Ryder for any suspicious activity.

That had been the perfect moment to locate Sam's access code, while he was in Ryder's office ranting, and not in view of a monitor where he could potentially see her lifting his password.

Sneaky? Yes. But her gut didn't trust Sam, and she would stop at nothing to get to the hidden files she knew were there. They had to be there.

Because Bianca believed only one thing at this point.

Ryder had not killed J. K. Kearn.

Beyond that, he claimed he'd been trying to help the prison guard.

She had a feeling that if she reviewed that video with him, he could show her where to look for the truth.

Her mind might have just now decided that Ryder Van Dyke was innocent, but her heart had been leading the charge to prove it for a while now.

Stupid organ with a sketchy track record that had no place on this mission, but her body refused to listen to sound advice when Ryder was around. One look into those silver eyes and she wanted to take away all the pain hiding behind them, to feel him close to her.

She was not a one night stand kind of woman, but she was honest enough with herself to admit she wanted things from Ryder she shouldn't. He'd awakened her libido when she'd questioned its existence and had her constantly wondering what was on the other side of those hungry looks he gave her.

At the tenth floor, the car hesitated and the panel started flashing.

Bianca's stomach lurched. She reached for the emergency button, but the world dropped away beneath her.

She stumbled backwards.

Alarms screeched inside the elevator. A mechanical voice announced, *"Warning! Warning! Vehicle descending too rapidly."*

She yelled, "Stop! Stop! Stop!"

"Warning! Warning!" Lights flashed on the panel.

Her feet felt light as the floor dropped faster.

"No!" she screamed then stumbled to her right and pounded the buttons.

The elevator picked up speed.

"Stop!"

It did.

Bianca slammed the floor hard. Her head bounced against a wall.

Everything went black.

CHAPTER 29

BIANCA'S MIND WHIRRED with images. She stared up at daylight from the bottom of a well, then random numbers flew past her mind's eye, scrambling and spinning until they turned into the shape of a skull. Next a masked team dressed in black grabbed at her. She cringed, unable to back away

An urgent voice pierced the mêlée of visions.

"Bianca! Answer me!"

She blinked her eyes. How long had she been out? She couldn't see anything but endless black. Oh, God. She was blind.

A red light on the wall blinked above her.

She released a big sigh of relief. Not blind. The lights were out.

"Bianca! Bianca, can you hear me? Talk to me, dammit!"

Ryder—yelling at her from a speaker.

"Ryder?" She grabbed her head. It felt like someone had used it as a baseball.

"Bianca, was that you? Speak up so I can hear you."

She cleared her throat. "Ryder, it's me. The elevator broke or something. I'm stuck somewhere. The power is off."

Bianca thought she heard low words akin to a prayer of thanks murmured in the speaker.

"Are you hurt, Sweetheart?"

There he went with that sweetheart business again.

Idiot that she was, her heart flip-flopped in reaction, and the voice that said her heart was lame and needy could just keep its stupid insecure mouth shut, because right now she could use some comforting.

She moved her arms and legs, expecting to be paralyzed. Nope. Just achy—and the effect of that morning's attack was finally setting in because she was sore everywhere. "Got a knock on the head but I'm okay. Maybe a few more bruises."

The four-letter words coming through the speaker this time could *not* be misconstrued as a blessing.

"Sit tight. The car stopped between floors. I've got people working on it. They're close to getting the doors open.

She must have been out for a while.

Using the blinking red light to navigate, Bianca crawled to the doors. Voices rumbled on the other side then one male voice roared, *"Get that damn thing open. Now!"*

She knew exactly who owned those vocal chords. For a former military man who'd been cool under fire throughout the preliminary hearing and was known for his ruthless self-control in the Army, Ryder sounded seriously close to the edge at the moment.

The doors peeled apart about three inches for an instant and then slid a couple feet wider. Light burst through the opening, blinding her.

She covered her eyes with her hand.

"Bianca, are you hurt? Can you move your arms and legs?"

"Everything seems to be working okay."

"Can you climb out or do you need me to come in and get you?"

When she squinted, Ryder's worried face popped into view just above the floor of the car. She took a breath. "I can climb out."

"Okay, Sweetheart. Turn around backwards and stick your legs out first. Don't worry. I'll catch you."

When Ryder dropped out of sight, Bianca peered over the edge of the opening. The elevator had stopped about six feet up. Ryder stepped off a chair and moved it out of the way.

Bianca rolled over on her stomach and scooted backwards, trying to keep her skirt from riding up her butt. She slid through the gap between the doors, trusting Ryder not to drop her.

Her feet floated in mid-air until her waist cleared the edge of the elevator floor. As soon as her feet dropped toward the ground, Ryder's arms wrapped around her legs.

He bore her weight, easing her down his front until her feet touched ground. When she swung around, six men in security clothes and overalls shuffled nervously behind him. Every pair of eyes watched Ryder with the wariness of being in the same room with a dangerous beast.

Ryder held her tight, but she felt his hands tremble. "Are you really okay?" His normally whiskey-smooth voice sounded raw. "I'll get you to the hospital and have them—"

"No, I'm fine, really. Please don't make me go there. Can we just go home?"

He kissed the top of her head. "Yeah, let's get out of here." Ryder kept her tucked close to him, protectively, as he issued orders. "Shut this thing down and have all the elevators checked before anyone gets on another one."

"Yes, sir," echoed around the room.

She was still woozy as Ryder guided her to the stairwell, stopping twice on the way down to check on her, offering to carry her.

No. She would not be seen carried from the Van Dyke building. Not something an FBI agent wanted in a personnel file.

But the minute they reached Ryder's black Shelby, Bianca drooped onto the seat.

In two days, she'd been assaulted, kidnapped, threatened over a cyberattack and dropped who-knew-how-many floors in an out-of-control elevator.

Another two days of this and she'd qualify for hazardous duty pay. That was a lot of coincidences.

Murdock would tell her there was no such thing as a coincidence on a mission.

Bianca scrolled the events through her mind, looking for a common denominator in all this.

The obvious one was Ryder. But why would he try to kill the one person who could help him? Was someone trying to set him up as the most obvious suspect just like he'd been set up as the most likely shooter in the Kearn killing?

Everyone knew her and Ryder's schedule, including Lady Anne who clearly kept her finger on the pulse of her family. Janeen was conspicuously missing today, but Terrence had been around. Lady Anne might be having Ryder followed.

The old biddy could just as easily have someone tail Bianca.

Then there was Hubrecht, ruler of his own corner of the free-enterprise world, suspected of funneling weapons—and probably money—to terrorists. But why would he try to kill Bianca if he wanted to find the leak in his company?

Did he *really* want her to find that?

Sam Long had her in his virtual sights and Kale Carter ran security. Her suspect list was getting as long as Ryder's.

As for Ryder, he'd had plenty of opportunities before now if he'd wanted her out of the picture, which still made no logical sense. But who would want to kill her in the Van Dyke building when it meant putting VDE in the hub of an investigation and a media frenzy?

Looking at it that way pointed the finger at Ryder setting up his father. Bianca could not see that making sense, with Ryder's freedom dangling by threads. That left the next logical jump.

Was someone trying to set up both Ryder *and* Hubrecht?

Ryder had not sent her on her own down that elevator. But only she and Ryder knew that, and even someone watching on a video feed wouldn't have known that *she* chose to ride down by herself in spite of his concern. They would only have known that she was in the elevator alone.

Ryder had nothing to do with the elevator falling.

But the rest of this crazy group were all suspect.

Bianca rubbed her forehead.

Tomorrow. Nothing would get decided tonight.

One thing was sure. Not finding a solid clue or lead on the terrorist connection or Kearn's killer today had struck a blow to their mission. If Bianca failed to pinpoint who was funneling money and guns to the wrong people, her first field assignment would be a dismal failure of gigantic proportions.

But failing Ryder would be epic.

Every day she failed put him one day closer to returning to a cell.

If that happened, her life would never be the same.

She knew in her heart that with enough time inside VDE, she could find the evidence that would gain his freedom. She *had* to uncover that grain of truth he needed.

Because she could not stand by and watch him walk back into that prison.

Ryder clenched the wheel. His fingers dented the soft leather cover he'd installed years ago to make handling the skinny steering wheel more comfortable for his large hands.

He checked on Bianca for the fifteenth time in two minutes.

How many times had he yelled into that damn speaker, silently begging for her to answer? His lungs constricted again, recalling each time she'd said nothing.

The elevator security camera had gone out with the power, and when he couldn't see her, a million possibilities had chased through his mind, starting with Bianca not being alive and ending with her body broken into irreparable pieces. He swallowed against the sick churning in his stomach.

The elevator hadn't dropped all the way, thank God. It had stopped after falling eight floors. That would lead him to believe the cables hadn't been cut, but that the computer had been reprogrammed to create a fall. He had no doubt that the elevator technicians being called in tonight would find a simple glitch that someone left in the system just to satisfy their search.

Bianca shifted in her seat. She was uncomfortable but trying to hide her pain.

He tried again to reason with her. "We really should get you checked out at the hospital."

"It's just aches and pains. They'll go away." She moved her shoulder. "Been there, done that, and it's not as bad as last time."

"What do you mean?"

"When I was a little girl, someone had put a sheet of plywood over an old well at an abandoned house near my dad's property. The wood was rotten. I stepped on it and fell into the dried-up well."

"How old were you?"

"Twelve."

He thought back on her hesitation to ride down thirty-four floors in an elevator. That was why. She was terrified of falling. A terror reinforced by tonight.

Had that incident been a message to Bianca about stopping the cyberattack?

Or a threat because now she was inside the VDE files?

He ran a hand through his hair. The last thing he wanted to do right now was add another reason for her to worry, but he needed her to be alert to the possibility that this had been intentional. He cranked the radio to a volume that would cover their conversation, then he said, "I don't think what happened with the elevator was an accident."

She became very still. "Why would you say that?"

"Someone jumped you on your run this morning, and now an elevator with a perfect maintenance record and no previous mishaps falls with only you in it." He tapped his fingers on the steering wheel, burning the last of the adrenaline rush as he thought. "The emergency backup light in the elevator failed. The maintenance crew on site said the battery was checked last week. It was charging just fine." He curled his hand into a fist and set it on the stick shift. "Someone's targeting you."

"Then we're on the right track." Bianca hadn't panicked or started wringing her hands. Instead, that analytical mind had started processing. That was impressive as hell, considering undercover field ops were *not* what she was trained for.

Who wanted to hurt her? Why?

The easy answer would be to get at Ryder.

He'd been alone so long that he wasn't accustomed to sorting through a problem with someone else, but they were in this together. "But coming after you doesn't make sense. Why not target me? Unless someone figured out what you were doing inside the VDE computers?"

"No. I would have noticed someone tracking my electronic moves and why would Hubrecht do this after he basically gave me his blessing to dig?"

"I wasn't talking about him necessarily." Ryder twisted the leather steering wheel cover back and forth, ruminating. "Hubrecht Van Dyke has a lot of faults, but this makes no sense even if he's found us out. He's smart enough not to draw attention to himself or VDE."

Any way Ryder looked at the picture it was skewed. Had Sam or Kale been behind the elevator falling?

"Do you think Hubrecht ordered Kearn's death?" Bianca asked.

Ryder fought conflicting thoughts on the man who had raised him. "At one time, I'd have bet my life that Hubrecht wasn't that kind of man—wasn't capable of ordering the cold-blooded murder of another businessman, crooked or not, but now I honestly don't know."

Someone had ordered a professional hit on a VDE competitor. A person with deep pockets and connections. Ryder glanced over at Bianca and speculated, "What would be the motivation? Could it be the stolen weapons plans?"

"Maybe. Then as a smokescreen, he asks us to find the VDE traitor who stole the plans and sold them to Kearn."

Or was the motivation to acquire a failing company when J. K. wouldn't come to the bargaining table?

Could Sam Long's posturing have all been for show to hide his real agenda? What about Kale who said little and moved like the former Delta Force soldier he was?

Who else in the Van Dyke family could be gunning for Ryder?

Lady Anne had never pulled punches when it came to her hatred of Ryder, but would she go to these extremes to get rid of Ryder's non-blueblood wife? Did she think harming Bianca would influence his decision to stay or leave?

If that were the case, Lady Anne would be right.

Ryder would take Bianca anywhere necessary to keep her safe, but then he'd come back to make someone pay.

What about Terrence or Janeen? Why would either of them harm Bianca? Janeen had everything she wanted whether Ryder was in the picture or not, but she'd always been protective of Terrence.

Then there was Terrence. Lady Anne and Janeen resented Ryder for being a threat to Terrence's position in the company, which had proven to be true if Hubrecht really was putting Ryder over Terrence. But Terrence seemed relieved to have Ryder close by to help.

Terrence *had* brought Bianca into the office today, but she said he'd only done so after she pushed him to get her past security.

Ryder scrubbed his face with his hand, tired and drained from the day. He cut another look at Bianca who had slumped over against the window. Asleep.

Understandable. Her day had been a lot worse than his.

When he parked in front of the family home, Ryder lifted a still-sleeping Bianca into his arms and carried her into the house passed a distressed Edward. Ryder waved him off with a shake of his head, never stopping until he laid Bianca on the bed. Once his eyes adjusted to the dark room, he slipped her strappy sandals off and flipped them to the side.

Bianca didn't stir.

Ryder unbuttoned her blouse and eased her limp body out of the sleeves. A silky beige tank top glowed in the dark. No bra. His mouth dried at the thought that she'd been wearing only this beneath her clothes all day. He checked as he unzipped the side zipper and slid her skirt off, to make sure she had on panties. Yes, and they barely covered anything.

The only reason he'd be able to catch any sleep tonight would be due to pure exhaustion.

He pulled the covers over her and kissed her hair.

Going back to prison had never been a consideration when he agreed to this mission. But now remaining free was an absolute. He could not walk back into a cell where he couldn't protect Bianca. And before he left, Ryder had to know that she would be safe. That someone would not continue to target her once he was gone.

He'd risk anything, except her.

CHAPTER 30

CHATTON LEANED OVER the laptop on her hotel desk and reviewed the electronic files she'd paid dearly for, but quality intel didn't come cheap. She read through Van Dyke shipping logs for three international weapons dealers.

Three highly suspicious operations.

She was familiar with all of them from her work with MI6, and from having gathered every speck of intel she could on her uncle's death. He'd traveled to the US under the guise of a winter ski vacation in Colorado, and there he'd been killed. A week after the shooting, the media moved on to something new and his story fell to the side.

Local law enforcement still held the case open, and the FBI had gotten involved since Abbot had been a British diplomat, but there'd been nothing to indicate his trip had any political or business significance.

Most telling had been his clean hotel room.

Professionally clean. *Operative clean.*

No housekeeping staff sanitized a room that way.

Whoever killed Abbot had removed everything pertinent to his real reason for coming to the US. Chatton had arrived too late to find anything of use at the hotel. His briefcase had been gone through and there were no fingerprints on the sides, only the handle. Her uncle had always lifted his briefcase by the sides when he placed it on a desk to work. She could see it in her mind clearly as she went over it again and again.

She lifted the shipping documents her uncle *might* have had in his briefcase, given his real mission in the US, which she'd figured out after combing through his electronic files. She hadn't been able to connect the documents to anything specific until J.

K. Kearn was killed. Kearn's name in the news had triggered a memory from her uncle's notes, and she'd gone back through them. They showed Kearn Industries as a serious potential threat to Van Dyke's hold on a significant Dubai arms dealer's business.

Still, none of that had gelled until Ryder Van Dyke was arrested for shooting J. K. Kearn. She'd spent a considerable amount of money for evidence that proved Ryder was the shooter—evidence law enforcement often didn't bother to obtain—but nothing had panned out.

If she believed Van Dyke had killed her uncle, she'd have grabbed him by now for a private discussion that would involve his pain tolerance level, but Van Dyke's case stank worse than spoiled cod.

He was not the shooter.

Too many inconsistencies between *his* character profile up until the Kearn killing and the profile of the person who could—and would—have made that hit. Did The General really believe Van Dyke had committed the murder?

Or was The General trying to screw with Chatton?

Not much of an effort if this was the best he could do.

Nothing beyond circumstantial evidence against Ryder Van Dyke had surfaced.

But then he'd walked out of prison a free man.

Chatton scrolled further, again cross-referencing financial records of three dealers. One in Dubai, one in Germany and one in Turkey. The one thing they had in common was buying from Van Dyke Enterprises, which wasn't that strange.

Kearn Industries sold to two of them but had not been able to broker a deal with Dubai. After giving that one closer scrutiny, Chatton had found a strange pattern in the Dubai arms dealer's buying habits.

Nothing in the report had flagged any illegal activity, but the financial records were a whole different story.

Dubai was paying for more inventory than the arms dealer was receiving.

That pointed a suspicious finger at Van Dyke Enterprises for Kearn's killing and would warrant an FBI investigation.

What if the FBI had decided to take advantage of Ryder's facing a death penalty or life in prison and made him an offer no one in that position would refuse?

Taking that one step further, what if the person who killed Kearn had also killed her uncle over a conflict related to an arms agreement? Someone inside VDE.

Chatton had a task for Ryder Van Dyke.

If Ryder was truly a free man who had not killed Kearn and his new wife had cut her ties to the FBI, then this information would never reach him.

Ryder had been working with Slye when he was arrested. All Chatton had to do was feed this information to the Slye group and see if it went anywhere. If Ryder was working undercover, Chatton was sure Slye would be involved since Sabrina Slye had hired Ryder an attorney and stood by him throughout his time in prison.

If Ryder got his hands on this information, he'd have to put two and two together to see the possible lead on who had framed him. A person who would not stand by and allow Kearn to knock VDE out of a thirty-million-dollar deal, over half of which was tax-free money sent to an offshore account.

Ryder would prove his innocence if he was still under the FBI's thumb, and that would lead Chatton to the person behind her uncle's killing.

She downloaded everything onto a memory stick and tucked it inside the zippered sleeve of her leather jacket. She grabbed her motorcycle helmet, sliding it on.

With temperatures in the fifties, this would be a prime night to get out of Buckhead and take a ride down to College Park. The sooner she got this info into the hands of someone with Slye, the sooner she'd have her answer on Ryder Van Dyke.

CHAPTER 31

RYDER GRUNTED WHEN Bianca snuggled up against him. Rubbing that soft backside against his throbbing erection.

He'd turned down the room's air conditioning because she'd been shivering earlier, a delayed shock reaction maybe.

The warm room should have prevented his having a half-naked woman in his arms. Yes, he could have rolled her back over away from him, but what fool would turn down holding *this* woman? He'd never said he was a saint and doubted even a real saint would back away from Bianca in a silk top and panties.

Not if he was a male saint.

Ryder rubbed his fingers in lazy strokes over her arm. She had creamy soft skin. He'd made love to more women than he wanted to count when he'd been in college, most of whom he'd forgotten as quickly as they'd forgotten him.

Ryder couldn't recall when he'd spent so much time in bed with a desirable woman and not ended up completely naked.

And sweaty.

She moved her arm, adjusting her position against him.

His hand fell to her hip just as she shifted her bottom. Again.

He clenched his teeth until she settled. Every brush of her sweet buns against his erection reminded him this was only going to get more painful if he didn't move away.

He must have a masochistic streak he never realized because he stayed right where he was. Unable to keep from touching her, he caressed her hip and played with the edge of her bikini panties. He stared up at the ceiling, wishing he could make use of the monster erection tenting his boxers.

Life had dealt his heart enough blows. There should be no soft spot left. A tested and battered muscle normally strengthens to rock hard, impervious to assault.

But his abused heart had softened where Bianca was concerned.

Enough that he couldn't take advantage of this and seduce her. It would be so easy. He'd seen the flare in her eyes when they'd danced near the fire.

She smelled fresh and womanly. After confinement in a prison cell with a convict who'd never been introduced to soap or deodorant, Ryder had sworn that once he was out, he'd never share space with another person.

On his next whiff of Bianca, he closed his eyes, enjoying the feel of a woman in his arms. *This* woman, who charged into battle, got in his face when she thought he needed to be taken down a notch, and kissed like an angel.

Staying turned on constantly around her was miserable, but he wouldn't intentionally use her or hurt her.

Or let anyone else.

Over the last five months, Ryder had thought the word mercy had vanished from his vocabulary. But then the guard in the prison yard had suffered a heart attack.

Look where mercy had gotten him.

That he still possessed a sliver of conscience surprised him.

Bianca rolled over to face him and snuggled up to his chest. He draped an arm across her, his hand touching the exposed skin on her back. She tossed a leg over his thigh.

Sweat beaded on his forehead.

With another shift, she barely missed brushing up against the bulge in his shorts.

Close call there.

But then she squirmed as if trying to get inside him, but the action turned into her pocketing his erection between him and her heat.

He had ten seconds to either get the hell away from her or peel off those panties.

Ryder grasped her at the waist and lifted her off him. Cursing softly, he dumped her gently on the mattress and got up in the semi-dark room, headed for the bathroom.

"Are you up?" Bianca called out, her voice thick with sleep.

Oh, hell yes, I'm up. And steel hard.

"Ryder, uhm, everything okay? Anything I can do?"

He paused, let out a frustrated breath and said, "No. Go back to sleep." *Or I'll finish what you accidentally started.*

Bianca was here for several reasons. Sating his raging libido was nowhere on the FBI's list.

Hands off from now on. Hands off, lips off, in fact all body parts off.

She made a pained sound as he was closing the bathroom door. He shoved it open and stepped over to the bed. "What's wrong?"

"Nothing."

Then why had she said that through clenched teeth? He leaned a hand down on the bed to support his weight. "Tell me the truth."

"I'm just achy."

He could appreciate that. "Where?"

"Everywhere."

He only ached in one place. "You want some more aspirin?"

"Not until I eat something, or I'll be sick. And I'm not hungry right now so don't bother anyone. Sorry, just go back to what you were doing. I didn't mean to make noise. I'm fine. I'll deal."

That was classic Bianca. She would rather be in pain than inconvenience someone. "Sit tight. I'll be right back."

Ryder stepped into the bathroom and twisted the faucets on the deep Jacuzzi tub. It was oversized to fit the six feet of height he'd reached by his junior year of high school. He drummed his fingers on the edge of the marble while he waited on the tub to fill, then added foaming bath crystals. He cut the faucet off and left the nightlight on to keep the bathroom semi-dark.

When he leaned down to ease his hands under her back and knees then lift her into his arms, Bianca hardly stirred. Should he let her go back to sleep?

Another groan of misery escaped her.

He headed for the steaming Jacuzzi.

At the tub, he stepped over the rim, settled down into the hot water and pushed the button to start the water jets.

Bianca jerked awake. "What are you doing?"

"Soaking away some of your pain." He positioned her between his legs and wrapped an arm around her, pulling her back against his chest.

A completely different moan slipped out this time that sounded like pleasure.

"See? Doesn't that feel better?" he murmured against her neck and kissed her skin.

"But we have our clothes on."

"You want the other option?"

For a heartbeat he thought she might say yes. What he wouldn't give to hear *yes* right now.

"Uh, no."

"In that case, sit back and enjoy."

"Ryder, I can feel you against my back. It's obvious that this can't be fun for you."

"Ignore it. I'm trying to."

Bianca evidently was in serious need of soothing, because she melted back against him. She didn't complain in body language or in words. Blasts of warm water charged against them from all angles, easing muscle aches and bruises.

It did nothing for the throbbing pain in his groin.

She wiggled that damned bottom again, rubbing his already aching erection. A wave of heat rocketed up his center and threatened to blow the top of his head off.

Both of them.

Ryder was going to grind his molars into dust at this rate.

Another stroke like that last one and he'd be the first person to enjoy this party.

She'd kept him in a state of constant arousal since the minute he'd stood next to her in the strategic planning session and got a deep breath of female.

He forced his thoughts away from his discomfort and focused on easing hers. He massaged her arms, working his fingers under the straps of her top when he got to her shoulders. She angled her head to each side, giving him access to her tight muscles, an unspoken permission to continue.

At nineteen, Ryder had dated a professional masseuse who taught him how to touch a woman in all the right places. Moves that would guarantee him access to the *hot* spot.

There would be no going to Bianca's hot spot, except in his fantasies. But he could use what he knew to loosen her strained, tense muscles.

Working his busy fingers along her arms and back up to her shoulders, he drew the tension from each taut muscle, no matter how small or hidden. He finger-combed through her lush, auburn hair, playing with each strand as he gently separated the locks.

"My side is sore," she whispered.

He moved his hands to massage her sides, careful to not press hard enough to hurt her. She let out a little gasp and said, "My abdomen aches, too."

Lifting an eyebrow at her that she couldn't see, he slid his hands around to her front, moving the foam floating on top of the water. Flexing his fingers, he slowly rubbed up and down, struggling not to sweep his hands up to touch her breasts.

She slid down in the water, and he almost came from the friction of her back against his hard penis. He grabbed her out of knee-jerk reaction to stop her from moving.

His hands landed on top of her breasts.

Fuck. Now what was he going to do?

Another noise escaped her, and it shot all the blood left in Ryder's body to his groin. He tried to move his hands. Really tried. But they cupped both of her breasts, and his thumbs scraped the soaked silk covering nipples that were hard and happy.

"Oh, God," she gushed.

Was that a yes, keep going? Tell me it was a yes.

Sweat drizzled down the side of his face. She was panting, but that might be because his hands were still teasing her nipples. He pinched gently and she arched.

Holy mother of...

He had to make sure she was onboard with where this was going. "Bianca—"

"Yes?"

Kissing her neck, he kept playing with her breasts and smiled over the chill bumps. She couldn't be cold because she was hot as a firecracker. "Sure you want this?"

He ran his fingers lightly over her nipples that arched up to his hand, answering his question. But he needed to hear it and know she wouldn't regret this tomorrow. "Bianca?"

"*Yes!*"

When he moved one hand away from her breasts, she grumbled, "I said yes."

He lifted the edge of the soaked material, sliding it above her breasts and turned her until she lay across his left arm. "Open your eyes."

When she did, the passion roiling through her hazel eyes shoved every thought out of his head except having her.

He lowered his head and suckled one nipple.

"Oh, that ... yes." She shook and gripped his shoulders, holding him there, making a sound that Ryder wished he could capture to take with him forever. He licked the nipple then grazed his teeth over the turgid bud. His free hand smoothed down over her bikini panties, one finger moving against her mound in a circular motion.

She pushed her feet against the edge of the tub, leg muscles tight, but he held her in place as he slipped a finger inside her panties and delved into the wet heat.

"Ryder!"

He didn't let up, moving to give attention to her other breast. They were the perfect size. She had dusty pink nipples that turned darker the more excited she got.

The hell with it. He gave a tug on the sheer bikini panties, and they ripped away. She gasped, but he dragged a finger through her folds, killing any complaint, then he flicked his fingertip gently back and forth, testing her hot spot.

She cried out.

Oh, yes. Target acquired. His finger delved back inside her, and she sucked in a sharp breath. Her legs opened wider, and he pushed two fingers inside, pumping them in and out.

"Please ..."

He lifted his head from her breast and kissed her, unleashing all he felt in that kiss. Her mouth was made for loving. Seeing her this turned on had him breathing hard now, too. "Tell me what you want."

"I don't care."

That moron had made her insecure about her sexuality. Ryder said, "Yes, you do. Tell me what you want."

"I want ... you to touch me everywhere."

She was keeping something from him. "Look at me."

She opened her eyes and he saw it. The fear that she would say or do the wrong thing. He wanted to mangle the guy who had been so careless with this woman. Ryder pulled his fingers out of her and toyed with her folds. "There? Do you like that?"

"Oh, yes."

When she started shaking and her body tightened, he moved from there to touch her breasts. He held his palm above her breast, barely touching the tip of her nipple. "What about there?"

"Yes." That had been an anguished *yes*.

Her feet were still against the edge of the tub, anchoring her spread legs. Using his legs, he lifted her until one of the jets rushed over her mound, driving across the folds.

She clutched at his shoulder and moved her hips up and down in the spray. "Oh, oh ... yes." He smiled and used the arm holding her to reach the breast on her left, which allowed him to suckle the other one. Her legs shook with strain. She was getting close. He reached a hand underneath to avoid interfering with the water jet and plunged two fingers inside her heat.

She was trembling with need and that was so damned hot. He pinched one nipple and scraped the other one with his teeth, all the time pumping faster.

Her hips paused. She arched, legs shaking until she cried out, pushing up and down against his hand. When her body slumped, he was shaking himself.

That was the most unbelievably gorgeous thing he'd ever witnessed.

When her breathing returned to normal, she mumbled, "I, uh ..."

"What, Sweetheart?"

Her hazel eyes were large and surprised. "That's never happened before."

"Tell me you mean you've never gotten off with a spray jet before?"

She shook her head. "With anything ... or anyone."

He knew he wasn't going to like the answer to this question, but he had to know. "How long were you with the idiot?" He didn't have to clarify who.

"Four months."

The magnitude of what she'd shared floored him. Ryder could only begin to imagine how miserable sex had been with some bastard who hadn't cared enough to take her to orgasm. He'd abused her every time he touched her.

Ryder wanted to spend endless months showing her just how amazing and sensual she was. He didn't have months. He might not even have days, but he had now.

He held her to him, running his hand over her face and hair, kissing her soft lips that welcomed his mouth. He laid her back in his arm where he could kiss her pretty breasts again.

She made an "mmmm" sound.

He kissed his way back to her neck and raised his head, waiting for her to open her eyes. When she did, he said, "You're so beautiful and so damn hot. Don't ever let anyone make you believe otherwise."

She joked, "Even if I'm not trophy wife material?"

But he'd heard something else that sounded like disappointment. "Why would you want to be that?"

Shrugging and looking self-conscious, she looked away. "Every woman wants to feel attractive and special."

He caught her chin and turned her back to face him. "Baby, I said you weren't trophy wife material because you are so much more than that. You're brilliant *and* beautiful. Arm candy is everywhere, but a woman like you is priceless."

Her mouth dropped open.

Had she really thought he'd found her lacking? How was he going to convince her—

She lunged forward and kissed him with unbridled enthusiasm, taking his breath away. Her tongue tangled with his, demanding everything he had and more. There was the woman she'd been hiding from men, unwilling to risk being humiliated again.

Ryder held her head, savoring the kiss that pulled him deeper into trouble with every breath. It took a minute before he realized she was straddling him. He peeled the wet silk top the rest of the way off her.

She reached down and grasped him. One stroke and he practically came out of the tub. He grabbed her hand. "Been a long time. Remember?"

"So, what are you waiting for?"

He fucking hurt he wanted to be inside her so bad, but he was fooling himself if he thought he'd last three strokes in her heat.

She leaned down and kissed his chest.

He held his breath, not wanting to stop her, but he couldn't let her keep it up or his nuts were going to burst.

Her fingers moved over his arms and down to his waist, like fairy fingers on his skin. She shifted and slid her hand between them until she gripped him.

He stilled.

She stroked up and down once.

His entire body trembled.

She raised her head. "My turn."

"Yours won't last long."

"We'll see."

Oh, hell. That had sounded like a challenge, but she had no idea how little it would take.

She pulled her hand away from his penis and he thought about begging. Her hands were pushing his chest. "You asked what I wanted? Lean back and close your eyes." She lifted his arms to the edge of the tub. "Keep them there."

He wanted to smile at her authoritative voice, but he was in too much pain to find anything funny.

Having her first orgasm had empowered her.

But if she didn't touch him soon, he was going to fight a true battle not to lift her up and shove her down on top of him. But he had no condom, and beyond that, he wouldn't take the control from her.

Dropping his head back, he closed his eyes. Anticipation of when she would finally touch him again was driving him mad.

She tugged his boxers. He lifted and let her take them off. He heard a wet *splat* hit the bathroom floor.

Her fingers trailed down his chest then one hand wrapped lightly around his penis and the other cupped his sac.

Oh, shit. He clenched her between his legs.

She stroked slowly up, stopped and swiped a finger over the head of his erection. Then her fingers cupping his sac massaged carefully.

She stroked down just as slowly, and his chest muscles constricted. She shifted forward and her breasts rubbed against his chest then lower as she kissed his nipples.

Part of him wanted to chuckle at her sinister teasing, but the other part was ready to offer her anything to move faster.

After another slow stroke up and down the length of him, she scooted back again, forcing his legs to release her.

Her fingers glided over the insides of his thighs with the unsure touch of a novice, and nothing had ever felt so erotic. When her fingers grasped his penis again, she did so with confidence, but still not staying long enough.

His body turned into one taut muscle, straining. His voice was raw, muttering incoherent thoughts. Like maybe he should have considered a hand job before climbing in here with her.

She was moving tantalizingly slow all around his groin then she suddenly began to stroke him in earnest.

He could swear his body levitated.

Her fingers caressed his sac, and it was all over. The orgasm imploded his brain. It was so powerful, he lost touch with consciousness, but he was pretty sure he roared his pleasure.

Good thing no one lived in this part of the house except him.

When the molecules in his body came back together and formed a human again, his lower half was back underwater and Bianca was draped over the top of him, wrapped in his arms.

He kissed her hair, and she made a soft snoring sound and scrunched closer to him.

Chill bumps pebbled on her skin and, this time, it was because the water had cooled.

He pushed the button to turn off the jets and checked to make sure he had feeling in his legs again before he stood up with her. Her legs hooked around his waist and bam, he was hard again. No surprise there.

Stepping out of the tub, he grabbed a bath sheet and wrapped it around her, then sat on the edge so he could dry her.

She made a half-awake reach for the towel, mumbling, "I can dry myself."

He wouldn't let her have it. "Don't cheat me out of this simple pleasure."

She was quiet while he finished.

When he took in the remorse in her eyes, he ran his knuckles over her cheek. "What's wrong?"

"I'm so sorry."

"Why?"

"For my part in sending you to that hellhole."

He wanted to say that he didn't hold her responsible, and she didn't have to apologize, but just the fact that someone *had* apologized wrapped his chest in warmth. "Thank you. I don't blame you for doing your job."

"But you're right. Ryder, we stopped looking when we found a neat fit for our evidence. I'm going to search back through all of it and find whatever we missed, because it has to be in there."

He doubted anything obvious would show up, but he would like to see that evidence himself. That might be expecting too much from Bianca who was still a rule-follower by nature, but before the week was out, he intended to ask.

She yawned.

Smiling, he lifted her in his arms and strode to the bed. "Think you can sleep now?"

"Yes. I'd make you put me down, but my legs are noodles."

After depositing her on the bed, he turned to walk away.

"Where're you going, Ryder?"

"To sleep somewhere that I won't hurt you unintentionally."

"Come back here."

He'd normally bristle at being ordered by anyone, but he liked this take-charge side of her. He stopped at the edge of the bed. "What do you need?"

"You. Here with me. I trust you, but you need to trust yourself."

"I can't guarantee I won't ... do something bad."

"I can." She patted the mattress next to her. "If it happens again, we'll talk about it then. Fair enough?"

The correct answer, the only answer, was no, but he looked down into the deep well of those hazel eyes and fell in headfirst.

Once he settled and had her back tucked up to his chest, he wrapped a protective arm across her. She reached up and hooked her fingers around his forearm and let out a contented sigh.

"Thank you." The words popped out without him thinking about it.

"For what?"

"For tonight. I never meant to touch you this week."

"If you hadn't, I might've never known what making love could be like."

"But you know what I'm facing in a few days. That we may never see each other again after this week." He should have thought about that before he let things go so far in the Jacuzzi. But thinking hadn't been possible when she was in his arms.

Her fingers tightened on his arm. "We'll find a lead soon."

Ryder didn't want to remind her that she hadn't found even a hint of anything suspicious in all the hours she'd spent looking today. He didn't want to dampen her happiness and tell her the reality was that someone had covered their trail so well it would take a miracle to find Kearn's killer.

He hugged her instead, holding the only miracle he'd ever known in his arms for what little time he could have her.

CHAPTER 32

MARGAUX RUBBED HER eyes and walked into the meeting room at Slye headquarters where there'd better be coffee.

"The Duke have trouble sleeping?" Nick Ferrari asked, using the nickname that annoyed her. He was of Mediterranean descent with brown eyes so dark they appeared black and thick eyelashes a woman would kill for. Sexy packaging with bad wiring. He was a wild card. No one knew exactly what he would do at any given time, but Nick came through at times when no one else could.

That didn't stop her from wanting to pull out her Sig and warn him about using that stupid nickname again.

"I sleep like a baby," she lied. Margaux hadn't slept soundly since asking Nanci to work on this mission. They'd never had differences until now, but they'd argued last night. Margaux got that Nanci's duty was to the FBI first, but Nanci could've told Margaux that she had a way to communicate with Bianca.

Lack of good intel pissed off Sabrina.

Pissing off Sabrina was never good for a person's health.

Not any more than pissing off Margaux or anyone else on the downstairs Slye teams. Tidy corporate security jobs were arranged *upstairs* in the street level offices, but the black ops missions to protect national security—or anything Sabrina deemed worthy of her dark ops teams—were handled down here in the soundproof basement.

Margaux filled a mug with black coffee and turned to find Josh, Dingo, and Tanner walking in. Josh Carrington always had the put-together look of a man accustomed to money, which he had aplenty, where Dingo melded into any dark shadow even in broad daylight. Josh and the Aussie went way back with Sabrina—like back to when they were little kids.

"You look like you could use a full body massage," Tanner said with a twinkle in his baby-blue eyes. "Let me know if I can lend you a hand."

Margaux took a sip of the hot brew, holding his suggestive gaze as she lowered the mug. "Speaking of your sex life, if you change hands in mid-stroke does that make you a polygamist?"

Tanner grumbled something about liking his women sweet in the morning.

Dingo opened his laptop and started typing. Josh thumbed keys on his smart phone, and Nick ignored everyone.

Sabrina entered the room holding a small flash drive up in one hand. "I found this on my desk this morning."

Everyone tensed because Sabrina did not have an open-door policy. Margaux had an inkling that privacy might've come at a premium for Sabrina growing up, because it had sure as hell been that way for Margaux, and she protected her space just as ruthlessly.

No one entered Sabrina's office unless invited in. To get there, you had to go through former MI6 Intel tech Amanda Talifero, who would step away from her keyboard long enough to hurt anyone who tried to enter Sabrina's inner sanctum.

Margaux asked, "Any sign of B&E?"

"No." Sabrina closed her fingers around the flash drive. "Professional job, which is saying a lot considering our security system."

Dingo stopped typing and looked up. "Someone went to a lot of trouble to make a statement about delivering that. Video feed was altered. Our codes can't be easily hacked. The skill required to get in here is—"

"CIA level," Josh finished.

"Wasn't *him*," Sabrina said, ending any further conversation on "him."

Margaux knew enough about the history of Sabrina's core team to know they'd been screwed over on a mission Sabrina was running for the CIA two years ago. But Margaux had no idea who "him" was or why he brought on an angry glare from Josh.

Sabrina moved on at her usual speeding-bullet pace. "Dingo will reset all the security today. After looking this over, I doubt we'll have a return visit, but I want the pass codes changed daily until Ryder's mission is completed."

Tanner asked, "Did the intel fairy leave you something special?"

Sabrina handed the flash drive to Dingo, instructing him to make two copies, then she answered Tanner. "Financial and inventory records on three international weapons dealers who do business with Van Dyke Enterprises. The two in Germany and Turkey also buy from Kearn Industries, but not the one in Dubai. It's going to take some time to go through all this, but it's clearly someone sending us information on this mission."

Margaux scrubbed a hand through her hair. "How long? We're running out of days at this point."

"That's why we need to get this to Ryder and Bianca now."

Nick piped up. "You give that to the FBI, they'll edit out what they don't want passed on. Hell, they might sit on it for a couple of days first."

Sabrina nodded. "Right. That's why Margaux is going to give it to her cousin to pass to Bianca." She took the flash drive and a dupe from Dingo then handed both copies to Margaux. "Nanci has to give this to Bianca first, then she can have the second copy for the agency."

Shit. This was going to be a worse argument than last night's with Nanci, but Sabrina was one step from shooting someone over Ryder's situation.

Margaux nodded. "Got it."

This was going to be ugly, because Nanci would balk at not taking the intel to Murdock first and Margaux wasn't leaving until she got what she wanted.

CHAPTER 33

BIANCA STEPPED INTO the mega-blaster shower the next morning. She was still bruised and sore, but she felt as if she'd left her body last night for an amazing little vacation to OMG land.

Water hit her from every direction and all she could think about was Ryder taking her to climax last night while water surged against her.

She refused to regret what she'd done and, make no mistake, that had been her doing. Ryder hadn't crossed the line with her. She'd pushed him over it.

Soaping up a thick washcloth, she started at her neck and shoulders, but the minute she dragged it across her breasts they perked up and her nipples pebbled.

How was she going to get through today thinking about sex all day long?

The glass door opened and closed.

Two arms came around her and his large hands took the washcloth from her. His husky voice rasped against her ear. "Looks like you got stuck in one spot."

Decision time.

Okay that was a total lie since her body had already made that decision for her. She shivered with anticipation. "I could use some help."

His hands started moving, slowly washing her breasts. She ached for him to toss the cloth away and use his hands on her. He was hard and that thick ridge pressed against her back, making her wet between her legs.

Then he was washing that very spot, moving the soapy cloth

between her legs, gently washing back and forth over the sensitive folds. Her knees were shaking.

He moved away, bringing the cloth to her back and working his way down to her butt cheeks, sliding it between them.

She put her hands against the wall in front of her for support and he moved down one leg, then the other.

Then the cloth was gone, and his soapy hands were on her hips, one sliding forward to barely touch one of her breasts. He rolled the nipple between his fingers, that tiny touch ripping heat from her breast to her womb.

His other hand slid between her swollen folds that were so sensitive it only took a touch for her to climb on that ledge again. "Don't stop."

"No chance, Sweetheart."

He moved to the other breast and left the first one begging for more. She was going to be in tears soon if she didn't get relief.

His voice wrapped her in a sensual blanket as he described each part of her body in erotic detail. She'd never look at herself in the mirror the same way again. His hand finally held her breast, massaging and teasing one then the other, but it was his fingers sliding across her slick folds and zeroing in on the nub connected to all the nerves in her body that was spinning her out of control.

The orgasm exploded through her. She would have fallen if he hadn't abandoned her breasts to hold her up against him, never letting up between her legs until she was gasping.

He wrapped her in his arms and held her, kissing her neck while water cascaded down from every direction. It was like making love in the rain.

When she could stand again, she turned to Ryder. Water rushed across that incredible body. An Adonis in a waterfall.

She reached up, wrapping her arms around his neck and kissing him. His tongue pushed past her lips and played with hers, tempting her with all the things that tongue could do.

There was no mistaking that he wanted her. His penis was hard and thumping against her stomach. What a heady moment to be standing in a shower with a man like Ryder, knowing he wanted her.

And wanting him back. He'd shown her what a man and woman could share. She pulled back, breathless. "We aren't doing this unless you can, too."

His eyes sparkled when he said, "I don't know who stocked the drawer where I used to keep them, but I found condoms."

Easing back away from him, she glanced down to find him already sheathed. When she looked back up, she gave him a cocky smirk. "Pretty sure you were going to use it, huh?"

Even his shrug was sexy. "I can always take it off and toss it."

She enjoyed the teasing but understood that he was giving her an out if she didn't want to do this. A painful memory flashed into her mind, and she forced it away, refusing to think of *him* while she was standing here with Ryder.

Water ran down her face and into her eyes. Ryder's hands came up, to hold her face. The warmth in his voice soothed her as much as him saying, "Don't ever think you owe any man anything. I'm fine with throwing the condom away and dealing with this myself. I know you were hurt physically and emotionally. Watching you last night was a gift to be cherished. I'd like to find the asshole and show him what a man like him really deserves, but right now all I care about is that you only do what you want."

She didn't want to fall in love with this man. There were so many reasons not to, but her heart had come out of hibernation because of him. Lifting up on her toes, she said, "Here's what I want. You inside me."

He didn't move at first, just stared at her as if he hadn't heard her right. Then he kissed her and as he did, he lifted her up. She wrapped her legs around him and moved against the hard ridge between them.

He held her with one hand and turned her back against the wall, freeing a hand to reach between them. His mouth devoured hers, kissing her as if the world would end before he could finish. His fingers were magic, stroking her until she was humping his hand.

His hands went to her waist, lifting her and breaking the kiss, but his gaze held her captive as he slowly eased her down until she felt his penis prodding at her opening.

"Just relax and tell me if anything hurts," he said. He held her with one arm and reached down, feeding himself inside her inch by inch.

The muscles in his neck stood out from the toll going slowly was taking on him.

She tensed at the fullness, but then his fingers were touching her and teasing the mass of nerves between her legs. She dug her nails into his back, wanting to feel that release again. Everything inside her reached for it ... and she peaked all at once.

Somewhere during that moment, Ryder had slid all the way inside her and started moving.

She could feel his arms taut with trying to be careful.

He ground out, "Are you ... okay?"

"Not exactly."

"What exactly then?" He sounded pained.

"I want you to do it harder."

"Fuck." He started pumping into her, each push shoving her up against the wall.

She gripped him, holding on, with only his satisfaction in mind, but then her muscles started contracting again and the pressure built. Her thighs locked tighter around him, and she squeezed against the friction of him driving in and out of her.

A wave of ecstasy crashed over her.

Ryder gave a powerful shove and went rigid, letting out a guttural shout, then kept pumping until he finally dropped his head on her shoulder, heaving breaths.

She held his head against her protectively, wanting to keep him here safe in her arms.

The water continued to rage, shielding them from the world for now.

Ryder lifted his head, his eyes searching hers for ghosts of past experiences.

She smiled. "I stand corrected. I do like sex."

The smile he gave her in return was one she would remember for the rest of her life. There was the man she wanted to stay with. There was the man she had to save.

This was the man her heart had chosen for her.

But nothing in the VDE computers had given even a tiny

inkling of hope. She hadn't said so to Ryder, because she wasn't giving up.

But she had orders for this mission that Ryder couldn't be privy to.

Murdock didn't want Sabrina Slye or Ryder to know that the FBI suspected Hubrecht Van Dyke of more than selling weapons illegally. They suspected someone at VDE of financing terrorist activities. With time running out, Bianca had to choose between pursuing information on Kearn's killer that she doubted they'd find at VDE and flushing out how Hubrecht, or someone else at VDE, was funding terrorists.

She owed her agency and Sara Lynn to perform the job she was sent to do, but she couldn't watch Ryder walk back into a prison either.

CHAPTER 34

BIANCA STARED AT the elevator doors that would open any minute. She'd have to ride up thirty-two floors to the top of Van Dyke Tower. *Don't throw up.*

"Are you sure you want to do this?" Ryder asked in a voice too low for anyone but her to hear even though four other people waited for the elevator to the corporate floors. They were probably thinking about how they'd spend their Friday night, not the least worried about the elevator falling.

Ryder had brought Bianca up the stairs to this point so he could inquire about the elevator at the lobby security desk.

All was fine. The technicians had found a small glitch in the computer program.

She would not throw up.

Ryder stood so close to her shoulder she could smell the spicy cologne he had on. His fingers gave a little squeeze at her waist. "Sweetheart, you don't have to do this."

"I'm fine," she assured him. Why didn't elevators have those little bags airplanes supplied for motion sickness?

"I can have a car take you home."

And that was why she had clammy hands, and her mouth was dry as a cotton ball, because she had to ride this elevator to the top floor if she wanted access to VDE's electronic files again. She could walk up thirty-two floors, but then she'd be so worn out she'd have to crawl the rest of the day.

"Really. This is fine." She gave Ryder a smile she hoped would convince him.

She'd faced her fear of sex last night and look how well that had turned out. Too good, because now she didn't think she could share that intimacy with anyone else.

Technically, she could.

Emotionally, she couldn't.

She should have known she couldn't treat it like an experiment. She wasn't built that way, which was why Bernard had pushed all the wrong buttons with her when he tried to bully her into treating intimacy like a sporting event with a new challenge every night.

Had he gained her trust, like Ryder had, she might have been open to experimentation and adventure, but in hindsight she'd realized Bernard had been a selfish pig. He'd never wanted to build trust or nurture feelings.

He'd wanted a subservient female.

She'd been naïve, not submissive.

The elevator doors opened, and she ordered her feet to move forward. Ryder's hand touched the small of her back. He moved her over to the corner and behind the other four strangers, basically shielding Bianca from everyone by the way he positioned his body.

Doors closed. The car started going up.

Her heart began its own rendition of war drums. She wasn't going to be able to do this.

Ryder hooked an arm around her shoulder and nuzzled her neck.

She hissed at him, "Ryder!"

"What?" His nose skimmed over her neck. "You smell so good I'd like to eat—"

"Stop it," she whispered, looking to see if anyone had turned to glower at them. Nope. The other four people faced forward.

His fingers were squeezing her arm then moving up to her shoulder. "Maybe we'll stay in for lunch. Eat in my office. You know, something quick."

His words were spoken in a smoky voice and loaded with innuendo.

How could words alone cause her breasts to ache with wanting Ryder to touch them after all they'd done this morning? Her boobs should be ready for a break, but they were worse than two puppies begging for attention from Ryder.

An instant replay of this morning flipped through her mind.

Ryder's hands finding places that she wouldn't have thought could turn her on. That familiar ache starting again.

Wrong frame of mind for walking into the VDE offices. She had a job to do, and Ryder was not helping.

She turned to him and got up close. "You're being inappropriate."

"I don't care."

"You should."

"Why?"

Because he needed this job? No. Because it might tarnish his business image? Laughable. "Because you represent the company."

"No, I don't. Terrence is the proper one. He can represent the company."

He had a point, but his fingers were making her forget what *her* point was. "Don't, uh ..."

"Don't what?" he asked in his bedroom voice that was driving her almost as crazy as his fingers that had moved to her waist. "Bianca?"

What had she been talking about? Him. "Don't you care what people think?"

"No." He kissed her hair, and she gave up.

A bell tone sounded, and the doors opened.

Ryder curved his arm around her shoulders and chuckled. "See? We're here."

She stepped into the top floor of VDE and shook her head. He'd distracted her to keep her from panicking over being in the elevator.

"What's so funny?" he asked.

"You."

He lifted an eyebrow at that.

"You were talking trash just to keep my mind off the ride up."

"It worked." He strolled ahead and opened the door to his office, holding it for her.

"Yes, but now those four people think we're going to have a quickie at lunchtime."

"Then they would be right."

CHAPTER 35

THE MONEY WAS great, but this was turning into the biggest bullshit job Munk had ever taken. Even for top dollar, this was a bigger headache than it was worth.

Paying for additional operatives on a mission wasn't unusual, but he'd had to bring in an electronics genius just to override the programming on a fucking elevator. And he'd had to pay prime money to get that operative there and inserted into Van Dyke Tower within his client's stupid three-hour window. He'd bill the client and tack on a nice upcharge, but what a roaring pain in the ass.

He should just kill the bitch and be done with this game.

But his reputation was at stake. He would never bail on an assignment until the job was completed, but an op like this would cost triple in the future. Enough money to price himself out of the market for anything but a clean kill.

Munk dialed his client.

"Yes?"

"Last night went without a hitch, but I could have used a little more notice." Munk pushed the sheer hotel curtain aside, making note of overcast skies.

"Like I had much notice? I'm just glad that Ryder was the only one at the offices with her. Makes him a prime suspect once something does happen to Bianca."

Munk took that opening. "When are we going to finish this?"

"What's your rush? You're being paid well."

"Got another project coming up soon."

"Not until after Sunday."

"What's happening then?" Munk did not tolerate surprises for any amount of money.

"It doesn't concern you. All you need to know is once I green light you to kill Ryder, you might want to wait to see what price is put on his head before you kill him. Could end up as a nice bonus."

That smacked of setting Ryder up as a terrorist, which would fit for this whacko. But Munk didn't trust this psychopathic client not to sacrifice Munk in an attack. "Where is this Sunday event happening?"

"Not on this continent, so don't focus on that."

How could Ryder be blamed for the attack? Munk would wait to see what fallout happened after Sunday before deciding how to move forward with Ryder, but Ryder would die. He owed Munk. "What about Bianca?"

"Once I give you the go ahead to take down Ryder, Bianca is all yours to do with as you wish. A win-win. But until then, this operation is still about giving her reason to think Ryder wants her dead."

Munk ended the call.

His client could be a pain in the ass, but he'd given Munk reason to smile.

When the time came, Ryder would finally pay his debt to Munk for what Ryder had done in Iraq, and Bianca would serve as interest earned on the debt.

CHAPTER 36

RYDER COULD FEEL Bianca's frustration threatening to explode soon. She did everything she cared about with passion, even digging for information that might prove him innocent of a crime her initial research condemned him of.

Digging, but not finding.

"I don't understand this," Bianca murmured.

Ryder lowered the file he was reading that she'd printed out so they could both get through the load of information. He'd have to shred it all before he left today.

Bianca said something under her breath that had an acidic sound.

Had she just cursed? Ryder found that amusing. "What'd you find?"

She bent her elbow and propped her chin on the heel of her hand. "Nothing, nothing and nothing."

No surprise since he'd found pretty much the same.

"That's not entirely true," Bianca amended. "From what I can tell, VDE is as solid as Hubrecht claims so I don't see a motivation based on financial problems. And I can't find where any inventory has gone suspiciously missing through theft or destruction."

"But the FBI is certain VDE weapons landed in the wrong hands."

"Yes."

Ryder shook his head. "I don't see someone at a lower lever than corporate getting weapons out of VDE without notice. That being the case, how is Hubrecht, or someone else, hiding their illegal dealings with so many eyes and hands crosschecking inventory and shipments?" He considered another possibility.

"Hubrecht could be testing you—or us—to see if you'll tell him if you do find any evidence in the files."

"Maybe Hubrecht thinks I still have ties, even personal ones, to the FBI and wants to prove his company has nothing to hide."

Ryder took it another step. "Or Hubrecht *does* have something to hide, and he wants to see if he's buried it deep enough."

"I have more questions than I started with." Bianca's disappointed gaze reached out to Ryder. Her expression mimicked his thoughts. She was one of the best at what she did, but she couldn't find intel that wasn't there.

She chewed on the corner of her lip. "We're running out of time. *You're* running out of time. I should have found something by now."

She was blaming herself for not saving him.

He would not let her take on that guilt. If they didn't clear him of this murder charge, he had to make sure she did not walk away carrying that burden.

He got up and circled the desk.

In the few days they'd been together, especially the last two intense ones, he'd learned enough about her to know she took this as a personal defeat. Stepping behind her, he placed a hand next to the keyboard, which brought his face alongside her cheek. He inhaled, wanting to soak up the sweet scent of Bianca. He would never get that out of his system.

Correction. He'd never get *her* out of his system.

He kissed her cheek then her ear and nuzzled her neck.

She smiled. "You're not helping."

"Yes, I am. You're smiling." He kissed the base of her neck, glad she'd taken off her navy jacket, even though it brought out the gold in her eyes. She preferred formal attire. It gave her confidence when in truth she didn't need the armor. But under that jacket, she wore an ultra-feminine white silk top held up by two thin straps.

He licked the edge of her ear. "Stop thinking so hard."

"*Ryder!*"

"What?"

"Stop killing my brain cells."

"You can afford to lose a few thousand and still blow away the competition."

"As a geek?"

"As a woman who is as intelligent as she is hot." He lifted the back of her hair and kissed her neck, grinning when she shivered.

That brought on a wider smile. "I see how you earned your Silver Tongue Devil pin."

"You haven't heard anything yet." He spun her around and braced a hand on each chair arm, hovering close, almost nose-to-nose. He said, "Stop worrying. We'll find something."

Hope burst into her eyes. "You think so?"

Not really, but that was all he could give her right now. "I'm sure. If *you're* sure the VDE Woden rifles were found where you said."

She nibbled on her bottom lip. "I'm sure of it."

Again, he had that sense that she wasn't sharing everything. "You've been working on this a long time."

"Two years."

That sounded significant. "Were you assigned this or did something draw you to these cases?"

Indecision wicked in and out of her gaze. "I transferred to the department researching these attacks. My best friend was killed while on a humanitarian trip. Van Dyke Wodens were found there and in two other attacks. We have to find out how they're being supplied and stop the line of domestic aid to terrorists."

"What was her name?"

"Sara Lynn." Bianca squeezed her eyes closed then opened them. "She shouldn't have died there."

He wanted to say something that would ease the pain of losing her best friend, but words wouldn't heal that wound. Still, he tried. "Sounds like she was doing something she cared about."

"She was." Bianca stared at the desk. "But she wouldn't have gone if I hadn't pushed her, then I got sick and couldn't go. I should have—"

"Don't do that, Bianca. That's one thing we learn in combat. If we don't learn it, we lose our ability to make decisions we *have* to make—in the moment—to do our jobs. Don't blame yourself for not being there to die with her. Do you think your friend would have wanted that?"

She didn't answer.

Now Ryder understood what was driving Bianca besides her job. An obsession for justice because of a loss. Could he blame her? No, but had that obsession clouded her judgment when she'd been building a case against a Van Dyke?

She raised heart-broken eyes to him. "I'm sorry."

"Why?"

"Because now I think I couldn't see past my need for justice when I was researching and analyzing evidence on your case."

There was his answer. "You were doing your job. You didn't tamper with evidence or create what wasn't there. I told you. I don't blame you. We'll keep looking until we find something."

She lifted her hands to each side of his face. "I won't stop no matter what."

That determination would have thrilled him at the onset of this mission, but that was when he'd only been worried about his own ass. Now he had serious concerns about her safety. He'd anticipated getting her inside VDE covertly so that no one would know she'd been the one to breach the firewalls and dig through the files. He hadn't expected Hubrecht to give her access.

What would happen when this mission ended, and they found no evidence to give Murdock? Whether Ryder went back to his prison holding cell or not, Bianca would become a significant target. If she wasn't one already.

Hubrecht would regret his decision to trust Ryder.

Would he retaliate?

Who would protect Bianca if Ryder wasn't here to do it?

She had no idea how dangerous this op was. If someone harmed her, he'd ... kill them.

He would hunt them down and ...

"Ryder, look at me." Bianca's voice broke through the traffic jam in his mind. Her fingers grazed his skin with an ethereal lightness that pulled him back from the dark edge.

Her touch tamed the beast that hovered inside and lived to strike back at any given moment.

How could she see past the darkness inside him to reach out and call him back to the surface?

Why wasn't she backing away like any sane person would do?

She pulled his face down to hers and kissed him with her signature sweetness that set her apart from so many cynical women he'd dated.

He scooped her up and sat in her chair with Bianca in his lap before she could protest. His mouth sought out hers, daring her to sacrifice the kiss to complain.

Special Agent Brady might have, but not when Bianca was in charge.

She could ignite faster than a short dynamite fuse and touching her was just as explosive.

His hand went straight to her breast.

Her fingers gripped his hair, dragging his mouth harder against hers. "I loved it when you took me hard this morning."

Damn it. His erection had shot up the minute he'd touched her. Another comment like that with her sliding her bottom against him and he'd shoot his wad right now.

"*Mr. Van Dyke?*" called out from the speaker on his phone.

Bianca froze as if someone had unplugged her.

Ryder cursed and reached over to press the button on his phone so he could answer Jenny. "Yes?"

"*There's a delivery for your wife.*"

Suspicion raced up his spine. "What kind of delivery?"

"*A man with roses.*"

"What the f—"

Bianca slapped a hand over his mouth, stopping his angry outburst.

He glared at her. She lifted an eyebrow, daring him to snap at her, then gave him a have-no-idea lift of her shoulders. A gleam of humor entered her eyes.

Had he really just acted jealous? He pressed the button again. "I'll be there in a moment."

"*Yes, sir.*"

Bianca jumped out of his lap and started straightening her blouse. He should be glad they'd missed out on the quickie at lunch since a snack wouldn't have been nearly enough of her, but waiting sucked, too. He wanted her any time, any place.

"Wonder who it is?" Bianca whispered as she smoothed her hair back into place.

That's right. He had someone suicidal outside his door, because any man who brought Ryder's wife flowers had a death wish.

But Bianca isn't your real wife.

Screw that. She was until this mission ended. Until then, she *was* his. Ryder cupped his eyes. He was losing his mind.

"What's wrong?" Bianca asked.

What's not wrong? "Nothing." He took a minute to adjust his pants, thought about going back to prison and wham, instant limp dick. Not totally, since Bianca was still pulling and tugging at her clothes, which made him want to take them all off.

Ryder strode over to the door and shoved an intimidating glower into place before whipping it open, prepared to demand answers.

Jenny was quick to call out, "Sorry, Mr. Van Dyke. He told me I could only tell you it was a man with roses."

A tall guy with coffee-brown skin in a business suit tailored to fit his lanky frame stood with a huge bouquet of roses. He took one look at Ryder's face and roared with laughter.

Not the response Ryder had expected. "What's your fu—"

"*Ryder!*" Bianca snapped from close behind. "You're in an office."

He swung his anger at her. "I know where I am."

"Then don't curse. Especially not in front of Jenny." Bianca had her hands on her hips, her jacket straight and was leaning toward him with one hell of a mean look of her own.

Ryder was O for two at intimidating anyone right now.

He ignored her and turned back to the loon who was still laughing until Ryder took a step toward him.

Delivery guy backed up quick. "Hold it, mon," he said with a Jamaican accent. "Just joking with ya."

"So those flowers are *not* for my wife, right?" Ryder suggested with enough menace to have made an enemy wet himself.

"Well, yes, they are. I just wanted to screw with you again."
This time, the delivery guy spoke without the accent.

But Ryder had caught something in the Jamaican twist that
made him look closer at the guy half hidden by a dozen roses.
The brown eyes and long nose seemed familiar, too, but it was
the crooked front tooth that brought his memory into sharp
focus. "Larry?"

"Hell, yes. Now, can I give these to your lovely woman?"

Jenny tried to smother her laughter with her hand, but it didn't
work.

Bianca stepped past Ryder. "Yes, you can. Thank you. It's
Larry, right?"

"Yes, ma'am. Larry Morant."

"You obviously know Ryder. Why don't you come in?"

She took the vase and walked back into Ryder's office.

Feeling as though he'd just stepped through a wormhole into
another world, Ryder followed her, grumbling, "You don't mind
him cursing?"

"He was smiling when he cursed. You weren't."

Female logic. The perfect example of an oxymoron.

Larry walked in, pushing the door shut behind him. "I like
this one, Ryder. Much better than those bobble heads you dated
in school."

Ryder was still getting over the shock of seeing Larry here. At
Van Dyke Enterprises. Didn't Larry hate Hubrecht?

When Bianca offered Larry a seat, he refused. "I can't stay. I
was downstairs when the flowers showed up and thought it'd be
fun to yank Ryder's chain."

Just like Larry used to do when he and Ryder were best friends,
before Hubrecht shipped Larry and his family to the other side
of the country. Ryder couldn't act like this was normal. "What
are you doing *here* of all places?"

"I work here." Larry stopped smiling. He shoved his hands in
his pants pockets and looked away then back at Ryder. "I would
have come to see you, you know, at the prison, if I'd been in
the country, but I was in England for the past year. Just got back
yesterday in fact. I'm so sorry about what happened to you."

"Thanks, but I still don't understand how you could work for a man who ran you and your family out of town."

"It wasn't like that, Ryder." Larry lifted his skinny shoulders in a stiff shrug. "Your dad knew I was involved with a drug dealer."

"You were?"

"Yep. I didn't want you to find out, because I knew you wouldn't approve. The money was better than anything I could make at a job back then. Your dad showed up at my house one night—"

"Over off Bankhead Highway?"

"Yep. That dump in the ghetto. Talk about shocked to see Mr. Van Dyke there." Larry paused as if in thought, then said, "I was pissed at him for a long time after we moved to Oregon. I mean, talk about being out of place. But my dad had a better job than he'd ever had, and my mom was able to stay home, which helped because of her arthritis. And I got a degree."

Ryder leaned back against the front of his desk, trying to shove this new information in around all the reasons he'd been angry with Hubrecht since high school. "Did you get a scholarship?"

"Sure did."

"Good for you."

"But I have Mr. Van Dyke to thank for my engineering degree. He picked up the difference in cost and that allowed me to finish faster."

"He gave you the money for school?"

"Yes, but with a stipulation."

That sounded more like the man Ryder knew. "Always strings attached with Hubrecht."

"No, man, not like you think. VDE actually covered the difference. In trade, I agreed to work at VDE for my first three years. So being sent away was the best thing that ever happened to me." Larry looked embarrassed. "Except for losing touch with you. Your father was afraid I'd be a bad influence on you and get you into drugs. I had to agree not to contact you, or we'd lose everything he'd helped us get. By the time he believed I was a changed person, you were gone off to the military."

What could Ryder say to that? He'd suspected something illegal when Larry showed up with a fat roll of cash one week. The following week Larry had disappeared.

Ryder had taken Larry camping a few times and had intended to plan a trip that week so they could talk, but now he doubted his words would've had as much effect on Larry's future as Hubrecht's actions.

Maybe sensing Ryder's debate on what to say next, Larry went in another direction. "Remember that cabin we broke into up near Rabun Gap?"

Ryder cringed at having that brought up in front of Bianca and quickly amended, "It was empty, and we were caught in a raging storm." He turned to Bianca. "We left it clean, and with money to replace the broken window."

Larry turned to Bianca. "He was no hoodlum back then. Ryder here tried to keep me straight." When Bianca gave him a smile a woman saved for stupid stunts boys pulled, he winked at her and turned back to Ryder. "Anyhow, I bought that cabin last year so we can go there without breaking the law."

"You're kidding me."

"No. I'd just gotten the place set up so I could telecommute from there when Mr. Van Dyke needed me in England. We're opening a partnership over there. Give me a week to catch up here and we'll go camping in style." Larry cut a knowing look at Bianca. "Or you two can use it when you want."

"Damn, man. That's great. Thanks for the offer." Ryder wished he had the kind of life where he could accept Larry's invitation, but Ryder's future was one big black hole right now. "Success looks good on you."

"Thanks." Larry gave Ryder a once over with those same friendly eyes Ryder remembered from school days. "Glad to see you back."

Ryder wasn't sure if Larry meant back in the States or back at VDE. A long time ago Ryder had told Larry there wasn't enough money in the world to get him to work for Hubrecht. "For now."

The cell phone clipped on Larry's hip buzzed. He checked it then pressed a button and looked up. "Gotta run, mon."

Grinning, he stuck his hand out. "Let's grab some beers next week. I should be caught up by then."

Ryder gripped his hand. "Love to." If he was a free man.

Larry held his gaze for a minute then grabbed him in a bear hug. "Missed the hell out of you."

Emotion clogged Ryder's throat.

Larry backed up, waved at Bianca, and left, shutting the door quietly behind him.

Bianca asked, "Is that the boy you told me your father made disappear years ago?"

"Yes."

"Not what you thought, huh?"

"Nope." Ryder didn't want to think how else he might have misjudged Hubrecht back then and didn't want to talk about it. He turned to the roses. "Who sent them?"

"Aunt Nan congratulating me on our wedding. She didn't have an address other than here." The music was on as usual, but Bianca clearly wasn't taking any chances. She mouthed the letters *F-B-I*.

Ryder went over and told Jenny to hold his calls. Not that he had anyone wanting to talk to him other than the press—and they couldn't get past her even if they somehow, miraculously, got this far into the building—but it gave him the cover of locking his door when he closed it. He walked back over and dug through the roses even though that would be too obvious.

He cupped the entire bunch in his hands and lifted them out of the beautifully painted vase. The green foam floral brick the stems were stuck into came into view, and Bianca whispered, "Jackpot."

Ryder held the flowers as Bianca grabbed scissors from his desk and started snipping the florist tape wrapped around the foam.

Bianca pulled off all the tape from around the brick then gripped on each side of the thin cut line and pulled.

A USB flash drive sealed in a watertight plastic casing fell out.

Ryder shoved the foam brick and the flowers back into the vase.

Using the scissors, she freed the memory stick. "It appears we have a gift." Moving around the desk, she inserted the key into the USB port and a box appeared saying she was using an unsecured USB device that is not allowed. "Crap."

"What's wrong?"

"Your father has cyber security that prevents the use of memory sticks that aren't whitelisted. Some companies used to block their USB ports, but that ended up being more headache than it was worth then software came along that prevented use of unauthorized USB devices." She ejected the memory stick. "That means VDE's authorized USB devices are encrypted to fit their company policies.

"Hubrecht said nothing about that," Ryder mused. "He wants us to find his leak, but that doesn't mean he trusts me, or you, when it comes to downloading his company information. How are we going to get information out of here without leaving a trail?"

"I don't need a flash drive to get information out of here without him knowing it," she boasted more to herself than anything.

He touched her chin and turned her head to him. "Is that so?"

"Yes, but I didn't mean to sound arrogant."

"It ain't braggin' if you can do it. I think your badass side is sexy."

Bianca rolled her eyes. "You think everything is sexy."

"When it comes to you, yes."

Her cheeks pinked adorably. Clearly ignoring him, she lifted the empty case she'd pulled the flash drive from and peered into it. She stuck her little finger inside and twisted, pulling out a small piece of paper that read, "Any and all info on shipments to Ukraine, Germany, and Dubai."

"Looks like Aunt Nan covered the possibility that you couldn't get into the flash drive right away." He took the paper and blacked out the text, then flushed it in the bathroom connected to his office. He made a mental note to take the flowers with him when they left so no one would find that hollow foam.

Bianca sat back down. "Let me finish going through calendars for the past year."

"What are you looking for?"

"Anything that pings with dates from my files."

"I can't get over how much you can retain."

"Sometimes it's a curse," she mumbled, typing then leaning in. "That's interesting."

"What?"

"I found someone's trip to Steamboat, Colorado last February."

He wasn't seeing the connection. "What does that have to do with weapons?"

"Nothing that I can see right now, but the dates coincide with when the British diplomat Edward Abbot was shot near the private home he'd rented in Steamboat."

"So?"

Bianca stopped and lowered her voice even more when she turned to him. "I'm looking for a tie between Kearn's shooting and this one, because the same weapon was used for both."

"That proves someone else could have killed Kearn."

She shook her head slowly, regret pushing her words. "You were looked at for Abbot's murder, but the investigation turned up that you were renting a house at Lake Sinclair in Georgia during the same time. Investigators canvassed the area heavily, trying to pinpoint a time you were gone long enough to make the shot in Colorado, but there were enough sightings of you that it didn't hold up and with the lake house so far from a major airport the travel time wouldn't work. There wasn't enough to even justify questioning you."

"Shit." That just made all this even more important. Ryder crossed his arms, thinking. "Much as I'd love to find a link to the killings, it's still coincidental for a lot of people to be in Steamboat in February, not just a VDE employee."

"I'd agree if this person hadn't changed travel plans at the last minute and spent an exorbitant amount to leave an hour before the diplomat was killed in the same way as Kearn, right down to the ammo." She lifted her eyes to his, hesitating for a moment before she added, "My people believe the diplomat was there to discuss an arms contract."

Which meant Bianca might have found the person who contracted the hit on the diplomat and Kearn.

"Who went on that trip?"

"Sam Long."

CHAPTER 37

"THE GOOD NEWS about Chatton off on a rabbit chase is that she can't interfere with our plans," The General told Wayan as they flew thirty-thousand-feet above the earth in a sleek Boeing 747. Things had been so much simpler when Czarion consisted of only him and Wayan.

Back before Chatton showed up with one of the five artifacts to decipher Orion's Legacy. She hadn't brought the thing with her, but she'd produced enough documentation to confirm she had the broken Celtic cross and it was *the* one.

Wayan let out a polite sigh. He was often underestimated because of his boyish face and slight build, despite impeccable suits made by the finest tailors in the world. "She has become a complication. I am sure she had a hand in the failure of my laser unit."

"I agree, but she was on another continent when the laser was activated so we don't have any way to hang it on her. She might have helped that Slye bunch stop the laser from crashing the airliner somehow, but I'm betting she's not too fond of them now that I think she's convinced one of their people killed Edward Abbot."

"Why is this diplomat important to her?"

"I don't know. Yet." But The General would find out. He owed Chatton serious payback for that stunt she'd pulled at the Pentagon. "We just need to be careful around her."

"My anti-aircraft laser will be tested again at some point when she is no longer an inconvenience. But our operation this Sunday is far more critical. This will be a one-time-only opportunity."

The General nodded his understanding. "Everything's in place. The Komodo has delivered Van Dyke Wodens to the second team and is the only person who can be tied to the bombing."

Pausing for a slug of his drink, The General set the glass on the table between them and continued. "On the heels of the first explosion, my people will be part of the Guardia di Finanza who respond, and I have officers in decision-making positions who will insure my people stay on scene."

"The detonations cannot disrupt—"

"I. Know. The secret underground chamber will be undisturbed. Our artifact will remain safe." The General tolerated Wayan's constant micromanaging and obsessing over details because Wayan would be of use down the road. For now, The General would allow the Chinese power player to question everything. When the time came, Wayan would know who really commanded Czarion.

Wayan touched his tie as if to straighten it, but merely tapped the knot with his finger. "I would prefer to be there myself for this one."

Five-foot Asian guy? "You might stand out as part of an Italian counter-terrorism unit." The General let obvious sarcasm edge the comment.

Wayan's eyes narrowed into slits, and the black centers shifted with a deadly slide toward The General. "I find your humor wearing."

I find you just as annoying, but I'm not complaining so what have you got to bitch about? "You should lighten up, Wayan. Life is short."

"As is our time together. For this, I give thanks," Wayan countered. "You are sure of this Komodo?" he asked for the tenth time.

"Yes, I like the way he operates, supplying weapons to his own personal terrorist squad for the past couple of years. The Komodo knows nothing about our men on the Guardia di Finanza, only that his men are to rush inside as soon as the third bomb goes off."

"The Guardia understands the priority."

The General liked being interrupted about as much as he liked having every detail questioned. Not at all. "Yes, our select group of Guardia will be carrying Van Dyke Wodens in addition to their own weapons, so when the smoke clears, the authorities will have nothing but the bodies of Komodo's men, who will be holding the *same* Woden rifles that mowed down the Swiss Guard defending the Vatican. Our men will drop those Wodens at the scene before the authorities show up."

Listening with an intent look on his face, Wayan pointed out, "But you said you have not met this Komodo in person."

"No, Komodo only knows the Banker and the Banker agreed to never meet Komodo in person. The Banker works through electronic communication primarily, only meeting in person when he deems it necessary." The General's one-way emails to the Banker couldn't be tracked back to him and the Banker triple deleted emails from the server, just as The General did on his end. "Komodo was behind the three terrorist attacks I briefed you on. His track record speaks for itself."

The General didn't pause or Wayan would question the Komodo's track record. "But enough about him. Casualty count for this Sunday is estimated at three thousand of those attending the inauguration for the new pope. As a bonus, taking out the new pope will pay an outstanding debt we owe to our Italian friends. In my country, that's called killing two birds with one stone."

Wayan showed as much enthusiasm as a man having a colonoscopy with no anesthesia. "Our team inside the Vatican must find the scroll with the inscription within twenty-four hours."

That might not be realistic, but there was no point in arguing with Wayan about something that had yet to occur. "They know."

"The timing is imperative," Wayan pressed. "This event will bring many national security agencies to focus on the Vatican."

"Some will blame it on the Bilderberg group." The General loved how conspiracy theories sometimes played in his favor, especially when he knew firsthand there was some truth to the rumors. Influential government representatives and financial icons made up the Bilderberg group suspected of altering the course of the world from behind closed doors.

"Perhaps. You are quite certain no attention will be drawn to either of our governments?"

"Yes. I haven't told you the best part of this plan."

The slight angle of Wayan's chin indicated he was greatly intrigued in contrast to his simple, "Oh?"

"As soon as news of the attack hits the media, I'll feed intel to the FBI that will put them on the trail of the Komodo. He won't last long once *they* go after him."

CHAPTER 38

"I FOUND SOMETHING," BIANCA declared softly since Ryder was picking up the remnants of Thai food he'd had delivered. Nothing like a Friday night to quiet the corporate floor of a major company. Everyone had left for the day, but music still played in Ryder's office, and they spoke in hushed tones. She loved music of all kinds, but after three days of nonstop music playing in the background, she was sick of it.

When could they get out of here and find somewhere quiet?

"Good, because we're leaving soon. It's almost midnight." Ryder walked behind her and leaned down, sending her a whiff of him. No cologne today, just the warm scent of his skin, a nice musk that she was coming to recognize all too easily. He read over her shoulder. "What is this?"

"An email that bounces if you hit reply, which makes me think the two parties have a one-way email for each other that's bounced through a series of servers."

"This belongs to someone in VDE?"

"Yes, but I haven't been able to nail down who. Took me a while to find this and it was only after I started searching for deleted emails still on the server. I've been digging through everyone's communication for the time periods around Kearn's killing as well as the British diplomat's shooting plus the timeframes when weapons might have been shipped prior to attacks."

Murdock would expect her to look for a connection that would lead the FBI and CIA to the terrorist in charge.

"That doesn't say anything about weapons."

"No, but there was another email before this ..." She hit a few keys then pointed. "This one lists a date and a specific time two years ago that payment would be deposited."

He followed her finger, reading. "Got it."

"That date and time was ten minutes after the bombing where my friend was killed." Ryder stared for a long time. "Show me the other email you had up first."

She did and sat quietly as Ryder read.

HALF HAS BEEN WIRED. SECOND HALF WILL BE DEPOSITED AT 0100 BASED ON SUCCESSFUL PROJECT EXECUTION ON SUNDAY. FAILURE WILL COME AT A PENALTY, AS AGREED.

He straightened. "Same exact verbiage. Something is happening this Sunday."

She looked up at him. "Looks like it to me."

"Any guess who this might belong to?"

"There's a K at the end of the email. I'd need to get on the physical computers to crosscheck some things, but the emails were sent and received after ten at night in every case, sometimes after midnight. The only person logged on here at VDE when these were opened, and the replies sent, was Terrence."

"*Terrence?*" Ryder put his hand to his forehead. "He's ... he's not capable of this."

She wasn't ruling out anyone. "There's the possibility that someone is sending from his computer, but Terrence also processes international shipping orders late at night."

She was proud of how she'd managed not to let her hands shake. There was the lead they'd been looking for. She had to get this information to the FBI once she figured out exactly what was happening and where it was happening.

Ryder looked sick. She could appreciate that. She'd feel the same way if she'd just realized someone in her family was aiding terrorists, but Bianca was not going to allow anyone else to die the way Sara Lynn had.

Someone would finally pay.

She took Ryder's hand. "I know it's hard to consider."

Ryder shook his head. He frowned the longer he stared at her computer. "It's not that. I already told you that everybody is suspect, even Janeen and Terrence. But Lady Anne put her foot down a long time ago about Terrence's hours. She mandated that Terrence could not be here more than six hours a day because of his health. He's never had the stamina to stay out late. That's why I said he's not capable."

"What's wrong with him?"

"He has ITP. Idiopathic Thrombocytopenic Purpura. It's a rare autoimmune blood disorder that Terrence used to call his purple disease because he bruised so easily. Hubrecht has given in to Lady Anne on practically anything to do with Terrence that didn't affect the business, because of his illness. One reason I went to see Kearn when Terrence asked was because I'd gotten an email from Janeen that said Terrence came home from Switzerland depressed and wouldn't share what the doctors said. Janeen thinks he's dying because he went immediately to update his will."

"That's so sad." Bianca studied on why Terrence would come to work late at night. "Maybe Terrence is determined to show Hubrecht he can do the job and doesn't want to be around people during the day, so he sneaks in late at night."

"Maybe." Ryder did not sound convinced.

Bianca had turned back around and started closing out files when she stopped. "He's here."

"Who?"

"Terrence. He just logged on."

Ryder moved around the desk.

She jumped up. "Where are you going?"

"To find out who *is* logged on."

"What if it's your brother?" she asked, coming around the desk.

He waited at the door. "What if it's not?"

She conceded the point, but to be honest she'd feel much better about walking in on Terrence than a lot of other people at VDE who were much more threatening.

"Stay here," Ryder ordered.

"Have you not figured out that I don't take orders from you?"

"Please."

"Nice try, but no." She hurried over to catch up to him.

Jaw set, Ryder strode ahead of her, exuding confidence that he could handle anything they faced. She hoped so since the person behind those emails might also be the one who had framed him.

Her heart had taken up kickboxing in her chest.

She'd like an injection of his confidence, but with or without it, nothing could stop her from finding out who was behind the terrorist attacks.

CHAPTER 39

RYDER LIFTED HIS hand in a silent order for Bianca to hold up when he reached Terrence's office door.

It was ajar and a light was on inside.

Could his brother really be involved with terrorists?

Why?

When he heard the clack of keys being hit inside the office, Ryder gently pushed the door open to make sure someone wasn't waiting with a weapon.

Janeen sat at Terrence's desk, typing away, oblivious to anything else.

Ryder stepped into the office. "What are you doing?"

She jumped and grabbed her chest. "What the hell, Ryder? You scared the piss out of me."

Was that because she was guilty of something?

Before he could say more, Janeen slapped her hand on the desk. "Don't you dare tell anyone about my being here."

That sounded guilty as hell. "It depends on why you're sneaking into the office after hours."

"Because I can't come in during the day and do this."

He noticed her sparkly outfit. Had she come here from partying tonight? Or did she just *look* as though she'd been out on the town? "You need to explain what you're up to."

"No, I don't. Not to you."

"Maybe Hubrecht would like to know about you coming in."

"So, you and dear ol' Dad have bonded? Gotten to be buddies in just a couple of days?" She sat back, showing the rest of her dazzling outfit. "Why would you create problems for Terrence?"

"Does he know you're here?"

"Of course, he does." She angled her head and sat forward.

"I don't like your tone. Are you implying that I'm *guilty* of something?"

"Are you?"

"Yes. Working for free."

"Why?"

"Because no one has enough brains to hire me here and someone has to watch out for Terrence. You sure as hell didn't. You just did your usual and walked away, not giving a damn about the fallout left in your wake."

His shoulders tensed at that after all he'd gone through. "If you mean when I went in the Army, I did that *for* Terrence."

"Keep telling yourself that. Our father was harder on Terrence than ever once you were gone."

"I thought leaving would give him a fair chance. He wanted to be here. I didn't."

Janeen's gray-blue eyes accused Ryder of being the hub of all the family trouble, just as Lady Anne had dumped on his head every day of his life. "If that's the case, then why'd you come back? Especially after all the trouble you caused with Kearn."

"*Me?* I wouldn't have been in the wrong place at the wrong time if not for once again trying to help Terrence."

"Don't try to convince me that Terrence knew what you were going to do."

Ryder started to protest that Terrence had called Ryder asking him to meet with Kearn, but Janeen knew about that. She was getting at something entirely different. "You think *I* killed Kearn?"

She stared him down, not giving an inch.

He had nothing to say to that. She really believed he was a murderer.

Bianca zipped inside the office and stepped up next to Ryder, hands fisted in her crossed arms. "What kind of sister are you? Do you have reason to believe Ryder could have killed anyone in cold blood?"

"That's precious coming from you," Janeen taunted. "Didn't you testify at his preliminary hearing? Weren't *you* the one who laid out a convincing string of evidence on how the bullet was a 300-grain *Scenar*, heavier than the bullets normally used for the .338 Lapua round because Ryder preferred it for his *custom* McMillan rifle? A very *unusual* rifle, of which *all* had been accounted for except Ryder's. You sold *me*."

Ryder tasted the disgust in his mouth. "You were at that hearing."

Janeen's smile came out as a sneer. "You think I'd waste my time and sit among the unwashed to do that? No. Sam got the transcripts. He and Kale went over everything. Kale had his doubts, but Sam believes you did it."

Screw Sam. "I didn't have the weapon once I left the Army."

Janeen snapped her fingers. "That's right. It was *stolen* from your issued gear the same week it was shipped home. The week *you* arrived home." She cocked her head as if mocking a confused person. "Another amazing coincidence, right?"

Bianca took a step forward, but Ryder put his hand out to stop her. He had real concerns about Bianca's safety around his sister at this point.

Bianca shot him a don't-interfere look then swung all that compact energy at Janeen. "I did lay out that evidence, but then I found conflicting evidence that cleared him of the charge."

"Just because he found a way to your heart through your panties doesn't mean you're going to convince me."

Bianca's cheeks were flush with color.

Janeen smiled knowingly. "What Sam and I can't figure out is how Ryder got out of prison, because neither one of us is buying this marriage crap. Did he promise you plenty of money or is he paying up at night?"

Ryder was done with listening to this poisonous spew. "When did you become such an evil bitch?"

"Oh, I've always been one. I'm just more impressive now."

"You haven't explained why you're here at night."

"And I don't intend to. Not to you." Janeen smiled. "Sam knows I'm here. That's enough."

"Maybe Hubrecht needs to know."

Janeen wasn't frightened. No, her face contorted with a snarl. "You just can't let Terrence get a break, can you? Telling Hubrecht will ruin any hope Terrence has with this company. Do you have to destroy his entire life? If you must know, Terrence has trouble concentrating. It's the medicine he's on now. Every time he comes back from Switzerland, he's on something different. I stop in and process his international shipments, so nothing hits a snag." Janeen's voice had softened when she spoke of their brother.

Another reminder to Ryder that he had never belonged in this family. Janeen had been civil as a sibling when they were younger, even used to take him to the range with her now and then, but every time Terrence had a conflict in school or struggled to please Hubrecht, Janeen, and Lady Anne had left no doubt about whose fault that was. Ryder's.

Bianca asked Janeen, "Why don't you just work for VDE? Then you could be here during the day to help him."

"Because my father won't hire me. Doesn't see my value or potential." Eyes teeming with resentment, Janeen turned to Ryder. "Not like he does for the bastard son who walked away then returned after a stint in the joint. Isn't that what convicts call it? The joint?"

Instead of rising to her bait, Ryder turned the attack back on her. "How's Hubrecht supposed to see any potential when you party all the time and never finished college?"

"And you finished?"

No, but he'd gotten another education in the Army. "We're not talking about me."

"And we're not talking about me." She turned to the computer, typed a couple of keys, then grabbed her sparkling handbag off the desk and stood up on four-inch heels. She headed toward the door. "Just so we're clear, I don't need a degree to design weapons. I know them inside and out. I'm the one who found the flaw in the XM-28 Woden. I caught it before they had the final molds made for the production lower receivers."

Ryder had never known that about her. "You want to design?"

When Janeen reached Ryder, she paused. "Find that hard to believe? Shows how little you know about me, too." She shifted her attention over to Bianca. "I've heard about your mad computer skills, but I just locked down Terrence's computer. I'll know if you touch it."

Bianca had a half-smile on her face. "Actually, you wouldn't, but I have no interest in his computer."

Janeen muttered something to herself that sounded like arrogant government agents and told Ryder, "If you tell our father about this, you will regret it."

"Threatening me?" he asked in a barely audible tone.

"Yes. And you know I can back it up." She sashayed past him and out the door.

Ryder walked out of Terrence's office with Bianca at his side. She asked, "Is your sister capable of ordering a hit on a competitor?"

"She wouldn't have to."

"Because she could do it herself?"

He hesitated, then backtracked mentally. "I could be wrong about that. Not about her taking the shot. That, she could do. But as much of a bitch as she is now, it still takes more than shooting skills to carry out a hit. It's the stealth and evasion techniques that are harder to come by. The discipline and patience to wait for the target to show. Hard to imagine Janeen with those." He kept walking back toward his office. "Let's get your stuff and get out of here."

"I want to get back on the computer. She said something about finding a flaw in the weapon prototype, and that she knew the weapons design inside and out. That would mean she had access to the plans, right?"

"I'd think so."

"If that's the case, then we will probably see the plans accessed late at night from Terrence's computer."

"What are you getting at?"

"She said Sam knew she was here. Sam was in Colorado when the diplomat was killed. The same shooter was at both locations, which begs a question. Where was Janeen during the time of both shootings?"

Ryder enjoyed a fleeting moment of hope before it was overshadowed by what this would do to Terrence and the rest of the family if Janeen was involved. He didn't like the woman she'd become, but could she truly have killed Kearn? The sight of blood had always turned her stomach. Plus, she was always so righteous in her beliefs about right and wrong.

But could she have *ordered* the hit? If she hadn't, who had?

And why, because it appeared that what Hubrecht had said was true about Kearn being the one in trouble, not VDE.

CHAPTER 40

BIANCA SHOULD BE falling on her face after so many hours on her feet, but she couldn't tamp down the excitement she felt from what they'd learned tonight.

Ryder drove out of the parking garage onto streets that were quiet even though it was barely Saturday morning. He rolled down his window and stretched his arm out in the cool night air that buffeted the inside of the car.

Punching in a local country station on the radio, he asked, "How tired are you?"

She'd just stretched her arms up and behind her seat. "My body's tired, but my mind is racing. Why?"

"I need some fresh air."

He had hardly been outside of a building or vehicle since he'd left the prison. Sensing how much he craved freedom tugged at her and made her want to fight even harder to prove his innocence. She'd never be able to give him back what he'd lost, but she wanted to give him his future. "You mean go somewhere outside we could talk without background music?"

"Exactly."

She wanted quiet, too, and outdoors was always the perfect choice. "I'm all for it."

They rode in comfortable silence for twenty minutes. She caught him checking his mirrors constantly and assumed his relaxed posture meant no one was following them. Her faith in his abilities was such that she rolled her window down and dropped her head back to enjoy the breeze blowing her hair.

When Ryder slowed the car and the terrain changed from smooth highway to bumps, she sat up. "Where are we?"

"At the Chattahoochee River."

It was dark as the bottom of a well at night and all she saw in the glow of the headlights was a dirt road and thick trees. "I don't see a river."

"You will once we get out and walk about fifty feet." He parked in the narrow stretch of ground that appeared to have been beaten down by thousands of vehicles parking here over the years. Maybe hundreds of thousands.

Ryder grabbed a flashlight from the glove box and climbed out.

Bianca grimaced at the loud sound of opening and closing their doors. It had to carry a distance in this stillness. "Can you see where we're walking?"

"Not afraid of snakes, are you?"

"They shouldn't be moving around with it this cool, but I still don't want to walk up on a Cottonmouth."

Ryder had rounded the car without making a sound and flicked on the light that blazed with plenty of candlepower. "You *do* know about being in the woods. You ever do any hunting?"

"Took my first eight-pointer when I was thirteen." Skinning it had been a chore, but Daddy had been so proud of her. She'd taken the meat to a family of six who'd needed the food. Her daddy never killed an animal for sport, only to put meat on the table. She lived by the same rule.

Ryder's voice rumbled next to her face. "Damn, you just get sexier by the minute. Like when you use your true accent."

She stilled, feeling like she'd been caught. "What are you talking about?"

"You sound entirely different now than when you're around Murdock."

She relaxed. "Oh, you mean sounding Southern? I thought it would work better with your family."

He chuckled. "You do pull off Southern, and it's sexy as hell, but I hear country come out sometimes—"

"No, you don't." She clamped her lips shut because she sounded defensive.

"Yes, I do. I've caught it a couple of times when you were talking to your mama." He took her hand, leading them toward the tree line. "And I like that accent best. It turns me on."

She hoped her blushing cheeks didn't glow in the dark because they were so warm. Ryder said the most outrageous things. Bernard had thought she was a country bumpkin because she liked being out in the woods, and he'd said a woman hunting was a total turnoff. But Ryder found it sexy. He liked her country roots.

She wanted this man and knew he cared for her, but she wouldn't ask for something he was in no position to give.

Ryder was too honorable to make promises he couldn't keep.

Until he was cleared of the charges against him, he wouldn't consider talking about a life with her. Plus, he'd been wronged so badly throughout all of this, that he had no reason to trust anyone, especially someone with the FBI.

But she made a vow to herself that regardless of what happened by the end of this operation, she would not stop until she cleared his name and gained him the freedom he deserved.

Then she'd find out whether he was willing to explore what they had together.

He led her through a tunnel of light cut by the flashlight through the black forest. Ryder's grip on her hand tightened. She could feel his excitement.

"It's been a while," he said more to himself than her.

"Somewhere you came to make out at night?" she teased.

"No. This was all mine. I never brought women with me when I came to the river."

She was touched that he'd brought her. "Why did you come down here?"

"To hear my thoughts and breathe fresh air and listen to the river."

She heard the rush of water as Ryder stepped from the trees onto the bank of a river that stretched over two hundred feet across to the other side. The river ran downstream to her right and below an interstate overpass. Bloated from recent hard rains, the fast-moving current doused any traffic noise.

Ryder flipped off the flashlight, but light from the interstate filtered down to outline his profile. He stood with his eyes shut as if absorbing the outdoors.

She wanted a picture of him like this, at peace.

No, she wanted to see him like this forever.

After a long minute, he opened his eyes and turned to her. "I would live outdoors if I could."

Those words shouldn't have cut her to the bone, but they did. She'd seen the wounds on his body and knew of the beating he'd suffered when he first entered prison. Locking him away in a tiny cell would be like stuffing a Bengal tiger in a dog carrier and expecting him to live that way.

It was difficult enough for someone who *had* committed the crime that landed him in prison, but heartbreaking to think about someone who suffered that fate who didn't deserve it.

Ryder stuck the flashlight in his back pocket and reached for her. She missed his touch any time he was even a few feet away and moved into his arms. He hugged her, running his hand up her back and rubbing his face against her hair.

He whispered, "Stop doing that."

She pulled back. "What?"

"Beating yourself up over what happened to me. I can see it in your eyes when you do. At the hearing, when you were cross-examined, you said you just gather information. You don't pass judgment."

"But I was convincing."

"That's your strength and you'll be just as convincing when we find the truth."

She wasn't sure she could handle the weight of his trust. What if she let him down and didn't find enough answers? What if she couldn't figure out what was going to happen on Sunday? What if they locked Ryder away and someone managed to kill him in prison this time?

Ryder turned her in his arms and started kissing the back and side of her neck. He shoved her jacket aside to nip her shoulder, making her laugh. "Is that your answer to everything?"

"Sure, unless you want to have sex, then I'll defer to answer B."

"You're crazy."

"About you."

"Really?" She wanted to bite her tongue. She hadn't meant to say that.

His kisses changed from tickling her to a tender touch of his lips on her shoulder. He stopped kissing her and swayed to the lulling music of the river with his arms wrapped around her. "When this is over—"

Bianca heard something strike a tree next to them as Ryder shoved her to the ground. She whispered, "Was that a—"

"Bullet."

Another bullet struck the tree closer to the bottom of the trunk. Bark flew off, hitting her on the cheek. The shooter was using a suppressor. She kept as calm as she could with her heart racing and looked across the river. "Where is he?"

"In the woods."

"Between us and the car?"

"Yes." He shifted her to the other side of him, putting himself between her and the shooter.

The next shot hit the dirt next to her leg.

Ryder wrapped her in his arms. "We've only got one way out of here."

"Where?"

"The river." He rolled them into the water.

She gasped at the cold water that stole her breath. It felt like being wrapped in a coat of ice.

Ryder had a grip on her arm. "Don't panic at the cold. We'll be okay."

Bullets struck the water around them.

Being cold just fell way down on her list of concerns. The current shoved them downstream at a rapid pace. Bianca paddled her feet to help Ryder keep them close to the bank. He had on boots that had to feel like two concrete blocks once the water filled them up.

They battled to stay afloat in the current until they were swept under the interstate overpass, then Ryder tugged her to his right. She hit her knee against a hard surface and yelped.

He fought the current, dragging them, finally, to the bank a quarter of a mile downstream. He shoved her up out of the water and climbed out behind her, chugging air with labored breaths. She couldn't talk for trying to breathe, then her teeth started chattering.

He pulled off his boots and poured the water out then put them back on. Stripping off his leather jacket, he wrapped it around her.

"You'll get hyp ... pothermia," she protested.

"I'll be warm once I start moving." He stood and pulled her to her feet. "Can you walk?"

She nodded rather than try to talk without her vibrating teeth biting her tongue.

He hugged her to him, then started walking her away from the river. "The lights through these trees are for an apartment complex."

When they reached the backside of a two-story apartment building, he moved her over between two large bushes where her back would be protected by the wall. "I want you to squat down and stay here while I go back and see if I can get to the car."

"*No!*" She grabbed his shirt.

"*Shh.* Keep your voice down," he told her softly.

She did, but still argued, "You'll get shot."

"Give me more credit than that, Sweetheart."

Okay, he *was* former Special Forces, but that didn't make him bulletproof. "Can't we go to the office for this place and call someone?"

"Who would we call? We don't know who at VDE or in my family is behind this. If we call the FBI or Slye, this mission is over." He was quiet then said, "Maybe we *should* call your people."

Was he serious? "No. I'm not giving up."

"I don't want you hurt."

"Murdock won't let you stay at VDE without me."

"I know, but you'd be safe if we called this off now."

Ryder was willing to abandon his chance at finding proof he hadn't killed Kearn just to keep her out of danger? Her heart squeezed at the idea of him not ending up free from all this, and then the crazy organ turned into a gooey mush when he said things like that. "Then give *me* some credit for being able to deal with the risk." She put her fingertips on his lips. "I trust you to keep us both safe. Go get the car and I'll wait."

He kissed the fingers at his lips. "Promise me you won't move until I come back."

She hunkered down. "Promise me you'll come for me."

"Always." Then he disappeared into the woods.

CHAPTER 41

RYDER TOOK OFF his boots and left them next to a tree he could locate when he returned to the apartment complex, then worked his way back upstream along the bank. His feet were freezing on the cool October ground after the dunk in river water.

What he wouldn't give for a night vision monocular right now. And a weapon. Those shots had all been closest to Bianca. Someone might be trying to kill her, but he doubted it. The shots were suppressed, which meant the shooter was likely no amateur. His hunch was they were trying to scare her.

Pushing low growing brush aside, he forced his mind to stay on the threat and not how much he wanted to mangle the bastard trying to hurt her. When he passed beneath the interstate overpass, he waited a couple of minutes, listening and watching.

Nothing. He wove his way up the access road until he could enter the woods that bordered the dirt road to the river. It didn't take long until he reached the parking area. He could see it under the sliver of a moon now that the clouds had cleared.

There was his Mustang. No broken windows. No slit tires.

A motion-activated bomb?

His gut said that was too overt. It didn't fit the pattern for this threat.

He slipped silently through the night until he could crawl up close to the car. Pulling out his keys, he used the tiny LED light to check the undercarriage. No sign of being tampered with or anything attached.

He'd left the windows down, which allowed him to reach in and flip a switch on his dash that killed the interior lights even with the door open. He'd made that modification when he dated girls who stayed out past curfew. When he dropped them off, they wanted to sneak out of the car without any lights coming on.

He eased the door open and slid in, then cranked the engine, threw it into gear and peeled out, slinging a dirt wake behind him.

No shots hit his car or came through the open windows.

That reinforced the sick feeling that he could no longer ignore. Bianca was clearly the target, and he couldn't keep her safe. Not here.

After making sure no one followed him, he returned to the apartment complex, parked, and sat there a moment to watch for any movement. When nothing stirred around the buildings, he got out and opened his trunk to find a backup flashlight. There was a leather tool bag the size of a small tote that didn't belong to him even though it was worn and dirty as if used for a long time.

He checked for wires, then opened the bag carefully and looked at the tools for a few seconds before it dawned on him the bag was not as large on the inside as it looked on the outside. Pulling out all the tools, he felt the bottom give in a squishy way. His fingers ran around the seams until he found a velcroed edge he pulled apart.

Five thousand in cash and a K-bar knife.

Had to be a gift from Sabrina. Her people had very likely inserted past VDE's security to do this today. The money hadn't been left as incentive to run, but to give Ryder backup when they had to keep their distance.

Sabrina's team was taking risks for him.

Ryder's team.

The level of belief that everyone at Slye held in his innocence grew more humbling every day they stood in the gap for him.

As quickly as Ryder wondered why they hadn't left him a handgun, he dismissed that thought. Sabrina had sent him a weapon that left no powder residue, no ballistic evidence, and could be wiped clean. The woman was a scary operative he never wanted to cross. She was as tough as they came and a striking woman.

Bianca was tough in that same way, and easily as beautiful, with a mind just as sharp. She had skills and was solid under pressure, with the same ability to put a puzzle together at lightning speed. But there was one significant difference.

Bianca was not as deadly as Sabrina.

But Bianca didn't need to be so long as she was with Ryder.

He searched the car for any tracking device on the exterior since he'd had it out of the garage over the last two days. The only true way to check for a tracker was with an electronic scanner, but he didn't have one available, and bottom line, he wouldn't remove it if he found it.

He wanted the bastard to follow them.

He hurried around the building to find Bianca.

Who was not where he'd left her.

Add frustrating to tough and beautiful.

Ryder turned, searching the area where security lights barely reached. He started for the woods and had just reached the first tree when he heard someone stepping on twigs and fallen leaves.

Head down, watching where she stepped, Bianca strolled almost right up to him before she stopped and caught herself mid-shriek. "How do you do that?" she asked as if accusing him of something unfair.

"Do what?"

"Just appear without making a sound?"

"You weren't paying attention."

"Yes, I was." But the guilty note in her voice said otherwise.

"And you wouldn't have had to be watching out if you'd stayed where I left you."

"For your information," she said, taking a threatening step toward him, hands going to her hips. "I barely avoided being seen by a security guy walking around. The minute he left, some lady came outside to walk her dog, who would've nailed me no matter how still I was. I hightailed it to the woods, but I've been walking back and forth to stay warm."

Now he felt even worse for leaving her wet and cold, but he hadn't had a choice. He reached for each side of his jacket that swallowed her and tugged her to him, feeling the tension in his chest ease the minute she snuggled up against him.

She was safe. That was all that mattered.

She shook with a hard chill.

He kissed the top of her head and snaked his arms around her back, giving her his heat. "I warmed the car on the way here. Let's get you out of this air and into some dry clothes."

She nodded and turned toward the parking lot with his arm around her shoulders. Bianca noted, "At least at this time in the morning, no one at the house will see us walk in looking like drowned rats."

"They aren't going to see us anyhow."

She pulled away and turned to face him, a frown marring her smooth forehead. "What are you talking about?"

He had one chance of selling this to her and if he said they were leaving because he needed somewhere he could keep her safe, she'd balk.

"Bianca, someone is taking shots at you. It might be the shooter who killed Kearn, and I can see him wanting to retaliate against you for getting me out of prison. Or it could be that someone in VDE sees you as a threat to their illegal weapons deals. I want to go somewhere that we can see him coming. I can't defend us here with no way to set a trap."

She thought on that for a bit then said, "So you want me to play bait to draw him in?"

"Not in a million years." Ryder was sure the person who'd drawn a bead on Bianca would follow. One on one, Ryder could stop the threat. "I didn't find a tracking device on the car but I'm betting there is one. You're already a target. I want to lead him somewhere that we have an advantage over the threat. I'll use your phone to leave a message for Hubrecht that we've got a lead on his leak that we need to check out."

"What if *he's* the perp and putting us up to finding the leak is just his way to test me to see if I really can get into his files and to see if you're on his team or not? He might see our leaving like this as a threat."

"We'll know once I get my hands on the shooter, but until then Hubrecht would be foolish to move against us without finding out what we know." Ryder still couldn't reconcile the idea of the staunch patriot that he'd known growing up as

Hubrecht Van Dyke with the idea of that same man supplying arms to terrorists, but he wasn't ruling out anything with so many possibilities.

"True. At this point, it could be anyone and based on what happened tonight at the office, I'm thinking Janeen and Sam Long might be working together. I'm not ruling out Kale either since he has access to everything."

He'd considered that after the encounter tonight. "I don't care who it is right now. If our leaving rattles the person we're looking for, then maybe when we disappear, they'll panic and make a mistake. I'll be ready for whoever comes for us."

At the car, Bianca stopped him with a hand on his chest. "If we leave Atlanta, Murdock will send someone after us. He'll think you're kidnapping me."

"Not if you convince him otherwise."

"Are you on crack? What am I supposed to tell him? That we decided to go on a honeymoon after all?"

Ryder backed her up against his car. He put a hand on the hood and leaned in, his lips an inch from hers when he said, "You said you needed time to go through everything you've found. We'll go somewhere no one can interfere."

Her eyes went to his lips. She swallowed and breathed faster. "Yes, but I, uh, don't know if he'll go for that."

Ryder couldn't help himself. He kissed her just to taste her again, but one taste didn't satisfy him. Never would. When he ended the kiss, he added, "In that case, tell him we do need some honeymoon time. *I'm* all for it."

CHAPTER 42

"RYDER AND BIANCA have left."

"You mean the city?" Munk scowled into the phone receiver and thought up a choice way to kill his client as he rode back down the elevator, he'd just ridden up from the hotel parking garage. He should be knocking down a shot of smooth whiskey right now, not heading out to fix his client's screwups.

"Yes, the city."

Did Ryder think he could escape? Munk should have taken the shot when he had it and to hell with this client. "I just spent the night traipsing around the woods, taking *missed* shots. That's fucking bullshit and not what I do."

"Ryder left a message that he'll be back by Monday. Some bunk about needing a couple of days together, but I don't believe it. I'm sure he's running to keep her safe, which is perfect if you can find him before Sunday."

What was going down on Sunday? Munk's extra sense, the one that kept him alive, was telling him this operation was falling apart and that he shouldn't be anywhere near his client when Sunday rolled around.

Munk said, "Give me the word and neither one of them will be a problem." He'd do the woman first while Ryder watched. He owed his old buddy a special treat.

"No!" his client snapped. "Ryder has to be alive on Sunday. That's non-negotiable."

"What about wifey?"

"I'd thought for sure she'd break by now and show her hand," his client went on. "She can't really be in love with Ryder, which leaves some arrangement either between the two of them or between her and someone else. I'm not ruling out that she's still with the FBI either. Her and Ryder's jaunt out of town may play in our favor."

"Just know that this changes everything," Munk warned. "I can't be expected to control the outcome of accidents when there's no time for thorough planning. One, or both of them, might end up severely hurt."

"Fine, but just don't kill Ryder until I say so. With Ryder and Bianca out of the public eye, this will be a perfect time to grab her and find out the truth behind this scam marriage. I need to know if she's still with the FBI. If Ryder really believes she got him out of jail, then he'll be so busy keeping an eye on her he'll eventually make a mistake. First, you'll have to find them."

Glad to have his hands untied, Munk grinned. "Looks like you owe me a bonus since I have a tracking unit attached to Ryder's car."

"With his background, he'll find it."

"Not this one. It's concealed in a false lug nut."

"How'd you do that?"

Munk tossed his duffle bag into the sport utility he'd rented. "You pay me to make these things happen. Not give tutorials."

"True," his client conceded. "Get your hands on Bianca as fast as you can and let me know when you're ready to move, because I want to talk to her myself. You can do what you want once I get the answers I'm after, but make sure she can't talk to anyone once you're done with her. Bianca will provide one more criminal charge against Ryder."

"Why would that matter when it sounds like you've got something way worse planned for Sunday than a simple kidnapping and murder to pin on Ryder?"

"Millions will hate him for orchestrating the Sunday attack. But there are those who will not easily accept that the Ryder they knew could do that. However, everyone can hate a man who brutalizes and kills a new wife who sacrificed all for his freedom. If Bianca *is* working undercover for the FBI, they'll never admit it and will do whatever it takes to make him pay for harming one of theirs. And if by some chance Ryder escapes after Sunday, the FBI will turn all its resources loose on him."

In that case, Munk should bill the FBI for services rendered when he dumped Ryder's body in a visible area of Atlanta, because Ryder would not slip through Munk's hands.

"Just remember that final payment is based upon satisfactory performance."

Regardless of how all this played out, payment *would* still be rendered. If not, Munk's client wouldn't like the way he collected bad debts.

CHAPTER 43

SUNRISE THREATENED IN the eastern sky as Ryder carried bags from the Wal-Mart in Suwannee to his Mustang. The only time to shop in a supercenter on a Saturday morning was before daylight.

Bianca listened to her iPod through the new headphones he'd gotten her. She'd finally admitted the iPod was customized for short-distance transmissions.

He asked, "Hear anything from Nanci yet?"

"No." Bianca let out a heavy sigh. "I have to get in touch with Murdock before we leave town."

"Based on what you told me about your last contact with Nanci, she'll find you while we're on the way." Dragging that out of Bianca had been tough. Ryder could appreciate that she'd been told not to share anything with him, but Murdock hadn't known that Ryder could be trusted. Bianca understood the folly in withholding vital information when they had a killer on their trail.

Maybe he was reading too much into her being quiet when it could be nothing more than exhaustion.

"But if Nanci doesn't make contact with me, Murdock will send a team to intercept us somewhere."

Ryder argued, "He wants evidence of the weapons deal too much to do that without checking first to see if the op is still moving forward."

Bianca glanced away when he mentioned the evidence. That raised a flag of concern again.

She buried whatever thought had brought on her moment of hesitation. "But we're already at the outer limits of what could be considered northeast Atlanta. I should've heard from Nanci by now."

"We won't become suspect until we head north of Suwanee. Murdock will think we're up here to visit the VDE production facility."

"I hope you're right, because our game is over the minute the FBI show up." Hazel eyes loaded with concern met his. "Everything may change once I tell them I suspect a threat on Sunday."

"Not until someone figures out who or what is in jeopardy. We don't even know the time zone yet to pin it down to a country. If Murdock was smart, he'd bring in Sabrina's team to help find the target."

"He won't."

"Then Murdock had better hope his people find it if you and I don't."

"My team can't know anything yet, but Murdock will alert Homeland Security. That will put more resources on this."

Ryder loaded the bags into the trunk, keeping his eyes on everything in the parking lot. "That brings up another thought I had."

"What?"

He opened her door, waiting as she sank into the seat. "Can you download agency files on the case against me?"

She didn't answer, didn't even look up at him, just stared straight at the windshield.

Ryder had been hoping for a shot at those files all week, but she was reluctant, and he had an idea why. She had to be stressing over constantly graying the lines between helping him and upholding her oath as an FBI agent. "I might see something in the files no one else would notice, but if you're not—"

"Sure, I can get my hands on the files." She raised her hand when he started to say more. "I believe in your innocence and once we find the truth, I'll have all I need to deal with Murdock."

Where had this woman been all his life?

He leaned down and kissed her. A gentle kiss to tell her how much she meant to him when he couldn't say the words yet. Not until he was free. "Thank you."

She nodded.

Once he had them rolling, he ran through a fast-food place for breakfast-on-the-go and Bianca had just finished her breakfast burrito when she put her hand on one of her earphones. "Nanci?"

Ryder kept his eyes on the road, trying his best not to appear troubled, but he didn't feel nearly as confident as he'd sounded when he'd told Bianca that Murdock wouldn't snatch Ryder out of a knee-jerk reaction. Truth was that Ryder had no idea how Murdock would react, especially if Bianca didn't convince her boss to allow Ryder to leave the city.

Bianca's face fell as she listened. "Tell Murdock to give me a chance to explain first.

Nope, that didn't sound optimistic at all.

Ryder eyed the road for any vehicles approaching at high speed and cut his gaze to the dark sky for an incoming helicopter.

Murdock would send everyone if he thought Ryder was running.

CHAPTER 44

"MURDOCK IS MOBILIZING a team to come after Ryder," Nanci said, sending cold fear washing over Bianca's exhaustion. "What's going on or can you talk?"

Bianca saw her future and Ryder's freedom crashing into a brick wall if Murdock thought Ryder was forcing her to leave town. She tossed a quick glance at Ryder's hooded expression and pressed the secret transmit button on her electronic device and told Nanci, "No. I'm traveling voluntarily. We're on to a lead and it's big."

"What lead and does this mean that Ryder knows you're talking to me?"

Bianca took another step out on the limb supporting her career. "Yes, Ryder knows I'm talking to you, but things have changed drastically, and I can't work with my hands tied. Tell Murdock that I believe there's a terrorist attack planned for Sunday."

Nothing came back from Nanci's end.

Bianca looked at her device, but there was no way to tell if she had a signal or not, so she was relieved when Nanci spoke again.

"Where and when is this attack?"

"I only have the when. It's O-one-hundred on Sunday, but I don't have a time zone to know what country the threat will be in so I'm thinking we start with the US."

"Okay, what do you want me to tell Murdock about what you're doing today?"

"I've copied files I need to go through with Ryder, but we can't do it around the VDE offices or at his family's home without the risk of someone catching us. Ask Murdock to give us today and tonight. If we figure out who or what is the target for Sunday, I'll call Murdock immediately, but I could use another set of eyes on this. Since we can't let the research department in on what we're doing, I'll give you the password for the vault that has all the files."

As soon as Bianca repeated the password, Nanci said. "Got it. I can be home in an hour where I can work on my computer if Murdock doesn't have different plans for me. Where are you headed?"

Bianca didn't want to admit she had no clue and went with what Ryder had told her. "A cabin in the Rabun Gap area."

"The transmitter in your iPod is not very powerful, because of the size needed to hide it. Murdock has a unit like mine, but if you're more than a few hundred yards away, no one will be able to hear you."

"Hold on." Bianca turned to Ryder. "How close can the agency people get to the cabin without tipping someone off?"

"Anything closer than a mile is careless. Further away is better."

Oh boy. She told Nanci what Ryder had said.

Nanci came back with, "I'll inform Murdock. He won't be happy, but we can't risk blowing your covers by getting too close."

"He's got to trust me and give me room to do my job."

"Agreed."

"Besides, we'll be safer than we were in Atlanta where Kearn's people might get to us again." Bianca watched for a sign from Ryder that she'd used a solid argument, but he wouldn't look at her.

"That's another thing, Bianca. Murdock doesn't believe Kearn's boys were behind the kidnapping."

"What do you mean?"

"Murdock has had someone inside Kearn Industries since J. K. was killed. The FBI plant was looking for evidence to convict Ryder."

Oh, God, please tell me they don't have more evidence against him. "And?"

"The agent on the inside has done better than expected. She's gotten close to one of the brothers and found out that J. K. *acquired* VDE weapons plans."

Bianca's did not let on that she already knew this, but it was hard to hide her gut clench over the FBI *now* also knowing. She put on her agent face, hoping it would show in her voice, to show an interest in this new information. "Acquired how?"

"Our FBI plant believes Kearn had someone steal the plans that VDE has in development for a smaller ground-to-air missile launcher a month before he was killed. That only improves the case against Ryder."

Bianca agreed, but only as a matter of logic. Her heart would never accept that he did it. "Anything else?"

"Murdock is sure Kearn's people didn't kidnap you two."

"How can he be so sure?"

"Because the agent inside Kearn Industries told him the Kearn brothers got into a big argument this week when the oldest one suggested catching Ryder and taking him somewhere they could get answers. The two younger ones convinced him that Ryder was too dangerous to tangle with and that they would not let up on the FBI until someone was brought to justice. The older brother finally conceded it was a stupid idea and our agent has been screening all communications at Kearn Industries. She found nothing about a kidnapping."

"Then who could it have been?" Bianca knew she didn't want that answer, but that drive inside her to find the truth demanded she be willing to consider all information.

"Murdock is convinced that the Slye team kidnapped you so they could get to Ryder with information, money, maybe a weapon. That's why Murdock is going apeshit right now."

Bianca recalled the money Ryder produced when they bought two buggies full of things at Wal-Mart. She'd taken the list to get food, clothes, and other basic things while he said he was going in search of materials to set up a security perimeter around the cabin. She'd looked through Ryder's buggy for a weapon even though he'd have needed a background check for one, but all he had were several rolls of wire and other hardware.

Where had the money come from? She'd assumed wealthy people kept cash around and Ryder had gotten his hands on some of it. The FBI had given him the twenty-five dollars all prisoners received. Bianca *had* figured that Slye gave Ryder the hundred-dollar bill that he'd pulled out of his shoe when they needed a cab, but Ryder's bank accounts had been frozen by the government so the cash he was carrying around could have come from Slye.

Bianca had a thousand dollars the agency had given her, but when she'd offered her credit card or cash, Ryder had said he had money from his father.

His father or Sabrina Slye? Bianca asked Nanci, "Is that the only reason Murdock thinks that?"

"No. He had someone keeping tabs on Sabrina's people, because Murdock doesn't trust them not to help Ryder in some way. He said Sabrina and five of her people couldn't be found during the time you were kidnapped. He asked Sabrina later and she told him she had a business to run and was not subject to his scrutiny. If he wanted her help, say so. Otherwise, not to waste her time."

Had Ryder's team kidnapped her? The breakfast Bianca had eaten threatened to come up. If that was the case and Ryder had kept that from Bianca, then he'd been playing her this whole time. The ramifications of that turned her in her stomach.

How much of what he'd said and done was an act?

Was that why he'd been intimate with her? To gain unquestioned trust? It had worked.

She had to finish up with Nanci. "I hear you. Please tell Murdock that I've got this. We've finally gotten a break. Give me the time I need to find answers."

"If no one shows up in the next ten minutes, take it as his approval to move ahead."

Bianca left one earplug in so she could monitor the iPod for a little longer.

Ryder kept checking his rearview mirror and the side mirrors. "She's dropping back."

"You know which car is hers?"

"Yes."

Because he was trained far better for these kinds of operations than she was.

Ryder turned to her, questions bombing his gaze, but he only asked, "Are we clear?"

"We'll know in ten minutes."

While she waited through a tense silence of what felt like the longest ten minutes of her life, Bianca considered the best way to find out the truth about her kidnapping. Asking him would be a mistake.

He'd deny it. Then where could she go from there?

Ryder threaded his car through light traffic as the interstate ended and they continued through heavily wooded country with rolling hills that reminded her of home.

Fifteen minutes had passed. She drew a breath of courage and watched Ryder carefully when she told him, "I know Kearn's boys had nothing to do with kidnapping us. I know who did."

He was dead still. The way she imagined he could be for hours and days while waiting to make a sniper shot.

When he didn't say anything, she decided to go for broke. "Why didn't you tell me your Slye team kidnapped us? Why did they do that? Why did *you* do that? To terrify me?"

"No." Muscles in his throat flexed and his fingers gripped the steering wheel. "I would never scare you unnecessarily."

But he hadn't denied her accusation. "But you would go along with it."

"Bianca, it's not what you think."

Oh, God. Murdock was right. Bianca didn't give into the hurt welling up inside her. "Really, because I think I'm pretty clear on this. You made a fool of me with my agency. With my boss. You let me believe I was in danger."

"You *are* in danger."

"Oh, yes, that's right." She snapped her fingers to emphasize what a ruse this had become. The joke had been on her. She'd given her heart to another man who'd stomped on it. "Someone is trying to kill me."

"Yes," he said with a fierce growl. "Which is why I need you somewhere I can keep you safe."

"*Oh, cut the crap, Ryder!* This has all been a scam to convince me I can trust you." She was fighting hard to sound mad and hide her pain. She would *not* break down in tears. How could he do this to her? "I'm supposed to believe that someone's hunting *me*. But they haven't managed it yet, have they? How strange that someone who supposedly killed a British diplomat *and* J. K. Kearn can't seem to hit one woman. Lot of near misses. Was all that necessary to gain my trust?"

He turned shocked eyes to her. "You think all these attempts on your life are *my* team? You dropped *eight* floors in an elevator." His voice was getting louder with each word. "Do you really believe I would allow *anyone* to harm you?"

"I don't know what to believe after finding out you lied to me about the kidnapping."

The lost look on his face would have been funny if not for the sick punch to her stomach. This changed everything she'd believed about Ryder. Her heart still protested that he was innocent of the Kearn killing, and the diplomat's death. But how could she trust him after he'd played on her fears that way?

His attention was back on the road ahead of him. He raked his fingers through his hair. "Let's just get this out in the open. Are you going to sit there and tell me you've been straight with me about all the things you've been doing? That you've held nothing back? Because I'll tell you right now, I know that's not true. I knew about your iPod the first day, and I know you haven't been honest with me about this case."

Busted.

He swallowed hard. "I'm sorry about the kidnapping, Bianca."

"But you're not sorry about lying to me."

"Yes, I am. I didn't plan to, and I didn't want to. But I owe Sabrina and the team for supporting me when nobody else did. Murdock—and you—were looking at me with blinders on. Nobody in your agency was going to do anything they thought would help me, whether I was innocent or not. I was a means to an end for you. Slye did that so they could ... talk to me."

He'd just held back information again by not telling her what information they had shared. He clearly didn't want to tell her.

She hadn't told him about Murdock being behind the cyberattack on VDE's computer systems, but she was a federal agent. This was her job. She could understand his loyalty to

DIANNA LOVE

his Slye team, especially Sabrina, but holding that back meant Ryder didn't trust her.

Holding out on him about the cyberattack meant she didn't trust him either. That might even things out between them, but it was lose-lose for at the same time.

What had made her think there was a future for two people with so much mistrust between them?

She didn't know and needed some time to think this through, but heartache or no heartache, they had to stop a terrorist attack first. She managed to keep her voice from cracking. "I will keep my end of this and comb through the files to find anything I can. And I'll let you look through the evidence gathered against you."

"Thank you." His words came out low and with a dose of disappointment that only added to the ache in her heart.

He was disappointed. Well, so was she.

Understatement of the century. Yes, she'd kept things from him, but the one thing she hadn't done was sleep with him out of some ulterior motive. He'd used that kidnapping to win her trust. It wasn't a stretch to grasp that he'd sleep with her for the same reason.

That's what high-level field operatives did, right?

So *not* what she was or would ever be.

Bottom line? No matter which way she worked it around in her mind, she'd never be able to look at what they'd done together in the same way. Never be able to kiss him or make love with him without wondering if he was doing it to get her help.

Some trust lost just could not be regained.

Her heart cracked into two pieces as the hard reality hit her. Nothing they'd shared had been real.

She swallowed hard and added, "When this is done, regardless of the outcome, I don't want to ever hear from you again."

"Wait a minute—"

"No, you listen to me." She gripped the dash when she turned to face him. "I thought I could trust you."

"You can trust me," he said quietly. "Just as much as I can trust you."

Fair was fair since she hadn't been totally honest either. But she'd believed he really wanted her, but now ...

"I thought—" She choked on the words. She'd thought he was different, like no other man she'd ever known and once they found the truth that he'd want what she did.

To have more than a few nights together.

"Say it." He reached for her hand and wrapped it in his. "Just tell me what you want, Sweetheart."

That endearment had meant so much and now it just hurt like hell to hear it. She pulled her hand away, fighting back tears she would not shed in front of him. "Nothing. I just want to finish this job."

He looked away, but not before she saw agony that reminded her of the first time she'd seen him in prison.

That knocked the last of the wind out of her sails.

The silence that followed for the next thirty minutes practically suffocated her. She tapped her fingers against the door handle, missing their easy camaraderie of the past days. Not enough to be willing to let go of the hurt that was choking her, but she couldn't spend another minute in this car with him.

She wanted to cheer when she saw a sign for a convenience store and gas stop ahead. "Pull into that gas station."

Ryder looked at her, surprised. "What?"

"Gas station. Please pull in."

Ryder wheeled into the empty, pot-holed lot past two gas pumps and parked to the side of a single-story wooden building with a screen door and a faded sign indicating they were at the *Stop & Get It*.

When Ryder killed the engine, Bianca held out her hand palm up in an understood request for the keys.

He blinked at her. "Do you really think I'd leave you out here alone?"

"No, but then I'm not a good judge of people these days. I didn't think you'd play me for a fool, either," she said, swallowing the pain.

Ryder's mouth flattened into a hard line, and a muscle in his jaw twitched, but his eyes pleaded with her. For what? Forgiveness? Understanding for his position maybe?

On a logical level, she did understand his being loyal to Slye, but forgiveness? She had taken one for the team to do this mission, and she *had* shared things with him in defiance of Murdock's orders. Not everything, but still…

Ryder was looking to the wrong person for absolution.

She kept her hand out, patiently waiting.

Ryder pulled the keys from the ignition and placed them on her hand then leaned back, arms folded.

She was stuck half in and half out of the car, drinking in his profile. He'd catered to any need she'd had for the time they'd spent together. They still had hours ahead of them to spend going through files. She was dying inside, but she could do polite.

"Do you want anything?"

He lifted his head and leveled her with the same hungry look that had crashed through her walls last night and this morning. "They can't sell me the one thing I want."

Don't even think about taking that bait. "Okay, be right back." She dug money from her purse and shoved the cash into her pants pocket. Why carry her purse?

Ryder had been accused of murder, not theft.

An insane rationalization, but he'd done that to her. Turned her into a crazy woman, because all she wanted to do was climb across the console into his arms.

Bianca yanked the screen door open, rusty springs creaking. Rows of canned goods and household products lined one crowded shelf after another to her right. Country music on a low volume drifted from behind the counter along with a whiff of cigarette smoke.

She picked up a bottle of water, meandered around for another minute until she had a grip on her emotions, then strolled to the cashier who rang up her purchase and wished Bianca a nice day.

Too late for that.

Outside, Ryder leaned against the front fender of the car with a cell phone at his ear.

Her cell phone, dammit.

Who was he talking to? Sabrina Slye or someone else on that team? Bianca would let him talk, then the minute she saw

Murdock, she was handing her phone over as proof that Sabrina did not keep her end of the deal.

Murdock could have at her.

When Bianca got close, she heard Ryder say, "That works for me."

He stepped over to open her door.

Bianca stood there, waiting for him to end the call and return her phone, but Ryder just kept talking with an easy nature and strolled back around to the driver's side. He kept opening his mouth as if he was trying to get off the phone then he'd quirk a smile.

"I've never done that, but I'm willing if you don't mind taking on a rookie," Ryder said, settling behind the steering wheel.

A rookie? At what? Bianca looked at his face. He seemed genuinely happy. What could make him so upbeat in the middle of the mess they were in? Maybe he was shading the truth in some way with her back around.

Ryder extended his hand palm up.

Bianca lifted the keys from her pocket before dropping into the passenger seat. She was handing the keys to Ryder when he said, "Fried chicken and pole beans would be wonderful."

Bianca froze. "*Who* are you talking to?"

Ryder held up a finger on his other hand while he nodded then covered the phone and whispered, "Your mama. She's asking me—"

Bianca grabbed his wrist and wrenched it to her then ripped the phone from his hand, struggling to calm herself before speaking. "Mama?"

"Hey, Baby. What happened to Ryder? I need to know what else he likes to eat for Sunday dinner. Your daddy is goin' to take him fishin'. Can you believe your husband's never fished? Daddy got a big laugh out of that, wants to know when Ryder's goin' to be here."

Oh, no, no, no. How could Bianca's life continue to deteriorate before her very eyes? "Mama, I'm coming to visit in a week or two, okay? We'll work everything out then."

"That's fine. Just call me before you head up so I can bake a peach cobbler. Did you know nobody's ever made Ryder a peach cobbler? And he loves peaches, but you probably know that."

Tears stung her eyes until she realized how much worse this would be once Bianca had to tell her parents the truth about their *son-in-law*. Bianca blinked away the threat of tears. "No, I didn't know that, Mama. I'll call you soon, but I really have to go."

"Okay, baby. Tell Ryder goodbye and we can't wait to meet him."

"Bye, Mama. Give Daddy my love."

Bianca punched the off button. Her heart beat hard in her chest. She'd eventually have to face her parents as a disgraced daughter, because they wouldn't understand why she'd had to marry him or why she had to be divorced. But that was her cross to bear. Ryder, the FBI and the world could do anything they wanted to her, but not to her parents.

How could Ryder promise to visit and make this even worse for her to face her parents?

She turned on him, raising her finger as a pointer to emphasize each word in a soft voice that shook with anger. "Don't you *ever* speak to my parents again. Don't you realize what they think?"

"We were just having a conversation," he said, his tone quiet.

"Jerking me around is one thing, but do *not* screw with my family." Didn't he understand how hard it was going to be to face her parents after this? She'd envisioned taking him home to introduce to them in person. Now she'd have to explain how she'd lied to them *and* married a man for the sake of this mission. She'd never forgive herself for their hurt.

"I wasn't screwing with them. Your mother's a nice person and I enjoy talking to her."

"*Nice?*" Her voice rose. "My parents are *exceptional* people. They are loving and loyal. And they believe everything you tell them. I can't help it if you have a poster family for dysfunctional relationships, but I do not."

She drew a breath, her hands fisted. "When this is over with they'll be hurt. It's going to be bad enough for me to tell them that I will technically be divorced, because they don't believe in divorce. But when they find out you aren't really my husband

and you didn't really mean what you said, they're going to be crushed. They think you are their son-in-law and they already care about you, dammit."

Ryder wisely remained silent, because she wasn't done. Not by a long shot.

"Not for you, for the FBI or even for my country will I allow you to hurt my parents any more than I already have by doing all this. Have you got that?" Her voice shook with emotion she couldn't hide. "Why did you even answer the phone?"

"Because you said your father had a heart condition and I didn't want you to miss a call if it was about him."

The truth in his face sucker punched her.

Great. Now she could add guilt over that.

She clenched her hands into fists and released them, trying to gain control. She was coming apart at the seams. Unable to process the emotions flying through her, she clamped her mouth shut and turned to stare out the window.

CHAPTER 45

RYDER MANEUVERED HIS Mustang carefully over the rutted dirt and gravel road to Larry's cabin, a growing sense of dread curling in his chest. He downshifted a gear when the incline changed and hoped no trees had fallen over the road during the time Larry had been away.

Bianca hadn't said a word for the last forty minutes. She'd never forgive him. Had he really thought his future would include her? Dreams belonged to other men.

There was no place for dreams in the bleak future of a man with a murder rap hanging over his head.

When the car finally broke through the dense foliage into a clearing, the log cabin was just as he remembered it except for a few improvements. The roof had been replaced and land around the cabin had been mostly cleared so the encroaching woods and underbrush were seventy yards away, which was a positive for seeing someone approach.

He parked right in front of the cabin nestled among a few big old pine trees and oaks in the center of the cleared area. "Wait for me to—"

Bianca jumped out of the car faster than if he'd hit an eject button rigged for her seat. She walked away, arms crossed and angry as a pissed off hornet.

Ryder slapped the steering wheel and scowled. What an unbelievable mess. One he wouldn't be able to straighten out until she cooled down, if then.

She was right.

He'd broken her trust, unintentionally, but the damage was done. But he needed for her to understand that protecting his team by not divulging the truth behind their covert action did not mean he'd lied to Bianca about anything else he'd said or done with her.

He hadn't used her.

Everything about the intimacy they'd shared was real. What he felt for her was real. Wanting her was as real as it got.

That had nothing to do with sex, though being inside her had been like visiting another universe for the first time.

He wanted all of Bianca, the entire package, right down to her family.

Allowing Bianca's mother to believe he was her son-in-law might have been wrong, but he couldn't help it and in truth, he hadn't wanted to.

Her mother wanted to know what he liked to eat. The joy in her voice had been intoxicating, warmed his heart. Her motherly interest had touched him in places he'd thought were dead. Places that had never been given life. Both of Bianca's parents were sincerely excited to meet their new son-in-law.

He'd wanted to be that son-in-law and to be part of a family where someone actually looked forward to his visit and planned a meal just for him.

No one had ever done that for him before.

How could he explain to Bianca what that felt like when she'd had it her whole life?

Bianca's father had been just as enthusiastic, yelling in the background that he was taking Ryder fishing. Her father had his buddy making a new pole just for his son-in-law.

A lump lodged in Ryder's throat.

He'd never been special to any family.

No one had ever given a damn about him, but Bianca's parents did. They'd already welcomed him into their hearts.

And for the first time in his life, he wanted to belong to a family like that and to be that person her parents couldn't wait to meet.

But he wasn't that person. He was the man who had wounded their daughter.

Ryder made his way to the porch and stepped up next to her, expecting another volley of anger thrown at him. He deserved that, but it didn't happen.

He swallowed against the misery in Bianca's face and the regret in her gaze. Seeing that regret was worse than any injury he'd suffered in prison.

He lifted a hand to brush the tears from her cheek.

She drew back and he died a little when she cringed away from his touch. He'd made mistakes in his life, but none he'd ever pay for more than hurting Bianca. Guilt and disappointment knifed through his gut.

"Don't." She shook her head.

"I'm sorry, Bianca. I would *never* intentionally hurt you or your parents. I agree. They are exceptional people who deserve a son-in-law much better than me."

She stared at him, confusion scrambling through her face for a fleeting moment before she swiped the tears away. "Are you sure Larry will be okay with this?"

"Positive. Give me a minute to hunt up the extra key. It's going to be in one of a couple of places."

She nodded, her expression still closed down.

Ryder surveyed the house for an alarm system. None, but that was no surprise considering it was too remote for any responder to reach quickly even with an immediate call to the police. He walked around the back and searched until he found a thorny bush surrounded by poison ivy. Ryder used his boot heel to knock the dirt loose around the base of the plants and hit a hard chunk in the ground.

The lockbox with a key was right where he'd guessed. Larry had once told him that was the only way to hide a key.

When Ryder came back around, Bianca was at the rear of the car and had the trunk open.

He unlocked the front door to the cabin and walked out just as Bianca struggled to lift a pile of bags.

He took all of them out of her hands.

She scowled. "I can carry bags."

He gave her a withering look and walked away, depositing the bags on the saddle-brown leather couch in an open great room that spilled into the kitchen.

She started setting up the laptop he'd bought.

Ryder took in the room. "If Larry upgraded this place so he

can telecommute, there has to be some internet access, but it's not going to be hardwired because there's no landline."

Without looking up, she said, "Maybe he has a satellite connection here or in his car."

Ryder could stand here being invisible as Bianca withdrew before his eyes or go search for Larry's internet access. Losing her and what they'd shared was killing him. He turned toward the stairs, figuring Larry had an office on the second floor somewhere.

What was he going to do about Bianca?

Ryder had wanted a rookie agent without the hard edge of someone who'd been in the field a long time. An inexperienced woman so it would play in his favor. Someone who could be a convincing new bride.

She'd turned out to be so much more.

He forced the ball of remorse back down into his chest.

Bianca was off-the-charts brilliant, resilient and so full of heart she'd found a way into his. Until meeting her, his only desire had been freedom, but now he realized the truth. Freedom would be nothing without her.

On the other hand, if he didn't regain his freedom, this distance between them might be for the best.

For her.

He coiled his fingers, wanting to pound something. He'd gone for months without speaking more than five words to anyone in prison. His soul was withering from an hour of her silence.

Bianca needed space to be angry, but for her sake they had to find some mutual ground for completing this mission. Until she became a target, he'd never given a second thought to leaving if it came down to no other choice.

But now he had to put her safety above all else.

If he left, would that end the threat to her?

He had to know for sure that she'd be safe before he vanished. There was still a chance the real killer would be found, but Ryder had to plan for the reality of that not happening for a very long time. Maybe never.

He found Larry's office and, just as Bianca had suggested, Larry had high-speed satellite internet. He headed downstairs determined to thaw her chilly disposition. One kiss would do it, but one kiss would lead to a hundred more because he wouldn't be able to keep his hands off her.

At the bottom of the stairs, he paused.

The great room was empty. Her laptop sat open on the coffee table. Everything was too quiet.

Ryder raced around the corner and looked in the kitchen.

Empty. His heart shifted into overdrive.

"Bianca!" Ryder crossed the kitchen and slung the back door open. "*Biaannca!*"

"What?"

He heard her loud snap but could see nothing except a forest of trees surrounding the cabin and a tin outbuilding. She stepped from behind the building with an armful of wood.

Damn. Couldn't the woman stay out of trouble for ten minutes? "What are you doing out here alone?"

"Don't get in a tizzy, Ryder." She strolled up to the small porch.

"Give me that." He took the wood from her. "If you want anything else out here, I'll get it." He carried the wood inside and dumped it in a black wrought iron holder that sat next to the stacked-rock fireplace.

She dusted her hands. "I grew up in the country. This is the real me. I'm accustomed to taking care of myself."

The finality of her words struck home.

She didn't need him or his help.

Not once the threat hanging over her was gone. For a short time, she'd believed that she did, and he'd reveled in being the man she turned to. It didn't matter. He wouldn't lower his guard until he knew she was no longer a target. "I don't care. While you're here with me, *don't* go outside alone."

"Don't start issuing orders." She crossed her arms and stepped forward. "You got away with it when I thought we were both after the same thing."

"Dammit, Bianca, this isn't about who's in control and we *are* after the same thing. But I don't want you hurt."

"Really?" she said dryly, one beautiful eyebrow lifted. Strands of loose hair dangled around her ears. A rose blush colored her cheeks. "Little late for that."

Go ahead. Twist that knife another turn. His insides were already destroyed.

He scrubbed his face, feeling the burr of a beard shadow under his fingers. "We need to talk."

"No. We just need to do our jobs. Or at least, I need to do mine." She walked past him to the kitchen where she started futzing with the coffeemaker.

He called over to her. "I'm going to set up a perimeter. Stay in the house." No response from the kitchen, so he added, "Please."

For that he got a hand wave dismissing him.

She kept throwing one wall up after another. He'd let her build all she wanted for now, but by the end of the day he would invade her emotional fortress.

They weren't parting ways until they'd gotten a couple of things straight. First, he had to get her to understand what she meant to him. Everything else after that was unimportant.

But he couldn't broach that subject until he found something in Bianca's files that would prove his innocence.

CHAPTER 46

BIANCA OPENED YET another file, ignoring the blanket of doom that had settled over the great room.

Not that Ryder had given her any indication that he was giving up, just the contrary. He'd been reading through pages of information Bianca had printed. Larry's office rivaled a small business setup.

But she'd found nothing in the VDE files she'd been reviewing for the past five hours, and Ryder hadn't said a word.

Not one word.

Of course, she'd told him in a huff earlier that she didn't want him to talk to her ever again, so maybe he took it to heart and decided to give her what she wanted right now.

So why was she complaining, even if it was only to herself? This way, Ryder couldn't purge his conscience and somehow turn this rift around as her fault.

Bernard's first default had been to blame anyone but himself, which generally meant dumping on her. Just like Bernard had made her believe any perceived shortcomings in the bedroom had been her fault.

That had been before Ryder, who knew how a man should treat a woman, especially in bed.

Then how can you continue to compare Ryder to Bernard?

She couldn't. They weren't in the same league, not even the same hemisphere.

Granted, Bianca may have Ryder to thank for solving a ginormous personal problem, but he'd created a bigger one.

Now that she'd been with him, she didn't want another man.

She tapped the key that scrolled the document back to the beginning since she had no idea what she'd read of the last three pages. What good did it do to find out she was capable of a full emotional and physical relationship with a man just to realize she only wanted it with the wrong one?

The one who had stepped between her and danger.

The one her parents couldn't wait to meet.

The one who made her insides melt with a look.

When she'd accepted this op, Bianca had considered the physical risks, but not emotional ones. If she'd kept her defenses in place, she wouldn't be nursing a broken heart right now.

Too bad. Her heart would have to wait on mending until she found the terrorist's target.

She read back over the last two pages and paused to study an email reminding her of the one that had noted a Sunday threat, but still nothing identified who the K signature referenced.

"I'll be damned," Ryder muttered from the kitchen.

Bianca twisted around to find him pushing a drawer in and out. "This thing was stuck the first time I tried it, but it healed itself. Working fine now."

"It didn't heal itself. I fixed it."

He sent her an arch look. "*You* did? Why?"

"It wasn't hard. Just needed a slide adjustment. Larry probably hasn't had time to spend on the small stuff, because the coffee pot wasn't working either. It had a short in the cord. Took ten minutes to fix. I figured it would be a good way to say thank you."

Ryder studied her but didn't give voice to the question behind those silver eyes. "Looks like Larry furnished this place with secondhand stuff, which seems odd. He must be making good money at VDE."

"Not that odd. The table and chairs look refinished. Larry might like working with his hands. It's not always about money. When you refinish a piece of furniture or repair something that's been tossed aside, you put a part of yourself in it. I found a stash of tools in the laundry room."

Ryder had that look again, like he was trying to figure something out. He closed the drawer and leaned a hip on the counter. "Do you like doing that? Refinishing furniture?"

"Furniture, appliances, toys."

"Why? Do you sell them?"

"No. I just can't stand to see something of value thrown away because someone wasn't willing to put a little love and effort into giving it a second chance." She didn't want to talk about her hobby or about the families around where she'd grown up, who needed so much more than she could provide in the few hours she now had to devote to the charity she and Sara Lynn had started so long ago. Leaning back, she stretched and groaned.

The sound of his footsteps coming toward her sent her heartbeat into a crazy rhythm.

He sat down near her. Not next to her, but close enough she could reach out and touch him. But she kept her hands to herself, where they belonged, and asked, "What'd you find?"

"That the evidence against me is pretty convincing."

She hadn't thought she could feel any worse, but it hurt to hear the resignation in his voice. He'd broken her heart, but he deserved his freedom and so much more for what he'd endured. "We're not done, Ryder. I have more files to go through. We'll find the truth."

"The truth is that I couldn't have made that shot, but it doesn't matter at this point."

Hearing him sound so defeated was almost as bad as the thought of his going back to prison. She sat her laptop on the coffee table and leaned back. Would he finally tell her why he'd left the Army? "Let me be the judge of whether it matters. Why couldn't you have made that shot ... other than the moral reason?"

He stared into the fire he'd built, quiet for so long she wondered if he'd really tell her. He said, "I'm not capable of hitting a live target with a rifle anymore."

He'd said that the first time she'd met him in the prison, but could he really have lost *that* ability?

"Did you change your mind about your role in the military, Ryder?"

He understood Bianca's confusion. He'd faced even harder questions when he'd decided to take an early out. Leaning back on the sofa, he searched for the words. "No, it's not like that. I'll never stop believing in what I did—what we do—as soldiers. Our military protects all of us, and the world, from vermin."

"I agree and I believe you. What happened?"

He hadn't discussed his last military op with anyone after leaving the Army. His life as a sniper encouraged few friendships. He'd pushed people away for so long it was automatic.

So why not shut this down?

Because Bianca was sincere. She'd had a poker face when they first met in the prison, but she hadn't been able to hide her emotions from him after their first kiss. He heard the honest interest in her voice. She cared.

That she still had the power to care moved him.

She'd been brave enough to let herself be vulnerable with him last night. If he ever hoped to earn back her trust, he had to be willing to take the same risk. Trust her with what he hadn't been able to share with anyone else.

"On my last mission, my spotter and I spent days following the target, a terrorist who'd captured nine US soldiers that he brutally tortured for weeks, then killed. Our intel showed his organization was growing and his bombs were getting more sophisticated. It was a matter of cutting the head off the snake. The target kept himself surrounded by children. We finally got a clear shot. The second my spotter said 'send it' I touched the trigger."

Black dots flashed in his vision at the memory of what happened next. He took a couple of breaths as Bianca waited silently.

"A child, maybe four years old, came out of nowhere and jumped up in the target's lap at the same second I squeezed the trigger. The bullet barely missed his head below that scumbag's eyes. A millisecond kept me from killing that little boy. Now every time I look through a scope, I see that kid." *And I still see him every time I close my eyes.*

"Oh, Ryder." Bianca's hand was on the one he'd dropped onto the sofa between them. She laced her fingers through his and just when he thought his heart had shut down, it started beating again.

"I was of no use to the SF team after that, couldn't pull the trigger. I opted out at the next opportunity." He sat there, letting her simple touch comfort him. Looking over at her, he found her eyes bright with unshed tears. "Even if that was of any use as a defense, which it's not, I never told my CO or anyone else the real reason I was leaving."

"We aren't done looking."

He'd always love her eternal optimism, but there were no new cards to play. "I've been through everything you printed out for me and it only convinced me that I won't beat this charge without a confession by the killer."

"That's why we have to prove someone else killed the diplomat."

She was all hope and heart. He couldn't stand another minute of not touching her and lifted a finger to her cheek. Would she back away again?

She didn't back away, but her eyes were still wary with unresolved conflict. She said, "We have to keep searching."

He dropped his hand and nodded. "What have you found?"

"I downloaded so much the other night, I just now got to some emails similar to the ones noting Sunday, which we're assuming is an attack. I found more cryptic references to an upcoming event, but nothing that helps. Nanci is going through this, too, but I haven't seen any message posted in the vault from her."

"Why didn't you use the vault for communication while you were in VDE instead of taking the risk of running on the streets to talk by using your iPod?"

"Because downloading to a vault carries risks. I hadn't intended to use a vault until we ran into Janeen yesterday and my gut told me that was our lead and I needed to secure the intel. Once I downloaded everything last night, I spent just as much time triple wiping the hard drive so I didn't leave a trail from VDE to the vault. Even with all that, there's a risk that someone might find it if Hubrecht has people with serious electronic forensic expertise."

She pulled the computer back to her lap and started typing again.

He slid over closer, causing her to pause briefly. When she didn't protest, he looked over her shoulder.

She explained as she typed. "I ran through all the travel records of the top tier executives, including Sam's, for Kearn's killing. Sam was on the West Coast and he had no communication with Kearn. Your brother and Hubrecht were the only two who talked to J. K. Kearn prior to the shooting."

"What would Hubrecht's motive be for having Kearn killed if Kearn Industries really was in trouble six months ago?" Ryder wondered out loud.

Bianca's fingers stopped typing.

She knew something she wasn't sharing. He'd kept the truth from her about the Slye team kidnapping, so how could he expect her to share something she was probably shielding for the FBI? He couldn't.

His silence must have weighed heavier on her than his words, because she heaved a long sigh and said, "J. K. Kearn did steal weapons plans from VDE. It happened a month before he was killed."

Well, fuck, that just put a cherry on the government's case against him. "Have you known this all along?"

She shook her head slowly. "Found out when Nanci called."

He believed her and sensed there was more, but he wouldn't ask for what she couldn't give.

Bianca looked down at her hands that were folded in front of her laptop. When she lifted her head, he saw resolve and regret in her gaze. She said, "I haven't been entirely honest with you either. The FBI was behind the cyberattack at VDE. That morning I went running, I made contact with Nanci through my iPod unit. Murdock wanted me inside VDE by 5:00 PM that day and he had a plan to help me gain Hubrecht's trust. I didn't know what it was when I walked into your office. I promise."

Ryder's jaw clenched. "I'd like to wring Murdock's neck for putting you in a volatile situation that could have gone bad, with no backup from your agency." More than that, he felt hope gather in his chest over her admission. "But thanks."

"For what? Taking you to task for being loyal to your people when I had to do the same?"

"You found out about the kidnapping from Nanci instead of me. I wanted to tell you, but I couldn't. I'm sorry for that."

She swallowed and nodded. "Okay."

His hope faded when Bianca started typing again, but what had he expected? That she'd just forget she'd been terrorized for no reason?

She paused to read, then pulled her fingers back. "That's odd."

"What?"

"I've been comparing the financial information from the flash drive on those three international arms dealers with the orders VDE actually shipped. This one in Dubai makes no sense. The Dubai broker paid more money to VDE at times over the past two years than they received in inventory."

"How much more?"

She looked at him with excitement that came from a breakthrough. "From one to two hundred thousand dollars more in some months. They're paying for invisible inventory ... or invisible weapons. This has got to be it. The lead we need to prove VDE is selling to terrorists or to someone who is brokering to terrorists."

"Who handled those shipments?"

She didn't hesitate. "They all originated in Terrence's office, at midnight or later. The additional payments are going to an offshore account."

Ryder felt kicked in the nuts. "While I was busting ass to protect this country, my own family was aiding the enemy. Janeen and maybe Sam, too."

Bianca nodded. "But none of this includes you. If we can tie this up, then Sam being in Colorado at the same time as the diplomat throws a whole new light on that killing."

"But not Kearn's."

"True, but the FBI is convinced that whoever shot the diplomat is the same one who killed Kearn. Ballistics matched."

Ryder should be glad to find a tiny hope at clearing his name, but he'd never wish prison on anyone. He tried to imagine Janeen there and it sickened him that she might've thrown her life away.

"Let me load this into the vault and ..." Bianca leaned closer to her laptop, eyes scanning quickly.

"What's up?"

"Nanci has gone through all those emails that I just got back to, and she found a bank account referenced. She also said she found a time zone for the attack referenced. She has to run everything past Murdock first, but for me to keep checking."

Bianca turned to him, a smile lighting her eyes. "I hope this is the break we've been looking for. Once Murdock looks at all this new evidence, I believe the focus of our investigation is going to shift to Sam Long. His position at VDE allowed him the means and power to make these deals. He authorized Janeen to covertly handle shipments from Terrence's computer. His visit to Colorado is suspicious and he might have been retaliating against Kearn for stealing the weapon design."

"Why set me up?"

"Because as much as you refuse to accept it, Ryder, I think Hubrecht really wants you back in VDE and that would have threatened Sam. You would have noticed his dirty deals eventually." Her optimism was infectious when she said, "There's enough here to make Murdock look again at your case. He's a good man who's committed to what he does."

Ryder reached for her hand, the one with his ring on it. He'd told Sabrina and Murdock to not share that the ring had been his mother's, because he hadn't trusted Bianca not to use that somehow as leverage against him. When this was over, he would tell her how the ring and his Mustang had been his two most cherished possessions.

That was until he'd found Bianca.

Now he wanted her love more than anything. But he was afraid to tempt fate and say anything until they had hard evidence.

She leaned toward him and that was all the encouragement he needed. He cupped her head and brought her lips to his, kissing her with everything he felt inside. Could he really believe that this nightmare might be over?

Her hands were on his chest, sliding up to circle his neck.

Had she forgiven him? He had no way to fix this beyond saying again, "I never wanted to hurt you."

She paused and looked at him with her heart in her eyes. "I know. I'm sorry for thinking you did."

That was all the forgiveness he needed. He kissed her with the depth of everything in his soul.

He held her head and kissed her forehead, her cheek, her eyes, then smothered her lips again with his, sliding his tongue in to meld with hers.

Kissing her again was like coming home.

He moved the laptop to the coffee table and hooked his hands around her waist, lifting her over to straddle his lap.

She ran her hands through his hair and pulled him closer. When she leaned in and brushed her chest against his, he took the hint and slid his hands beneath her T-shirt, up to cover the soft mounds filling her lacy bra. She gave a lusty sigh. Shoving the T-shirt up higher, he popped the front clasp on her bra and dipped his head to taste paradise with his tongue.

Her pretty pink nipples budded, and she arched into him.

She moved her hips, rubbing his erection. He grabbed her hips. "This is not going to take long if you keep that up, Sweetheart."

"This would be a good time for that lunch quickie you promised me because we have until the computer dings. I set it to let me know when Nanci downloads into the vault."

"In that case ..." He peeled her warm-up pants down and slipped his hand inside, going straight for the center of her. He touched the damp folds, sliding his finger through her heat until he went for the spot that would take her over the top.

She made that sound that drove him crazy. "Please, Ryder, now!"

He sucked on her breast and licked the tight little bud. She quivered on the edge until he pushed a finger inside her, slow at first then faster in sync with her breathing.

Her orgasm was beauty in motion.

He'd never wanted her more.

She fell to his chest, clutching his shoulders. He held her to him, thankful to have her back in his arms. Now if he could just keep her there.

She mumbled, "You. Now."

"The condoms are upstairs. We'll get to me soon."

The computer dinged.

She sat up, staring at him. "Everything from my waist down is shot, but fingers can type."

"I doubt that you're shot from the waist down." He fondled her breast and she moaned.

"I'm so freakin' addicted to you."

He chuckled, determined to keep her hooked.

"Help me climb off of you or Nanci will wonder what happened if I don't get right back to her."

She tugged her top back into place, and he helped her pull her pants up, then lifted her over to sit beside him again.

She told him, "I'm showering as soon as this is done."

He'd be right there with her. He hadn't wanted to lead her on with thinking they could have more if he was either locked away the rest of his life or on the run, but once she finished processing everything with Nanci, Ryder could tell Bianca how much she meant to him.

That he'd fallen in love with a woman who turned him inside out with a smile.

Bianca shook her hair out of her eyes and grabbed the laptop, hitting keys the minute it landed in her lap. "Nanci says she found a reference to the time zone in another email as CET." She frowned. "What's in that time zone?"

"From France to Germany and Sweden to Italy."

"How are we going to find the attack target in all that?" She scrolled and kept reading. "Nanci said the account given in the emails signed by K for the transfer of payment on the Sunday attack is the same offshore account the Dubai arms dealer transferred the additional funds to each month."

Ryder felt hope build in his chest.

Someone in his family had betrayed him in the worst way, possibly with the help of Sam Long. Ryder compartmentalized those emotions to keep his focus on giving Bianca and Nanci any aid they needed.

"And," Bianca went on. "Nanci found out what K stood for. It's ... oh, my God, no."

"What's wrong?"

Her face lost color.

"Bianca, what is it?"

"Nanci found an email that is older than the others. It listed the K as Komodo."

If he had any doubts about being set up by a family member, that crushed them. The FBI would still be after someone at VDE, but this could be construed as connecting Ryder to the illegal weapon sales.

He just realized that Bianca's reaction didn't make sense. "Did you know that was my nickname when I was a kid?"

"Yes." She said that as if the word had been squeezed from her lungs. "Terrence mentioned it when we had lunch."

That still didn't explain why she was so upset, unless ... "Does Murdock know it was my nickname?"

She swallowed. "Not ... yet. But there's more."

His blood ran cold at the way she said that. "What else?"

"The email with the Komodo signature was sent a week before Kearn was killed and stated specifics plus assurances that Sunday would be accomplished no matter what because the Komodo had people in place across the world. That email was sent from the server for what we have as your personal email address."

Reality hit Ryder square in the chest.

Not only could he not prove his innocence, but he was also going to be charged with treason against the United States.

Bianca's eyes shone with tears she fought to hold back and everything she felt for him was written across her face. "This isn't the end, Ryder. I love—"

He stood up and stepped away. "That's it then. This mission is over." He couldn't let her say she loved him no matter how much he wanted to hear those words roll off her lips. What he had to do was bad enough. He was willing to live with the pain of losing her and knowing she'd hate him for the rest of her life as long as she was safe.

And free to love again.

The idea of another man touching her turned Ryder's heart black, but he owed it to Bianca to cut any tie and give her a chance at happiness. She deserved better than being in love with a man whose life expectancy was dwindling by the minute.

But he would find who robbed him of a chance with Bianca and, when he did, Ryder would exact payment tenfold.

She stood and reached for him. "Ryder?"

He backed away, hands up. "Whoa, we both knew my chances of ending up free were slim. You're amazing and the sex was incredible, but this thing between us has nowhere to go. I'd kill for one more time in the sack with you, but I don't want your people walking in here and catching me with my hands on you. Murdock would have them toss me in the Hole. Getting laid isn't worth that."

Agony ripped through his chest at the devastation in her face. He'd just reduced what they'd had to cheap thrills.

He couldn't do this to her.

He *had* to do this for her.

Her lips moved with silent words until she sputtered, "You can't mean that."

"Look, Bianca, don't make too much out of our time together. It was off-the-charts hot and you're a sport for all that you did, but—"

"A sport?" she said in a shuddering breath. "That's all I was to you? Bed sport?"

His chest was so tight he wasn't sure he could draw enough breath to speak, but he shrugged. "Don't get offended, babe. I don't mean to make light of all this, but I'm not cut out for picket fences even if I was free. You're hot as a firecracker and sexy as hell and ..." He rubbed his chin in thought, pausing to give his next line just the right timing. "You know what? We might have time for one more quickie."

"Screw you!" Her eyes bulged with tears.

Please don't cry, Sweetheart, or I'll cut my own heart out and give it to you to stomp on. The damned thing belonged to her anyhow. He pulled the blank mask into place that had gotten him through five months in the pen. But he wouldn't be able to keep this up for long if Bianca broke down.

Now he had to ask her for a favor on top of all that.

He softened his voice to get this one boon from her. "I'm sorry if you misunderstood my intentions. I really didn't mean to make you feel bad."

Her jaw trembled then hardened with the words trapped inside.

He hoped she was disgusted enough with him that she'd want a few minutes alone. "Think I could talk you into letting me take one last private shower before you call in the troops?"

Squaring her shoulders, she gritted out, "You have ten minutes."

A life together had never been in the cards for them. He'd been crazy to even entertain the idea, but she'd come to mean more to him than life. For that reason, he couldn't leave her crying her heart out for a wanted man on the run.

He wouldn't have much of a lead since he had to stay until Murdock's people showed so Bianca would be protected. Now that Ryder realized he'd been set up for far more than a murder, he understood why someone had been targeting Bianca.

They knew Ryder would take her out of the threat zone.

If he went back to Atlanta with Bianca, she would be at risk again, but if he disappeared it played into the hands of whoever was pulling the strings to frame him.

That still didn't ease his guilt over hurting her.

He was every bit the bastard he saw reflected in her eyes, meaning this charade was working.

Now a stronger and wiser woman who knew to expect more from a man as her partner, Bianca would survive this and have a real husband one day.

That pissed Ryder off when he had no right to be pissed.

Her eyes turned into angry slits. *That's right, Sweetheart.* She had it straight in her mind now. He was the son-of-a-bitch she was itching to call him.

Heading for the stairs, he turned his back on the best thing to ever touch his life.

CHAPTER 47

BIANCA WAITED UNTIL Ryder's footsteps on the stairs faded before she folded in half and landed on the sofa. She dropped her face in her hands, fighting the sobs that were crawling up her throat.

A volcanic heartbreak waiting to erupt.

Not yet. Not here.

She would finish this mission and send her report, just as soon as she could stop the shaking that had started in her legs.

Don't make too much out of our time together?

Just drive a stake through her heart. That's what it would take to make her stop loving Ryder in spite of everything he'd said. How could she still care for a man who *admitted* he'd only pretended to care for her?

She'd made yet another mistake—a huge one.

Her original plan after Bernard had been to dive into work at the agency and swear off of men since her father was the only honorable man she knew.

Time to go back to her original plan.

But she wanted answers before she left here. Bianca sent a message to Nanci that she would be in contact soon about picking up her and Ryder, but to wait on her call to send anyone. She made it sound as though Ryder trusted her and that Bianca was close to gaining more intel, that she wanted to squeeze as much as she could from him while things were relaxed between them.

What a whopper.

Almost as big a whopper as her marriage.

Trust your instincts, Baby Girl.

Daddy's words whispered through her, warming her insides,

and filling her with the confidence that came from knowing she was loved, no matter what. The kind of open and unconditional love Ryder had never known.

What were her instincts telling her?

He's an honorable man.

Why would an honorable man treat her so callously? The Ryder she knew wouldn't do that unless ... he was trying to protect her.

Ryder wouldn't want her waiting for him if he had to go back to prison forever.

But he'd sounded so convincing just now.

He'd sounded convincing when he'd told her he'd never wanted a woman the way he wanted her.

She closed the laptop. Bianca's head pounded with the beginning of a blinding headache that she couldn't afford to have right now. She walked into the kitchen to dig out some aspirin from one of the Wal-Mart bags on the counter.

Trust your instincts.

Hers were telling her that Ryder was as honorable as she believed, and that he did care about her. More importantly, he deserved her love.

She felt a peace settle over her that did more for her headache than any aspirin. She was going to go upstairs and tell him that no matter how hard he tried he would never be able to push her away. That she loved him, and he had one person willing to fight for him and his freedom until her last breath.

A tiny noise caught her attention. It struck her as out of place.

The hair on her arms stood up.

She lifted her head to listen for whatever had put her on alert. Ryder wouldn't sneak up on her and he'd told her the little bell he'd placed just inside the door would ding constantly if someone entered the area he'd secured.

Was there really someone after her?

Or were they really after Ryder?

She tiptoed over to the door that opened onto the back porch and squinted to see if anything moved in the woods.

Nothing. She took a step back and bumped against a body. A hairy arm whipped around her neck, locking her against him.

Kicking her feet, she sucked in air to scream his hold tightened to cut off her air.

A deep male voice whispered, just a breath away from her ear. "Careful. Someone wants to talk to you, but I can kill you any time if you cause a problem. Make a sound and I'll snap your neck or stay quiet, and you live a little longer. Your choice."

CHAPTER 48

BLOOD ROARED THROUGH Ryder's ears and pounded in his veins. His chest hurt so much he was sure it was because his heart had exploded into a thousand pieces.

He hurried to dig out the K-bar knife from where he'd tucked it inside the small duffle he'd brought up.

Janeen and Sam had done this.

She'd even put Terrence at risk by using his computer. That's what shocked Ryder most of all. Janeen had been fiercely protective of Terrence for his entire life.

Why had she done this?

How had Ryder not realized his sister was a psychopath? How had he missed that kind of pure evil during all the years he'd lived with her? Had it been Lady Anne's influence? Or had Sam corrupted Janeen? Turned her into someone who sympathized with terrorists?

It couldn't be about money. Janeen had more than she could spend.

She resented not being asked to join VDE. Was she doing this to get back at Hubrecht?

Then why screw Ryder?

What did I ever do so wrong to Janeen to deserve this?

He would never forgive Janeen for a lot of things, but the most criminal was what he'd been forced to do to Bianca downstairs. As bad as prison had been, watching Bianca's misery was worse.

She loved him.

That was gone. Everything that mattered to him was lost.

He stowed the K-bar knife in his boot in case the FBI showed too soon and he had to drop the duffle and run. He carried his and Bianca's bags back downstairs and paused at the last step. His blood chilled at the silence.

Had Bianca gone outside again, after he'd told her not to?

Dropping everything at the base of the stairs, he called, "Bianca?" He spared a glance at the fireplace. Still plenty of wood stacked to the side.

He stepped around the corner. No one was in the kitchen.

A bottle of aspirin sat open on the counter.

Her short boots were still sitting by the end of the sofa and her jacket hung on a hook by the door.

There was no way his common-sense country girl would have left the house barefoot and without a jacket in October.

Heart pounding, Ryder ran over to the door and slipped outside. He hurried to check the multiple wires he'd run around the cabin that should have triggered a bell inside the house to ding when it was tripped.

The wire had been cut in the only spot that would disarm the entire perimeter.

His mind started processing the odds of someone locating the one point necessary to disarm his system without having tripped any detector.

In that moment, everything gelled. The shootings. Motive and means. His time in Special Forces, and the contracts he'd executed for the CIA. The other snipers he knew. The timing. The ballistics. His heart hammered in his chest.

All that time he'd spent in the Hole, all those hours spent considering who would have the skills to frame him, and *still* he'd never put it together until this—until his perimeter was breached.

Any man who'd been with him on black ops missions would know Ryder's preferences for securing a perimeter—specifically how he would've secured *this* one.

But Ryder had met only one man during active duty who would know that, plus be able to make the shot that killed Kearn—and who would do it for money.

Munk.

Munk would have made the hit on Kearn for no money. He would've done it just to frame Ryder, because Ryder had cost

Munk a contract with the military when he figured out that Munk *enjoyed* killing.

Way too much.

That animal had Bianca.

CHAPTER 49

BIANCA PANTED, STEPPING high quickly to keep from being dragged over a log. She had on thick socks, but it was little protection against sharp sticks and rocks.

Who was this guy?

His iron-hard fingers were locked around her right arm, hauling her along with no regard for the forest undergrowth clawing at her.

Panic threatened at the edge of her mind. She would beat it back by getting information. "What's this—"

He dug in his boot and wheeled on her. He snarled, "One warning is all I usually give. This will make two, a record for me." The fast-paced hike had not winded him at all. Tall, bulky, but very strong, he had a long-barreled, bolt-action rifle slung across his chest she had no doubt he could handle with lightning speed if she tried to break away.

The struggle to stay upright while being dragged across the rugged terrain sucked the wind out of her rising hysteria.

Think! If Ryder was in this fix, what would he do?

He wouldn't be in this fix.

He'd have known before this man got close and disarmed him. Okay, that opportunity was long gone.

Ryder had said she was the one in danger. *I should have believed him.*

She came up with nothing useful as the guy yanked, pushed, and threatened her for a half mile before they finally stepped out of the trees to a view of sloping hills that spread out before her.

A black sport utility was parked nearby. But sitting prim and out of its element on the rough, grass-covered ground was a crimson-red Jaguar.

Terrence?

Not Janeen?

Terrence leaned against the car, arms crossed, casually waiting. Upon their approach, he stepped forward, meeting them halfway to the car, a smarmy smile in place.

"So, you're behind all this," she charged. Her kidnapper's grip tightened. She winced.

"Let up, Munk," Terrence ordered. "We don't want her damaged ... yet."

Munk released her.

Bianca rubbed feeling back into her wrist and threw a scathing look at her captor until he rotated his thick head. The dead-flat eyes of a sociopath stared back at her.

If she hadn't taken his warnings to heart before, she did now.

Keep them talking. Buy time.

She angled her gaze from a face that nightmares were made of to one she'd love to knock the smile off of. "What are you going to do, Terrence?"

Ryder would find her.

Promise me you'll come for me.

Always.

Whether or not he really did care about her, Ryder was a man of his word. He would come for her.

"I assumed this marriage had to be trumped up, but I couldn't figure out if you were just a geek that Ryder seduced or if you were an FBI plant."

She glowered at him.

"Setting Ryder free threw a kink into my plans until I realized I had a new opportunity, which only got better when it was clear he actually cares for you."

Bianca laughed, hoping it had a disheartened sound to discourage Terrence. "Boy, did you get that one wrong."

"I'm not as easily duped as my father, so save your effort."

"Are you and Hubrecht in this together?"

"Be serious. My father is so clean he squeaks." Terrence's eyes flicked up and around as though he waited to see someone else. "But Ryder has never made a true commitment to any woman, which means he *should* be on the run by now. If he is, he owes me for giving him a head start."

Nausea rose in her throat. Ryder running?

He might if he thought that was the way to bring in the FBI.

The FBI wouldn't be coming to save her until Ryder's chip moved far enough away from the cabin to become suspect.

After that message Bianca had left for Nanci, they might think she was taking a walk with him, but Ryder didn't know about that message.

She couldn't imagine how anyone could disarm the chip inserted that close to Ryder's spine—or cut it out—without seriously injuring Ryder, but she knew without a doubt that if Ryder decided to escape, he'd have that part figured out.

Which meant the FBI would be busy chasing him with no idea where Bianca was.

No. She refused to believe Ryder would do that with her in danger. Whatever troubles were between them, he'd earned her trust, and she wouldn't take it back now. But she hoped he'd call in the FBI and wouldn't play the hero since he had no weapon to use against Munk and Terrence.

As terrified as she was right now, she had a deeper fear. If Ryder came for her, he'd be killed. And if Munk killed her, she'd never get a chance to prove Ryder's innocence.

Terrence chuckled. "Did you really not consider that he would run? The FBI can't keep a leash on someone like Ryder. Not a man who was in Special Forces." He turned to Munk. "Right? You worked with those guys. You know what they can do."

Munk said nothing, just stood by looking scary.

Terrence was screwing with her. He had to be. If he really believed Ryder would use this opportunity to escape, wouldn't Terrence and Munk be hunting for Ryder?

Then again, she had no idea what went on inside Terrence's screwed-up mind.

Bianca held out little hope of being found, but she'd keep Terrence talking to buy as much time as she could. "Why are you doing all of this?"

"You're the one who has to answer questions, not me."

"Come on, Terrence. I know you aren't going to let me live."

That sounded far more confident than the petrified woman inside her who wanted to scream for help. "Putting this together took genius. Satisfy my researcher's curiosity."

He shrugged. "We can't leave just yet. What do you want to know?"

Playing to his ego worked. She could use that. "It can't be the money. You have to be worth millions, maybe billions. Or maybe you aren't."

"Oh, I am, and I will take VDE to even greater heights. But defense spending will rise only as long as there are conflicts and events like the one tomorrow. My father is too set in his patriotic ways to understand the need to keep arms in the hands of the opposition if there is to be a demand for weapons on our side. It's simple mathematics."

Dear God. Terrence was behind the attack planned for Sunday. *He* was arming terrorists to generate more demand for weapons for allies. "Why are you dragging Ryder into this?"

"*You* dragged Ryder into this part when you turned him loose."

"I don't understand."

"Ryder being in prison for murder was only one part of his fall from grace, and it was working brilliantly until you screwed it up." His lips twisted with a heinous smile. "But now that he's free *you've* made it even easier for me to show Father just what a loser Ryder is when his golden boy is credited with tomorrow's attack."

Terrence had destroyed Ryder's life just to disgrace him in front of Hubrecht? Bianca's skin chilled at the calm way Terrence spoke of mass murder. She didn't know Hubrecht very well, but her gut told her that he cared for his adopted son. "Your father will never believe that about Ryder."

"Perhaps," Terrence allowed. "Either way, I win. Once Ryder and my dear father are gone, all of VDE will be mine. Then it will become a true family business when I bring in Janeen."

"So, she's in on this?"

"Janeen? No, unfortunately, she inherited my father's values." Terrence nodded at Munk who took a step toward Bianca.

She jerked away, searching for some opportunity to save herself.

Munk was creepy, but Terrence was certifiable.

"Don't make this any more difficult, Bianca," Terrence warned.

Moving faster than she anticipated, Munk snatched her arms and pulled them behind her. She couldn't yank against him unless she wanted to pull her arms out of their sockets. She had nothing to lose, so when Munk started to drag her away, she yelled at Terrence, "You did all this because you're *jealous* of Ryder?"

Fury seared Terrence's gaze. He lifted a hand at Munk.

Munk growled.

Bianca twisted to look over her shoulder. This time, Munk gave Terrence the stink eye.

"Let's get something clear, Bianca," Terrence said. "Ryder is all that *my* father ever cared about, but *I'm* the real son." He pounded his chest. "Ryder was accepted from the first when I should have been number one, but my father hated me. He adopted a bastard and treated him like flesh and blood."

Okay, Terrence had a valid point and family counseling for this bunch might require a building full of psychiatrists, but this?

"Now the world will see my power even if I can't take credit tomorrow," Terrence bragged in a voice devoid of humanity.

"I doubt that." She had to push him to find out the target, but even if she did, then what? She had no mobile phone, and no one knew where she was.

"You doubt me?" Terrence shouted, taking a step forward and backhanding her across her face. "You'll eat those words when scenes from Rome are on every news outlet." His voice changed to a singsong taunt. "Oh, but you won't be alive to see that. Pity."

"Ryder will figure out it's you and come for you."

Terrence leaned in and kept his voice whisper soft, and his eyes blazed with excitement. "Actually, I'm banking on him coming for *you*. When he does, he'll walk into a trap, just like he did when he went to see J. K. Kearn."

CHAPTER 50

RYDER STUDIED THE scene, seething. Munk was a dead man. The bastard had dragged Bianca through the woods to Terrence.

His brother.

How could it be Terrence? And why? Ryder had always defended him. He'd gone into the Army believing it would clear the way for Terrence. When and where had his brother hooked up with Munk?

Doesn't matter. Focus.

Getting Bianca out of here alive was priority one.

Where was the damn FBI? Weren't they tracking his chip? He'd expected them to show up any minute and have to race to keep ahead of being captured before he found Bianca.

Ryder moved with stealth through the low brush, easing closer. Exposing himself wouldn't save her. They'd just kill Bianca before he could reach her. He should've searched for her damn phone before leaving, but the minute he'd realized that Munk had Bianca, Ryder had been in a rush to catch up before Munk hurt her.

Terrence slapped her.

Ryder lunged forward, then caught himself and held still. If he rushed out like a madman, Munk would drop him with one shot.

What he wouldn't give for a weapon right now.

He searched around his feet and found a small log three inches in diameter. It could be a weapon, but he had another use for it.

CHAPTER 51

BIANCA LICKED THE coppery taste of blood from her lips and shrugged as much as she could with her hands pulled behind her. She told Terrence, "If you're right about Ryder, then he should be long gone by now."

She hoped so, because more than anything else, she didn't want him dead. But she knew in her gut he was hunting for her at this very minute.

"If not for you, I'd agree," Terrence mused. "Never saw a weakness in him before, but our little terror campaign exposed a side of him that was unexpected. Loving a woman can soften a man's spine."

Loving a woman?

He'd been considerate and protective of her while they were together. He was honorable. She believed that. He cared for her, and he'd probably faked that last little scene to give her an out, but he didn't love her.

If he did, she'd spend her life proving his innocence and waiting for them to have a chance.

Either way, she'd never stop until he was a free man.

She'd gotten over Bernard, but in hindsight she could see how that hadn't been real love. Not in comparison to what she felt for Ryder. When she'd finally realized that Bernard was only in it for what he could get from her, a switch had flipped in her heart.

She'd never be able to just turn off her love for Ryder.

"You done?" Munk asked Terrence. "Time to kill her."

Bianca jammed her foot back against Munk's knee and he cursed but didn't go down. Instead, he punched the side of her head, knocking her sideways.

Terrence shouted something as she hit the ground and stars flew through her vision.

Protected from the line of sight by a cluster of thick bushes, Ryder ran out of options when Munk hit Bianca. Ryder stepped out slowly, carrying the small log. "You want me?"

Munk whipped the rifle around, aiming it at the center of Ryder's chest.

Terrence laughed. "Well, well. Finally joining our party."

Munk grinned. "Good to see you, Van Dyke."

"Sorry, I can't say the same. I should have put this together sooner. You went to the hospital in Switzerland after your failed mission."

"I didn't *fail*, asshole. The unit let me down."

"No, they didn't." Ryder continued moving forward slowly, keeping an eye on Bianca in his peripheral vision. She raised her head slightly and nodded, letting him know she was okay. Thank God. Ryder kept Munk's attention on him by arguing the facts. "You jeopardized the mission. You were told to stand down, but no one realized you'd developed a taste for killing. Your screw up cost a good man."

"Casualty of war. I paid a price, too."

"No. A casualty is unavoidable. Don't even compare the other men to yourself. The Army cut you loose, but they should have hung you. Besides, it looks like the hospital did a good job rebuilding your ear and cheek. Having your ear blown off was your own fault."

"At least I can still make the kill shot. Heard you pussied out after your last target." Munk grinned. "Got that out of your spotter. Bet you thought he'd never tell your secret. Took some incentive. He only told me ... right before I killed him."

Ryder's gut contracted into a sick knot. He'd heard his spotter died in a bombing. No autopsy to determine if his friend—a decorated soldier with two kids at home—had been tortured then murdered.

He couldn't dwell on that now.

"But advantageous for me," Terrence interjected, clearly not happy to be ignored. "Had Munk not been in Switzerland when he was, we would not have met." He sent Ryder a sly smile. "Enough of old-home week."

"Do you really want to end your days like this, Terrence?" Ryder needed to know why Terrence had done this. "Why not enjoy what little life you have left?"

Terrence bellowed with laughter. "That's golden."

Ryder chanced a quick look at Bianca who had pulled her legs up under her. She lifted her gaze, eyes sharp. He hoped she'd be ready to run.

"Save your tears, dear brother. I'm not dying."

"What?" Ryder jerked back to the conversation.

"I went to Switzerland for pain treatments, thanks to the problems I've had since birth because of that bitch who gave you life."

Ryder could see the hate in Terrence he'd not noticed before when his brother had played the weakling. "Have you spent your life blaming my mother for going into labor early? Lady Anne was the one who wrecked the car. If not for that, my mother would have lived, but I never blamed you for that."

"You have no grounds to hold anyone responsible for your life but the slut who bore you."

Ryder couldn't win this argument. His mother had been promiscuous and ended up pregnant, but Lady Anne was in a wheelchair and Terrence had health problems because of the wreck. Not Ryder's mother.

But the point in keeping Terrence talking and Munk focused on Ryder was to give Bianca time to escape.

She'd managed to move a few feet away and was still sliding a little at a time, but there was no close cover other than the trees at his back.

No point in arguing when Terrence didn't want to hear the truth. Ryder said, "You want me. You got me. Let her go."

"I don't want you dead yet," Terrence explained. "As for your new wife, she's become a bonus in my plan. I want you to suffer as I have."

"I get that you have pain, Terrence, but I didn't cause it and you aren't dying." Ryder changed tactics. "Does Lady Anne know about that?"

"Absolutely not. I can't afford to lose Mother's indulgence."

Munk shifted his stance, antsy. "Cut the crap. Let's get this done."

Terrence's face distorted with anger and a vein stood out on his forehead. "I have waited a long time and paid a fortune for this moment. I will not be rushed when I can finally enjoy reaping the reward of years of work. Shut the fuck up."

Ryder held his breath. Munk had killed for far less than that. To break the tension, Ryder asked, "How'd you do it, Terrence? How'd you convince doctors to tell Lady Anne you were dying?"

Terrence morphed into a man all too happy to boast about what he considered his superiority. "Lady Anne made Hubrecht fund the clinic in Switzerland when I told her how amazing they were. The director of the clinic and I had a nice win-win agreement. Their clinic not only treated my condition, but going there afforded me a perfect setting for making deals in my private quarters."

For the first time in months, Ryder took a really good look at Terrence. He didn't look sickly so much as scrawny.

"See, I'm the one who is on the ball, not you, Ryder. I'm the one who orchestrated all of this, right down to arranging for Munk to make your shots."

"Shut up, Terrence," Munk growled.

That's when Ryder took a close look at the bolt-action rifle hanging from the cord attached to Munk's vest. There was his McMillan, stolen the same week he'd been discharged. It still showed bits of the camo paint job he'd applied at his last desert duty station.

When the Army canceled Munk's civilian contract two years ago, based on Ryder's recommendation, Munk went ballistic, threatening payback for Ryder. Terrence must have been orgasmic when he met Munk in Switzerland and stepped in to feed the mercenary sniper's lust for blood and money.

How much blood had those two spilled in all this time?

But did Terrence understand just how deranged Munk was?

Munk swung around to check on Bianca who went perfectly still ten feet away. Ryder prepared to rush Munk if he lifted his weapon, but he just stared at her as if he were trying to decide whether she'd moved or not.

Ryder shouted, "Munk's right, Terrence. You can't control a machine like him."

Munk whipped back around, weapon ready.

Terrence chuckled. "Of course, I can. He's only a hired gun."

Ryder cut another look at Bianca who was sitting upright now. Good girl. She'd slowly moved onto her knees, appeared ready to move. Now would she just do what he wanted for once? He tried his best to warn her with his eyes. She blinked hers in response, as if she were tuned in to his every move.

Munk stood halfway between Bianca and Terrence, so Ryder was the only one who could clearly see everyone in play. But there was no way for him to get through Munk to Bianca. The best he could hope for would be to draw Munk and Terrence into an argument to give Bianca time to run.

"I'd be careful, Terrence," Ryder warned. "I know Munk. He takes orders from no one."

Munk grunted an assent.

Terrence found that hilarious. "Munk will never be a problem to me. I know all his dirty little secrets. Like the job you did in Bangkok, right Munk?" Terrence smiled over at his hitman. "He's *my* killer. He jumps when *I* tell him."

"*Shut up!*"

"Careful, Munk, or you won't get your bonus." Terrence shifted his arrogant gaze to Ryder and tilted his head. "See? Just like a trained monkey."

Munk's eyes churned bright and deadly like the centers of two volcanoes ready to erupt. He swung his rifle at Terrence, who went wide-eyed.

Bianca jumped up and dove at Munk, hitting him in the stomach as the bullet exploded from the rifle and hit Terrence in the gut, knocking him back against his car.

Terrence slumped to the ground.

Ryder rushed Munk and yelled, *"Go, Bianca!"*

But did she listen?

No.

CHAPTER 52

RYDER SHOT STRAIGHT ahead and dove at Munk as he turned on Bianca.

Munk's instincts must have kicked in, because he twisted back in time, toward the greater threat.

Ryder shoved the rifle muzzle upward as he barreled into Munk.

If Bianca hadn't jumped away, they'd have crushed her.

Ryder hammered blows at Munk, trying to get to his weak shoulder, but he must have had a bionic rebuild, because it was like beating on a brick wall.

Munk plowed his meaty fist into Ryder's body, getting in solid hits. Munk kicked his side and he kneed Munk but connected with a groin cup.

Just as Bianca had described the guy who had attacked her on her run.

This bastard would never hurt her again.

Bianca ran over and grabbed Terrence by the lapels of his suit. "Where's the attack going to be on Sunday?"

He tried to smile but it turned into a grimace.

She shoved her hand against the hole in his abdomen and he gasped in pain. "Tell me or it will get much worse. What's your pain tolerance like, Terrence?" She pushed harder, surprised to discover this side of herself. But she had to stop the deaths planned for tomorrow. If someone had gotten to Terrence sooner, Sara Lynn would be alive today. How many men, women and children would die tomorrow if authorities didn't pinpoint the location in time?

She dug her nails in around the wound.

Terrence cried out, "Stop."

She wished Ryder was doing this instead of her. He'd know how to make Terrence talk, but Ryder and Munk still battled.

And based on the blood pooling underneath him, Terrence might not live long.

Ignoring her bloody hand, she threatened, "Ready for more?"

"No." Terrence's voice was thin.

"Who's your contact?"

"You ... will never ... find him."

She shoved her fingers deeper into his abdomen and he cried out "*Noooo!*" but his voice was getting weaker.

"Then tell me *where* the attack will be."

"Rome." He was gasping for air.

"Got that. I want the exact location." She grabbed his collar and shook him. "Where? Who?"

Tears poured from his eyes. "Please. No pain. Please."

She was so disgusted to be doing this. She moved her hand back to his wound.

The minute her fingers touched him, Terrence gasped, "Vatican."

Bianca jerked back, shocked only for a second and yelled, "Who's the target?"

"Pope."

Her hands shook, but she couldn't back off now. "Why kill the pope?"

"Money."

Shit! "Who's your contact, Terrence?"

"Shut up you idiot!" yelled from the fight.

Bianca turned around.

Munk wrenched his rifle free and swung the butt. He caught Ryder on the temple and knocked him back a step, then Munk turned the rifle on Bianca as he worked the bolt action.

Ryder roared and dove at Munk with a knife in his hand.

Munk shot, then used the rifle to block Ryder.

Bianca felt the burn in her side as she was knocked backward into Terrence who grunted, then didn't make a sound.

CHAPTER 53

RYDER STRAINED TO shove the knife into Munk's throat, but it was like fighting a bull with arms. One who hadn't spent five months locked in a cell. They hit the ground, rolling down an incline. Munk had one hand choking Ryder and his other hammering fists at Ryder's head. Ryder blocked but couldn't keep that up forever. Ryder rammed his hand down to shove the blade at Munk's heart, but the bastard twisted his arm forward.

That move sliced the razor-sharp blade across the sling on Munk's shoulder, leaving the rifle behind as they rolled over the edge of a six-foot drop.

In midair, Ryder drove the knife into Munk's side and twisted before they hit hard and fell apart. Face down, Ryder sucked in air. He had to get up. He flipped over, expecting Munk to be on him with the knife.

But Munk was backing away, holding his side.

Adrenaline gushed through Ryder. He shoved up to his feet and took a step toward Munk.

Munk clutched the bloody knife in his hand and called out, "She'll bleed to death if you keep coming for me, but I'm good if you are."

Bianca. Ryder stopped short. He shook with wanting to kill Munk, but Munk had already made it thirty feet away and was right. Bianca was bleeding out the longer he took.

Ryder backed up to the ledge they'd fallen over and spun around, vaulting up on top to grab the rifle. When he turned around on one knee with the rifle at his shoulder, Munk had disappeared over another drop.

Fuck!

Ryder raced to Bianca and tossed the weapon down.

God, no, please.

Blood saturated her shirt where her hand was pressed to her side. He jerked off his jacket then his shirt and wadded up the shirt to staunch the blood flow. Then he wrapped the jacket around her.

Her voice was raw. "Did you get Munk?"

Ryder shook his head. "I want you alive more than I want him dead, tough girl." He could try to drive her out in one of the vehicles, but she needed a helicopter, and the FBI would not be far away. The log he'd carried in was a few feet away. He ran to it and lifted it behind him.

Bianca realized what he was doing and cried, "No, Ryder!"

If the FBI were hanging back for any reason, damaging the chip would bring them running to his last location. He whacked at the chip and gritted his teeth when he hit his spine. He took a breath and swung harder, feeling something burn on the left of his spine. That had to be it.

Ryder saw Munk race up the hill on the other side of the valley, probably taking the straightest route to another source of transportation he had as backup, since the closest tree line was on the right.

Munk knew Ryder couldn't make the kill shot so he wasn't even heading for cover.

In fact, he was probably laughing his butt off as he ran.

Back at Bianca's side, Ryder lifted the rifle and flipped out the legs on the attached bipod.

"Ryder ..." Bianca reached for him, and he leaned down to where she was.

"Shhh. It's okay—"

"You don't have to do this. Murdock will find him."

Ryder realized she was saying she'd give up Munk rather than have Ryder face shooting a live target again. "He'll go underground, Sweetheart. And he'll come back for you. He won't leave a witness alive. I can't go back to prison knowing he can get to you without me here."

He dropped to the ground, prone. He moved quickly, making instinctive judgments that came as natural as breathing. Nine hundred, fifty yards plus across the valley. He dialed the windage and elevation into the scope without even looking at the settings, then pulled the stock tight into his shoulder. Two deep breaths, then he set the crosshairs on his target in the failing light.

His hands shook.

This bastard had tried to kill Bianca, and he *would* come for both of them again.

Not happening.

He clamped down on his mind and tuned out everything except the target he could barely see climbing the grassy hill. In another ten seconds Munk would disappear over the next rise.

He squeezed the rear trigger to set the front one, and adjusted the rifle, holding it over his target by four mil-dots. He set his finger against the edge of the front trigger and felt the nerves in his stomach flare to life.

What will you do to keep the woman you love safe?

Anything.

He gently touched the front trigger.

The report sounded and the familiar recoil punched the stock deeper into the muscle of his shoulder, then ... Munk fell to the ground, grabbing his upper thigh. The femur—and maybe the hip—was likely shattered. Munk rolled back down the hill and behind a tree, out of his line of sight. No kill shot, but if the bullet didn't hit a femoral artery the FBI should be able to capture Munk since he couldn't do more than crawl.

Ryder leapt to his feet and rushed back to Bianca.

He'd seen the eyes of soldiers who'd taken a bullet and were going into shock. But this was Bianca. Ryder's whole body shook as her eyes drifted shut.

"Wake up, Sweetheart. Don't close your eyes," he begged and pressed on his shirt where it covered her wound.

Tears ran down her face.

He kissed her forehead. "I know it hurts, but they'll be here soon."

Shouts surrounded them. Men and women flooded in from the woods, guns drawn.

Whump. Whump. Whump. There was the helicopter Bianca needed. Wind whipped the ground.

ATVs crashed into the clearing.

Ryder didn't move his gaze from Bianca, whose eyes fluttered open then closed again. "Open your eyes, Sweetheart."

"Back away from her," a deadly voice barked from behind Ryder.

"She needs a medic."

Two rifles came into view, one on each side of his head. "Move."

He'd do anything if they'd just take care of her.

Ryder stood slowly with his hands up. He took one step back and was knocked to the ground. Flex cuffs were snapped on his wrists and ankles as medics rushed over to Bianca.

Two men lifted Ryder and carried him away with him yelling at the top of his lungs for them to let him stay until she was stable.

His pleas were lost on Murdock.

CHAPTER 54

CHATTON DRAGGED MUNK a hundred yards to the tree line, and there she dropped his legs. She left his hands flexi-cuffed and propped him in a sitting position against a tree. He shifted his weight onto one hip, clearly trying to take pressure off the gaping wound in his upper thigh.

Munk groaned. "You sure are going to a lot of trouble to kill me."

She pulled out her Italian accent. "Me? I do not want to kill you. I want my money."

"What the fuck are you talking about?"

"You took my hit."

Munk squinted at her, eyes glazed with pain. "You're in the business? Who are you?"

She'd dressed the part in all black leather, including gloves, and carried a suppressed HK UMP submachine gun. The compact weapon with its folded stock was slung across the front of her body and hung inside her open leather jacket. "I do not have time to exchange business cards. You cost me half a million US dollars."

"When?"

"You killed my target. Edward Abbot in Colorado last February. Was *my* job." She thumped her chest. "My people are not happy. They think that sloppy work was mine. Took much trouble to explain."

"Sloppy my ass. That's the way the client ordered the job."

"I do not care. You have a choice. Pay me or die."

"Hey, baby, I'm all about business. Can you get me out of here?"

"Of course."

"Then let's get moving and we'll deal."

She walked around and made a point of looking out at the scramble of FBI agents on scene across the valley. They were still pouring into the scene but would send agents to hunt for Munk soon. Turning back to him, "You do not call *this* sloppy?"

"Again, not my fault." He clenched his teeth when he slid down the tree a little farther. "Stupid client with too much money wanted it done *his* way."

"I hear you talk about working with him on Sunday job, too, yes? I want in on that."

"Hey, let's not get overly chummy here. I'm not in on that crap."

She squatted, producing a knife she used to prick the skin under his eye.

"Stop that shit!"

"You have cost me a prime job plus money and time to find you. I want payment and in on your connection." She flicked her gaze over him. "If you heal, we could work together. I could teach you much."

"Arrogant bitch, aren't you?"

She stuck the tip of the knife at his throat. "I do not like to be called names."

"Hold it, babe. No problemo, okay?"

She smiled. "Who paid for diplomat?"

"That squirrely bastard I shot just now ordered the diplomat hit."

That was useless since it appeared from her surveillance that Terrence Van Dyke was now dead. She gave Munk a look of disgust.

That weasel Terrence had killed Chatton's uncle just to set up his brother. Not to wipe out another descendant in her family line. But information was better than gold. She would squeeze all she could get out of this lump of flesh. "So, you do not know who pays for Sunday job." She stood. "In that case, I have no use for partner with you. In fact, I do not see the value in taking risk to get you out of here. I will give you my phone and you will make the money transfer now."

"No, wait. I *do* know who is behind the Vatican attack."

She arched an imperial eyebrow at him. "Oh?"

"Someone called the Banker."

She'd heard that name before. Those bastards. She smiled. "Gracias."

Munk gave her an ugly grimace that might be an attempt at a grin.

She lifted her weapon and double-tapped his forehead, then walked away, covering her tracks as she did.

CHAPTER 55

MARGAUX STEPPED INTO her apartment Sunday afternoon, dog-tired.

Bianca was safe and the FBI had J. K. Kearn's killer, but Ryder had been sent back to prison.

Sabrina had practically set headquarters on fire with scorching curses. Murdock did admit that even though she was shot, Bianca had been a crazy woman in the helicopter, demanding that Murdock agree to review evidence against Ryder on the death of the prison guard.

Not much, but it was something.

Exhausted, Margaux dropped face down on her bed, clothes, and all. She should have gone by Nanci's place tonight to make amends for calling in a personal marker from when they'd been teens *and* for putting her cousin in a tight spot with her agency. She would, but not right this minute. Nanci was in a temporary apartment on the northwest side of Atlanta that belonged to the FBI. On the opposite side of the city from Margaux's apartment in Decatur. And to visit her cousin meant Margaux would have to insert covertly to keep from putting Nanci in the position of explaining who Margaux was if someone saw her.

That would be tough to do since Margaux didn't exist, not even to her family. None of them, except Nanci, knew she was still alive. Her cousin had protected Margaux's identity and existence all this time, in spite of working for a government agency.

How had she repaid Nanci?

By taking advantage of their relationship. This work turned Margaux into a machine some days, fixated on nothing but getting the job done.

She might have gone too far this time.

What if Nanci doesn't want to speak to me again?

Margaux felt her chest squeeze at the possibility. She'd always had Nanci when she'd had no one else. *Don't be ridiculous. Nanci said she'd never stop loving you just because you're fucked up.*

The muscles in her chest eased. Her cousin *would* get over being pissed, because they were closer than two sisters, but Margaux couldn't do that again. Ever. Nanci had done her a favor and stretched the parameters of her sworn oath to the FBI to help Ryder.

Fuck it. She'd go tonight, but she needed a shower and a clean set of clothes first. Did she have any? And she'd like to eat. Tomorrow would be better once she had ten hours of sleep to make up for being awake practically nonstop all week. With *enough* rest, she might even be able to make up with Nanci by spending a day looking at antiques.

Crawling through sewers to catch a felon would be more fun.

Excuses, excuses.

"I'm a shithead." She was a tired shithead, but she was going to climb the side of a building and get her ass chewed. Just needed ten minutes to catch a catnap and she would go.

Her phone rang. *Shit.* Margaux rolled over and reached for the cell phone in her back pocket.

Nanci. *Damn.*

Margaux hit the button for speaker, prepared to grovel. Before she could give a greeting, Nanci shouted, "*How did you get in my house and what do you want?*"

Margaux launched herself off the bed, gripping the phone, and ran for the door.

A male voice said, "It's not what I want. It's what my boss wants."

"What?"

"He wasn't happy about you sharing financial information."

No, I did that, Margaux wanted to scream.

The man continued, "I'm here to deliver a message about people who snoop."

Avoiding the elevator, Margaux took the stairs two at a time, her heart beating wild enough to burst by the time she descended three flights to the ground floor.

Nanci's voice shook. "What message?"

Keep him talking, Nanci. Margaux was running all out.

"Never screw with the Banker."

"Who's the Ba—"

Two muffled shots struck with a soft *thud, thud*. The phone sounded as if it had been dropped.

Footsteps walked across Nanci's tiled floor.

Skidding to a stop, Margaux wheezed, "Nanci?"

There was a gasp of air, then silence.

Pain stabbed her midsection. Margaux fell to the ground, bent over and gripping her stomach. Rage and agony exploded in a scream.

Nanci was dead.

CHAPTER 56

BIANCA SET THE bottle of medication aside. The pills were useless against her real pain, the one that had been eating a hole in her chest since she woke up in the hospital with no Ryder.

She could tolerate the ache in her side. The bullet had sliced across her side just underneath a rib. It had bled like a son of a gun, but she'd been lucky the powerful round hadn't hit her solidly. Lucky she hadn't died.

She hadn't, thanks to Ryder. That ache started again, not the one in her side, but higher in her chest.

There wasn't enough morphine in the universe for that kind of pain. She needed to get away from here and give her heart a chance to grieve.

"Are you ready to go?" Murdock strolled into her hospital room where she'd been under guard for thirteen days for her protection.

Just another Friday. Nothing like the day two Fridays back when she was still with Ryder. "Sure."

"You did a hell of a job."

Two weeks ago, she'd have wallowed in happiness at a compliment like that from her boss, but she couldn't drum up the strength to be happy. "Thanks. Any word on Nanci's killer?"

"Not yet, but we're working on that."

She nodded. Nanci's death had been a professional hit, thus the reason for guards on Bianca's room, but Sabrina Slye had shared something with Murdock that convinced him Bianca was no longer under threat.

Bianca had told Murdock on the way to the hospital to not tell her parents she was wounded and risk giving her father a heart attack.

He'd promised to tell them she would be in debriefing, which might take a week or more and she'd get in touch with them when she was free. Bianca would sort out the rest when she went home.

Murdock was unusually quiet when he normally rattled off orders nonstop. "You're clear to leave, if you're sure you can drive."

"I can drive." She couldn't raise her left arm very high without pulling on the stitches, but after surviving last week, she was pretty sure she could handle an automatic transmission.

When Murdock picked up her bag of clothes and toiletries, Bianca followed him down the hall. She had her personal items from her travel bag in the cabin, but not her prepaid phone.

Murdock hadn't brought up that sticky issue so she wouldn't either.

He kept talking in an easy tone as they walked out. "VDE has been cleared of any wrongdoing since we have your statement on Terrence Van Dyke and Aldwin Taylor aka Munk."

She could never think of Munk as Aldwin. It didn't fit the cold-blooded killer found later in the woods with two shots between the eyes.

Another professional hit. "What about the Dubai arms dealer? Did you figure out how he was getting the weapons?"

"He had molds for the Woden lower receivers out of the first test run weapons. Terrence got the mold out of VDE and shipped it to Dubai. They made the lowers with no serial numbers, but a consistent flaw matched the ones we inspected at the Van Dyke manufacturing and testing facility. Once the Dubai broker had lowers, they purchased the other parts from random dealers to assemble complete weapons."

She was floored by the work that had gone into illegal sales. Terrence was probably brilliant. Just evil. "Was Sam Long involved?"

"No. His ski trip was a vacation and he got called back to an emergency that was traced back to Terrence. Just another person who got used in the setup."

She hoped Murdock was including Ryder as one of those people who was used and set up. "What happens now in Dubai?"

"It's done. From what I understand, the CIA had a parallel op going on in three countries where they suspected Van Dyke as well. Seems that the CIA got their hands on the same financial information we did for Dubai."

Bianca jerked her head up fast at Murdock. "How?"

"I had a visit from a man who gave me a name that I'm sure isn't real. He's a spook after all. Definitely CIA. He gave me info from his resources, and we compared notes to wrap up this case."

She fought the insatiable urge to ask about Ryder. He'd been cuffed and taken back to prison. Somewhere during her drug-induced first twelve hours in the hospital, she'd grabbed Murdock's arm and told him Ryder had been set up, that the emails came from Terrence who was the Komodo.

Had Murdock reviewed the prison video or just agreed to keep her calm when she'd been bleeding in the helicopter? Would he read too much into it if she asked about Ryder this soon?

Ryder had broken her heart in a way that couldn't be fixed, but he deserved justice.

"About Van Dyke," Murdock started as they exited the doors to a chilly October afternoon in Atlanta.

She noted that her Ford Explorer was parked on the curb, being watched over by an agent she didn't recognize. "Which Van Dyke?"

Had Murdock's lips twitched?

Her boss clarified, "Ryder Van Dyke. Munk's rifle was the murder weapon for J. K. Kearn and Edward Abbot. That cleared Ryder of the charge against him for Kearn's death."

That didn't mean Ryder was free. Since Murdock brought up this topic, Bianca felt safe in asking, "Did anyone review the video of the guard's death?"

"Yes, and when the techs slowed the frames down there were two seconds of Ryder's hand holding the guard's radio. That was enough to determine he *had* been trying to get help for the man. Plus, a snitch in the prison ratted out the men responsible for the attack on the guard. He was terrified of those two after Ryder left and wanted them out of there."

The breath she'd been holding released with all the tension in her body.

"Took until early this morning to get him released, but he's free."

Ryder would not spend another day locked away. Tears burned at the corner of her eyes, but she squeezed them into submission.

Murdock opened the passenger door to Bianca's SUV and tossed the bag in on the bucket seat. He walked around to the other side and opened the driver's door, waiting for her.

When she stopped in front of him, Murdock said, "Because of your efforts we located the funding vein for the terrorists and prevented an attack on the Vatican that could have killed the pope and thousands of men, women and children."

"It wasn't just me. I was the rookie in this operation and Ryder was the one with skills. I couldn't have found that information, or stayed alive, without Ryder's help. He deserves as much or more credit."

"He'll be compensated."

How could you compensate a man for all that Ryder had lost?

Pain stabbed her chest, and it had nothing to do with her injury. "Speaking of that, do you have my, uh, divorce papers?"

"No. Ryder hasn't signed them yet."

"Why not?"

"He disappeared the minute he walked out of prison. Probably back with Sabrina's team, which means I have no idea where to reach him. I got the impression from Sabrina he was gone on a covert op. I left the papers with her, and she said she'd get them to Ryder, but if he doesn't sign them just let me know."

"He will." She forced the sadness back into the hole in her heart and twisted the ring that someone had put back on her finger while she'd slept last night. She couldn't bring herself to take it off yet, but admitted, "This ring is his."

Murdock waved her off. "Ryder left word that he wanted you to keep that. Said it was yours."

Her heart stuttered. Had Ryder given her this beautiful ring to keep because he'd felt guilty for getting her involved in this mission?

He couldn't have given it to her for any other reason. Could he?

Dammit. Why was she still determined to read more into what happened between them? She shrugged to hide the emotions wallowing around inside her. "It's probably not worth much, but I hate to keep something that isn't mine."

Murdock chuckled wryly. "We talked about having Lloyd's of London insure that ring. It's a Van Dyke heirloom, been in the family since the mid 1800's."

Bianca stared at the rock on her finger. "He can't give me a family heirloom. Good Lord, Hubrecht has probably been worried to death about this thing."

"It's not Hubrecht's. It belonged to Ryder's mother, who left it for him. He said it was the one thing that would definitely convince his family you were really his wife."

On the drive to lunch with Terrence, Ryder's brother had told Bianca only two things meant anything to Ryder. His car and something his mother had given him.

He gave me his mother's ring. Her heart did a backflip in her chest. Did that mean he ...

No, he doesn't love you so just stop it. Tears welled up in her eyes and she blinked hard to keep them from falling. Ryder had walked away from everything, including her.

If he'd wanted her to keep him *and* the ring, he'd have found a way to be here even if Murdock wouldn't share her location. Nothing so simple would have stopped Ryder. Bianca squeezed her eyes to stem the waterfall she'd been holding back for twelve days, kidding herself that he was just going to show up and tell her he loved her.

Ryder had tried to protect her every step of the way just as hard as she'd worked to bring him justice.

She was safe and he was free. Mission accomplished.

He felt responsible for her being stuck as his wife and getting wounded. She would not allow him to give her this ring as some sort of payment but taking it off was going to rip her in half.

She didn't want the ring.

She wanted Ryder. That had been a fool's wish.

He was gone and knew how to vanish forever. She swallowed the hurt and pulled the ring off, handing it Murdock. "I don't want this and ..." *Without Ryder's love it means nothing.* She shook her head. "Please send it to Sabrina. She'll get it to him."

Murdock accepted the ring and slipped it into his coat pocket. "Any message you want me to relay?"

The idea of Murdock passing along a personal message was surreal. Bianca gave him the truth. "Yes. Just say it was never mine to keep." She made a move to get in.

"One more thing, Agent Brady. I'd like you to transfer to my anti-terrorism team here."

Her mouth fell open. "Really?" Brilliant. Now he could recant that decision based on her inability to form a coherent response.

"Really." He actually smiled.

Then she considered what she'd just been through. "Just so we're clear, I'm not cut out for field work, Sir."

"I might argue that point if you had more training, but that's not the position I'm offering you. I want your analytical and computer skills."

She was being offered her dream position. She should sound more excited, but the best she could do right now was to force a smile and say, "Thank you, Sir."

"Can I take that as a yes?"

"Absolutely. I just need a day to go see my family and I can be back."

"You still have to rehab that injury and you need some down time. Call me in two weeks and we'll talk."

"Yes, Sir."

"Are you sure you don't want to reconsider keeping the ring, Brady?"

She shook her head, still confused over Ryder's offer. Swallowing past the lump in her throat was difficult. "No, Sir."

Sliding behind the steering wheel, she settled into the seat carefully. Her side still hurt, but if she took it easy the ache was bearable without pain meds. She cranked the engine and drove away while she still had her act together.

The ring bothered her. She wished she'd seen him one more time.

But who was she kidding? There would never be closure so long as Ryder owned her heart.

He just didn't know it, because they'd parted on bad terms without her getting a chance to tell him she'd been wrong to lose faith in him even for a brief moment. She was not the woman she'd been two weeks ago, and she owed that to Ryder. She was a stronger woman because of what she'd learned about herself around him.

It would take a while, maybe forever, to go on without him, but she would never be sorry for falling in love with him.

Everything else was going to be all right.

Now, to figure what to tell her parents about why she'd gotten married and divorced. Some people would laugh at her concern, but her parents trusted her to make a wise decision in choosing a partner and to do the work it took to make a marriage successful. They wouldn't understand why she'd had to marry for her job and would still think she'd fallen in love with Ryder.

Divorce would be tough enough to explain without having to tell them the son-in-law they were dying to meet didn't exist.

How had she screwed up so badly?

Idiot that she was, all she could think about was driving to the Slye offices and begging Sabrina to tell her where Ryder was so she could see him. Touch him. To tell him it was okay that he didn't love her, because she had enough to last a lifetime for both of them. She wanted one more kiss.

One more time to look into those molten silver eyes.

She reached for the box of tissues in the console as the first tears rolled down her cheeks.

CHAPTER 57

CHATTON CALLED THE General at a hotel where he was staying in Chicago just to piss him off, because everyone in Czarion had agreed to not use phones.

He answered, "What?"

"Take you away from something important?"

"You know better than to call."

As if she cared? "It appears that you're still in my debt since Ryder Van Dyke was not the shooter."

His sigh said he'd like to choke her to death, but he gave a wicked chuckle. "You get my message about passing along information to the wrong people?"

Her extra sense went on alert and came up with only one possible message. Chatton had installed a listening device at Nanci's house and had heard the exchange before Nanci was shot.

She ignored his amusement. "Why the theatrics?"

"So that you never make the mistake of thinking I miss anything, because I have eyes on everything."

The General needed to be taught a lesson. "And here I thought you weren't subject to something like emotion, but I clearly pissed you off."

No volley came back from him. Chatton smiled.

When The General finally spoke, his words came out chillingly soft. "Being a spook does not make you invincible. Keep that in mind."

"No, it just makes me deadly." She hung up.

Arrogance can be fatal, General. He'd just confirmed that the Banker worked for him. Wayan and The General thought they could toy with Chatton.

Nanci Tyler had a cousin and friends in the espionage business. Maybe they needed a tip on which direction to look for Nanci's killer.

CHAPTER 58

B IANCA SWITCHED THE radio off, tired of music after all
afternoon on the road.

Facing the music was getting closer by the minute. She still
hadn't come up with anything to tell her parents.

An annulment would have been simpler, but a sheet of paper
wasn't the issue. She couldn't face her parents and lie to them. If
she said the marriage had been annulled, that was the equivalent
of saying she hadn't consummated the marriage.

There had been plenty of consummation. It wouldn't matter
to a lot of people, but honesty with her mama and daddy was
something she valued.

She turned off the paved road onto the packed dirt road that
led uphill to her parents' house. Now she stared straight into the
blue-black clouds threatening rain.

"Rain, Sara Lynn? I always think it means you're happy when
it rains, but you wouldn't be happy to see me this miserable."
Bianca grabbed a tissue and wiped her eyes. Mama and Daddy
would still know she'd been crying.

They'd taught her to follow her heart. Following her heart this
time hadn't been wrong.

She would explain to her parents that she'd married for the
good of her country and apologize for being divorced, but that
she wouldn't take it back even if she could. She'd never be
sorry she married a hero for the sake of justice.

Mama and Daddy would still love her, and they'd tell her
she'd find the right man to give her heart to one day, but there
was little danger of that unless the impetuous organ got a kick-
start.

She drove slowly up the bumpy incline through an archway of

tall trees with half their branches bare. Gold-and-rust-colored leaves floated down, swirling in the rising wind, a precursor to the storm that was brewing.

She rounded the next curve and the simple frame house she'd grown up in came into view. That house might not be much to look at, but it was perched on a cliff with a breathtaking backdrop of the Shenandoah Mountain range, the easternmost band of the Appalachians. Her sturdy vehicle growled as she drove onto the hard-packed, dirt front yard.

Oh, no.

A handful of worn vehicles cluttered the grounds.

Their neighbors had turned out like this was a celebration. She needed time before she faced people who weren't family. She fought a wave of nausea and took a swig of water from the bottle in the console.

The clouds dropped lower, surrounding the ridge.

She didn't care. The rain would help hide her tears.

What had Daddy told her as a teen? *You gonna play, you gotta pay.*

Time to pay.

She stepped from the car and checked her clothes for crumbs. She'd eaten a package of crackers on the way here. Maroon pullover and jeans both clean. No reason not to go in the house.

Fat raindrops hit her on the head, face, and arms. "No reason to dump a bucket right now, Sara Lynn," Bianca muttered softly.

Two of her daddy's buddies sat on the corner of the porch in rocking chairs. They smiled when she started toward the house. One yelled toward the screen door, "Bianca's home."

Great. As soon as she finished explaining to her parents, she could tell their friends about the farce known as her life.

Little water bombs smacked her harder and splatted into the dirt around her.

A dozen steps from the porch she halted.

Her mama and daddy stepped through the open door, grinning like a star had arrived. Little did they know their daughter was a fallen star. Soon to be a drenched one.

She tried out a smile to see how much it hurt. Not bad.

Kind of like grinning with a mouth full of thorns.

Before anyone said a word, a tall figure stepped out of the house and around her parents.

Bianca's smile faltered, and her throat tightened when her gaze locked on a pair of sparkling silver eyes.

Ryder ambled down the steps like he'd lived in the country his whole life. She knew better.

He never slowed even as rain splattered him until he stopped in front of her.

"What are you doing here?" she asked, her throat raw.

He lifted a hand to her face. "In this family, we don't divorce."

CHAPTER 59

WATER RAN OFF his face and soaked his clothes. Ryder barely noticed. He'd caught his first deep breath since being dragged away from Bianca when she was wounded. The only image that played over and over in his mind was that last image of her bleeding and going into shock.

She was in shock again, but not from being near death. With her finally so close, he trembled with the need to touch her.

"Why are you here?" she asked in a hoarse voice that sounded as if she'd been crying.

That gouged another hole in his heart. "I needed to explain some things."

She started shaking her head. "Don't feel guilty about what happened. Me getting hurt wasn't your fault."

He couldn't take another minute of waiting. He lifted his hands to hold her face and fought a groan of happiness at touching her again. "It was my fault that you ended up in the line of fire."

She wrapped her fingers around his wrists and tried to shake her head, but he stopped her by saying, "I'm sorry—"

"I know you didn't do any of that stuff I accused you of."

The crazy woman couldn't keep quiet long enough for him to get to the part where they could kiss and make up. He put his finger on her lips again. This had to be said.

"I'm sorry for so much, Bianca, but most of all for letting you think our lovemaking was anything less than miraculous."

Her lips parted in a soft O he wanted to kiss, but not until he earned back that right. "When it looked like I was going to be accused of treason, I didn't want to leave you caring for me. I wanted you happy and to have a life even if it was with someone else, but I ended up lying to both of us."

Her fingers tightened around his wrists. "If that was a lie, then what's the truth?"

"That I love you so much I can't give you up."

She started crying. He pulled her into his arms and all at once he was at peace. Having this woman next to him was all he needed. All he'd ever want. "Don't cry, Sweetheart. I never meant to hurt you and I'll never be able to make it right."

Pushing against his chest, she lifted her head. "You just did when you told me you loved me. You wouldn't let me tell you in the cabin."

His voice was raw. "So, tell me now. Please, God, tell me you still love me."

"I do love you." She pushed up and he met her halfway, kissing her with all the love that had been bottled up inside him, just waiting for a woman this amazing. His arms tightened, holding her closer, afraid of losing his only reason for breathing.

Never happen. He would fight the world to keep her.

When someone on the porch catcalled, she started laughing and pushed against him to look up in his face. "We look like drowned rats."

He took her in with one slow look and said, "You're beautiful soaking wet."

Her lip trembled and her face looked like it was going to crumble.

He was confused. "What'd I say wrong?"

"Nothing. Sara Lynn used to tell me that if a man really loved me, he wouldn't care if my hair got wet."

"She was right." He stepped back and took her left hand, lifting it to kiss her ring finger.

She regretted her hasty decision this morning. "I gave the ring to Murdock to send back to you through Sabrina."

"That's not a problem, but there is something you have to do for me."

"What?"

"You'll see." He kissed her again and turned them to face the porch full of grinning friends and family. His chest tightened with happiness. His family.

The storm had slowed to a gentle rain.

On the way to the house, Bianca said something under her breath that sounded like, "I'm glad you approve, Sara Lynn."

CHAPTER 60

SIX HOURS LATER, Bianca stared up at a lock of tawny hair that fell across Ryder's forehead. She brushed it away from his eyes and the simple touch made her heart beat double time. "You don't have to do this. I don't need this."

"I do. I need for you to know we're married because I love you." Taking her hand, he kissed her palm and sent heat streaking up her arm. "My life would have been unlivable without you. *And* your family."

Ryder had taken a helicopter to reach her parents' home before Bianca arrived. He'd put his silver tongue to the test when he'd sat down to explain about the wedding and what he could share about the mission with her parents. He'd even told them how he was worried Bianca wouldn't forgive him for letting her think their time together had been a casual affair.

Ryder said he'd never been so scared as when her daddy stuck a finger in his face and said, "If you ever hurt my baby again, I'll come after you with a filet knife."

To which, Ryder had replied, "If I'm stupid enough to screw up the best thing that's ever happened to me, I'll slit my own throat."

Bianca didn't have the heart to tell Ryder that Daddy's threat had been literal. He would filet an errant son-in-law.

Daddy and Mama had welcomed Ryder into the family *if* he could convince Bianca to take him back.

Cocking an eyebrow at Bianca, Ryder asked, "What's so funny?"

She didn't want Ryder sleeping with one eye open, worried about her daddy skinning him alive. Instead, she said, "The idea of you fishing with me and Daddy."

"I'm not a city boy, Sweetheart."

There went her heart again, dancing around in her chest at the way he said *sweetheart*. "Oh, I know you're in your element traipsing through the woods or any other terrain when you're hunting the enemy, but me and Daddy been fishing since I was little. He always wants to wager on who catches the most. You *might* distract *me* with all that sexy Alpha thing you do, but Daddy'll put you on your butt when it comes to catching fish."

She'd expected him to show his competitive side and brag how he was up for the challenge. But his eyes turned smoky, and his voice got deep. "I can handle losing to your dad as long as I have you to nurse my wounded ego."

He kissed her before she could laugh at that. He touched her constantly. Always careful of her injury, but she'd given little thought to it since hearing three words from him. Love was the best pain medicine.

She regretted giving Ryder's ring to Murdock.

Ryder kissed her lips once more then touched his lips to her forehead and said, "I don't know how much longer I can wait."

"Patience, love."

"I'm all out." Ryder smoothed his hand over her hair that was now dry and falling over her shoulder. He growled something to himself and reached for her again, careful not to muss the lacy peach dress Mama had bought her this week for the celebration they'd planned.

The kiss turned Bianca's legs to jelly. She grabbed his arm, enjoying the muscle beneath his suit.

When he pulled away, they were both breathless.

She warned him, "You shouldn't be here. It's bad luck to see the bride."

"My luck has been nothing short of miraculous since the first time I met my bride."

Would he always be a silver-tongued devil? "We're really doing this again?"

He nodded, grinning. "This is the one that counts."

"We *are* still legally married."

"That was paperwork. This is about vows from the heart and with family." He cupped her face. "I vow to try to be the man who deserves you. I vow to love you until the end of time. I vow—"

She put her fingers on his lips. "Save it for the ceremony."

"You're going to hear it again and again."

"I won't need the words. I know you love me."

He sighed with total contentment. "You scare the hell out of me some days. Your determination to save me almost got you killed. I couldn't survive if anything happened to you. I'm proud of the FBI agent you are, but after seeing you shot—" His Adam's apple bobbed with a hard swallow.

Unable to finish his sentence, he looked away until she turned his head back to her.

She had to take him out of his misery. "I forgot to tell you. I'm being transferred to Murdock's team, but only as an analyst."

He couldn't have looked more thrilled. "Is that what you want?"

"Yes. I want to have a life with you, not play 007. Besides, you'll be undercover with Slye operations and that's enough time away for both of us. If I was doing the same thing, we'd never see each other."

"As long as you're happy with Murdock's offer."

"I'm getting my dream job and my dream man. How can I not be?"

The door to the small bride's room on the side of their country church opened and her mama scowled. "What are you doing in here with the bride, Ryder?"

Bianca muttered, "Now you're in trouble."

"I was calming her down," Ryder told Mama who rolled her eyes.

Mama turned around and nodded at someone then backed out of the way and Bianca's daddy entered.

Ryder stopped rubbing his thumb over her fingers when Daddy narrowed his gaze at him standing so close to Bianca. "Papers don't mean nothin' to me, son. Actions do. You ain't her husband *yet*. Not 'til this is done. Best you get out front and be ready, so you don't miss the main event."

Ryder answered with a humble, "Yes, sir." He strolled toward the door where he shook hands with her daddy, then Ryder looked over his shoulder with a wink and disappeared into the hall.

She took her daddy's arm and couldn't believe how nervous she was. She'd already married Ryder.

But this was for real. This was forever.

When the wedding march sounded and they entered the church, everyone was standing. Bianca's eyes locked on Ryder.

The love pouring out of his face threatened to turn her into a waterpot. As she neared the front, she searched the groom's side where Hubrecht Van Dyke stood in front of the varnished pew. Next to him were her kidnappers, aka the Slye black ops team, and Murdock. But Hubrecht Van Dyke had been the big surprise.

His limousine had scrunched rocks across its undercarriage when the driver pulled right behind her Explorer an hour after she'd arrived at her parents' house.

Ryder had swept her next to him, within his protective embrace.

Hubrecht had given them both an appraising look as he'd marched up her parents' front yard and announced, "I missed the first ceremony. I would like to attend this one."

Mama and Daddy had stepped forward and shaken Hubrecht's hand, which was when Ryder found out her parents had called his, because as Mama said, "That's what family does."

Bianca's heart went out to Hubrecht. He hadn't said a word about Terrence, but he looked older, as though the pain of losing his son had increased his years. Hubrecht was not an easy man to get close to, but Bianca would never forget the moment when Hubrecht shook Ryder's hand and said he was proud of Ryder.

Ryder finally admitted to Bianca that he'd been wrong about Hubrecht, because of the way Terrence had manipulated all of them. But Ryder was ready to give the man who had raised him a chance at being his father. He wanted to meet with Janeen and try to mend that rickety bridge, though he didn't have high hopes.

As Bianca walked up the aisle toward the altar, her gaze danced over to Hubrecht who had turned with everyone else to watch the bride's entrance. He winked at her, shooting a happy bolt through her heart.

Ryder *was* loved by someone in his family.

Her daddy stopped in front of the altar and passed her off to Ryder. To be honest, the ceremony was more blur than anything until Ryder took her finger and slid his mother's ring on her hand, for real this time, and said, "With this ring, I thee wed forever and a day."

THANK YOU FOR reading my book! I would really appreciate a review of any length where you purchase e-books. I hope you loved meeting Ryder and Bianca. Ready for Margaux to take off locked and loaded for vengeance? She planned for everything except going up against the one man who can destroy her, but first they have to save the world. Keep reading for an excerpt of Kiss The Enemy.

You're invited to join my reader group where you are not inundated with emails and your information is NEVER shared. Visit: AuthorDiannaLove.com/connect

Keep reading for a sneak peek at
KISS THE ENEMY

 SLYE TEAM BLACK OPS

KISS THE ENEMY

DIANNA LOVE

Kiss The Enemy

Going rogue from Slye to take down a mastermind who killed her cousin in a recent mission, Margaux barges into a deadly operation where she becomes the inside link for any hope of preventing the destruction of a huge US city. Her only chance for survival and success lies in the hands of her enemy, the last man she should ever trust.

"Action, adventure, romance, the tension is off the charts." ~~Goodreads

CHAPTER 1

MARGAUX DUKE EXITED first from the unmarked van parked on an empty side street in east Atlanta two blocks from tonight's target. She lowered her night vision monocular into place as the rest of the six-person team spilled out behind her.

Black figures melded into the dark shadows and chilly night, all armed and deadly.

All moving on her intel of a meeting for payoff on a suspected terrorist attack to be carried out in Atlanta.

Wednesday.

Today, as in less than twelve hours.

The meeting was going down in sixteen minutes. Margaux had shared every detail her snitch provided, with the exception of her hunch on who was making that payment.

At one time, her intuition would have mattered.

Not these days.

Sabrina Slye's voice came through the comm sets everyone wore. "You're absolutely *sure* about this intel, Duke?"

If this was about getting retribution for Margaux's dead cousin, Nanci, she'd go on much less dependable intel. But this was about stopping a terrorist and she would not walk the team into danger for just a gut feeling. Sabrina had never questioned Margaux's resources.

It rubbed that she did now, but Margaux pushed the mic switch clipped to her black molle vest and answered, "Yes." She spoke in a soft whisper. The throat mic picked up the vibrations, and the sound came clearly through the earbuds of the team. "This came from my number one contact. He's never been wrong in three years."

No one else said a word. Tension pulsed through the silence.

That was telling in itself when any other time Nick and Dingo would have been ragging on her that she'd be picking up the beer tab if this was a bust.

She hadn't been invited to share a beer in months.

She added, "This is the same informant who gave us accurate intel on the submarine sabotage we averted in Kitsap last December." An attack planned for Naval Base Kitsap on the Kitsap Peninsula in Washington, no less.

"Ten four." Sabrina's brisk voice moved on with, "Time check. O-one-hundred." She counted seconds until everyone on the team gave an affirmative.

Sabrina ran covert teams for secret national security operations under the cover of Slye, an elite corporate security agency. A tough, but fair, leader who had zero tolerance for her agents going rogue for personal vendettas. She'd leveled Margaux with a steely gaze when she'd reminded the entire team of that unbendable rule just ten days ago.

Message received.

Stop focusing on the Banker, a broker for international terrorism.

Ryder Van Dyke's deep voice cut in on the comm unit. "One vehicle just arrived at Strident Global Imports." There was a pause while they all waited to hear more, then Ryder said, "No one's getting out of the car yet."

Ryder was team member number seven. He had a sniper position on top of the building across the street from an import company where the meet was expected to happen.

The snitch had discovered a link between Tio Giovanni, the ruthless leader of a New Jersey crime syndicate, and this import company, which accounted for the location of this meeting.

What was the mob doing for a terrorist?

Margaux could feel Sabrina's gaze drilling through her confidence. She could not screw up the deal she had with Sabrina, the only person left who knew Margaux's true identity. More than anything, Sabrina had helped her reclaim her life and had known how much Nanci meant to Margaux.

The team knew Margaux based only on what Sabrina had built for her identity. As for FBI Special Agent Nanci Tyler, the team had only known that Margaux had a rapport with a contact in the agency, but one that had to be kept secret. They understood her loss when Nanci was murdered, but not that it had been like losing a limb.

Margaux had been spending her off-time—and her money—hunting for the Banker. But when Sabrina finally made it clear that Margaux had to let go of her quest for vengeance, Margaux paid heed, because Sabrina was right.

The Banker had cost her enough.

That's why Margaux had told her snitch she was no longer paying for intel on the bastard.

Tonight was about protecting innocent people and doing her part.

If this operation went sideways, which was always possible with one pulled together this quickly, she would take a bullet for Sabrina or anyone else on this team. Of the six elite operatives in this unit, Margaux was the only one truly expendable. With Nanci gone, no one would mourn her death.

She shoved that load of guilt back down in the cavity her heart used to fill and checked her Sig Sauer M11-A1 holstered beneath the black windbreaker. Her jacket might look like the FBI type, but hers had no agency initials and this wasn't a sanctioned government mission.

Hell, this hadn't even been a mission eighty-two minutes ago.

Ryder came back on the radio. "Three males exiting the sedan. One is staying by the vehicle. The other two are at the door of Strident and ... they're entering the code for the alarm system. No other vehicle yet."

That meant the first group was connected to Strident.

Sweat trickled down Margaux's back with total indifference to the cold front sweeping Georgia in early May. Adrenaline pumped hard enough through her veins that she was numb to anything as insignificant as the temperature continuing to drop since midnight.

No mistakes.

Sabrina's tone sharpened. "Heads up. Dingo goes with me.

White Hawk backs us up at the entrance. Nick's with Duke at the rear with Tanner as backup."

A bad feeling niggled at Margaux, that sixth sense an operative paid attention to if she wanted to walk away to fight another day. Maybe it was a case of doubting herself after Sabrina had questioned Margaux's intel. She shook it off, getting her head in the game where it belonged when the team needed her.

Ryder had an update. "Second vehicle parking in the lot. No one exiting yet."

"Everyone ready?" Sabrina asked.

Affirmatives followed all around, but Sabrina would hold off sending them until both men were in the building in case one decided to blow up the other.

Nick Carrera stepped across Margaux's line of sight, standing a couple inches taller than her five-ten height. The only part of him showing through the black ski mask was a flicker of white around the eye not covered by his monocular, and his unsmiling mouth.

Margaux would question Sabrina's choice for her partner du jour if not for Margaux's having butted heads with everyone else for months.

Not that she didn't like Nick. He was a solid partner, and he didn't butt heads. But Nick played by Nick's rules and was a bit of a wildcard on a mission. It was hard to say exactly what he'd do in any given situation, but he did make things happen that often defied all probability.

Of course, he just as often did so in a way that created a lot of chaos along with the positive results.

Dingo Paddock stepped over to show Sabrina something on his smart phone. The Aussie's ski mask covered spiked blond hair that looked out of place against skin the color of weak tea.

White Hawk, a Cherokee female operative and new recruit, stood off to the side. Dark brown hair cut short on one side and chin length on the other framed an oval face with high cheekbones passed down from generations of Native Americans. She was quiet, but in a way that said she was constantly engaged in threat assessment.

Word was that White Hawk had a knack for languages.

And for tailing a suspect.

Nick said she practically turned into a ghost when she shadowed someone.

Ryder finally said, "Three suspects exiting the second car, leaving one man out front, two heading into the building."

Sabrina announced, "Move out."

Dingo, White Hawk and Sabrina left as one pack. Margaux, Nick and Tanner Bodine took off in a different direction to approach the building from the rear. Out in public, Tanner was a big rambling cowboy with an easy smile, but at night he could move like the wind when stealth was key.

Margaux entered a dark stretch of alley that had been used as a john for the homeless if that stink was any indication. She widened her stride until she reached the tall chain-link fence surrounding the back lot of the global marketing company. Tanner stepped up and snipped an opening large enough for his wide body, which left plenty of room for her and Nick to slip through.

Sabrina's hushed voice came through the comm. "Guards at entrance contained. Ryder has confirmation on identity of the New Jersey suspect as Tio Giovanni. Black hair, slender build, five-nine. Both guards positively identified as known enforcers for two separate crime syndicates."

Margaux blinked at that news. Dingo could run facial recognition software *if* he was at a computer and *if* he had decent images. Had Sabrina sent someone ahead to set up a live feed at the front of the import company? Even so, Dingo didn't have that access at the moment, and Josh Carrington, the other techno whiz on the Slye team, hadn't been available tonight. Amanda, the research dynamo Sabrina had snaked from MI6 last year, was on vacation.

That would mean the images were very likely being sent to Ryder's personal electronic superpower, an electronic analyst genius at the FBI who also happened to be his wife.

Sabrina would be pulling out all the stops to confirm as much as possible before sending in agents.

Tanner hung back as Margaux and Nick approached the building.

Nick spoke softly, asking, "Alarm status?"

Dingo's voice came right back. "All clear, mate."

If the alarm had been reset once everyone was inside as a security measure, Dingo had just disarmed it.

Nick moved silently up the metal steps to the rear door of the warehouse and went to work on the lock while Margaux covered his back.

When his hand touched her shoulder, she turned to enter a dark space that would be impossible to navigate without night vision gear. She took the lead, weaving her way with soft steps around forklifts and pallets stacked with merchandise covered in plastic wrap.

She stopped at the corner of tall metal shelving lined up in rows. A mirror set of towering gray structures loaded with inventory ran along the other side of the building, creating a wide walkway down the center.

There was enough space for two forklifts with eight-foot-wide loads to easily pass each other.

Or for two men to meet in the center of the building sixty feet away and discuss destroying parts of this city. A single mercury vapor light glowed bluish-white overhead, leaving the rest of the warehouse in pitch dark.

Nick eased forward and peeked over her shoulder. A guard stood two strides behind each respective boss.

Margaux assessed the room. Lots of metal angles for bullets to ricochet against.

But there were only two exits.

Dread clawed along her neck. *Why?*

This felt rushed, which couldn't be helped since there was no way to plan for when intel would arrive. Besides, this was what Slye excelled at—moving on a hot tip without red tape, then fading into the shadows so alphabet agencies took the credit.

And taking on missions that stopped powerful criminals.

Margaux's snitch had given her pieces of intel that alluded to the Banker making the payoff tonight. But not enough information to say for sure.

Eight months ago, Sabrina would have been open to the

possibility of going after that bastard on a good hunch, but not after a source—translation, Sabrina's friend in the CIA—said agencies had been tracking the Banker's ties to international terrorist events for years. According to her source, there was no intel to support the Banker having entered the US at any point in the past or present.

There were no known photographs of the Banker, and Sabrina's CIA friend had shared that the Banker was believed to presently be holed up in Germany.

That settled that, which was why Margaux didn't bring up the bastard's name and draw Sabrina's ire again.

Margaux's new goal was regaining the respect she'd once enjoyed before she'd let an obsession make her team think she'd gone rogue. She hadn't, and no way would she allow her personal issues to end with letting her team down.

Sabrina ordered, "Stand down. The second suspect can't be confirmed as a known terrorist."

Nick muttered, "Fuck."

He took the word right out of Margaux's mouth. She eyed the two men who were now shaking hands as if their business was concluded. The pause that followed stretched until Sabrina said, "Margaux I need any other intel you've got on this guy. *Anything* else from your snitch I can use."

Son of a bitch. Decision time. Margaux swallowed and made a leap of faith, whispering into her mic, "My snitch said this *might* involve the Banker, but he did *not* have confirmation. I dismissed that as insignificant since we were told the Banker is not in this country."

But the snitch had argued that this terrorist was rumored to have put out a hit on an FBI agent eight months ago for interfering with his operation. That fit the description of the hit on Nanci.

"What are you saying?" Sabrina asked.

Margaux regretted all the months she'd focused on the Banker, because right now everyone had to be thinking he was at the core of her investment for this op. She said, "There *is* a chance the unidentified suspect could be the Banker, which would explain not being able to confirm identification as a terrorist. I didn't tell you because it was only speculation and that was never the point of this op. This is about stopping an attack on Atlanta."

Silence answered her.

She glanced at Nick.

He rolled his eyes, an action she was sure the rest of the team mirrored at this same moment.

Nick didn't activate his mic when he whispered right at her ear. "How long have you been suicidal?"

Margaux left her mic off as well to answer him in a hushed voice. "How is this suicidal with an entire team?"

"I didn't mean this." He nodded to the left toward the targets. "I meant stomping on Sabrina's last good nerve."

"I'm not saying it's him." She paused, wishing she were anywhere else right now. "But what if it is?" Regardless of what happened eight months ago, if this was the Banker, they had the chance to take down someone who brokered the deaths of thousands, and they all knew it.

"Hey, I'm in."

And just like that, Nick was at the top of her favorite partners list.

Ryder's voice came on the comm. "We've got company. A sporte ute pulling into the drive. I count at least four inside. Time to move or get out."

Margaux held her breath, not sure what she hoped Sabrina would decide, but if they pulled back, they'd lose the terrorist and Giovanni, and maybe sign the death warrants for thousands of innocent people.

Sabrina finally said, "Op is a go." She paused then ordered, "Move in."

Margaux nodded at Nick then she slipped around the corner with Nick on her left side. She aimed at the guard on her right. Nick would take the one on the left.

Giovanni turned to speak to his guard.

Dingo and Sabrina would be approaching from the front, one covering the terrorist and the other watching Giovanni. It was imperative to bring those two out alive.

Everything sharpened in Margaux's surroundings. Time took

on a life of its own, slowing until everything came into laser focus.

Sabrina's booming order ripped through the room. "Hands in the air. Now!"

Did they do that? Of course not.

That would have been too damn easy.

Both guards spun, shooting toward Dingo and Sabrina's positions as they did.

The terrorist sank into a squat, and Giovanni dropped to the floor, rolling away, but he had nowhere to go beyond the shelves.

Margaux took out her guard with one shot to the head.

Nick hit his target but missed the kill shot only because Giovanni knocked the guard into the shelves where he continued unloading his magazine.

Bullets pinged against metal and the smell of gunpowder filled the air.

With the rapid-fire reverberating, the unknown terrorist must have decided the only threat was coming from the entrance, which had to be why he made a dash for the rear of the building.

He was in his forties, twenty pounds overweight, and must not have been able to bring a weapon into the meet because he had yet to pull one.

Even better? He was heading straight for where Margaux waited. This was too good to be true. Finally, something was going right.

She told Nick, "I got this."

The shooting stopped. Pounding footsteps were the only sound interrupting the sudden silence.

Eight feet from where Margaux hid in the shadows, the suspect looked up as she stepped out. His eyes bulged with shock then rage. She moved forward before he could react and put her weight into the motion, taking advantage of his forward momentum. She hooked an arm around his neck to clothesline him to the ground.

He hit hard. Crack-your-skull hard.

"Get up you piece of shit," she ordered and kicked him in the side.

He groaned and grabbed his head. "You fucking …"

"The word you're looking for is bitch."

"You're a woman? You *sorry whore*. You're gonna burn for this."

She smiled at him and squatted down. "We'll see who burns."

Sabrina came striding up with an HK 416 in her hands. "All clear. Guards inside neutralized. Giovanni is contained. Backup has the four new arrivals restrained and hooded outside. "

Margaux searched his face for something that screamed merciless killer, but nothing magically pinged to identify him. Was this the Banker?

"Do you have any clue what you just screwed up?" the suspect on the ground mumbled in a pain-filled voice.

Margaux prompted him. "By all means. Tell us what you were here to negotiate."

He turned to her, his face twisted with more hatred than she thought a human capable of expressing visually. "You just fucked a two-year deep undercover DEA operation that was one day from success. I'll see every one of you buried for this."

Sabrina demanded his superior's name. When he gave it, she looked straight at Margaux and cursed.

The agent's eyes rolled back in his head just as Ryder's voice came over the comm in clipped, urgent tones. "Four Atlanta police units pulling up out front. Two unmarked units in back. Alphabet agencies. We're burned."

Blood rushed from Margaux's head so fast she saw stars.

She was alive because no one knew she existed.

If she got arrested, she was as good as dead.

For all *KISS THE ENEMY* links, visit AuthorDiannaLove.com for all retailer links or order a copy signed and personalized at DiannaLoveSignedBooks.com

You're invited to join my reader group where you are not inundated with emails and your information is NEVER shared. Visit: AuthorDiannaLove.com/connect

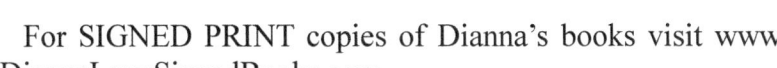

For SIGNED PRINT copies of Dianna's books visit www. DiannaLoveSignedBooks.com

The Slye Team Black Ops romantic thriller series is 'completed' (great for binging!)
Book 1: Nowhere Safe
Book 2: Honeymoon To Die For
Book 3: Kiss The Enemy
Book 4: Deceptive Treasures
Book 5: Stolen Vengeance
Book 6: Fatal Promise

Note: *Last Chance To Run,* Prequel to the Slye Team series, is free with the box set: Slye Team Black Ops: Prequel plus Books 1-2

Praise for *SLYE TEAM BLACK OPS series*

"Engrossing, thrilling and wonderfully steamy...a pitch-perfect suspense that will keep readers breathless..." The Romance Reviews

"I could not put this book down...Once again Dianna has thrilled my suspense taste buds..." After Hours Rendezvous

"It seems with each book this series gets better...(Love) has an uncanny ability of always creating wonderful characters that you care about... This was such a beautiful romance..."
~~Barb, The Reading Cafe

"I fell in love with the characters in this book. This story is chock full of action, white hot romance, shocking twists and intelligence."

~~Trina, After Dark Rendezvous

Acknowledgements

NO AUTHOR CREATES without a great support team and I have the best, starting with my husband, Karl, who has always believed in me and makes it possible for me to do what I love.

Steve Doyle has spent many hours sharing his vast knowledge gained as a Special Forces soldier, especially when it comes to all forms of weapons. Additionally, he reads every story and his feedback is a tremendous help. Any mistakes made or adjustments for fiction are my own, because everyone who helped me went above and beyond the call to give me the best information.

One of those people who helps me ferret out important details is my assistant and intrepid traveling companion, Cassondra Murray, who is in the trenches with me every day whether it's reading early rough drafts or proofing final edits or juggling the massive amount of office work that happens behind the scenes of producing a book.

Much appreciation goes to award-winning author Mary Buckham who brainstorms with me during the year when she isn't writing on her own Invisible Recruit series.

Thanks also to enthusiastic early reader Joyce Ann McLaughlin who makes me smile with her fun comments and keeps me straight with her sharp eyes.

Judy Carney's first copy edit read catches all those things you scratch your head over not seeing and she smiles the whole time, making it a pleasure to work with her. I want to shout out to Hope Williams who is an early reader as well when I need it.

Thanks to Kim Killion for another rockin' cover and to Jennifer Jakes for formatting the pages and exorcising gremlins.

Thanks also to Leiha Mann, Su Walker and the RBLs for supporting all authors!

A special thanks to Tina Rucci who recently went through the story and caught things that were missed earlier.

About The Author

New York Times **Bestseller Dianna Love** once dangled over a hundred feet in the air to create unusual marketing projects for Fortune 500 companies. She now writes high-octane romantic thrillers, young adult and urban fantasy. Fans of the bestselling Belador™ urban fantasy series will be thrilled to know she has a new spinoff series - Treoir Dragon Chronicles, which is also completed. Dianna's Slye Team sexy romantic thriller series wrapped up with Gage and Sabrina's book–Fatal Promise– perfect for bingers! She also has HAMR Brotherhood romantic thrillers and a new League of Gallize Shifters paranormal romance series. Look for her books in print, e-book, and audio. On the rare occasions Dianna is out of her writing cave, she tours the country on her BMW motorcycle searching for new story locations. She lives in the Atlanta, GA area with her husband, who is a motorcycle instructor, and with a tank full of unruly saltwater critters.

Visit her website at www.**AuthorDiannaLove.com** or www. **DiannaLoveSignedBooks.com**